SHADOWDANCE

ROBIN WAYNE BAILEY

SHADOWDANCE

Copyright ©1996 by Robin Wayne Bailey

COVER ILLUSTRATION: PAUL LEE
DESIGN: MICHAEL SCOTT COHEN

Borealis is an imprint of White Wolf Publishing.

WHITE WOLF PUBLISHING
780 PARK NORTH BOULEVARD, SUITE 100
CLARKSTON, GA 30021

PRINTED IN CANADA

For Stephen Pagel
with more thanks than I can say;

For Scott Tansey,
who was there when I began this,
and John Leininger,
who danced by as I finished;

For Diana,
who saved my life by teaching me
my first dance movements;

And for Louis Falco, Robert Joffrey,
Murray Louis, Yuriko, Loyce Holton,
Ann Brekke, Jean Ford, and others,
who through their instructions
certainly saved my soul.

At midnight's bell
All sleeping souls rise up entranced
To prance across the nighted world;
They whirl and leap
And, shrieking, fly and fly around the moon
Until they swoon and tumble down to hell—
Which is their mortal shell rejoined.
And waking,
Some remember with a timid shaking
How a dream is but a dream, no more.
But you and I,
Who love to fly, embrace the dark with jubilance
And fling ourselves each night into this
Shadowdance.
For what is earthly walking, running?
When a cunning music calls
We fall into a metronomic trance,
Ascend with a graceful spin, and begin to
Shadowdance.

CHAPTER 1

ROBIN WAYNE BAILEY

INNOWEN DRAGGED HIS crippled body desperately through the darkness and the mud, ignoring the chill, whipping wind and the rain that pelted him. His hands were sore and bloodied from pine needles and thorns and sharp stones. Still, his fingers dug into the road, seeking purchase as he hauled himself a few more painful inches, stripping more flesh from elbows already raw and oozing. His breath came in ragged gasps; he cried out again and again for help, but through the thunder and relentless deluge, his voice came as a weak and pathetic whimper.

Who's there to hear me, anyway? he thought forlornly. Yet for the sake of his guardian he cried out, hurling his shouts against the tempest as he dragged himself with piteous determination through the miserable night.

A blast of lightning, a cobalt flare bright enough to penetrate the tangled canopy of leaves and branches, tore open the sky. For an instant, Innowen saw the narrow road stretching before him and the trees on either side that loomed like mighty soldiers of an era before the Age of Man. *Help me,* he begged them. *Help Drushen! Don't let him die! If only I had legs to run for help!*

Darkness closed in again. Thunder ruptured the heavens, and a wind ripped through the forest. At first, in that rasping rustle, he thought the trees had answered his prayer and torn themselves from their roots, that they would sweep him up from the mud and, awakened from an ancient hibernation, march to Drushen's aid. But that was only fever or a moment's wild dream. Neither spirits nor gods answered men so easily. Save for the deafening crashes and the rain and his useless cries, the forest kept its silence.

He couldn't stop a gush of tears. He didn't know how much time Drushen had, how fast the venom in his veins would work. If only Innowen had legs to run! The village of Shandisti was not too far for a man with legs. Or Lord Minarik's keep; his soldiers might help.

But Innowen's legs were worthless. Filled with despair and self-loathing, he pounded his fist against the road, splashing mud in his face and eyes. Without Drushen, he would be alone in the world. How would he get by? He shouted again with a force that left his throat raw. *Help me, help!* But not a soul traveled the forest road on such a night as this, and if any gods rode the wind, they offered him no solace.

For Drushen's sake, he swallowed his fear as best he could and struggled on his belly toward the village, eating the mud that filled his mouth, wiping rain from his face, with only the lightning to show him the road.

Half a man, that's all he was. Not even that; barely a man at all. He hated himself for his useless legs and for his tears, all his weakness. Now he hated the world because soon Drushen would die, and he, Innowen, would be left alone.

On the verge of exhaustion, he used that hatred like a whip to lash himself onward. Weeping, he dragged his body another inch, clinging to the barest shred of hope while a small part of him prayed. *If Drushen dies, let me die, too, here, exposed in the storm.*

In heaven, they would be together again, and Drushen would take care of him forever.

"Look here, my lady." A deep voice said suddenly out of the night. "Quite a worm we've found wriggling in the mud."

Innowen looked up just as a bright flash tore open the night and stung his eyes. For an instant, fear gripped his heart, but that emotion yielded suddenly to wild hope as a pair of riders splashed cautiously out of the darkness.

After-images of the lightning dazzled his vision, and he wiped a hand over his eyes. A huge white horse stopped so close that its hooves splattered him with mud. Raising up on his elbows, he stared in wonder at the leather breast strap so richly studded with gold and silver, at the elegantly worked bridle that tinkled with bells and precious glimmering jewels. With an impatient snort, the horse shook its streaming mane, then lowered its head as if to investigate him.

He saw the horse's rider perched high on a soft, beautifully woven cloth-of-gold riding pad. Just as suddenly, he perceived the eerie glow that surrounded her and lent gleam to the gems and luster to the metals on her tack. A warm, wondrous pool of light spread on the ground around her. Innowen felt it like a gentle wave on his skin.

Her hair shone with the same golden light, and it spilled over her shoulders. Her eyes, though, were black, full of a darkness so deep it shamed the night. There was no color in her cheeks, but her lips were redder than roses. They turned upward in a strange smile. One hand parted the folds of her cloak and fluttered to her throat, while her ivory breasts strained against the white silk of her gown. Upon that tender flesh, a ruby hung on a thin chain. It seemed to Innowen that the jewel burned with an inner fire and throbbed with something not unlike hunger.

Innowen caught his breath, unable to move or speak. He had seen few women in his life, and none at all like this one. The heart sprang out of him; he loved her at once. Yet he feared her, too, for he knew her name. In all of Ispor there could only be one such woman.

He gazed upon the Witch of Shanalane.

When she spoke, her voice was a velvet caress: "Vashni, get down and see what this is. If it really is a boy, then it's either mute or afraid of us." The red blossom of her mouth opened in a smile, exposing small, perfect ivory thorns. "We won't harm you, boy," she said, but her words didn't reassure Innowen.

A deeper rumbling answered the Witch. "I still think it's a worm, mistress."

Innowen recoiled as a huge demon rode out of the Witch's shadow on the largest, blackest mare he had ever seen. Lightning glistened on the creature's breastplate and greaves, which were made of black leather and fitted with rings of burnished bronze. As the demon swung down to the ground, Innowen saw the immense sword belted over one hip and the helm bound with a leather strap to his other. Dark braids tumbled over the demon's shoulders as he bent low, grasped Innowen's arm, and tried to jerk him to his feet.

Innowen gave a sharp cry of pain as his shoulder nearly separated from its socket, and another as Vashni, reacting in surprise, dropped him. The muddy road rushed up to meet him as he fell helplessly.

"He's lame," Vashni commented without emotion, looking down upon Innowen, who struggled up onto one bruised elbow. A grim smirk lifted the corners of the demon's mouth. "A poor night for a walk, anyway."

"Enough of your rudeness," his mistress ordered.

The Witch of Shanalane turned her dark-eyed gaze fully upon Innowen, and he froze, unable to look away. A shiver passed through him. Drushen, the storm, the forest, his anguish, all other thoughts suddenly dissolved. Only those eyes, of all else in the world, held any meaning for him.

She's drinking my life, he thought through a strange, blissful haze. His vision blurred, his senses swam, and he felt himself becoming tenuous and thin. *Let her. I give it willingly.*

But then she let him go—if, indeed, it had not all been his imagination. He shook his head and wiped rain from his eyes.

"We heard your wails even over the storm," she said. Her voice sounded sweeter, richer than the bells that jingled on her bridle. "Are you lost, boy?"

His face burned suddenly with shame: he had forgotten Drushen.

"My guardian is dying," he stammered, wishing with all his soul that he could stand on his feet to speak to this lady. Plainly, she didn't deserve her reputation. The aura that surrounded her was surely the golden light of goodness. Here was no thing of evil. He beheld no witch, but a goddess.

Innowen swallowed hard and continued, the words rushing from him. "He went to gather logs from the woodpile at dinnertime, and a serpent bit his hand. He barely made it back to the cabin before collapsing. I touched his skin—it was so cold! I had to try to get help, but as you see, I can only crawl. Then, this storm came up so fast!" Innowen broke down again and sobbed freely. "He may be dead by now, but please, Lady.

Drushen is all I've got in this world!"

Under her steadfast gaze, he felt like a bug pinned in the mud, like the worm for which Vashni had taken him. Again, unwanted tears sprang from his eyes, and he hung his head.

"Mistress," the demon said in a bare whisper, "the soldiers..."

The Witch's words came like shards of ice that froze the air. "The soldiers are my worry."

Vashni dared to say no more. He turned away, but he looked back just long enough to glare at Innowen with eyes of pure menace.

The Witch put a finger to her lips, considering. Her brow furrowed ever so slightly in a way that did not mar her beauty. "Put him over your horse," she said at last to the demon. "We'll see if his Drushen is alive or dead."

Innowen raised up on his hands and lifted his head as high as he could. "Thank you, Lady, thank you! Please, let's hurry!"

Before he could say another word, the breath rushed from him as Vashni seized the rope belt around his waist and jerked him from the mud. Innowen flushed with anger, feeling as if he'd been cut in two, as the demon heaved him roughly over the black mare's withers. What must the Lady think to see him treated like a piece of meek baggage! And the demon used no riding pad, but rode bareback. A sweaty froth coated the mare's hide, unpleasant and creamy warm against his skin.

Innowen bit his tongue to keep from crying out or protesting. He'd found help for Drushen. Only that mattered. For his guardian's sake he kept silent. A wrong word and they might shove him back in the mud. Where would he be then? Where would his guardian be?

The Witch of Shanalane addressed him: "Do you live down this road, boy?"

Innowen started to snap. He was no boy. But then he mastered himself. He could not be angry with such a lady. From his awkward position, he did his best to look up. "Yes, that way. Just off the road you'll see a narrow path. Drushen is a woodcutter, and we live in the deepwoods."

A burst of lightning illuminated the forest, and the wind suddenly bent the trees until timbers cracked and splintered. Innowen stared, wide-eyed, as a strange realization struck him. He held up his hands. "The rain!" he cried. "It's not touching us!"

The Witch smiled as she waited for Vashni to swing onto his horse and guide his mount up beside her. Innowen found himself nose to knee with this strange woman, and her scent swam intoxicatingly in his nostrils. "Of course not," she said. "It's my storm. It's supposed to slow my enemies, not ruin my garments. What's your name, boy?"

He swallowed again and told her.

"Innowen," she repeated with a small laugh. "Like *Innocent*." She looked toward Vashni, and Innowen heard the demon's low-throated chuckle. "Well, hold tight, my Innocent. We'll waste no time reaching your guardian."

He didn't get a chance to answer or to protest the nickname. *Boy* was bad enough, but *Innocent!* Vashni's huge mount lurched forward, bouncing him painfully on the demon's knee. Again, the breath rushed out of him with a whoosh; starry lights burst dizzyingly in his vision, and tears burned his eyes.

Still he felt good. Soon, he would be at Drushen's side again. He hadn't failed his dearest and only friend.

This time he had won a victory over his crippled, useless body, and his heart swelled with pride.

They raced with bone-jarring speed. Mud splashed up toward his face, never quite touching him. The storm smashed the forest, beat the branches of the trees until they hung thick with water. Yet no drop of rain dampened his skin.

The wind was a different matter. It stung his flesh and pulled his hair. He tried to look ahead, but he couldn't bear its force directly in his eyes. It filled his ears with a terrible rushing roar as it whipped past.

The horse's motion made breathing difficult. Innowen bounced helplessly, held in place only by Vashni's huge right hand, which pressed into the small of his back. Innowen's lungs burned until he feared he would cry out. Instead, he choked and gasped for what little air he could draw and bit his lip against any sound or outcry.

From the corner of his eye he glimpsed the Lady. Far ahead, she glowed like a wild torch in the darkness. Her hair streamed, and her cloak flowed behind her. At a bend in the road, her horse slipped in the treacherous muck, nearly unseating her, but she recovered easily, and her unexpected laughter drifted back to him like cymbals and wild bells on the night air.

Never in his young life had Innowen met anyone like her, and he knew in that instant that he loved her with all his heart. He couldn't explain his passion, and he wondered if it might be some strange magic. But he knew it with certainty.

Caught up in wonder, he almost missed the boulder and the old tree that marked the path to his cottage. The Witch of Shanalane sped past them. Only the

strange radiance that surrounded her gave Innowen any
warning as, for just an instant, his landmarks stood
illuminated against the gloom.

"Wait!" he cried. "To the right! Take the path!"

The Witch seemed not even to slow. She jerked on
her jeweled reins and wheeled her steed in an
impossible circle. Into the thicket, she briefly
disappeared. Then, her light could be seen winking
between the trunks and the branches and the leaves.
Nothing restrained her speed.

Innowen marveled at her courage. The woods were
thick along the path. A low limb would certainly sweep
her from the animal's back. Didn't she care?

Vashni's hand pressed him down with greater force
as they, too, turned onto the path. The world spun
crazily for a moment, and Innowen thought the black
mare had slipped. He screamed and dug his fingers into
Vashni's leg. The huge demon only chuckled as he
crouched low over Innowen, bringing his face close to
the horse's neck as they plunged into the woods.

The forest closed around them, but the canopy of
leaves seemed less dense than Innowen thought it
should be. There were no limbs to menace them, no
roots to trip them. He knew the path well; Drushen had
often carried him along it to the road where they would
meet and chat with travelers. But now the way was
clear. The trees seemed to bend away, to *part* for them.

Just ahead stood the cottage. Firelight trickled
through the cracks of worn shutters and through the
partially opened door. The Lady had arrived before
them. Her mount waited untethered, breathing heavily.
Her shadow moved within the cottage.

Vashni jerked his own horse to a halt, flung his leg
over Innowen's head, and jumped down. He hauled the

boy down and tossed him over one shoulder. At last, Innowen dared to protest—uselessly. The demon kicked the door open wider with the toe of his boot, glanced around disdainfully at the furnishings, and grunted before he deposited his squirming burden on a stool that stood beside a rickety table.

In the darkest corner of the cottage, a figure sprawled on the only bed. The Witch stood over it. Innowen noticed immediately that her strange glow was gone.

"Drushen?" he whispered, afraid his guardian might already be dead. "Drushen?"

"Shut up," the Witch ordered quietly. "He's very weak. We're almost too late."

Drushen struggled up onto one elbow. Ropes of black hair turning gray clung to his sweat-drenched face. His moist eyes gleamed as he looked past the Witch and spied his charge. "Child, my child," he managed thickly. "I feared the storm had claimed you." He clutched suddenly at the Witch's sleeve and pulled her closer. "Take care of my Innowen, please! He needs someone. I beg you!"

The Witch gently pushed Drushen back on the bed. "Hush. You'll care for him yourself." She tore away the sleeve of the old man's tunic and lifted his arm to better see the puncture marks of the serpent's sting, two tiny wounds just above the right wrist. Abruptly, she called to her demonic companion. "Vashni, get a better fire going in that hearth. I need warmth and light, and these few candles aren't enough." She gestured at the two sticks on the mantle with their pathetic flames. "Then bring my smaller riding bag. You know which one."

Vashni obeyed at once. Without a word, he gathered logs from a basket that sat near the door, thrust them into the hearth, and began to prod and stir the coals.

The Witch unlaced her cloak and started to cast it aside. Then, noticing Innowen on his stool, she changed her mind. "You're shivering," she observed, draping the expensive garment over him. "Don't worry, my Innocent," she whispered. "The old man will live. The bite is a bad one, but the venom hasn't yet reached his heart."

Innowen only nodded. He was back in his familiar cottage, the one-room world which made up most of his existence, and he had found help for Drushen. Although rainwater dripped from strands of his hair and ran into his eyes, and mud slicked his clothes and skin, he found comfort in these surroundings and security in the presence of this Lady who had stolen his heart.

He watched her move, dimly aware when flames began to crackle in the fireplace and the room began to warm. The Witch tied back her hair and never glanced his way as she worked. He couldn't see what she did, but she put her mouth to Drushen's arm several times and kissed his wound. She made a poultice of water and hot ash, and she stripped bandages from the sheet beneath Drushen's body. Sometimes her hands seemed to glow, but Innowen was unsure if that was magic or just the firelight on her ivory flesh.

Vashni returned with her riding bag. In the brighter firelight, Innowen saw he was no demon at all, and he sullenly chided himself for his fear. Beyond a doubt, though, Vashni was the largest man he had ever seen. Far bigger even than Drushen, who bulged with muscle from his wood-cutting. His garments, kilt and breastplate, greaves and arm braces, all glimmered with studs and rings of copper and bronze. The short, embroidered sleeves of a black linen tunic showed from under his armor. And that huge bronze sword still hung sheathed at his right hip.

He had seemed a demon in the storm, with lightning glimmering on all that metal. Innowen had never seen such armor before. Nor had he ever encountered a man he would have called beautiful. He dared to study Vashni's face. The features were perfect, though marked by a hardness that bordered on cruelty. His mouth was a thin cut above the chin, and his brows seemed to crag over deep-set dark eyes that glittered like splinters of black ice. But for the pair of braids, his hair was chopped close, and a short-trimmed beard colored his cheeks.

The Witch took the bag from his hand, opened it, and extracted a small wooden figurine. From a sheath at her belt she withdrew a small dagger and began to carve. The firelight rippled on the sharp copper blade as she worked, and Innowen leaned forward on the table to see better. But she turned, blocking his view, and quickly finished. She looked from the doll to Drushen, then touched it to his forehead and heart. With two quick motions, she stabbed the figurine's right arm, kissed its new wounds, and cast it into the fire.

The old man never made a sound. His eyes stayed closed in apparent sleep.

Innowen sagged against the wall, sure at last that his guardian would be all right. The Witch had said so, and he had watched her work some charm.

I love her, he thought again. He didn't understand, but he knew it without a doubt. Everything about her fascinated him. She was new and refreshing, and she made his world seem new as well. The cottage felt warmer, the furniture looked more elegant. The very woodgrain in the old walls seemed sharper and more vivid. He inhaled the air, and it tasted like the rarest essence. The snapping crackle of the flames made a music. The fire shimmered.

Her shadow! It danced upon the walls and the ceiling, going where it would, spinning and leaping whenever she moved, flitting around the cottage like an independent soul. The shadow glided delicately and with a strange quality, a kind of magical dance-for-two that only he seemed to witness. The Lady's every gesture embodied grace as she went about her healings, but her motions were brusque and purposeful.

Her shadow, though, was a piece of enchantment, blackness without darkness. One with the Witch, yet free, it elongated all her movements, drew them out and transformed them into pavanes and arabesques.

Innowen looked for his own shadow. It made barely a stain on the far wall, huddled on a low shadow-stool in a corner, all crouched down and formless. It didn't move, it didn't dance. It just sat there, two useless shadow-legs thrust out at funny angles.

Even his shadow was crippled.

A moan rose from the bed. Innowen glanced apprehensively toward Drushen, but the old man made no other sound. The Witch stood motionless at the bedside. Innowen swallowed. "Is he...?"

"Just sleeping," she answered, turning slowly to face him. She wore an expression of weariness as she drew herself erect. "He should awaken later in the day, and he'll be hungry. Feed him the broth that Vashni has prepared."

Innowen gazed toward the hearth. A kettle hung on an iron hook near the fire, and a rich aroma filled the cabin. He hadn't seen the big warrior prepare it. He'd been too involved in watching the Witch and her shadow, too wrapped up in his own thoughts.

Near Drushen's bed, a bowl of water sat on the floor. The Witch had used it to mix the poultice for his wound. Now she bent to pick it up, but as her fingers brushed the earthen rim, she froze. For a moment, she stood unmoving. Then her brow furrowed. She stooped closer and peered with keen interest at something in the water.

As if struck a blow, she suddenly recoiled. All color drained from her face. Her mouth opened slackly, and her eyes widened. Carefully, she picked up the bowl, cradling it in both hands, and stared into it again.

Innowen knew there was only water in the bowl. He didn't understand. What could she see in a bowl of water?

The vessel slipped through her fingers, and the thin pottery shattered. Water splattered the floor and the hem of her fine gown. The Witch didn't care. She whirled toward Innowen. With an effort, she composed her features into a semblance of calm. Slowly, she drew a long breath and knelt to meet him eye to eye.

"Do you know, my Innocent, why you cannot walk?"

Innowen hung his head, unable to meet her gaze for long. He looked, instead, at her shadow as it stretched across the floor, up the far wall, and back over the ceiling like a tenuous preening creature. He could talk to her shadow, if not to the Witch.

"Drushen said I was born this way." He swallowed hard again and trembled at her nearness. Yet the shadow on the wall encouraged him to speak, nodding its head as the flames danced in the hearth. "I never knew my parents. They left me on the road, exposed for the animals or the elements. Drushen found me and raised me, and we've been each others' only company ever since." Despite himself, a tiny smile creased his lips. "I can't do much to help around here, but I listen to his complaints and his stories, and we talk a lot."

The Witch of Shanalane touched his knee. It startled him, and he jerked, bumping his head on the wall. He couldn't avoid her gaze any longer. Her eyes burned into him, searing him, illuminating all his secrets. Was it her power, or was it his own fear? He didn't know, but he couldn't look away.

"Are you happy?" she asked, an odd question for one stranger to ask another.

Innowen stammered and blinked back the tears that threatened to come again. "I can't walk," he answered slowly. He tore his gaze away at last and sought her shadow. It flickered in time to the crackling fire, moving over the old rough wood with an eerie grace. "I can't dance."

A torrent of words burst from him, and his eyes flooded with tears. "I want to dance," he said bitterly. "Like your shadow there. Like the fire. Like the trees in the wind and the stars through the sky. Drushen dances sometimes, and the villagers in Shandisti dance when the harvest comes in. The animals, the birds, the grass and flowers—they all dance, they're all alive with motion." He pounded his fists against his unfeeling limbs. "But not me! Not Innowen!"

The outburst drained him. He sagged back against the wall and slipped sideways off his stool to the floor. He beat his legs once more, but weakly, ashamed of his tears and his infirmity, painfully aware of the beautiful woman before him and of his own unworthiness.

The door opened. Vashni peered around its edge. "We should leave now, Lady." He spared a glance toward Drushen's bed. "We've stayed too long already.

The soldiers...."

The Witch waved her hand, and Vashni fell silent. Leaning close, she took Innowen's face between her fingers and turned him toward her, forcing him to meet her eyes once more. He couldn't bear them, especially after his unmanly display. Yet she gripped his chin and compelled him to look.

"My poor Innocent," she whispered. "I saw your pain. I saw it in the water where the past and future sometimes reveal themselves to me. I see it now in your aura, which glimmers with misery." She released him, and her hand settled on his chest, just over his heart. "I saw your fate in that bowl of water, my Innocent." Her face came next to his, and the warmth of her hand spread all through him. "You'll walk, yes, and you'll dance. You'll dance the world away."

An arcane glittering like the flashes of tiny lightning bolts filled the dark wells of her eyes. Innowen's tears surged forth once more, humiliating him, the droplets completely beyond his control. He became a child again, a weeping baby in need of succor, muddy and filth-splattered. He slid further down, his back against the wall, until he almost lay on the floor. The Witch watched him; that only made him cry more.

"I—I love you," he confessed through his sobs. With a boldness born of shame, he reached up to touch her face, longing to brush his fingers over the milky paleness of her cheek. She was just beyond his reach, though, and he trembled as he drew his arm back. His tears continued, blurring his vision. "I don't understand, I don't know how, but I love you." He turned his face to the floor and covered it with one hand. "Help me," he muttered.

"I'll help you," the Witch answered, pulling his hand

from his face. "I'll help you to walk, and you'll dance as no man has ever danced." She rose and went to the door. Vashni was no longer there. She called his name, and he appeared instantly.

"Carry our Innocent out into the rain," Innowen heard her whisper. "Strip away his rags and let the downpour cleanse him. Make him fit to look upon our god."

Vashni's eyes snapped wide, then he furrowed his brow. "Lady, Minarik's troops know our direction."

Again, the Witch stopped him with a curt gesture. "This is too important," she snapped. "The storm will slow them, and if anyone finds us before I finish, you'll have to deal with them. Now do as I tell you. Then wait by the horses and keep a sharp watch. Go!"

Vashni shook his head, frowning, but he picked up Innowen with his usual disdain. "Stop that blubbering," he grumbled, giving him a shake as he carried him through the door.

The shock of the rain and wind did what Vashni's threat could not. Innowen had become used to the cottage's warmth. The cold stung him. He hugged himself and barely protested when Vashni dropped him on the ground, seized the back of his tunic and ripped it free in one swift motion. He opened his mouth to cry out, but no sound came.

The huge warrior loomed over him, and Innowen realized the giant was as soaked and miserable as he was. Raindrops pearled down his face, streamed from his lashes and chin, causing him to blink and wipe his face endlessly. "You want to shed that breech cloth, or do you need more help?" Vashni snapped.

Tremulously, Innowen unwound the breech cloth from his loins. He folded it self-consciously, watching as the dark warrior went to the Witch's horse, reached into another bag that was somehow bound to her riding pad, and lifted out a bundle of black velvet. Vashni's face seemed frozen in a perpetual grimace as he bore the burden back toward Innowen, slowly unwrapping it.

Innowen caught his breath. The velvet came free, exposing a strange wooden idol. Thick copper nails had been driven into it, perhaps a hundred, at all different angles. Innowen could discern no detailed features for the spikes that pierced its face and head. The gods of Ispor were many, but Innowen, who knew little of gods, had never seen its like. Its countenance sent a shiver up his spine.

Vashni set the idol on the ground and shot a glance toward the cottage. The door stood open, but all he could see was the Witch's shadow bent over that of the small table. It seemed to be writing something. He looked again at the weird god-figure and the copper spikes that impaled it, and dragged himself back a pace. The stern eyes of Vashni stopped him, and he sat up, trembling. The rain chilled his bare flesh; he hugged himself as much against his fear as for warmth.

The Witch appeared in the doorway, the glow from the fireplace lending her a soft aura as she hesitated on the threshold. Silhouetted in such light, it proved impossible to see her face, but Innowen felt her gaze fix on him.

She slammed her hand angrily on the door jamb. "Vashni," she shouted. "You fool! Not in the mud!" She disappeared inside again, only to return with the stool on which Innowen had sat. "Use this."

Vashni retrieved the idol from the mud with a muttered apology as the Witch placed the stool near Innowen's feet. Snatching up the scrap of Innowen's tunic, he wiped the idol clean of any filth before he positioned it carefully on the stool. That done, he went back to the bag on his mistress' horse to extract from it a mallet and a new copper nail. Under the Witch's watchful eye, he set these down on the stool with the same care and backed away.

The Witch opened her arms wide as if to embrace the storm. No longer did she hold the rain at bay with her magic. It drenched her, and her hair hung in thick ropes, and water rilled down her face and breasts and into her gown. She had not even donned her cloak. Her sodden garments clung to every rich curve of her body.

As she approached the idol, her lips moved in a soundless prayer or incantation. Giving no thought to her fine gown, she knelt in the mud. One hand reached out to grasp the mallet, and her voice rose a bit until Innowen could hear her words. They made no sense to him. She lifted her other hand in the air, and he saw that she clutched something.

A sudden flash of lightning revealed the piece of white cloth she gripped, perhaps a strip torn from Drushen's bedding. He remembered her shadow writing over his table. What had she scrawled on that scrap?

A powerful bolt ripped a jagged blue tear in the sky. Thunder boomed and echoed. A terrible shriek followed, chilling Innowen to the marrow of his bones, and he gave a little cry, too, out of startled fright. The Witch had made that sound. She threw back her head and howled again. The sky answered with more lightning and more thunder.

Suddenly, setting the mallet down and turning away from the idol, she glared at Innowen. Her eyes were two small heavens filled with their own wild tempests. They reflected the lightning flash as she came toward him.

Innowen stared, fascinated and terrified, and he began to shake with an uncontrollable trembling.

"You will walk," she said fiercely. "And you'll dance." The wind set her soaked garments to snapping, and the wet, tangled ropes of her hair blew back from her head and writhed like snakes in the gale. "How you'll dance!" she cried.

Terrified, Innowen looked from her to the idol, to the lightning crackling overhead, and back to the Witch. For an instant she was a monster, a horrible creature crouched over him, ready to devour. She was evil—a witch. All the villagers, all the people in the countryside, knew and feared her. She summoned storms.

Lightning exploded again, shattering the night. For a brief moment, a thousand shadows of the Witch stretched across the world, shadows that danced ephemerally before the returning waves of darkness washed them away.

Even so, he loved her. He did, with all his young heart. She had saved his guardian, and now she was saying that he would walk. She could make him walk! Witch or not, evil or not, he had to love her!

He swallowed his fear and met her potent gaze. "I want to!" he shouted over the thunder. "Make me walk! Do you have that much power?"

Her eyes burned. She leaned forward on all fours, her hands sinking into the mud on either side of him. "My god does," she answered darkly. She pointed back to the idol with a long, ivory finger that dripped with muck and slime. "He has all power."

The heavens fractured. Fiery lightning raced in all directions, turning the night into a cobalt lacework. Thunder rolled until the earth itself shook, and the trees bowed to the ground under a fearsome wind.

The Witch brought her face close to his, and in the flashes of lightning, Innowen saw nothing human. He screamed inwardly, but he refused to admit his fear. He loved her! Still, he recoiled from her until he lay flat on his back in the mud.

"He demands nothing of you," she said. Her warm breath caressed his lips, and the strange wild smell of her filled his senses as she stretched practically on top of him. "Only of me does he ask anything. The price is mine to pay." Her lips brushed ever so subtly against his. "At least for this moment."

Innowen could retreat no further. His breath came in short gasps. His senses roiled in confusion. For all his fear—and he could no longer deny he feared her— he desired her deeply! Her body pressed down upon him, hot and wonderful and frightening. He bit his lip and clenched his fingers in the soft mud.

"You will walk," she repeated, the words hissing between her perfect teeth, "and you will dance, and in time you, too, will pay a price." She pulled one hand from the mud and smeared it over his chest like a fine ointment. Her cold fingers drew small, teasing circles around his nipples and moved upward toward his throat. "But what is the value of a whole body, my Innocent?" she asked. "What would it be worth to be a complete man?" She hesitated as if expecting a response, but before he could speak she set a finger to his lips. "Shhhhh, no need, when we both know the answer."

Whatever she was, whatever the villagers thought her, she knew his dearest dream. "Make me walk!" he uttered breathlessly, doubting her even as he wished fervently to believe. "I want to dance!"

"I will," she promised. She held up the strip of

cloth in her hand. It was wet and muddy, but as she unrolled it, he could see strange writing. "This is my prayer," she said. "You will be healed and made whole." Her hand clamped on his right leg. Innowen could not feel her strength, but when she let go, his flesh showed livid white marks. "Have faith in my god, Innocent! Believe in Him!"

"I will!" Innowen shouted fervently.

She scrambled on her knees to her idol and picked up the mallet. Crumpling her prayer in one hand, she pressed it to the wooden body of her god. Next, she picked up the sharp copper spike, set it in place against the cloth, and drew back to drive it home.

The mallet struck, and the sky erupted. Thunder drowned out the sound of the impact as the nail ripped through the cloth and deep into the idol. Again, the Witch struck, and again the heavens cried with thunder. A third time she struck, and Innowen covered his ears.

Vashni appeared beside her suddenly with a small bit of burning wood from the fireplace. He cupped one hand around the flame to protect it from the storm as he knelt and passed it to his mistress. She looked over her shoulder at Innowen, then touched the brand to the edge of the cloth. Though it was soaked, it began to burn. The smoke rose even through the thick rain. Then it flared with blinding intensity, and all the nails in the idol's body began to gleam in the red heat.

The cloth quickly seared away. Not even an ash remained to fall on the stool. Still, the nails shone with heat-glow, and the air smelled of burning.

The Witch cast her small brand aside, and the flame died before it hit the ground. She rose, drawing her dagger from her belt. Standing over her idol, the image of her holy god, she set the razor edge to her wrist. The blade rippled with wild color as lightning lit the darkness. The thunder that followed covered any sound she made as she drew it through the flesh.

Blood splashed on the idol's head and streamed down among the nails, mingling with the ceaseless rain, staining the wood. Innowen cried out for his Lady, not knowing how deeply she had cut. The free flow of her life-fluid made him cry out again. She said nothing, though, just stared at the heavens and held her arm rigid while the blood pumped.

Suddenly, Innowen felt the power of her god upon him. The idol's eyeless face regarded him with a cold passion. He stared back, looking for a gaze he could meet, then clapped a hand to his mouth in disbelieving horror. Its chest began to heave as if it drew breath; wooden limbs stirred ever so slightly and seemed to pulse with tension.

He was only imagining it, he tried to tell himself. The lightning and the thunder, the fire, and the Witch's blood-letting all contrived to play this trick on his mind.

But no, he knew the truth. The thing exuded a fearsome, unimaginable life, and he was the object of its unnatural attention. He sat up slowly, supporting himself on his hands, unable to look away from the idol.

With a screeching wail, a new wind ripped through the forest. From deep in the woods came the crashing of huge old trunks as their branches snapped and shattered and they struck the earth. Over it all, Innowen heard a groaning and a wrenching that made him look up. A corner of the cottage roof reared against the night, bucked and writhed like a tortured animal, then blew away with the gale. A section of the west wall sprang outward, and another piece of the roof collapsed.

Innowen threw himself sideways on his elbows, twisting his body as he screamed. "Drushen!"

The Witch stood over him. Her hair lashed wildly behind her, and her ruined gown whipped and beat in the wind. Her voice stung. "Rise, Innocent!" she shouted, shaking her fists. "Save your Drushen. Get up and run to him!"

Innowen dragged himself through the mud, tears streaming, mingling with the rain that rilled down his face. "I can't!" he cried despondently. "Drushen!"

"Drushen!" she mocked him. Then she kicked him repeatedly until he rolled away from her and found himself again at the wooden feet of her cruel god. She positioned herself between him and the cottage, and Vashni took a position at her back. "Get up, Innocent!" she demanded. "My god has placed his hand upon you. Save your guardian, but I won't let you crawl to him. Get up! Walk!"

The wind swelled to greater fury. Even the Witch leaned into it to stand at all. Innowen stared at his home as yet another portion of the wall caved outward and another piece of roof tumbled down. He opened his mouth, but no sound came, so great was his horror.

He stared at the Witch. He loved her! How could she do this, save his Drushen only to let him die? She had been beautiful before when she worked her bedside mercies. But now, muddied and soaking and angry, she seemed hellish, and he knew that the villagers were right in their fears, and that he was a fool to love her.

"Get up!" It was the very voice of the storm coming from her. She shook her fist at him, and lightning crackled across the sky.

He looked at the idol with its many copper spikes, sure that it breathed now. It pulsed with horrid vitality, swelled and contracted. The nails stirred like quills. The thing watched him and bent its will upon him with a dreadful force.

"I can't! I can't!" he answered both the Witch and her god. "Help me!" He rose as high as he could on his hands, but she refused to let him crawl. Her sandaled foot pushed him back. Yet Drushen was still inside, and their home was crashing down. He had to save Drushen!

He screamed in fear and anger, and as he did, he pulled one knee under himself, the first movement his legs had ever known.

"Help yourself, Innocent!" the Witch cried with fierce urging. "Help yourself, and help your Drushen. But hurry! How long will the rest of the roof hold? How much time? Get up! Run!"

Ever so shakily, Innowen rose, barely aware of his miracle. Drushen filled his thoughts. He took his first lurching step, then his second. The Witch stood before him, and he pushed her aside, all his attention on the cottage door and the firelight beyond it. Vashni moved out of his way.

"That's it!" the Witch shouted gleefully. "Walk! Run! Dance! All you've wanted is yours now. Save Drushen. That's your task tonight!" She laughed, and the sound of it rolled even over the thunder. "But there's another task to come. I've seen your fate!" She laughed again. "Hurry, Innocent! Hurry to your task!"

He reached the door. One hand grabbed the edge of it, and he jerked away in pain, a gasp on his lips. A huge splinter protruded from his right palm. He wrenched it out, grimacing at the tiny well of blood as he cast the splinter down.

The foot of Drushen's bed was all he could see from the door, so he focused on that. Every step was a torturous effort. He balanced precariously on one leg, then the other. He had never learned to walk. How he managed it now, he didn't know. Maybe it was the god. But then, the god could have made it easier! Innowen had to think through every movement, and there was little time.

The wind raged around him, pushing him back, as it blew through the shattered sections. He glanced upward. The remains of the roof hung dangerously over his head.

Innowen fell suddenly, tripping in the debris that had been his home. Agony shot up his left arm. He raised it before his eyes, terrified at the sight of more of his blood.

The roof made a menacing noise. A thick beam dipped toward Drushen. Innowen forgot his wound and dragged himself quickly across the ruined floor, using his elbows as he always had. The Witch wasn't there to stop him. But when he reached the bedside, he clutched the rough wooden frame with all his strength and hauled himself once more to his feet.

He couldn't deny that the Witch had kept her promise—or that her god had kept it for her. He could stand. He could walk. But there was no time to ponder why or how. He pulled his unconscious guardian up and slipped his arms around the old man's chest. He took his first step backward.

And fell again. He kept his grip on Drushen, though, and they tumbled from the bed to the floor. Once more, Innowen struggled to his feet, bent over uncertainly, and seized his guardian by the wrists.

The room swam in circles as he straightened and began to drag Drushen through the rubble. Twice more he fell, the simple skill of moving backward eluding him. Each time, though, he rose faster and more surely. Through the door and into the storm he hauled the old man, falling yet again in the slippery mud.

He screamed in frustration. With a grinding noise, the remains of the roof collapsed. The walls followed, crashing down in a thick cloud of dust that the rain swiftly smothered. The only home he had ever known lay in ruins. A numbness filled him. He stared at the broken pile of timbers that had been a cottage, and at Drushen, who slept the undisturbed sleep of a child.

He looked for the Witch, but she was gone. So was her servant, Vashni, as was the idol. The little stool stood crookedly, alone in the cold rain, one of its three legs sunk deeper in the mud than the others.

He looked slowly down at his own legs, so straight and perfect, so strong, and his heart leaped. *He could walk! He was whole!* Suddenly, the cottage seemed a small price to pay for such a gift.

The Witch had said there would be a price. He drew a deep breath, unable to resist the grin that turned up the corners of his mouth. *What would you give?* she had asked him. What *would* you give? he asked himself.

He took a few hesitant steps, then flung up his arms and rejoiced. The cottage was, indeed, a small price. Drushen could build a better home, and they could both have beds. This time, Innowen could help!

The storm grew weaker, and the rain almost stopped. But the wind rose again, strong as ever, and the night wailed with its power. Innowen, still new to the subtleties of balance, turned into it and was blown over into the muck. He rose on his elbows at his guardian's side.

The wind blew through the forest, and the sound of its rush through the leaves, through the grass, took form in his ears and spoke to him in the Witch's voice. He shot a wild look around, searching for her, but she was not there. Only her words remained on the wind.

Dance, my Innocent, the wind said to him. *To walk, you must dance. Every night you must dance, or never walk again. Dance, dance as no one has ever danced. Dance the world away. Dance, dance, dance....*

The wind laughed and laughed, then fell suddenly and dissipated. The leaves rustled weakly as it faded away. For a moment, silence ruled. The rain ended. The barest hint of lightning flickered far away in the heavens. In the distance, the thunder gave a last rattle and died.

Innowen rolled over, his face close to Drushen's. The old man looked serene, his eyes gently closed. No trouble or worry creased his brow. He slept as if still in his bed, oblivious to the mud beneath him and to the destruction of his home.

Innowen planted a small kiss on his guardian's cheek and got to his feet. He had to think about shelter. Drushen couldn't be left in the chill all night. He looked around, wondering what to do.

Then, the words of the wind echoed in his head. *Dance,* it said.

He didn't know how.

Experimentally, he lifted one foot, pointed the toe, and tapped it on the ground. *There should be music,* he thought. But there was none. The leaves rasped suddenly as a fresh wind stirred with new gentleness through the branches. That was music of a sort, Innowen reasoned.

He drew back his foot, threw out his arms, and began a tentative turn, following it with another.

I can dance, he whispered softly to himself. *I can dance!*

The trees swayed with him, keeping time like great metronomes, and the wind rose again, but subtly, and it sounded ever so much like laughter.

CHAPTER 2

INNOWEN SAT WITH his back against the trunk
of an old tree. A thick, broken limb hung down to the
earth, providing the only shelter he could find from the
misty, intermittent drizzle and the wind that had turned
so chilly. Droplets of water from the leaves above fell
with annoying regularity in his eyes and on his face.
He did his best to ignore them and to forget the cold
muddy ground beneath him.

He gazed down at Drushen and brushed the damp,
graying hair back from his guardian's face. The
woodcutter stirred ever so slightly; the corner of one
lip twitched, and a hand settled on Innowen's knee.
Drushen slept in apparent peace, but the Witch had
warned he would wake hungry. Innowen thought of the
stew Vashni had prepared by the hearth. But the hearth
was only a pile of stones now, scattered among the ruins
of the cottage.

A dark blot in the greater darkness of night marked
where those ruins were. Innowen had dug among them,
hoping to find some bit of fire in the fireplace to carry
back to his shelter, just a small flame, a handful of coals
even, to warm Drushen in his sleep. But the collapse
had smothered the fire and his hope. He had only his
body to keep his friend warm, and he wrapped his arms
and legs around the older man and hugged him close.

But slowly, a strange sensation crept into Innowen's

legs. Dull needles pricked his flesh, a tingling that began at his ankles and spread upward. No matter how he rubbed and massaged, the sensation worsened until he could stand it no longer. He eased Drushen aside and leaped up, grabbing the tree for balance.

He took a hesitant step and fell with a sharp cry, fearing the numbness that filled his legs. Cautiously, he rose again, grabbing hold of the broken limb to support himself. If the Witch's magic had worn off, he would be a cripple once more. The thought terrified him. He took a couple tentative steps, never letting go of the branch, begging whatever god had healed him not to turn away from him now. He curled his free hand into a fist and beat it desperately against his thighs, trying to stir up feeling.

Little by little, the tingling stopped and Innowen's fear subsided. He let go of the limb and walked around the tree until he was sure of his step again. Had the Witch's god heard his prayer? He glanced down at his bare toes and wiggled them in the muddy grass, a marvelous feeling. A slow smile blossomed on his lips; he delighted in the newness of such textures under the soles of his feet.

The sheepish grin spread over his face, and he chided himself for his own ignorance. Now that his panic had subsided, he recalled how Drushen had occasionally rested from his work, settled back on his haunches to eat a lunch or to talk a bit, and how he would sometimes rise suddenly and complain that his legs had gone to sleep. The expression had never meant anything to Innowen before. The old man would beat and rub his legs until sensation returned, and he would smirk and mumble about getting old.

That was all that had happened to Innowen. The Witch's magic had not deserted him. He had only sat too long in an uncomfortable position, and his legs had gone to sleep. There was a sweet pleasure in the discovery that his once-dead limbs could do that. He grabbed the branch again for balance, then lifted his right leg, pointed the toe, flexed the knee and pushed straight out.

He smiled. Then he let go a gleeful laugh that rolled through the forest. It felt so good to laugh and to move his legs. He sat down, marveling at how his legs folded so naturally beneath him, and cradled Drushen's head in his lap. If only his guardian would wake so Innowen could show him his surprise!

A sigh escaped his lips as he leaned back and stared at the sky through the leaves of the sheltering branch. Gray clouds raced bleakly across the heavens. The palest crescent moon dared to peep through. A few stars winked briefly and disappeared.

Beautiful and frightening, he thought, *like the Witch.* He couldn't stop thinking of her. Her voice whispered to him on the breeze. The moon was her smile, and the stars were her eyes watching him from behind the clouds. The air smelled of her perfume. She had treated Drushen with kindness and mercy, and she had healed Innowen's legs.

Yet she had also destroyed their home and endangered Drushen's life after she had saved it. He remembered her in the storm and wind, seeming like nothing human, as she'd taunted and laughed at him. She'd seemed so gentle before, when she found him on the road.

Innowen didn't understand. He closed his eyes and

rubbed them with his fists, wishing that morning would come. Dawn couldn't be far off. He longed suddenly for the warmth of the sun and an end to the cold and rain.

A sound came abruptly from the path that led to the road. Innowen hesitated uncertainly, then untangled himself from his sleeping guardian and crawled from under his shelter. Five mounted soldiers rode out of the woods.

He leaped to his feet. "Help!" he called, waving his arms. "Please, help us!"

The riders halted, and five spears leveled on him as heads jerked his way.

Innowen stepped forward into plain sight so they could see he was weaponless. "Please help me!" he begged, lifting his empty hands toward them. "My guardian is ill, and the storm has destroyed our home."

The five riders approached him warily. Innowen could tell very little about them, since they wore cloaks and helms. They were big men, though, and obviously on edge. What were they doing on the road on such a night? And why had they turned off to take the trail that led to his cottage? He looked at the points of their spears and swallowed.

One soldier nudged his horse ahead of the others and stopped again before Innowen. The man stared downward without speaking. Innowen could barely see the gleam of eyes under the nose guard and the copper rim of the ornately fashioned helm. A crest of horsehair crowned its top and cascaded down the rider's back. Innowen stood before him, suffering the weight of that stare until the rider spoke at last.

"Where are your clothes, boy?" The voice was deep, yet soft and tinged with weariness.

Innowen felt the heat of embarrassment rise in his cheeks. Vashni had ruined his only tunic and taken his loin cloth. "I was asleep," he lied shyly, "and naked when the cracking of the roof beams wakened us. Drushen took a snake-bite today, not a fatal one, but he was still sick, and I had to drag him out of the cottage. There wasn't time to dress."

"Drushen?" The stranger's speech was like a rich, warm liquid. The sound of it fascinated Innowen, and he wondered at the face behind the helm. Never in his life had he met so many strangers in one day!

He pointed back to the broken branch that he'd claimed for shelter. "My guardian," Innowen explained. "He's under there. We took care of his bite in time, and he's breathing, but I can't wake him up."

The rider crooked a finger. Two of his comrades slid down from their horses in response and crawled under the makeshift shelter. Innowen watched them disappear, then looked up again. The man seated above him unlaced his cloak and cast it down to him. He caught it in both hands.

"Cover yourself before you catch a chill," his benefactor instructed. He glanced toward the remains of the cottage and drew his shoulders back in what might have been a soundless sigh. "We'll take you with us to Whisperstone tonight and try to get you settled in Shandisti tomorrow."

Innowen took a step back. "Lord Minarik's keep?"

The rider grinned. "Are you afraid?"

He stammered. "I—I don't know. I've never seen Minarik."

The man removed his helm and leaned forward on his horse's withers.

"Whom did you think you were addressing in this accursed drizzle?"

Innowen paled, taking sudden note of the man's exquisite garments—the lacquered breastplate and the embroidered sleeves of a linen tunic, the short kilt similarly embroidered, and the sculpted metal greaves that covered his lower legs. Innowen should have noticed as soon as Minarik had removed the cloak, but he'd been too startled to receive it as a gift. He studied the lord as best he could in the darkness. Minarik was younger than Drushen. There was the barest hint of gray in his hair, but none in the close-trimmed beard and mustache. His face was handsome, and his entire bearing conveyed strength and power.

A stray moonbeam rippled along the bronze point of Minarik's javelin as he balanced it across his bare thighs and rested his helm carefully on the shaft. "Now, I've got some questions, boy, and be mindful of my kindness as you answer."

Innowen licked his lips and nodded hesitantly, uncomfortably aware that he'd already lied to this man once. He was also aware of the veiled threat in Minarik's words. Of course, there had to be a reason why the Lord of Whisperstone was abroad on such a foul night.

There was a scuffling behind him, and he turned. The two soldiers emerged from under the overhanging branch bearing Drushen by the heels and shoulders. The old man slept on, oblivious to everything. Even when they passed him up to one of the other riders, who draped him unceremoniously across the shoulders of his horse, he didn't stir.

Lord Minarik drew Innowen's attention back.

"We've been following two fugitives," he said. "A woman and her champion. But this wretched storm has made a ruin of the roads and their tracks. As near as we can tell, though, they came down this path." His gaze bore into Innowen as he leaned even lower. "Did you see them?"

Innowen hugged the cloak around his shoulders and stared at Drushen, who hung limply across the horse between a soldier's thighs. He thought then of the warmth of Whisperstone's hearths and the safety of its walls, perhaps some food, and the bed his guardian certainly needed. And he thought of the Witch, who had healed his crippled legs.

"What have they done?" he dared to ask, meeting Minarik's gaze as steadily as he could.

"King Koryan was murdered two nights ago," Minarik answered sternly. "This woman and man are charged with the crime, and since they dwell within my borders I'm responsible for their apprehension." He straightened a bit, but his countenance was no less severe. "So tell me if they passed this way."

Innowen tried to hide his trembling. He owed a debt to Minarik for the cloak and for the care and shelter he had promised. Yet he owed a debt also to Vashni and the Witch of Shanalane. She had saved Drushen from the serpent's venom, and she had made his legs whole again. Surely, that was the greater service, even if Minarik was the lord of this land.

He stalled while his mind raced. "Then Kyrin sits on the throne of Ispor?"

Minarik snorted. "Koryan's first-born sits safe and dry at my table in Whisperstone eating my larder bare while I hunt for his father's killers. But never fear, he assures us of the depth of his grief. Now answer my question."

Innowen pulled the cloak tighter about himself to fight off a chill that had nothing to do with the weather. "How did great Koryan die?" he persisted. "You say it was two days ago?"

Minarik shifted impatiently. "You're too inquisitive, boy." he grumbled. "Nobody knows how he died, but they say there was such a look of terror on his face—as if he'd seen into the Underworld itself—that only the Witch of Shanalane could've done the deed."

Innowen gave no thought to his foolishness as he observed with an open scoff, "That's slight evidence, Lord."

A hand seized him by the back of the neck and lifted him to the tips of his toes. He gave a half-strangled cry of pain before Minarik waved his hand, and he was released. He shot a fearful glance over his shoulder and stared into the face of one of the guards who had carried Drushen out from under the shelter.

"You've seen her, haven't you, boy?" Minarik's gaze brooked no argument. Abruptly, Innowen felt a strange weakness in his knees and thought he would fall down. But the guard behind him settled a hand on his shoulder, steadying him, and Minarik spoke again. There was no anger in his voice, yet he was firm. "It's said that all who see her must love her." The barest hint of a sympathetic smile flickered on his lips. "And you have that look about you." The smile quickly vanished. "Nevertheless, you must tell me the truth."

Innowen listened to the wind, hoping it would speak to him again, tell him what to do. But the air was silent, the night suddenly still, as if the world held its breath to see what he would do.

At last, he nodded. "She saved Drushen," he admitted as the slow fire of shame warmed his face. Even as he betrayed the Witch, he tried to defend her. He clenched his fists in the fabric of the cloak and stepped up beside Minarik's knee. "Why would she murder King Koryan and then take time to spare an old woodcutter?" he said furiously. "Why would she do that?"

Minarik brushed a finger over his lower lip and gazed at him intently. "You say she saved your guardian?"

Innowen bowed his head and drew a deep breath. If he could do nothing more, perhaps he could gain time for the Witch by talking. "He was stung by a serpent, but she drew out the poison. She bandaged him, too, and her man made a stew in the fireplace. What sense does that make if she murdered Koryan?"

The Lord of Whisperstone scratched his chin. Then he crooked a finger again. A soldier rode up on his right side and wordlessly accepted Minarik's javelin and helm. Unburdened, Minarik threw a leg over the neck of his horse and slid to the ground. Folding his arms across his armored chest, he paced toward the ruins of the cottage. Innowen followed.

When Minarik spoke, it was half to himself. "Kyrin said she fled when he sent his men to question her."

"Question her?" Innowen sneered, "or apprehend her?" At once, he clapped a hand over his mouth. He had dared too much, to use such a tone of voice with such a great man. He flung himself at Minarik's feet. "Please, I beg you! Do her no harm!" He set his forehead on the toe of Minarik's muddy sandal and grasped his ankle in both hands. "You've shown me kindness, Lord," he cried, "with this gift of your cloak and your offer of shelter. But she saved my guardian's life. The Witch of

Shanalane can't be guilty of Kyrin's charge!"

Minarik bent down, gripped Innowen's arm gently and pulled him up. "You have seen her, then, as I thought," he said. "And perhaps you do love her even at your tender age." He let go of Innowen, turned, and walked back to his horse. "Well, it no longer matters. We'll not catch them tonight." He glanced up at the sky and wiped the drizzle from his forehead with the back of his arm. "Dawn can't be far off. My men are tired, and the rain has washed away any tracks." He took his reins, climbed astride his huge gray, and settled himself upon the animal's bare back. The soldier at his right side held out the javelin and helmet. Minarik took them and set the helmet on his head. "We'll return to Whisperstone and face Kyrin's wrath," he announced, beckoning to Innowen. "Come, you'll ride with me. What's your name?"

"Innocent," he answered without thinking, taking the lord's hand, allowing himself to be hauled upward. Minarik was strong indeed. He balanced Innowen between his thighs and wrapped an arm around his middle. Working the reins with one hand, he steered his horse around to face his soldiers.

"Forget what you've heard here," he told them. "We found these two in the storm, that's all. The Witch and her man are lost to us. If anyone questions you, shrug and blame it on her magic." He glanced at the racing clouds overhead and again wiped the damp mist from his brow. "I'm half-convinced she's responsible for this murk, anyway. Now, who's for food and a crackling fire?"

His four men grumbled agreement, and with Minarik taking the lead, they started back up the narrow path to the main road. Low branches swatted them smartly, and wet leaves licked their faces. Innowen shuddered, remembering how strangely different it had seemed when he rode this way with Vashni. But then he'd been slung over the horse like a piece of baggage. Maybe that was really why the limbs hadn't struck him, why the forest had seemed to shy away as they passed.

He sighed and shivered and tried to adjust himself more comfortably on the horse's wet hide. Minarik's arm tightened about him, and he leaned back against his benefactor. There was warmth in the older man, and Innowen had been cold too long.

〖〗

He had never been so far from home or so far down the forest road. To every tree and boulder there was a wonderful sense of newness that not even the darkness could hide. When the road began to widen, Innowen leaned forward eagerly. Despite the hour, he was not tired. He looked about with excitement.

The clouds parted briefly. A slender moon and a few broken stars lit up the world ahead.

Innowen caught his breath. Slowly, he raised a finger to his mouth and chewed the tip as he stared at the dark, magnificent shape ahead. While he had never seen Minarik's keep before, he had heard tales among the villagers in Shandisti. None of those tales had prepared him for such a sight.

Whisperstone reared defiantly against the heavens, hugging the moon's light to keep the night at bay. Dim candles and lamps bent to the same task, oozing dull amber radiance through the open shutters of the highest windows. Turrets and towers loomed like jagged teeth. Shadows shifted in the crenilations and among the battlements of its fantastic walls where small watchfires burned. Behind it, as if to provide an appropriate backdrop, rose the blacker bulk of a huge, rounded hill.

Impossibly, Whisperstone seemed to grow clearer to Innowen's vision as he gaped. He could make out the individual blocks of stone in the great defensive wall, the crumbling mortar, cracks that had become home to moss and lichen. He knew he couldn't possibly see so clearly in the darkness, yet the illusion persisted.

Then clouds obscured the moon once more, and Whisperstone seemed to fade. Only the pitiful lights in the windows and the watchfires remained like pale, inscrutable eyes that measured their approach.

Innowen trembled.

"Cold?" Minarik asked, his voice breaking the silence as gently as if it were an egg. "We'll be there soon. Dry clothes and hot food will chase away the chills."

Innowen didn't answer. *Not all the chills*, he thought, hugging himself. Whisperstone frightened and fascinated him. He stared ahead, both hoping for and dreading another glimpse of their destination. The clouds granted his wish. The moon lit up the keep once more with an icy white light, but only briefly before closing in again.

The night teased him like that. Several more times, the moon shone through only to be swallowed by the clouds. Each time, Whisperstone brightened and faded, as if it were not quite part of this world, but on a misty boundary between earth and unreality.

The road grew wider still. They passed a house set back among the trees, then another with a small forge in a shed beside it; the coals still glowed with dull red heat and exuded thin wisps of smoke. A little further along, several houses stood clustered together. There was a barn and a corral full of horses. The animals stood quietly and unmoving, disinterested as the soldiers rode by.

Innowen required no moonlight now to see Whisperstone. The road led straight ahead through its mighty, massive gates. On either side of it, small shops and cottages stood darkly silent. Innowen peered at the doorways and shutters for any sleepy faces that might peek out. But the village was still. No one and nothing stirred.

The immense gates stood open. A pair of guards kept watch at the entrance, clutching long, wooden-shafted spears with glistening copper leaf-shaped points. They looked thoroughly miserable in sodden cloaks, yet they pulled themselves to attention and saluted properly as their lord approached.

Minarik's small company passed through the gates and rode across a muddy expanse. It was more than a mere courtyard. It might have been a huge training ground or a vast common area. A few outbuildings, barely visible, nestled in the shadow of the great wall.

One of the gate sentries walked alongside Minarik's horse, lighting the way to the keep's entrance with a single oil lantern. Innowen caught his breath again when the dirty glow illumined a brief cascade of wide marble stairs that rose up between two huge, ancient, fluted columns. Just beyond the columns, a pair of ponderous doors stood shut. Hideous bronze visages peered back at him through the gleam, immense masks, he realized, hammered and embossed into the metal plating that strengthened and reinforced those doors.

And there was more. Demons danced and wild spirits writhed obscenely in relief around the masks, as if the artist had sought to depict some hellish orgy. In the lamp's flickering, the figures seemed to move, and Innowen clapped a hand to his mouth.

Minarik gave a low chuckle and squeezed the boy's shoulder. "Nothing to hurt you, son," he said. "Whisperstone was built in another age, long before my father's fathers came to own it. Men were superstitious in those days, and our home reflects many of the old beliefs. Those were made to frighten away intruders, but they're only the imaginings of a skillful artisan, nothing more." He squeezed Innowen's arm again. "You're much too frail and delicate for your age, boy." It was a soldier's appraisal, and Innowen squirmed. "You need some muscle and meat on you."

Innowen drew his shoulders up around his ears and gathered the cloak tighter around his throat.

Minarik scratched his bearded chin. "I'd heard that your woodcutter lived with a crippled lad. Drushen, you said his name was? How did that rumor get started?"

Innowen only shrugged. How could he explain his newfound ability to walk? It was easier to let the Lord of Whisperstone wonder. Rumors were only rumors, and in time, Minarik would surely dismiss the story.

"You've turned sullen," Minarik observed. He waited, as if expecting Innowen to answer. When Innowen volunteered nothing, he continued. "I've shut myself within these walls too long. I barely know the people who dwell in my corner of Ispor anymore."

Innowen twisted on the horse's bare back to see Minarik's face. The regretful tone of Minarik's remark surprised him, and his mouth fell open. He thought of his lonely cottage in the woods and the years spent with only Drushen for company. Except for the rare times when he accompanied his guardian to Shandisti to sell wood, that had been his world. But he'd been an invalid and a cripple. How could a man like Minarik, vigorous and full of a man's strength, how could he hide inside his walls when the whole world sprawled at his feet?

He saw something suddenly in the older man's eyes, just a brief flash, something deep and sad. A memory, perhaps, or an old hurt. Innowen bit his lip and turned away, knowing with a strange certainty that some mystery surrounded Minarik, something that haunted his heart and soul. He wished he had not seen it, that he had not looked in those eyes. It disturbed Innowen, filled him with an odd disquiet.

He jerked his head up suddenly and frowned. His imagination was running away with him. How could he know such a thing? Who was he to judge this man who had treated him so kindly? It was time to get a grip on his senses, on his reason.

He clenched his eyes shut and opened them, then he gazed again at Whisperstone, his lips forming a taut line. The keep was huge; he felt dwarfed and cold in its shadow. But it was only a keep, he told himself, an ancestral home for a long line of noblemen. In the darkness, it seemed to breathe with a palpable life. In the light of day, though, he knew it would be just a pile of stones.

Minarik eased himself back onto the rump of his horse and slid down to the ground. Then he held his arms out to help Innowen dismount. As soon as his feet touched the muddy earth, Innowen pitched backward, over-balanced. The horse started to bolt, but Minarik caught its reins and jerked hard with a low shout. The beast stilled at once, and he reached down and lifted Innowen from the mud.

"You're a clumsy boy," he said with a grin, "but, I think, a likable one."

Innowen's cheeks burned with embarrassment, and he looked despairingly at his fine cloak now splattered with filth.

"Don't worry," the lord said, laying a hand on Innowen's shoulder. He passed the reins of his horse to the sentry who carried the lantern and guided his young guest up the steps toward the pair of doors. Two of his soldiers surrendered their reins to the same guard and followed, bearing Drushen's unconscious form between them. "Gently," Minarik cautioned them.

The Lord of Whisperstone pushed open the doors and led the way inside. Innowen blinked as light spilled around him. The inner hall blazed with a brilliance provided by mirror-enhanced lamps. Behind each sconce a plate of burnished copper hung, intensifying and reflecting the lamps' fireglow. Innowen had heard of such a thing, but never seen it.

Minarik beckoned. "Come in, Innocent."

He frowned and hesitated. His feet were muddy and his cloak dripped. Whisperstone's floor was made of beautiful marble tiles. Minarik had left tracks, but then, it was his floor.

The lord shook his head with undisguised mirth. He dragged the sole of his sandal on the floor, leaving a thick smear. "I have many slaves and hired servants," he said. "Now come along."

Innowen swallowed, then stepped inside. The stone was cold beneath his bare feet. A small grin blossomed on his face. He'd never felt such a sensation against his feet before! Or any sensation until tonight. All the terror of Whisperstone fled before this unexpected reminder that his body was whole, that he had feeling where none had ever been, that he could walk. He wiggled his bare toes on the marble, unable to hide his delight.

"You're a strange one," Minarik said wonderingly, and Innowen noticed the curious expression his host wore.

He made a hasty excuse for his behavior as he went to Minarik's side. "I've never stood on such a fine floor." At least it was not a lie. He didn't want to lie to this man again. "We had a dirt floor in the cottage."

They walked down a long hall and turned into another. A huge, powerful-looking servant clad in a robe of white homespun hurried to meet them and to gather their wet garments. Innowen cowered away, rather than surrender his cloak. He was naked underneath; he didn't want to stand bare and dirty in this place where great men lived. The servant tried to snatch it, anyway.

Minarik saved him. "Taelyn, let him be," he ordered with a patient voice. "I gave him the cloak. Go, and prepare a room for him and his guardian. The old man is ill, so light a good fire, and get food and drink ready for them."

Taelyn shot a baleful glare at Innowen but bowed and hurried to obey. The two soldiers followed after him, bearing Drushen between them by heels and shoulders, as if he were a sack of vegetables. Innowen started to protest, but then he caught a quick glimpse of his guardian's face; it was composed in utter peace.

Innowen turned uncertainly toward Minarik. Was he supposed to go with Drushen or stay with his host?

"Are you tired?" Minarik asked.

He shook his head.

"Come with me, then. This is your chance to meet Ispor's new king." Minarik wiped a frown away with the back of his hand. "It's not the honor it should be, but young as you are, you may find some thrill in it."

He didn't miss Minarik's doubtful tone, and if the noble hid his frown behind a hand, he couldn't hide the creases that lined his brow when he spoke of Koryan's son. But Kyrin was king now, and respect was his due. It was not right to speak as Minarik had.

In their brief time together, though, Innowen had come to trust Minarik. If the Lord of Whisperstone disliked his new monarch there must be some reason. He, too, would be wary then, and form no quick judgment.

He wished that he had better clothes, any clothes, in which to meet a king, but he had no chance to remark on it. Minarik had already started down the hall. Innowen clutched the corners of his cloak and hurried after him, his bare feet making dull slapping sounds on the cool marble.

They turned into yet another corridor. Everywhere Innowen looked, weapons adorned the walls. Spears and leaf-shaped swords hung on pegs or stood paired in niches and alcoves. Lamplight gleamed on the bronze blades of crossed axes and on small, beautifully carved bows and flint-tipped arrows. There were weapons unknown to him, relics, he guessed, of another time or from far-off lands. A row of ceremonial shields lined one passage, each different in shape and ornamentation. He recognized few of the mythic creatures, nor any of the demonic faces beaten or painted upon their surfaces, but he thought they leered at him and followed him with their copper-glinting eyes.

"Are there ghosts at Whisperstone?" he murmured softly, afraid that his voice might echo in the corridors and disturb things better left alone.

Minarik didn't stop or answer, but his throaty chuckle did nothing to calm Innowen's fears. Innowen swallowed, took a deep breath, and walked a little faster in his host's footsteps.

The corridors twisted and turned until he thought he would get dizzy and embarrass himself by falling again. Yet he walked on and did his best to keep the swift pace without stumbling. The ornate workings and furnishings of the keep nearly overwhelmed him. In his young life he had never seen such opulence. Where there were no weapons adorning the walls, there were sculptures. Where there were no sculptures, there were friezes and frescoes. Without asking, Innowen knew they were the works of master artisans. Each was flawless, exquisite even to his crude and uneducated sensibilities.

A gentle music, the sweet high notes of a reed pipe, floated down the hall. It grew louder as they walked, and clearer. He listened to its enchanting purity. Each note was perfect. The tones rose and faded without wavering. Unthinking, he began to sway. He drew one arm gracefully up and over his head.

With a jolt of realization, he stopped himself. Because he walked a little behind Minarik, the lord had not seen, and he was thankful for that. Still, the music was lovely. He could barely keep from dancing; that was what he longed to do, had longed to do all his life, to dance.

He remembered where he was and put his desires aside. There would be a time to dance. This was not that time, though. He was in a great house with a great man, and on his way to meet a king. He lifted his chin and thrust out his chest, attempting to bear himself with proper dignity.

As he drank in the music, he swore he heard his name in the next three notes.

Minarik stopped abruptly, and Innowen ran into him. Inwardly, he cursed himself and started to apologize. But the Lord of Whisperstone had not even noticed. Instead, he stood stiffly, with fists clenched at his sides, and glared at four sentries who blocked a pair of oaken doors.

Innowen studied the four, quickly noting the short red-sleeved tunics under the leather breastplates on two of the men, which set them apart from Minarik's men, who wore chitons of green with embroidered short sleeves under their armor. The pair in scarlet smiled with smug contempt, while the other two looked down at the floor in shame.

A low, angry sound rumbled in Minarik's throat. Ignoring their spears, he grabbed the reds by their collars and hurled them away from the entrance. Innowen cringed away and flattened himself against a wall. Minarik's two men stepped back with stricken looks on their faces, uncertain of what to do. Minarik scowled at them, and they bowed apologetically out of his way.

Minarik kicked open the thin, wooden doors; they rebounded on the inner walls with a crash, and Minarik smashed them back again as he stormed through.

Innowen quickly followed, ducking under the arm of a sentry who dared to make a grab for him.

Apparently, the man lacked the courage to chase him. Or perhaps it was good sense that made him decide to remain at his post in the corridor.

This new hall was yet another amazement in a night filled with wonders. It was larger than his entire cottage and far more splendid. And the music! It swirled around him, overwhelming his senses. He spotted its source, a young girl at the farthest end of the room. She sat on a pillow playing her pipe at the feet of a man who he knew could only be Ispor's new king.

"You insult me, Kyrin!" Minarik's bellow rolled through the chamber. Startled by the force of Minarik's anger and awed that he would dare to address Kyrin so bluntly, Innowen forgot the girl and gave his attention back to his benefactor. "Do you fear my warriors, that you must add your own guards to my doors? Do you doubt my loyalty?"

Kyrin sat on an ornate, cushioned chair, which was positioned on a low dais against the room's far wall. He half reclined in it, with one leg thrown casually over an arm of the chair, and he peered at them over the rim of a flat-bowled kylix. "No insult at all," he answered, wiping a trace of wine from his lip with one finger.

To Innowen's surprise, Kyrin's voice carried with equal power, though he did not shout. The girl at his feet fluttered a note on her pipe suddenly, as if to draw his attention to the hall's nearly perfect acoustics. He looked at her, and their eyes met briefly before she glanced shyly away, lifted her instrument, and resumed her soft play.

"Unless it is to me," Kyrin continued, straightening himself as he put both feet on the floor. "I ordered two of my men to stand duty so that yours could join the search for that cursed Witch."

Innowen stiffened. Cautiously, he moved from behind Minarik and found a place near the lord's right hand. He took a harder look at this king. A scarlet cloak lay discarded in a heap on the floor near the chair. Several trays and vessels were also scattered about. Innowen studied the fine red robe that Kyrin wore, the mass of black braids that crowned his head, the richly oiled beard that hid the lower half of his face, the eyes that glittered darkly even over the length of the hall.

Who are you, he thought with slowly growing bitterness, to speak of the Witch and to dare hunt her through rain and wind. Even if you were king of the world, you would pale beside her.

"But they refused!" Kyrin rose from the chair, his hand clenching so tightly on the supporting base of the kylix that wine splashed over its rim. "As if your order took precedence over mine!" As suddenly as he had sprung up, he seemed to relax again, and he forced a smile. "Still, because it's your house, I spared their heads. This time." He took a sip from his cup and wiped his mouth again with the back of a hand. "Well, did you find her?"

Minarik sighed and rubbed his eyes with a thumb and forefinger. "Except for the few who remain on watch, all my men are scouring the countryside. But I tell you, Kyrin, this damned storm has spoiled any sign of a trail. The gods alone know where she is by now."

Anger flashed over Kyrin's face. With a visible effort, he mastered himself, bent down to the girl with the reed pipe, and placed a hand affectionately on her head as he whispered something in her ear. She put down her pipe and smiled up at him. He stroked her beautiful black hair and returned her smile. Slowly, she got to her feet, made a delicate curtsy to him and then to Minarik, hugged her instrument to her bosom and left the room.

Innowen stared after her, painfully aware of the absence of her quiet piping. The room seemed cold and still without her music. Even the air went stale, and what had seemed splendid before became plain.

"I ordered you to find the Witch!" Once the child was gone, Kyrin's rage returned. "I ordered you!" He rose to his feet and shook a fist at Minarik. "You dare face me empty-handed?"

Minarik sneered. "You'll find soon enough, boy, that it's one thing to order men, and quite another to order fate! Are you such a great king? Go tell the storm to stop, and tell the rain to leave her tracks untouched! Go on, I'll wait here!"

Kyrin purpled. With a shout, he flung his winecup at the Lord of Whisperstone. Innowen also gave a cry. Without thinking, he leaped in front of Minarik. The vessel struck him in the chest; red wine splashed his face.

A hand closed on his shoulder and pulled him out of the way, but Minarik spared no glance or thanks. He turned toward the doors instead, and called to one of his men. "Take my young guest to Taelyn," he instructed the green-sleeved guard. "He's prepared a room. Make sure the boy and his guardian are comfortable."

"Don't turn your back on me, Uncle!" Kyrin bellowed. "It's a mistake to turn your back on me!"

"So I've heard," Minarik answered darkly, turning from Innowen and resuming his argument with Kyrin.

Uncle! Innowen watched over his shoulder as the

guard led him out. Minarik and Kyrin faced each other. Like giants, they seemed to him, ready to bite and claw. The guard led him through the doors and out into the corridor. Shouting followed them and echoed through the keep.

"Is he really the king's uncle?" Innowen asked his guard. The soldier only grimaced and said nothing.

Whisperstone was a maze. One corridor turned into another. They went up, down, and under stairways. They met no other servants, and all but a handful of soldiers were looking for the Witch and Vashni. The oppressive silence unsettled him. He found himself thinking of the girl with the pipe again and of her music.

Ahead, a door eased open. Innowen recognized the servant who had met them earlier. "Oh, you're here, are you?" Taelyn said. "Well, good." He waved a hand impatiently at the guard. "Go back to your business," he said. "This young man is in my care now. Go on, I say." The guard departed, silent as ever.

The servant beckoned Innowen into the room. A rush of pleasant warmth swept over him. A fire crackled in the fireplace, and oil lamps burned in each of the four corners. A sweet scent wafted on the air; he couldn't tell its source, but he inhaled deeply.

"Over there," Taelyn said, "is a basin where you may wash." He indicated a low pedestal near the fire where a bowl and pitcher rested. "And here," he continued, leading him to a small table, "are fruits and strip-meats to eat and fresh water to drink. Your guardian is in the next room." Innowen followed him through a narrow archway into another chamber. "Your bed is also here."

He had never seen such finery on a bed before. The

idea of stretching his body upon it, weary as he was, almost appalled him. It was too fine! Only a single candle lit this room, but it was enough to tell the quality of the rich spread and the lush pillows, and the thick carpets that surrounded it all.

Drushen slept quietly on another bed on the shadowed side of the room. Innowen crept toward him, ran a hand over the beautiful quilt that covered his old friend, and sat down gently beside him.

The dim candlelight glimmered on the flecks of gray in Drushen's beard and dark hair. The old man's lids were pale and blue-veined. His face, though, had been washed and the filth combed out of his hair.

"Did you do this?" he asked over his shoulder.

Taelyn let go a too-loud sigh. "I couldn't very well have him soiling Minarik's sheets, and there was no one else to do it this time of night." He sighed again. "Or morning, I should say. Now, if you have no other needs, I'll wish you pleasant dreams and seek my own rest."

"Wait," Innowen called softly. "My thanks for all you've done. I will remember you to Lord Minarik."

That brought a chuckle. "Remember me to him? As if he could damn well run this household without me! You have much to learn, young man."

Innowen frowned at such rudeness, but reminded himself that he was a guest in someone else's house. "Then, I'll bid goodnight to Minarik's very important servant," he said with mock-courtesy.

Taelyn looked at him for a moment, then grinned, as if he actually appreciated Innowen's daring. "Servant?" he said, lifting an eyebrow as he pulled away the neck of his chiton to expose a narrow collar of black leather. "You honor a poor slave." Then he was through the archway and gone. In the other room, the door closed gently.

When Taelyn was gone, Innowen gazed down at Drushen and brushed his fingers over the old man's brow. The skin was cool and soft, a wondrous contrast to the woodcutter's rough features, the sharp bone lines, the traceries around his eyes and mouth. He sought Drushen's hand beneath the quilt and squeezed it. *Get well*, he wished. *Don't leave me alone.*

He rose from the bedside, went into the other room, and washed his body. When he was clean again, he took a fruit from the table and drank water. The air was warm, too warm. The only window was in the bedchamber, and the shutters were closed. Would Drushen get cold if he opened it? Perhaps he could risk just a crack. He crept over the carpets.

"Innowen?"

He turned away from the shutters at the sound of his name. His guardian stared at him from the pillow, smiling weakly.

"Drushen!" he exclaimed, hurrying to the bedside. He hugged the old man and leaned his head on Drushen's chest. "I was afraid when you wouldn't wake up. But you're all right! This is a night of miracles!"

Drushen's voice was barely audible. "Miracles?" he managed. Then he touched Innowen's leg. Though his eyes were filmed and bleary, they suddenly lit up with wonder.

"Yes!" Innowen laughed, springing up and spinning on his heel. "I can walk! The Witch made it possible. She healed you, too." He slapped his thighs. "Drushen, she's such a beautiful lady, and she made me a whole man!" Joyful tears began to leak down his face.

Drushen struggled up onto one elbow and swung a leg over the side of the bed. Tears misted his eyes, too, as he rose and reached for Innowen. "The gods!" he cried. "Thank the gods!" He flung up his arms.

But Innowen caught his old friend's arms and pulled them down to his sides and intertwined Drushen's fingers in his own. It startled him as he realized suddenly that he was as tall as Drushen, and he bit his lip. "Stop," he said. "It wasn't any of the gods we know. It was the Witch and some strange god from another land." He swallowed, abruptly fearful. What if the gods were listening? He knew little about Ispor's gods, but he knew all gods were jealous. Still, he dared to continue. "It is to that god I owe thanks, not to the gods of Ispor who made me lame."

Drushen looked at him oddly. "Witch?" He shook his head slowly. "What are you ranting about, boy? I dreamed of fire in my veins and a cool storm. There were voices. But a witch? The Witch of Shanalane?" They regarded each other uncertainly, and Drushen's face clouded over. Abruptly, though, he brightened again and caught Innowen in a fierce embrace. "I don't understand, but it doesn't matter. You can walk! Praise whatever god for it!"

They held each other for a long moment until Drushen sagged back onto the bed. Innowen remembered that the Witch had said he would be weak when he awoke. And hungry. He went into the other room and hurried back with the platters Taelyn had left.

Drushen waved them away. "I'm too happy to eat," he said, his voice only a whisper. "Perhaps later. But throw back those shutters, child. It's nearly morning. Let me see the first light of day."

Innowen obeyed, pushing open the shutters as far as they would go. The faintest hint of dawn colored the horizon. The sun promised to rise right in their window. They would watch it together.

For the first time in my life, Innowen thought, I will greet the day on my feet.

Slowly, the sun climbed over the edge of the world, spreading its brilliant fire. Never had it seemed brighter or lovelier. Higher and higher it floated. Drushen reached out, caught Innowen's hand, and gave it an affectionate squeeze.

The sun sailed higher, chasing away the last vestiges of night. It bathed Innowen's face with a fine warmth that spread like a rich wave over his naked chest, down his stomach, down to his legs.

Suddenly, Innowen folded like a broken puppet, striking his head sharply on the floor. With a small, despairing cry he blinked away the red starflashes that filled his vision. He tried to get up.

"No!" he screamed when his legs refused to move.

Drushen dropped down beside him, placing his arms around the boy. The fear in his gaze mirrored Innowen's own. His lower lip trembled as he tried to pull Innowen to his feet.

"They won't move, Drushen!" Innowen whispered, staring in horror at his useless limbs. "I can't move them."

Taelyn rushed into the room in his nightshirt. Minarik appeared moments later still in his wet riding garments. Together, they helped Drushen lift him onto his own bed.

"What happened to the boy?" Minarik asked, getting no answer from Drushen. Taelyn only shrugged.

Innowen clutched at Drushen's arm and pulled him closer, wide-eyed. "Don't leave me," he begged. "Please, don't leave me alone!"

"I'm right here," Drushen assured him. The old man crawled onto the bed and curled his body protectively around Innowen. "I'll always be here. I'll always take care of you." Weeping silent tears, he kissed the boy's cheek and brushed a hand over Innowen's hair.

Minarik and Taelyn stood uncertainly at the foot of the bed, casting troubled looks at each other, muttering words that Innowen didn't understand. He didn't care. He shivered against Drushen and stared at the window.

The beautiful sun sat perched on the sill, and he could hear it laughing at him.

CHAPTER

3

INNOWEN STAYED IN bed all day. Drushen brought him food, but he ate little. Minarik came to visit and sat with him, but he was clearly puzzled by Innowen's unexplained paralysis and sullen silence. Taelyn hovered around like a worried mother. Innowen refused to talk to any of them. He wanted only to be left alone, and when he was alone he cried slow, soundless tears and rubbed his unfeeling legs.

Beyond the open window, the sky segued from sweet autumn blue to somber twilight. A quiet wind blew into the room, touching him with the cool softness of a ghost's breath. He bit his lip and turned his face to the pillow. Drushen entered and worriedly brushed a hand along Innowen's cheek. When Innowen didn't respond, the old man lit a candle, set it on a bedside table, and left. Outside, darkness inundated the world.

With a sob, the first sound he had made all day, Innowen clutched his coverlet and drew himself into a ball.

A moment later, with a mingled sense of shock and excitement, he opened his eyes hesitantly and looked at his knees between his arms. He drew a sharp breath, then pressed his lips together, his tongue clenched between his teeth. His heart pounded. He lay utterly still, afraid to move, afraid it was only a dream, and in that moment he prayed to every god he knew.

He straightened his right leg, sliding it slowly upon the smooth sheets, and knew he was not dreaming. He straightened the other. Carefully, he sat up. The soles of his feet touched the carpet. The sensation of the cool, plush weave on his skin reassured him, and he wiggled his toes experimentally. Every muscle in his body tensed as he pushed himself off the bed and stood erect. He squeezed his eyes shut, expecting to fall, and peeled them open when his limbs proved themselves.

He moved cautiously toward the window, shuffling his feet, fearing to lift them too high. Something beyond the window called him. What was it? He leaned his hands on the sill and breathed deeply. Once more, the wind came to him out of the darkness like a chill, invisible serpent that twined over every part of his naked body. He felt it crawl over his face and chest, over his legs. He was alive again!

A gasp and a clatter sounded from behind him. He turned. Drushen stared, ashen-faced, his jaw open. At his feet, a silver tray lay turned upside-down on the carpet. A few scraps of meat showed under the edge, and a cracked goblet rocked beside it in a spreading pool of water. His guardian took two steps toward him, then stopped uncertainly, staring with fear-widened eyes.

"It's the night," Innowen said with barely controlled awe. He turned from Drushen and gazed past the sill again, out into the unknowable dark. No star burned in the heavens, no moon. There was only the void. "I don't think the Witch knows. But her god does."

"What are you talking about?" Drushen whispered. Fear thickened the old man's voice, and Innowen felt the distance between them like a wall. "What evil—"

Innowen cut him off. "It's not evil, Drushen." He

hugged himself as the wind fluttered over him. "It's the night. I understand now. The daytime is my enemy. Sunlight steals my legs from me. It makes them useless. But the nighttime is mine. I can walk from sundown until dawn. That is the gift of the Witch's god."

The carpet rustled as Drushen took another step and stopped again. He managed to utter, "A child of darkness? Is that what you've become?"

Innowen whirled. "I'm no child, Drushen. I'm tall as you, if not as strong. I've seen eighteen springs, and I'm no longer so helpless that I have to quietly suffer being called a *child*. I'm a man." He clenched his fists and turned away from his guardian to stare back through the window. It was another world out there, a world unlike his cottage prison, unlike this room in Whisperstone, totally different from the world of the daytime. "At least, I'm a man at night." He closed his eyes and opened them, then walked past Drushen into the outer chamber and toward the door.

"Where are you going?" his guardian called, hurrying after him. He caught Innowen's arm and spun him around.

Innowen started to snap, but stopped himself and sighed. He loved Drushen; the old woodcutter was the only family he'd ever known. He couldn't be blamed if he still treated Innowen like a cripple. In time, he would rejoice, too. "For a walk," Innowen said finally, laying a hand gently on the old man's shoulder. "I've never gone for a walk by myself before."

Drushen managed a weak smile, though his face was lined with worry. "Well, you'd better put something on," he said. He turned toward the table, which, the night before, had been laden with food. Someone had placed a small pile of folded garments there. His guardian lifted a pale blue chiton from the top, shook it once, and held it out to him. "This isn't our home, and you can't run naked around a grand place like this."

The fabric was an incredibly fine weave. Innowen had never seen its like. Drushen handed him another cloth of equal softness to wrap about his loins. Then he draped the chiton over Innowen's body, leaving the left shoulder bare, and fastened a small silver brooch that closed the right shoulder. The hem touched the middle of Innowen's thigh, but when he added a leather belt and laced it tight around his waist, it rose a bit higher.

"Look," Drushen said, crossing to the other smaller table where the water basin sat with an oinochoe jug. In his haste the night before, Innowen had not noticed the large copper mirror behind the basin. He stared at his own image.

He had seen his face as a water reflection when Drushen had carried him to bathe in the stream near the cottage, but never had he seen himself standing erect. He turned slowly, viewing himself from every angle. It was not his image, but the reflection of his *movement* that fascinated him. He noted with wonder how the muscles in his side rippled if he leaned a certain way, how tilting his head back exposed the veins in his neck. His chest was too narrow, he quickly decided, and his arms too thin, yet there was a grace in his body that surprised and delighted him.

"You'll become vain, boy," Drushen said from the center of the room. "You have the beauty for it."

Innowen didn't turn, but their gazes met in the polished metal. "The power of movement is a magic all its own," he answered. "I see that now. You've had that magic all your life, so you don't appreciate it. You don't see what a miracle it is to lift your foot from here," he pointed to a spot on the floor, "and put it here. And this is an even greater miracle." He rose onto the ball of his left foot, pirouetted with perfect control, and faced himself in the mirror once more. "But it's a magic utterly new to me, and it makes me feel..." He hesitated, looked sad for a moment, then pirouetted again. "I don't know. I'm almost glad that I could never walk until now."

"It's the Witch's power you feel," Drushen said darkly. "And nobody gives something for nothing."

At that, Innowen faced his guardian. "Don't they, Drushen? You found me on the road when I was a newborn baby, and took me in. You fed me and took care of me, raised me and loved me. What do you want in return?"

The hurt showed visibly in the old woodcutter's eyes, but he said nothing, only stared back silently.

"I'm sorry," Innowen said, relenting. "Just don't speak ill of the Witch."

Drushen hung his head. "Not if it upsets you," he agreed quietly. "But remember she is a *witch*. You know nothing about her, not even a name to call her by."

"No one knows her name," Innowen countered. "But I owe her no less, and somehow I intend to find her." He swallowed as he tugged at the hem of the chiton and adjusted his belt. "Now I'm going for a walk. Coming?"

Drushen smiled weakly again and looked askance. "I thought you wanted to go alone," he said. "You've never taken a walk by yourself, remember?"

"I've never taken a walk with you, either," Innowen reminded him, and he poked his guardian in the ribs playfully with one finger. "Not without being carried, anyway." He took a step past Drushen and opened the door. "Coming?"

Reluctantly, Drushen nodded.

They went into the corridor together, and Drushen pointed to the left. "That way leads back toward the Great Hall," he said, and that was enough for Innowen. The stone floor was cold against his bare feet, so he set a brisk pace. His guardian, though, had no trouble keeping up. As he had noted before, Whisperstone was a maze, and they were quickly lost. He wished momentarily that he'd waited to invite Taelyn to join them, or perhaps even Minarik himself. But he was in no hurry. It was only just nightfall. He had until dawn to explore.

Many of the corridors were dark, but some of them were lit with lanterns hanging on pegs, or by oil lamps suspended by small chains from beams in the ceilings. Innowen thought about simply appropriating one of the lanterns, but after all, this wasn't their home, and their host might take it unkindly. Instead, they made their way carefully from one pool of light to the next.

When they passed an occasional window, they stopped. Most were shuttered tight, but one or two were slender, open embrasures barely wide enough to stand in sideways. Innowen squeezed into one and looked out. On the wall far below, he could just discern the watchfires of the sentries. He wondered if they were Minarik's men or if Kyrin was still at Whisperstone, too. Except for Drushen and Taelyn and, briefly, Minarik, he'd seen no one all day. Where was everyone? Were they still hunting the Witch?

A chill wind blew suddenly on his body, forcing him back inside.

They continued on, up and down staircases, through corridors both narrow and wide, lit and unlit, and at last found themselves in the entrance hall before Whisperstone's great doors. There, lamps blazed in mirrored niches, casting a rich, warm glow. Innowen considered the several passages that branched from the entrance hall and chose the one he thought he'd walked with Minarik the night before. It occurred to him that he might find his benefactor if he retraced the steps they had taken together.

But as he started that way, a few sweet notes of music touched his ears. He stopped, and the music stopped. He'd heard that ethereal piping before, and he remembered the girl at Kyrin's feet. Another flurry of notes played on the air and faded. Innowen listened expectantly to the silence.

"It's beautiful," Drushen said when it started and stopped again. "Can you tell where it's coming from?"

Innowen shook his head, listening, hoping for more. "No, but I met the piper last night. She's as pretty as her song."

A cascade of music suddenly filled the hall. Innowen looked at Drushen, and the old man's face lit up. It didn't stop so quickly this time, either. The sound flowed around them in a joyful rush. "Beautiful," Drushen repeated, his voice a reverent whisper.

"This way," Innowen said, choosing the passage from which the music seemed to originate. He could feel it on his skin like a warm watery wave. His step lightened as he went; he could barely keep from dancing. The Witch had told him he had to dance to walk. But he held himself back, resisting each insistent note. When he found the piper, then he would dance.

After a series of turns, the passage led them to a half-opened door. A cool breeze blew inside, carrying the music with it. Just beyond, they found an inner courtyard. The walls of Whisperstone rose up on all sides, but the stars shone brightly overhead in a narrow patch of sky.

The piper sat in a small gazebo in the courtyard's center. Wrapped in a white feathered cloak to keep out the chill, she held her instrument to her lips and played, oblivious to everything as she swayed in time to her pipings. In the flickering light of the gazebo's two lamps, Innowen thought for a moment that he saw the very notes as they fluttered like tiny butterflies through the air. He blinked, and they were gone, just another odd hallucination inspired by her music.

It was the same girl he'd seen the night before at Kyrin's feet, but he still didn't know her name. She was lovely, though, and he guessed her age to be about twelve or fourteen. He watched as she played with her eyes softly closed. Two lamps, suspended on thin chains, swayed lightly in the breeze and cast a wonderful play of orange and red upon her features and upon her ivory fingers as she worked the holes of her pipe. Tresses of dark hair spilled from under her ample hood. She was small and slender, and as Innowen looked at her cloak of feathers, he could not help but think of her as a delicate bird.

Suddenly, she opened her eyes and saw them. The music stopped, though the pipe remained frozen at her lips. Slowly, she lowered it to her lap and turned her gaze shyly downward.

Her mouth, even in the lamplight, was a dark flower that gleamed with sweet dew.

"Our apologies," Drushen said, bowing. "We didn't mean to interrupt. But we heard you playing."

She said nothing, but Innowen saw the smile that so subtly parted her lips.

He walked closer and leaned on the gazebo's ornate wooden latticework. A leafy vine brushed his face, and he pushed it aside. The girl kept her attention fixed on her pipe and refused to look at him. Nervously, she turned the instrument over and over in her hands, then, realizing that she did it, stopped and gripped it tightly.

Innowen grinned. "Scholars say the world was created by music, that the stars and the sun and the moon were mothered in a grand symphony, that the trees and the river, the wind, the seasons are all expressions of a tender cosmic ballad." He hesitated. She was beautiful, this child, and her shyness touched him strangely. "If so," he continued, "then I think you were surely that musician."

She looked up slowly. Her lips formed the tiny hint of a smile as she regarded him from the corners of her eyes. "Do I look so old to you?" It was only a whisper, but her voice was as pure as her music and as sweet.

"The tune you play is the breath of the world," Innowen answered. "Stop playing, and we die."

Drushen nudged him in the arm. "Ispor's gods, boy, where did you ever learn this kind of talk?" To the girl, he said apologetically, "It's not my fault, that's for sure." He leaned closer to Innowen again and muttered, "It's a different kind of spell you're under now...."

Innowen didn't look at his guardian, but unobtrusively found the old man's toe with his heel and put his weight on it. Drushen yelped and pulled his foot free. "Forgive him," Innowen said, giving his attention to the girl again. "He's only an old man."

"That's unkind," she answered, her voice stronger than before. "He's no older than my father or Lord Minarik." She turned her smile on Drushen. "I think he's very handsome, and obviously quite strong. I've never seen such arms before."

Drushen blushed and bowed very low.

"Recipe for a woodcutter," Innowen mumbled. "Two strong arms, one weak mind."

"Recipe for an Innowen," Drushen countered, straightening. "One mouth, two broken sticks."

Innowen whirled, heat rushing into his face. Then, remembering they were not alone, he calmed himself. He didn't want to make a fool of himself in front of her, and he'd asked for that, after all. Back in the cottage, he and Drushen had always poked and jibed at each other. Mouth games, they'd called it. To their rare visitor it had sounded pretty vicious sometimes. But it had just been their way with each other, no holds ever barred and no harm ever meant.

Still, that one had stung him.

The girl glanced away again and rose to her feet. "I should go," she said.

Was that regret in her voice? Innowen turned away from Drushen. "Stay," he said. "Please."

She looked at the pipe in her hands, then at last met his gaze. Her eyes were large and dark, and they sparkled with reflected lamplight.

"What's your name?" he asked.

She lowered her gaze again as she answered. "Dyan."

"Dyan," he repeated. "Two more notes of beautiful music."

Drushen made a strangled noise, then covered his mouth and feigned a coughing fit.

"Your name is Innocent," she said. "I overheard

Minarik and Taelyn talking today. They said you were ill." She looked up once more.

He loved her eyes. "A passing thing," he answered. "I'm better now. In fact, I feel like dancing. Would you play for me?"

"Dyan!"

Her face went pale. Innowen spun around to see who dared to shout at her. Then he stiffened. Drushen shot a glance at him, his brow furrowing in question and confusion, and Innowen reminded himself his guardian had not yet met Kyrin. Ispor's new king marched across the courtyard toward them, his face full of rage. He thrust a finger at Dyan. "Get to your room, girl!"

Dyan fled, her feathered cloak rustling, the hood slipping from her head and her dark hair flying as she hurried over the smooth paving stones, through the door and into the depths of Whisperstone. Angrily, Innowen watched her go.

"You are Minarik's guests," Kyrin said with barely controlled menace. "But stay away from my daughter. You may have fooled my Uncle, but I know your kind. I know what you want." He gripped the hilt of his sword and exposed a portion of its bronze length. The lamplight rippled on its edge. "If you touch her, if you even talk to her again, I'll cut off your hands."

Drushen stepped between them, his hands clenching into huge fists, but Innowen caught his shoulder and tried to pull him back as the two men regarded each other, Drushen breathing rapidly, Kyrin's eyes burning with anger and challenge.

Finally, Kyrin sheathed his blade, though his anger did not abate. He backed off a step. "Your son has saved your life," he said arrogantly.

"My *son*," Drushen sneered, "has saved your teeth."

"Drushen, shut up!" Innowen pushed his guardian away and positioned himself between the two men. To Kyrin he said, "I didn't know she was your daughter. I heard her playing, that's all, and we exchanged a greeting. I meant no offense."

Kyrin's gaze burned into him. "Make sure you understand me, then. Stay away from her. She is uncorrupted, and I mean to keep her that way." He looked at Drushen, then back to Innowen. "This time I'll forgive his insult. It wouldn't be polite to sully my uncle's fine courtyard with common blood for so little reason."

He retreated a few more steps before he turned his back to them and set after his daughter.

Drushen gripped Innowen's shoulder. "You should have let me bend his spine a little, boy. Not too much, mind you, just enough to make him squeal."

Innowen embraced his guardian, knowing full well that Drushen could have carried out such a threat. But he loved this old man. It didn't escape his notice that Drushen had stepped between him and Kyrin. And now that he thought of it, his chest swelled with pride that he had done the same thing when Kyrin turned on Drushen. He could never have done that before when his legs were useless twigs. Now, though, he could walk, and he could stand beside his friends. He had the Witch of Shanalane to thank for that.

That reminded him. *To walk*, she had said, *you must dance*. He had not yet danced, and the night was passing.

"You would have bent his spine, would you?" Innowen said with a wry grin. "You'd have knocked out his teeth?" He clapped Drushen on the shoulder and made a show of straightening the woodcutter's tunic.

"You'd have done that to Kyrin, your king, king of Ispor?" He hugged Drushen and kissed his cheek politely. "I didn't know how much you cared for me."

Drushen pushed his charge back. "Kyrin?" he sputtered, his face clouding with shock at Innowen's news. "What do you mean, calling him king of Ispor? What happened to Koryan?"

Innowen bit his lip. Koryan was dead, but how could he tell Drushen without also explaining that the Witch of Shanalane was accused of his murder? Drushen wouldn't understand; he was already too upset about their meeting and what her magic had done for him. Yet he didn't want to lie to his guardian, either. He hated lying.

Drushen waited impatiently for an answer, and at last, Innowen made his choice. "Koryan is dead, that's all I know." He turned away and stared at the empty chair in the gazebo where Dyan had sat. "I'm only a woodcutter's waif. They don't tell me state secrets."

"But how did you find out?" Drushen pressed.

Innowen shrugged. "Minarik told me on the ride here. You were still sick and unconscious."

The wind blew down into the courtyard, making a low susurrus as it swept along the walls and over the paving stones. The gazebo creaked musically under the gentle force, and the green vines that grew on it rustled.

Innowen listened, then raised one arm gracefully. He leaned to the side and extended into a lunge. He stepped quickly through and drew himself erect as he raised his other arm and repeated the same phrase of movement.

"What are you doing?" Drushen asked uneasily.

Innowen closed his eyes. "Dancing," he whispered.

Drushen grunted, and Innowen heard the old man's steps on the stones as he moved out of the way. "I don't know any dance like that," Drushen commented.

Innowen didn't miss the strange edge in Drushen's voice, but he ignored his guardian. The wind was with him now, and from somewhere came an echo of Dyan's pipe. That was impossible, yet he heard it. The rush of the wind and the sound of her music filled his head. And there was the Witch's storm. The memory of thunder made a wild timpani that drove him. He spun and whirled as the pipe ascended an impossible scale, straining for notes undreamt of. He leaped, and the wind seemed almost to lift and buoy him. His muscles throbbed with energy, stretching in ways they never had before. Sweat quickly beaded on his skin; it ran in thick streams down his neck and chest until the chiton was soaked and clung to him like a rag.

Around the gazebo he moved, throwing back his head with every turn of his body, stopping before Drushen. He jumped, and his right leg described a perfect arc above his guardian's head. He pivoted three times on the ball of his left foot, stopped and clapped his hands together twice under the old woodcutter's nose. He whirled and stopped, leaped and turned and stopped. Each time he stopped, it seemed the world stopped with him and resumed its dance when he did.

He lifted one leg out before him and moved it to the side, a slow, perfectly controlled motion. The thigh muscle bulged with the effort. Sweat glistened there, catching the lamplight as he held it high. The muscle began to quiver, a delicious sensation, and he lifted the leg higher still, pointing his toe, extending his line as far as possible.

Suddenly, another movement caught his eye. With the lamps at his back, his shadow loomed on the far wall. It extended its leg just as he did, but that dark limb seemed to go on forever, reaching around the courtyard. He moved an arm, and his shadow moved, too, with an elongated grace, imitating his motion. He lunged, and it lunged, covering more distance, filling more space, mocking him with its immensity.

But Innowen would not be mocked, not by his own shadow. He challenged it instead, moving with a wild tempestuous frenzy, daring it to follow. It whirled as he whirled, leaped as he did. He couldn't defeat it, he realized. It was not a competitor, but a partner. They danced, his shadow and he, each the equal of the other, one black and ominous and insubstantial, the other in the light, gleaming with sweat-sheen.

He rolled his head back between his shoulders and stared at the small patch of sky visible above Whisperstone. Suddenly the stars were not stars at all, but the eyes of the gods all turned upon him. He danced for the hosts of heaven, danced until his heart was close to bursting.

He leaped and touched the ground, crouched like an animal, ready to spring again. He snapped his head to the side sharply. One hand shot upward to grasp those stars. And froze. The last burst of thunder shivered and rolled away. The last flurry of pipesong diminished and faded. The wind receded. Innowen sustained his effort until the final quivering notes melted away into the night.

Then the silence closed in upon him, and he sank to the ground. A small cry escaped his lips as he sprawled upon the cold stones and gasped for breath. He lay there for a moment, prostrate with exhaustion, too weak to move. Gradually, his heartbeat slowed, and the trembling left his limbs. He raised himself onto his elbows.

"What did you think?" he asked Drushen, his chest still heaving as he struggled to get out the words.

Drushen didn't answer. He stood mutely, hiding his face in his hands. His huge body shook all over. Innowen got to his feet and hurried to his guardian's side to see what was the matter. He slipped one arm around his old friend's shoulder. "Drushen, what is it?" he asked in a hushed tone. "What is it?"

Drushen took his hands from his face and regarded Innowen as if he were a stranger. Slipping free of Innowen's arm, he backed away a few paces and stared at Innowen again. His eyes were full of fear. Innowen went to him and tried once more to embrace him, to reassure him. Something about his dance had upset his guardian. But Drushen wouldn't let him near. He knocked Innowen's arms away when Innowen reached for him, and backed quickly toward the door. "No!" he whispered. "Stay away!" The old man lingered only a moment more, then turned and walked stiffly into the keep.

Innowen let him go. Alone, confused, he walked back to the gazebo and sat down in the only chair and tried to think. He didn't know what to make of the old man's reaction. Drushen had been afraid of him, Drushen, who had killed a wolf with his bare hands one winter when it attacked him at the woodpile as he fetched fuel for the fireplace. Innowen had seen worry on that rough, weathered face before. He'd seen desperation, and outright rage. But never had he seen Drushen in such a state. The unmistakable fear in his eyes, that had been plain enough to see. But there'd been something else, too. Something Innowen didn't understand.

He jumped up and ran across the courtyard. He had to find Drushen and learn what was the matter. The Witch had only healed his legs, that was all. That was nothing to fear. It was a gift, a blessing, even if he could only walk at night. Drushen had to see that. He had to.

He raced into the keep, back down the corridor they had taken to the courtyard and into the main hall. A sweeping stone staircase ascended to the upper levels, and he took the steps two at a time. The passages bent and twisted, seemingly without logic or reason. Sometimes lamplight illumined his way. Sometimes he ran in darkness. He began to fear that he was lost until at last he entered a familiar corridor.

He stopped just outside the door to his quarters and waited for his breathing to calm. Then he pushed it open quietly. Drushen was not in the first room. Innowen found him standing before the opened window in the second, staring outward, biting the knuckles of one hand.

"Don't come in," Drushen warned. "Go away."

"Drushen, I had to dance," Innowen tried to explain from the archway. "The music was so powerful...."

The woodcutter refused to look at him. "There wasn't any music!" he snapped, driving a fist against the stone wall.

"I heard it!" Innowen insisted. "The wind and Dyan's pipe and the thunder. Maybe it was in my head, I don't know. It had to be, because the sky was so clear. All those stars! I don't understand everything, yet. But why are you so angry with me?"

Drushen spun around. In the shadow it was impossible to see his face. Innowen wished uselessly that he had lit a candle or grabbed the lamp from the other room. His guardian came toward him with outstretched arms. "Angry with you, child?" But before he reached Innowen, the old man stopped and clutched his hands to his chest. There was still half the room between them. "No, I couldn't be angry with you. I couldn't." Suddenly, he covered his eyes and rubbed his fists in the sockets. "But what I saw! You were beautiful! It made me feel things! It made me... You made me want..."

Innowen moved swiftly, reaching his guardian and flinging his arms around his shoulders. "What, Drushen? What did you want?"

"Don't touch me!" Drushen pushed him back with a force that sent him sprawling in the middle of the floor. "You don't know! Gods, help me! I never would have! I never meant to!"

Innowen rose slowly, uncertainly, as Drushen took a step toward him. In the dim light that seeped from the other room, he saw his guardian's face and the anguish there. But there was more, too, and worse. Drushen's eyes burned with a dark desire.

"I never would have hurt you," Drushen whispered, coming closer, bending down. Innowen crawled back until the wall stopped his retreat. "I never would have. I promise I won't." The old man shook his head from side to side, but his gaze never left Innowen. "You shine like the moon, boy. You know that? So beautiful!"

Drushen's huge hands caught Innowen around the waist and lifted him as if he were no more than a doll.

Innowen pushed uselessly at his guardian, suddenly frightened and acutely aware of Drushen's powerful strength. "Drushen!" he screamed. The woodcutter didn't say anything as he carried Innowen across the room. "Drushen," Innowen appealed once more, resisting the urge to scream this time, trying instead to sound reasonable and calm. "Please, stop."

"I can't!" Drushen hissed, his breath hard and ragged. He laid Innowen on the bed, pinned him there with one hand, and lifted the blue hem of his chiton with the other. He leaned closer and placed a kiss on the boy's cheek.

"Drushen!" Innowen shouted as he tried to roll off the bed's far side. But a hand crushed down on his mouth, pinning him to the pillow, preventing any more cries. The old man loomed over him like a big monstrous cat, and Innowen was the mouse. He couldn't get free!

"Be quiet," Drushen urged with a terrible, certain calm. "I won't hurt you, child. But your dance! Oh, when I saw you dance." He spoke with a dreadful serenity as he unfastened Innowen's garments. Innowen squeezed his eyes shut, barely able to breathe for the hand over his face. He kicked and flailed to little avail, and the woodcutter ignored his feeble blows. A slight wind brushed over his suddenly naked flesh, and a hot hand began to massage his belly. "Dance for me, Innocent!" Drushen moaned softly. "Dance for me now."

Drushen bent down and kissed him in earnest. Innowen's head swam, and tears spilled from his eyes. The old man's hands roamed through his hair and caressed every part of him, creating fire wherever they touched, strange heatless fire that grew and spread all through him. He lay dumbfounded, burning with a terrible, dark fear and an awful pleasure. Too frightened to look, he turned his face to the pillow and covered his eyes with an arm. When Drushen entered him, he bit his lip, not daring to scream. The bed beneath him seemed to disappear; he melted into endless darkness, floated to a confusion of sensations, all beyond joy or pain, lost in a cruelly consuming tenderness.

He awoke later with the taste of Drushen still in his mouth. From the floor by the bed came a low, pitiful sobbing. Innowen listened weakly until he was sure of who it was. Then, he turned on his side to look. The woodcutter huddled on the carpets, clutching the edge of the bedsheet in one hand as tears streamed down his face. He looked up at Innowen.

"I'm sorry!" he said. "I couldn't stop myself. Innowen, I never would have hurt you!" Drushen got to his knees. His elbows pressed on the bed, and Innowen cowered away. "Forgive me," he begged. "I don't know what possessed me. Forgive me, Innowen!"

But Innowen slunk further back, his throat dry, his body trembling all over.

"Innowen!" Drushen stared in horror and shame. He extended one hand toward his charge while the fingers of the other clawed in the bedclothes. Abruptly, he let go a cry of pure anguish and leaped to his feet.

"I've got to get away," Drushen said in a stricken whisper. He shot a look wildly around the room, as a trapped animal might. "Far away from you before it's too late." He looked once more at Innowen, then fled. "I'm sorry! Sorry!"

Innowen heard the door wrench open, and Drushen's panicked footsteps echoed loudly in the outer corridor until they gradually faded.

He rolled onto his back, shut his eyes, and wept. Out of the darkness came the memory of Drushen's wide, pleading eyes to haunt and terrify him. Slowly, he curled into a ball and hugged himself. He burned all over with strange sensations, yet he felt hollow. His tears fell on the sheets, which were already damp with sweat. No matter how he tried, he couldn't stop them.

Alone, he thought forlornly, *utterly alone.* It was his greatest fear.

He turned over onto his back again, opened his eyes, and looked to the sky beyond the window. He waited for the sun to rise, and he waited for the life to drain from his legs. He waited for Drushen to return, and knew he would not.

CHAPTER

4

ROBIN WAYNE BAILEY

INNOWEN DIDN'T SLEEP at all that night, and the sun was high in the sky when someone knocked at his door. He didn't answer. After a moment, they went away. He listened to the receding steps, remembering Drushen. Sometime later there was another knock. He didn't want to see anyone, didn't want to talk, and shortly, the corridor echoed again with retreating footsteps.

It was almost noon when someone knocked again. He refused to answer, but this time the door opened anyway. Taelyn poked his head through the archway. "Are you awake?" he whispered. Taking a step into the room, he stopped, made a face, and pinched his nostrils shut with his fingers. "Oh gods!" he exclaimed in disgust. "You've soiled the sheets, young man. Couldn't you reach the slop jar? It's right under the bed!"

Innowen said nothing, just turned his head to the side on the pillow and looked away.

"Don't you play silent on me, boy!" Taelyn snapped. "You may be Lord Minarik's guest, but I'm the one who cleans up the messes around here. Now get out of that bed and wash yourself. Those sheets have to be scrubbed at once, or they'll never look clean again." He clapped his hands together sharply. "Move!"

Innowen closed his eyes. "I can't walk," he said without emotion. Languidly, he draped one arm over his eyes.

Taelyn came closer and bent over the bed. The

distaste on his face was obvious as he pulled Innowen's hands down and peered at him carefully. "Where's your guardian?" he asked, suddenly quiet, his anger fading, a note of concern creeping into his voice.

Innowen pulled his hand free and covered his face again. "Gone."

Taelyn stood there a moment. "I'm going to get Minarik," he said finally. "But first, a drink for you. You're feverish." He left Innowen's bedside, went into the other room, and returned with an earthen drinking cup and an ornately decorated hydria jar. He poured a half measure of water into the cup and lifted Innowen's head while he held it for him to sip. Innowen only moistened his lips a little and turned aside again. "I'll get Minarik," Taelyn repeated, setting both cup and vessel where Innowen could reach them easily.

Once more, Innowen found himself alone listening to the sound of fading footsteps. He stared at Drushen's unused bed on the other side of the room, then shut his eyes and shed thick silent tears until, at last, he drew his hand across his face and wiped his nose. Taelyn had gone for Minarik, and lying in his own mess was shame enough. He would not cry before the Lord of Whisperstone if he could help it. He pushed against the bed with his hands and drew his back up against the wall until he could sit up. Beyond the window, the day was bright and crisp, but it failed to cheer him. He pulled the coverlet up to his chest and waited, thinking of Drushen and fighting back the tears that threatened to come again.

Minarik touched his shoulder. Innowen had not heard him enter. He looked up into his benefactor's worried gaze, and then down at his own dead legs. Taelyn came in behind Minarik with an armload of clean bedding, which he set down on Drushen's empty bed before coming to peer over his master's shoulder.

"How are you, boy?" Minarik said, settling gingerly on the edge of the bed.

Innowen turned his gaze slowly back to the lord. Minarik looked terrible. His faced appeared drawn and sleep-deprived. Shadows circled his eyes, and dirt runneled the deep lines of his neck and brow. He smelled, too, of sweat and horse-froth, as though he had ridden some long distance. Yet he had taken time to come see his guest.

"The day passes," Innowen answered in a flat voice, realizing he owed Minarik the courtesy of a response. Still, he could generate no enthusiasm. His lids quivered shut, and he hugged the coverlet as a chill rippled through him. "Drushen is gone."

"I know," Minarik said quietly. "The gate guard told me he left in the middle of the night, taking nothing with him. He said your Drushen was weeping, and that he mumbled a name over and over as he passed through the gate." A hand brushed tenderly over Innowen's damp forehead and pushed back a lock of hair. "Your name, Innocent."

Though he tried to stop it, a droplet squeezed from Innowen's eye and glided down his cheek. He reached up to intercept it, but Minarik instead caught it with his fingertip and held it up to sparkle in the light.

"What passed between you and your guardian last night, boy, to cause you both such grief?" Minarik lowered his hand and wiped the bit of moisture on his tunic near his heart. "The love you bore for each other was plain enough. No father and son could have shown more."

Innowen remembered the pain of Drushen's hands

upon him, so strong, hurting, pinning him. Again, confusion and fear swept over him, so powerful, numbing. Yet he recalled also, one layer of memory over another, his guardian's anguish, his pleas for forgiveness, the sorrow and shame on the old woodcutter's face.

What had driven Drushen to hurt him?

He clenched his fists in the coverlet, struggling to make sense of it, knowing only that some dark desire had possessed his guardian last night and made them both its victim. How could he explain to Minarik? How could he tell such an evil truth, or speak of the deed that had been consummated under his roof? However he disliked it, he knew he had to lie again.

"We argued," he started honestly enough. "About the Witch, and about my legs."

Minarik stopped him. "You are crippled, then, as I'd heard." He nodded with sudden understanding as he lifted one of Innowen's arms and examined it closely. "I knew there was something odd about you. See? The calluses on your elbows where no normal man would have them. And the strange, careful way you walk as if any moment you expect to fall. This is the Witch's work, isn't it?" Minarik ran a hand along Innowen's thigh down to his knee. "She made you whole again."

"Only during the nighttime hours," Innowen said softly. "From sunrise to sunset I'm still half a man."

Minarik looked long and hard at Innowen, then turned away and rubbed his eyes with thumb and forefinger. After a moment, he turned back again, and his features settled into an expression of great weariness. "None of this explains why Drushen ran away."

Innowen drew a breath and let it out slowly. "He didn't know about the Witch's part in this. He thought it was some miracle from the gods. But last night I told him the truth." He looked up and met Minarik's gaze with directness. "Drushen's very superstitious, and he'd heard stories about the Witch of Shanalane. He said terrible things, and when I defended her, he said I was *abathakati*—tainted." Suddenly, he covered his face; he felt shame, but this lie was far better than the truth. "He *hurt* me." Innowen continued finally. He drew a deep breath and leaned his head back against the wall. That, at least, was no untruth. "And I hit him. I'd never done that before. He took it as proof of my utter corruption and fled." He rubbed a hand over his eyes and looked beyond the window. "Now I'm alone. Drushen won't come back, and I have no one."

Taelyn stepped closer. "Lord," he said, bending over Minarik. "You haven't slept all night. You should rest. I'll see that the boy is bathed and the room cleaned. The two of you can continue this discussion later."

Minarik waved him back, then rubbed his eyes as Innowen had done, and rose from the bedside. He shot a smile at Innowen. "You're not the only who needs a bath—I don't know which of us is worse." He sniffed himself and made a face before looking to his slave. "You're right, though, Taelyn. We can continue this, but after we've cleaned ourselves." He leaned down and rumpled Innowen's hair. To Innowen's surprise, he found he didn't mind. "You look after Innocent," Minarik went on, "and when he's presentable, carry him down to the courtyard. See that there's food waiting, too."

Taelyn protested. "You need sleep, my lord."

Minarik put on a patient grin. "You fret too much, old friend. I'm stronger than you think. Riding around pointlessly all night is admittedly a bit tiring, but it only takes an argument with Kyrin to stir the blood again, and mine's been whipped to a froth." He looked back to Innowen. "I'll join you in the courtyard shortly." Then turning again to Taelyn, "He doesn't look half as bad as you said."

Taelyn put on an exaggerated frown. "He perked up deliberately to make me seem like a liar."

Minarik's grin widened, then he shrugged and left the room. Taelyn followed his lord but returned moments later with the wash basin and a cloth. He poured water from the hydria jar by Innowen's bed into the basin.

"I like him," Innowen confided as Taelyn pulled away his coverlet and began to clean him. "But the villagers in Shandisti almost never speak of him. Why is that?"

Taelyn rinsed the cloth, wrung it, and continued his ministrations. "Minarik seldom leaves Whisperstone anymore, except to hunt. This business with Kyrin and the Witch of Shanalane has taken him farther from the gates of his keep than he's ventured in years and years. He entertains few guests, he visits no one, and he stays out of other people's business." Taelyn sighed. "He uses these walls to shut out the whole world."

"But why?" Innowen wondered aloud.

Taelyn shrugged. "A woman," he answered glumly. "It's always a woman, isn't it? Years ago he fell in love. None of us ever saw her, mind you. But nearly every night he would ride from the gates when the sun declined, and each dawn he would return. The horse would be half-dead, but his smile would be brighter than the sun itself."

Taelyn rolled Innowen onto his belly and wet the cloth again. The water was cool, and there was a welcome, comforting pleasure in being cared for. "It went on for nearly the whole of one summer. Then one night, Minarik returned earlier than usual. It was just before the stroke of midnight, and his horse was lathered as if he'd tried to ride the beast into the ground. He just left the poor animal standing untended at the gates and shut himself in his rooms. For three days he spoke no word to anyone."

"She rejected him?" Innowen asked.

"No one knows what happened," Taelyn answered. He dropped the cloth in the basin and set it on the floor beside the hydria jug. "When our lord finally emerged again, he was as you see him now, pleasant and kind, from all appearances a man for men to envy, and he went about his life completely as if nothing was amiss. But from that time on, he almost never left the confines of Whisperstone."

"And no one ever found out who the lady was?" Innowen persisted as Taelyn lifted and carried him to the other bed and set him down.

Taelyn only shook his head as he turned to strip away the soiled coverlets and sheets. "He never breathed her name."

"You never tried to find out?"

Taelyn frowned as he dropped the bundle of bedding on the floor. "My duty is to care for my lord and his house...."

"You did try," Innowen interrupted with a careful smirk.

Again, Taelyn shook his head. "No. It was clear Minarik wanted to forget some deep pain. What good would it have done for me, or anyone, to pick at his scabs?" He snatched up one of the clean sheets he had brought and snapped it in the air before spreading it upon the bed. Before it settled smoothly, though, he jerked it away. "Oh, this won't do at all. We'll have to leave the mattress to dry." He folded the sheet again and returned it to the fresh pile.

Innowen watched Taelyn as he worked. At first, he had thought this slave to be quite a gossip, so freely did he talk about his lord's personal business. But there was something familiar about the way Taelyn spoke of Minarik, some light in his eye, a particular set to his chin. And when Taelyn spoke again, Innowen failed to understand the words, for it was Drushen's voice that filled the room. He saw, then, the love that slave bore for master. But was it Drushen's dark love? That he couldn't tell. It was plain, though, that in Taelyn's heart there was room for nothing else but service to his lord.

Innowen wondered where Drushen had gone. Even though the hurt and shame of last night were not forgotten, he was worried about his guardian and feared he might never see him again.

"You're doing it again!" Taelyn said, snapping his fingers under Innowen's nose. "Minarik walks in and you're attentive as a new bride to her husband. Then he leaves, and you're in and out, just the way I found you, like sunshine on a cloudy day. Did you hear what I said?"

"I'm sorry," Innowen answered honestly, "I didn't."

"I said, you're too heavy for me to carry all the way to the courtyard. I'm no woodcutter, after all. I'll call two servants to take you down, though they won't be happy about it. Everyone's asleep after chasing about the countryside all night." He disappeared through the archway and returned with clean garments similar to the ones Drushen had given him the night before. "Put these on." He tossed them from the arch and was gone before Innowen could question him further.

Innowen dressed himself and waited. He tried not to think about Drushen, but time and again his thoughts turned to the old man, until a dark mood began to settle upon him. He shook himself, trying to resist it, but the mood only took a stronger hold. *What's to become of me without him?* he thought.

Two strangers entered his room and made short bows. They looked very tired, and Innowen realized that, like their lord, these men had been up all night.

"We're to bear you to the courtyard," one of them said, coming forward. The other followed, and together they lifted him upon crossed hands. Innowen draped his arms about their shoulders to steady himself.

"My thanks," he said courteously when they entered the courtyard and approached the gazebo. A second high-backed chair had been placed directly across from the other, and they lowered him carefully into it. The cushions were luxurious; he ran his hands over the finely padded arms.

Behind his bearers came three more slaves. One carried a small table, another a silver tray with goblets and an oinochoe jug decorated with an elaborate floral pattern. The third bore two serving dishes, one heaped with small meat cakes, the other with sliced fruit, dates and nuts. Innowen watched steam rise from the cakes and realized he was quite hungry. He licked his lips and inhaled the aroma.

"Lord Minarik will join you shortly," the last servant informed him. "He wishes that you help yourself until he arrives."

They left him alone in the gazebo. He stared at the warm cakes but decided to wait for Minarik. The table was close enough, though, and he filled one goblet. To his surprise he poured, not water, but wine. He had seldom tasted wine. Drushen had not been able to afford it.

No, he would *not* think of Drushen. He sipped the wine, savoring its potent, unfamiliar taste. It wasn't as wonderful as he'd expected, but he had a feeling he could grow to like it. He took another sip and gazed up at the sky, so blue and cloudless for this time of autumn. It was comfortably warm, too. He studied the walls of Whisperstone block by block as they rose high around him, noting with disinterest the small shuttered apartment windows that dotted its heights. He ran his fingernails over the chair arms and over his unfeeling thighs. At last, he munched a single date.

"Did you taste the cakes? I have the best kitchen staff in the land." Bearing a small bowl, which he placed on the table near at hand, Minarik stepped into the gazebo and smiled as he sat down in the chair opposite Innowen. He had bathed and changed. His garments were regal cloth-of-gold, and he shimmered like one of Ispor's gods. He poured wine into the other goblet, lifted it, then spilled a small quantity on the boards at his feet before he drank. The red liquid quickly ran between the cracks.

"Why did you do that?" Innowen asked, lifting his own goblet.

"Men die, are placed in the earth and become, in time, no more than the dust at our feet," the Lord of Whisperstone explained with a mixture of solemnity and amusement. "So spill a little wine to wet the lips of those who've gone before us."

Innowen considered Minarik's words, then tipped his own cup. No doubt the nobles had many customs, he reflected, which common people could ill afford. Most of the folks in his acquaintance would have blanched at such a senseless waste.

"Not too much," his benefactor cautioned with a grin. "The dead have a notoriously dull sense of taste, and this is a very rare vintage." He took another sip from his own cup, then set it aside and reached for the bowl he had brought. He lifted from it a wet, white cloth, wrung a bit of water from it, and leaned toward Innowen. Gently, he passed the cloth over each of Innowen's hands, then over his own, and returned it to the bowl. He reached for a meat cake. "Now try one of these," he suggested. "I promise you, they're wonderful."

They were indeed. Some were stuffed with bits of venison, others with pork or lamb. Some were seasoned with expensive spices that Innowen had never sampled. He ate four cakes and washed them down with wine. Then he ate four more. When his belly was full, he settled back in his chair. He couldn't remember ever feeling so stuffed. Nevertheless, he forced down one more cake for politeness' sake. It wouldn't do to let Minarik think his food was unsatisfactory.

While he ate, Minarik watched him. Innowen successfully ignored him while he eased his hunger. As he munched his last cake, though, it began to bother him. No word had been spoken during their meal. Innowen consumed his final crumb, licked his fingers, and waited patiently for his host to finish a last bite of fruit. When it was gone, Minarik leaned forward and refilled both their goblets.

"You've been very kind to me," Innowen said somewhat shyly. He tasted the wine once more, then put it aside. Rare it might be, and with food the taste was not too bad. But just to drink? Maybe he would grow to like it, and maybe not.

Minarik also set his cup aside. "Then maybe we can

be honest with each other," he said, settling himself more comfortably in his chair. "Tell me about the Witch of Shanalane."

Innowen frowned. "Is that the price for kindness these days?" he dared. "Betrayal? I know why you were up all night. You were hunting for her."

Minarik nodded slowly, his eyes never leaving Innowen. "I, my soldiers, my servants, any man who could ride." He hesitated, then put on a wry grin. "Except Taelyn. He hates horses, so I left him here to coordinate incoming reports."

"You didn't catch her, did you?"

Minarik snorted. "Of course not. She's long gone from these parts. You and I know that, but it's tougher to convince Kyrin." He looked away suddenly and drew a slow breath. "I'm not asking you to betray her, Innocent. Just tell me about her—how she looked, what she did, what she said. Anything you feel comfortable talking about."

Innowen regarded the man across from him, noting the change in Minarik's mood. Though he tried to disguise it, there was the subtle tension of a military man on the verge of gaining information. It was there in the way he leaned slightly forward in his chair while trying to appear relaxed, in the way he kept his hands unnaturally still. Innowen peered straight into his benefactor's eyes, wondering just how much he could trust Minarik.

"She was beautiful," he began cautiously.

The Lord of Whisperstone gave a barely perceptible nod.

"She glowed with an ivory light," he went on. "It almost hurt my eyes. Her lips..." He stopped, picked up his winecup and took a drink. He held the liquid in his mouth for a long time.

"Her lips?" Minarik pressed.

Innowen swallowed. "Like a flower," he answered finally. "Like a rose."

"She touched you?"

Innowen thought back. "I think so. I don't know. Maybe, when she healed my legs." He took another drink, unmindful of the taste.

Neither said anything after that, and Innowen grew slowly aware of the silence. He turned the cup nervously between his hands, stared at the ruby contents, and waited. Minarik sat with his eyes closed, his lips a thin, taut line.

At last, his host spoke. "Dark-haired. Dark as the night." Minarik said it as if it were a fact.

"Blond," Innowen contradicted.

Minarik pursed his lips thoughtfully as he shook his head. "What about your legs? You say she healed you, and I believe that. I know she's a woman of great power. Yet, now you're—" He almost said *crippled*. Innowen saw his mouth start to form the hated word, but Minarik caught himself: "—incapacitated once more," he finished tactfully.

Innowen leaned back in his chair and bit his lip. "She said I would be whole again, that I would walk." He gripped the arms of the chair suddenly until the muscles stood out on his arms. "She was half as good as her word. From sundown to dawn my legs are as good as any man's."

"And with the sunrise," Minarik interrupted, "you are crippled once more." He didn't dodge the word that time.

Innowen nodded.

"But no less a man," Minarik added with great

seriousness.

Innowen shrugged, then bit his lip again and closed his eyes.

As before, the silence grew between them. Innowen heard the rustle of the lord's crisp raiments and the sound of pouring wine as Minarik refilled his cup. The breeze whispered ever so lightly through the vines that grew on the gazebo. In the sky, a pair of birds fluttering over the courtyard called to each other, their song sweet and distant.

"You think you love her, don't you?"

The words cut the stillness and Innowen's heart like a fine bronze edge. He opened his eyes, and his gaze locked with Minarik's. "I know it," he answered firmly. "I can't help myself."

Something flickered in Minarik's eyes. Innowen froze, held himself perfectly still, not daring to move for a long moment. Then, slowly he let out a breath. With a sudden insight, he understood the bond he shared with Whisperstone's lord.

"You love her, too," he said gently. "She's the lady from your past, the one Taelyn told me about."

"Taelyn talks too much," Minarik answered, rising. He leaned against the side of the gazebo, and it gave a small creak under the burden of his weight. Abruptly, he changed the subject. "What do you plan to do, Innocent, now that your guardian is gone?"

"My name is Innowen," he calmly corrected. Then he put his chin into one palm and thought. "I've got to find her," he announced. "I don't think she knows that her magic went wrong, that I can't walk by day." He scratched his chin. "And she said something about seeing my destiny in a bowl of water. I think I want to find out what she saw."

Minarik folded his arms across his chest as he regarded Innowen. "What about your guardian?"

Innowen looked away. "I guess I have to find him, too."

Minarik picked up his winecup, drained it, and set it back on the table. "Wait here," he instructed, as if forgetting how unlikely it was that Innowen would go anywhere. He left the gazebo without another word, crossed the courtyard, and disappeared inside.

Innowen folded his hands in his lap and stared at them. He hadn't told Minarik everything. He hadn't told him about the dancing, how he had to dance to keep the Witch's spell intact. That was as much dishonesty as lying, wasn't it? He had never lied before he met the Witch. Since then, he'd told many lies, and one lie just seemed to lead to another. Could it be true, as Drushen had tried to warn him? Could her dark magic corrupt him so easily?

He gazed upward. Through the gaps of the trellis that made the gazebo's roof, the sun shone down and warmed his face. He stared at the sky, and suddenly he hated its soft blue color. He wished for the blackness of night, wished for life to return to his legs. Why hadn't the Witch told him about the sun? Had she even known? So many questions plagued him.

And now to find that he and Minarik were rivals!

He looked at the table with its platters of food, the goblets, the oinochoe jug, and the bowl containing the cloth with which Minarik had washed his hands, and he gave it a shove. It fell over, spilling everything. Wine pumped from the jug, a rich red stream that spread over the floor and seeped between the cracks of the boards. Some of the meat cakes lay in the flow and sopped up the liquid. Very quickly, they looked like old clots from hideous wounds.

Drushen, you bastard! Innowen slammed his fists on his unfeeling legs. *Why? Why?* He squeezed his eyes shut, but not to stop any tears. He was done with weeping. It was anger that filled him instead, burned him from the inside out, and when the fire was spent he leaned his head back wearily and sighed.

He didn't know how long Minarik was gone. But a shadow settled over him, and when he opened his eyes the Lord of Whisperstone stood there. "You fell asleep," Minarik said.

Innowen blinked as he righted himself in the chair. "I guess I did." He cast a glance at the mess on the gazebo floor. "I must have knocked the table over, too. Forgive me."

Minarik shrugged as he sat down. "The servants will take care of it." He looked askance for a moment, then faced Innowen again. "Do you have any idea at all who your parents were, boy, or what became of them?"

Innowen shook his head and answered with only a trace of bitterness. "Drushen found me on the forest road when I was a baby. My parents had left me there to die, rather than bear the shame of a less than perfect child."

There was an intensity in Minarik's face that made it hard to meet his gaze. "Now Drushen is gone," Minarik said, hesitating as if expecting some comment, but Innowen said nothing. "You say you want to search for the Witch. But how will you do that? You have no money, no one to look after you."

"I'll find a way," Innowen answered roughly. "You don't have to remind me that I'm crippled. I'm not! I'll walk by night to find her, and sleep by day. I'm not that much different from normal men. You live your life in the sunlight, but when night comes and you take to your bed, you might as well be crippled. The world doesn't begin and end with the sun."

Minarik gave him a hard look, and Innowen wondered if he had dared too much to speak with such anger. Yet he did not repent, nor did Minarik reproach him. "I have no son," the lord said slowly, "no children at all." His gaze never left Innowen as he took a ring from his finger. "I will adopt you, Innowen, if you agree."

Innowen's jaw dropped. Then he stuttered, "But I can't stay here! I have to find the Witch and Drushen!"

"I know," Minarik replied calmly, "and as my son, you'll have money, prestige, everything you need to help you. You'll have status and position. That will get you into places you could never go alone. You'll find my name is known in some lands even beyond Ispor." Minarik leaned back, bracing his hands on the arms of his chair as he smiled faintly. "Besides, I like you, and I sense that I can trust you."

Innowen looked at the ring in Minarik's palm as he considered such an unexpected proposal. He liked Minarik, too. There was a bond between them. He'd felt it from their first meeting. Was it because they both loved the Witch? Was she the thread that drew them together?

It was as if Minarik knew his thoughts. "I don't blame you for loving her," he said gently. "She makes you love her. Not just you, either, but all men. It's like a power." He took the ring between his thumb and forefinger and held it out. "Take it," he urged. "Wear it, and be my son."

Son. Drushen had never called him that. Innowen repeated the word several times in his mind, trying it on. He had never called anyone father before, either. Drushen had been Drushen. *Son.* He liked the sound of it. He bit his lip, trembling with excitement as he extended his hand. Minarik took it and slipped the band on his finger. "Son," he said aloud.

The sunlight glinted brilliantly on the ring. It was gold and exquisitely worked, fashioned in the manner of a bird whose wings enwrapped his finger. *Father,* Innowen thought, trying that word out, but he couldn't quite bring himself to speak it.

"Wherever you go in Ispor, that ring will be recognized," Minarik said, "and in many of the surrounding nations the great nobles will know it. I ask only that you wear it with honor."

Innowen turned it on his finger, studying the careful workmanship, the detail of feathers, the textured breast, the tiny fierce eyes. Almost, it seemed to breathe upon his finger, and he felt its warmth. *But it's only metal,* he told himself, *and Minarik's warmth from wearing it.*

"You'll find the Witch," the Lord of Whisperstone said, "then you'll come to me and tell me where she is." He hesitated, observing the stillness that suddenly filled Innowen, and the mistrustful expression that flickered over his face. "I would not hurt her," he added. "I promised you that. Trust me. But like you, I need to know."

Innowen thought for a long time, and Minarik did not break the silence. "I'll find her," he said at last, "for both of us. But first, you'll teach me things. I'll have to learn to ride, and you'll have to teach me at night. There are other things, too. There's much I have to learn about the world outside of Shandisti." He ran his palms over his thighs. "And my legs. Even at night I have trouble walking. These are sticks, twigs, but not legs. It's the Witch's magic that makes me walk, otherwise these wouldn't support me. Help me put some muscle on them."

Minarik grinned. "I think I'd better get used to sleeping days."

"You were used to it once," Innowen said, "when you

rode from Whisperstone every night to meet your secret lady." He leaned suddenly forward. "You know her name, Minarik," he whispered intensely. "Tell me her name!"

A mask of stone would have betrayed more emotion. Minarik regarded him evenly, his face half in shadow as the sunlight streamed down through the latticed roof of the gazebo.

"We love the same woman!" Innowen insisted. "Give me a name to call her by!"

Minarik slowly rose. "Wear my ring with honor, Innowen, as my father wore it, and his father." He nudged one of the goblets with his sandaled toe. It rolled across the floor and stopped against a soggy meatcake. "I'll send for servants to return you to your room. You'll want to rest before we start your education." He turned his back and started to leave. Then he stopped. Without turning, he spoke once more to Innowen: "Taelyn talks too much."

There was pain in those last words, too much pain. Innowen relented and lowered his head. He didn't watch as Minarik left him, but twisted the ring around and around on his finger, and listened to the sound of retreating footsteps.

CHAPTER

5

ROBIN WAYNE BAILEY

A TEPID NIGHT wind blew Innowen's long dark hair back over his bare shoulders. It played over his body, teased his berry-brown nipples. It caressed him with a lover's warmth, and he lifted his head higher as it kissed his throat, swirled down his chest and belly.

Pulling back on his reins, he brought his mount to a halt. Beside him, Razkili did the same. "What's wrong?" his companion asked, deep-voiced.

Innowen stared ahead into the rich darkness. The horizon formed a gently rolling shadow upon the yawning starlit sky. His gaze trailed upward through the moonless heavens until he found the Crown of the Gods, the brilliant milky band that stretched from one end of the nighted earth to the other. He closed his eyes and listened, expecting stillness. The wind made a delicate rush in his ears.

"Nothing," he answered Razkili. He drew a deep breath. The air smelled fresh, as it must have on the first night of the world. "I've missed Ispor."

"It's always good to come home," Razkili said with a nod. He glanced back at their pack horse, dismounted, and ran a quick check on the animal. Satisfied, he climbed upon the bare back of his own horse.

They rode on. Innowen eyed the darkness, leading the way with a sureness that would have amazed a day-dweller. That towering silhouette on his far left, that was Razor Mountain, so named for its sharp peaks and sheer walls. Passing it, they arrived at the bank of the River Semene, Ispor's longest river, which flowed from a spring in the more distant Akrotir Mountains. He smiled to himself as he steered his horse down a grassy slope and waded its shallow black waters.

Razkili spoke little as they rode, trusting Innowen unquestioningly to know the way. His gaze swept from side to side as he kept pace beside Innowen, but sometimes it turned upward to study the blaze of stars.

Just beyond the river at the edge of the Plain of Kenay, Innowen stopped again. He sniffed, rode forward a few more paces, stopped, and sniffed once more. Razkili came quietly up on his left, tightly gripping his reins and the packhorse's lead line. The look on his face was question enough.

"Blood," Innowen answered softly, warily.

"How can you smell blood?" his comrade asked, even as his right hand settled on the pommel of the sword he wore on his left hip.

"How can you not?" Innowen countered in a whisper as he searched the darkness ahead. "There's a lot of it."

They pushed on slowly. The night no longer seemed so friendly and welcoming. Despite the warmth of the wind, a chill crept up Innowen's spine. The smell of death hung in the air. Razkili, too, began to notice it, and he wrinkled his nose.

"Stop," Innowen said abruptly. Razkili obeyed without comment. Innowen's gaze swept the ground. He swung a leg over his horse's head and slid to the ground, but he clung to its reins, hesitant. He touched Razkili's right knee and passed them to him. Alone, he walked on.

He nearly tripped over the first body. Kneeling, he ran his hands over cold naked flesh, finding a sword still clenched in a lifeless fist. A few paces on, he found another body, then another, all naked. But the next one wore a breastplate of finely crafted leather, and upon its head was a helm of bronze.

Innowen straightened as Razkili rode up beside him, leading the horses. They exchanged looks, but no more. His friend dismounted, and side by side they wandered over the plain. Corpses and weapons littered the ground. In some places, the dead lay piled upon each other. Most were naked footmen, but here and there, they found an armored officer or nobleman.

Innowen picked up the shaft of a lance whose bronze point had broken away. Leaning upon it, he looked slowly around and let go a long sigh. Suddenly, he dropped the broken weapon and stared at his hands. A cold, black, viscous substance covered his palms. Blood, he knew, from some dead warrior. He wiped his hands on the front of his short kilt until they were white again. Yet the stickiness remained.

"Terrible," Innowen whispered.

"You've seen battle before," Razkili reminded curtly, his gaze sweeping the darkness.

It was true. There was little he hadn't seen in his travels, he sometimes thought. Small skirmishes, major conflicts, or tavern brawls and alley murders. Death came in many guises and for many reasons. He had learned that much. Still, this time it was different. This was his homeland. He rubbed his fingers together, wishing for water to wash them clean.

"Not in Ispor," he answered quietly. "These are my people." He bit his lip as he reclaimed the reins of his mount. Standing beside him, Razkili touched his shoulder in sympathy. "What's happened?" Innowen asked, unable to keep the note of pain from his voice.

He shook his head before he swung a leg up over his horse's back. Leaning on the animal's withers, he shook his head again. "I've been gone too long."

Razkili also mounted. "Or maybe you've come home too soon," he said with an air of foreboding.

"None of your Osiri philosophy, Rascal," Innowen muttered. "Not now."

Razkili shrugged and nudged his horse forward.

They left the battlefield behind and rode toward a range of hills. The wind fell silent. A strange stillness hung over the land. Even the steady clip-clop of their horses' hooves was muted by the thick grass and the soft dust. The smell of death, though, did not relent. It hovered in the air, clung to their hair and clothing like a cheap and sickly incense. Innowen fixed his gaze on the low, dark peaks ahead and tried to ignore it.

Neither of them saw the men that suddenly leaped up at them from the ground. The breath rushed out of Innowen as arms encircled him and flung him from his horse. He struck the earth, flat on his back, numbed. Hands grabbed at him, pinned him down. A great weight dropped on his chest, a knee, he thought, and a fist crashed against his face once, twice. He tried to focus on the face of his attacker, but his vision blurred. A third time the fist smashed down, and Innowen let out a dull cry, barely clinging to consciousness.

A scream sounded close to his ear. The weight toppled from his chest, and he was free. He gulped for air and tried to sit up. The clang of clashing blades rattled through him like thunder. Prone on the ground beside him, a huge man groaned and stirred, and his eyes fluttered open. Innowen determined at a glance that it wasn't Razkili. One of his attackers, then. He locked his hands together and slammed them with all his might against the man's nose. Bone broke, and black blood gushed out. The man shrieked and shuddered, and went still.

Innowen jumped up, pushing the pain in his jaw to the back of his mind. He quickly spied Razkili as his friend lashed out with his short blade and drew a dark line across a foe's unprotected bicep. Another figure ran up behind Rascal and raised his own sword to strike. Innowen gave no shout of warning, but leaped and drove his sandaled foot into the attacker's ribs. The air whooshed from the man, and he sagged to one knee, looking up just in time to catch Rascal's sword across his face.

Innowen whirled, trying to determine the number of their foes. Too late, he saw the dim flash of a pommel as it rushed at his head. He flung up his arms to ward off the blow. Still, it grazed his skull, and he fell sideways, catching himself on his hands. A foot smashed into his belly. With a gasp, he flipped over and sprawled face downward on the ground, his mouth suddenly full of dust and the acrid tang of his own vomit.

From the corner of one swollen eye he saw Razkili go down under the weight of three men. One trapped his arms from behind, while two more wrenched away his sword and caught his legs. Together, they lifted him and slammed him on the ground with bone-jarring force. Then they fell on him, pinning him down as they pummeled him. The Osiri cursed and spat and kicked until the blows took their toll. Finally, Razkili went limp. Unable to move, Innowen watched horrified as two of them then pulled Rascal up and held him between them, while the third continued to beat him. He let out a weak moan, hoping to draw their attention, but the answering kick to his head came from behind, from a foe he couldn't see. His chin snapped forward against his chest, and a red fire exploded inside his eyes.

Slowly, the fire faded, but the blackness that came after it was deeper and colder than any night he had ever known.

〖◫◫◫〗

Innowen awoke to a painful throbbing in his head. His face felt swollen twice its normal size, the skin stretched much too tightly. The sharp taste of blood yet lingered in his mouth, and a tooth wobbled dangerously when he touched it with his tongue. Gradually, another pain penetrated his fogged brain, and he discovered that his hands were tied behind his back. The ropes bit cruelly into his flesh, and there was little sensation left in his fingertips.

He opened his eyes and knew a moment of fear when nothing focused properly, but gradually his vision sharpened. Razkili's face was a mere hand's breadth from his own. He winced as he saw the damage to his friend's features. Rascal's eyelids were horribly swollen, and a red, crusty cut made a half-moon over one brow. His lower lip was puffy and blue. Streaks of blood had clotted in his handsome black beard.

Tears of anger burned in Innowen's eyes. What was happening in Ispor? What had he led Razkili into?

He rolled stiffly onto his back and surveyed his surroundings. A tent roof rose over him. A small campfire in the center of the dirt floor provided light and heat and shed smoke that rose through a hole in the roof. There was nothing else at all in the tent, no furnishings, no supplies, nothing to help him get loose.

Frowning, he lay still for a moment and listened.

There were sounds beyond the tent. Voices. Different voices, some close, some muffled and farther away. He couldn't distinguish many words, yet he grew sure he was in some kind of encampment. He remembered the battlefield he and Rascal had crossed, and he cursed himself as he wondered which side he had blundered into.

He drew his knees to his chest and worked his bound hands past his hips, down to his ankles and over his feet. He was still tied, but it was far easier to maneuver with his hands in front. He crawled to Razkili's side. "Rascal?" He kept his voice to a low whisper. Since someone had taken them prisoner, it seemed reasonable to assume a guard might be close by. "Rascal?" he said again. The Osiri didn't move. Innowen wiggled closer still, and drew the tip of his tongue over the cut on his friend's brow. The taste of Rascal's blood was no less bitter than his own, but he didn't stop until the wound was clean. A faint moan issued from Razkili's throat. Innowen whispered his name again.

One eye peeled open. Its black pupil drifted slowly around until it settled on Innowen's face. It took another moment still for the glaze to lift and recognition to come.

"Alive?" Razkili managed weakly, daring to crack a grin.

"Unless the underworld is a tent with a campfire," Innowen answered. He sat up, and though his clumsy fingers tingled and trembled with the effort, he untied the ropes that bound Razkili's wrists. His friend breathed a sigh of relief as his freed hands fell to his sides. Then the one eye closed, and Razkili went limp again. Innowen watched for long moments, full of worry. There was no more he could do for the Osiri.

At last, he moved into a corner away from the crackling fire and went to work on his own bonds with his teeth.

He was nearly free when Razkili lifted his head from the dust and looked at him. "Let me," he said thickly, and he pressed himself up on his hands and knees and crawled to Innowen's side. Although there was little left to do, Innowen held out his hands while Rascal fumbled over the last of the knots.

"What now?" he said when his wrists were free. He rubbed and massaged the raw chafings, easing his pain only a little by wetting the marks with his saliva, trying to ignore the fire of blood returning to his fingertips.

Razkili poked his head carefully through the tent flap and looked out. Quietly, he crawled back to Innowen. "We wait," he answered. "We're in the gods-damned middle of an army camp from the looks of things out there. We can run for it and probably get cut down—"

"Or we can hang around and find out what in all the hells is going on in Ispor these days," Innowen finished.

Outside, something rustled on the tent's crude fabric. Innowen made a grab at their discarded bonds as the entrance flap whipped back. He shot a look at Razkili and hid his hands behind his back. Razkili did the same. He wiggled up against the tent wall, drew his knees close, and hoped their captors weren't too observant.

Three men in dirty, ragged kilts and cloaks filed inside. Two grasped swords with short, leaf-shaped blades, which were badly nicked and in need of whetting. They positioned themselves on either side of their third companion, a tall man with features like hard stone and eyes that glittered in the firelight.

Innowen dared to meet his gaze and shuddered. The man's hatred stung him like a tangible force. He feared suddenly for Razkili and for himself.

"Get up," the man said, his voice gruff and unpleasant.

Innowen obeyed awkwardly, using just his legs with no help from his hands, trying to maintain his charade. Razkili rose more adroitly, but carefully kept his hands hidden behind his back. "I am Innowen, son of Lord Minarik," Innowen said slowly, measuring the effect of his words. He knew at once he'd made a mistake.

The man he faced glared at him. Then, a terrible smile revealed his small, broken teeth. "Well then," he answered with an unnaturally silken purr, "when I am done with you, I'll know where to send the pieces."

Rascal stiffened. For a moment, Innowen feared his friend would do something stupid. He took a small step closer to the fire, at the same time putting himself in Rascal's path. "Who are you?" Innowen asked, trying to appear reasonable. "What do you want with us? I've been gone a long time, you see. Is Ispor at war?"

Harsh, bitter laughter shook the tent. "The spy dares to interrogate his captors, does he?" The two guards imitated their leader, adding their own laughter. "Then know that it's Chohlit who holds your life like a grape on the palm of his hand." He brought his nose right next to Innowen's and glared. "Too bad I don't like grapes," he hissed. Stepping back, he turned to one of his men. "Drag them outside."

"You don't have to drag us," Innowen said, giving up his pretense. He held out the thongs that had bound his wrists and dropped them in the fire. "We're not spies."

Chohlit's face darkened with anger; his right hand

curled into a fist. Innowen tensed and prepared to duck a blow, but Chohlit whirled suddenly on one of his own men and knocked him to the ground. His rage did not abate so swiftly, though. He kicked the fallen soldier twice in the ribs, hurling curses and epithets with each blow. "Fool!" he railed. "I told you to tie them tightly. Again and again you fail me. You should be dead out there on the field, and some soldier worth a spit here in your place." Chohlit glared as his minion rolled over weakly. The poor man clutched his side and gasped, unable to draw breath. Still, he tried to scramble to his feet, afraid of his leader's wrath. When he rose shakily to attention, his face was a pale mask.

Innowen shot a look of warning at Razkili and put himself even more directly in his friend's path. It would be foolish, probably fatal, to attack Chohlit in the middle of an armed camp. *Stay alive*, he thought. *Wait for an opportunity to escape.* This, though, wasn't it. He turned his attention back to Chohlit and watched him warily, wondering what demons drove such a man.

"You were wise not to make a break," Chohlit said, meeting Innowen's gaze. His eyes were clouded with deep shadow as he looked across the fire, and yet the black pupils caught and reflected the flicker of the flame. "I would have caught you and hamstrung you and hung you by your heels."

"Over hot coals to roast slowly, no doubt," Razkili said suddenly. A smirk parted his bruised lips ever so slightly as he stepped away from Innowen. "You're the type. No imagination."

Chohlit's eyes narrowed to angry slits. Plainly, he didn't like to be mocked. He looked back at Innowen. "So, your puppet can pull its own strings. Good, there will be two voices to answer my questions, and if the answers don't agree we'll see if you can scream in harmony."

Razkili spat into the fire. "It takes a brain to appreciate good harmony," he answered, drawling his words. "But maybe we'll squeak a little for you. That should be enough to satisfy your musical sensibility."

Innowen shot an appalled look at his friend, trying to warn him to silence. Razkili ignored him, instead folding his arms and grinning at their captor with wry amusement, running his gaze up and down Chohlit and shaking his head. "I've known men like you before," he continued tauntingly, "on their backs with their feet fluttering in the air like birds."

Chohlit clenched his fists; his lips drew into a thin red slash. He took a step toward Razkili.

"Rascal!" Innowen started. "Shut…"

"Five copper *selats* a night they cost," Razkili added. "What's your price, soldier?"

Innowen's breath caught in his throat as Chohlit faced Razkili. The Isporan towered over his Osiri friend, more than a head taller. Innowen watched in apprehension as the two locked gazes, Razkili still grinning his irritating grin. Chohlit's huge arm rose with casual confidence, and his open hand rushed down.

"No!" Innowen shouted.

Razkili leaned away ever so subtly. His left hand came up, brushing Chohlit's descending right with just enough force to spin the bigger man around. Razkili's fingers clamped on Chohlit's windpipe as he kicked the Isporan's ankles. Both men fell to the ground exactly where the Osiri intended, and his hand shot out toward the fire. An instant later, a flaming brand hovered near Chohlit's eyes. "Drop them!" he hissed at Chohlit's guards as they brandished their swords. So swiftly had their leader gone down, the two hadn't even moved. "Drop them!" he ordered again, "or I'll roast this pig!"

One of the two, the man Chohlit had beaten, looked willing to pay the price. He swung his sword up, his face a deep grimace, his teeth clenched angrily. But the second guard caught his wrist, jerked the blade from his hand, and tossed it on the ground beside his own.

Chohlit tore at the hand on his throat. He raked his nails deliberately on Razkili's unprotected flesh, drawing blood, but the Osiri only tightened his grip. Chohlit groaned and gurgled and tried to scream. Razkili leaned all his weight onto his hand, shutting off even a croak. Then he bent down and whispered in Chohlit's face. "Scratch me again, and I'll burn the gods-damned eyeballs out of your sockets! You understand?!"

Chohlit's face looked like a swollen purple fruit. The veins in his temples throbbed visibly under the skin, and his eyes bulged as he stared at the menacing brand. Gradually, he let go of Razkili's wrist and lay perfectly still. Razkili, in turn, eased off the Isporan's windpipe.

"Pick up their swords," he said to Innowen. Swiftly, Innowen scooped the weapons from the dirt and took a position behind the two guards. He pressed the bronze points hard against their spines. "Hells, what kind of a rag-tag army is this?" Razkili cursed, looking up at his friend. "We've got to sneak out of here, and damned quick!"

"How?" Innowen said simply.

Razkili frowned. "Don't look at me. I've done my part." He gestured at Chohlit with the brand. "It's your turn to think of something."

"Thanks," Innowen answered wryly. "I would rather

have tried to talk our way out."

Razkili held the brand a bit higher, spilling more light onto Chohlit's features. "Does this look like the face of a reasonable man?" he asked sarcastically.

Innowen bit his lip. Then he tapped one of the two guardsmen on the bare shoulder with the flat of a sword. "All those bodies we found at the edge of the plain," he said. "It was some kind of battle? Is Ispor at war?"

The soldier looked to his leader for permission to answer, but Chohlit's face was swollen and screwed with pain as he sucked for the little air that Razkili allowed him. At last, the soldier shrugged. "Civil war," he answered bluntly.

Innowen's jaw dropped. "Rebellion against Kyrin?" he said, incredulously. "Who would dare?"

"These days?" the soldier answered with a smirk. "Who wouldn't? The man can't scratch himself without making an enemy. And everybody seems to have an army. That battle? We don't know who they were. They just came at us, no banner, nothing. It's dog eat dog, I tell you."

"Innowen," Razkili said impatiently. "Time to go."

Innowen drew a deep breath. He looked aside for an instant, then savagely smashed the pommel of his right-hand sword against the temple of the guard who had remained silent. That one fell with a groan face down in the dirt. He turned, ready to strike the second man, but the soldier held up his hand for mercy.

"I answered your questions, didn't I?" he said reasonably. "Suppose I just agree not to call out?"

"I trust you," Innowen answered, and he looked to Razkili, who nodded. The soldier grinned as he lowered his hands, and Innowen hit him with all his strength. "Like hell, I trust you," he muttered, gazing down at the sprawled form. He gestured at Chohlit with the point of a sword. "What about him?"

A wicked smile spread over Razkili's face as he looked down into Chohlit's eyes. "Time to die," he whispered, and his fingers dug into the soft flesh around the windpipe. Chohlit's already bulging eyes widened with pure terror, and he made a faint gasping wheeze. Too late, he grabbed for Razkili's wrist. In only a moment, he went limp.

"Dead?" Innowen asked.

Rascal shook his head. "Just out," he answered. "But I bet he'll be surprised to wake up in this world." He grinned unpleasantly. "He had that look in his eyes at the last minute, you know? His whole life flashed before him."

Innowen gave him one of the swords. "I think you enjoyed that."

Razkili winked. "Take your pleasure where you find it."

"More philosophy," Innowen mumbled with mock distaste. "Spare me."

"I might." Razkili answered, nudging Chohlit with a toe. "But he won't. I suggest we leave."

Carefully, they crept to the tent flap and peeked out. Razkili hissed between his teeth. A dozen fires burned in a wide circle. Bare-chested, kilted warriors moved in twos and threes, talking in low voices, chuckling over unheard jokes. Beyond the immediate clearing, smaller fires burned, and tents dotted the dark landscape as far as could be seen.

"It's still your turn," Razkili whispered. "Thought of anything yet?"

Innowen shrugged doubtfully. "Run?" he suggested.

Razkili pursed his lips tightly. "Let's try the back way," he said.

They lowered the tent flap, stepped over their unconscious former captors, and knelt down. Innowen drew the edge of his sword through the thin tent fabric. "We're lucky someone didn't see our silhouettes through this stuff," he muttered. "That fire's bright enough to show everything we're doing in here." He tugged open the slit his blade had made and peered out. Tents and campfires surrounded them, but there were fewer men awake and no brightly lit clearing to cross.

"Run?" Innowen said again.

"Walk," Razkili corrected. "Just like we belong here." They glanced at each other for a long moment. Razkili's dark eyes glimmered in the firelight, the sockets made deeper and more shadowy by the red glow. Beads of sweat gleamed in the valleys of his throat and chest, and his lips parted slightly. Innowen could almost taste the tension his friend tried so hard to hide. *Excitement*, Rascal would call it, *and thrill*. And if they got out of this and lived, Innowen thought, he might even agree.

"What's wrong?" Razkili whispered. "You have a peculiar look."

"I was thinking about the horses," Innowen answered. "Especially the pack horse. I'll regret losing the contents of those bags." He forced a half-hearted smile, then crawled through the rip into the warm, open night. Razkili followed, and they stood up.

Side by side, they walked with their short blades pushed through their belts. They avoided the campfires that might have illumined their faces and kept their sandaled tread as soft as possible on the dry, flattened grass. They muttered to each other in low voices, meaningless words, mostly, spoken for the benefit of the ragged men they passed, men whose kilts were little more than scraps tied around their loins, men without sandals, men whose rib bones showed through their skin even in the dim firelight.

"These men are half starved," Innowen murmured to Razkili. "Farmers and shopkeepers. Not professional soldiers at all."

"Don't be fooled by their clothes," Razkili advised sternly. "Look at their weapons. And look at their eyes; they're full of anger. There's no love here for your King Kyrin, and no man hates as much, or fights as hard, as a hungry man."

Suddenly, the shrill note of a horn rent the camp's quiet. Shouting rose from the clearing and quickly spread among the tents. Innowen started to run, but Razkili caught his arm. "No," he said. "They'll expect us to run. Instead, move with purpose and authority, and draw your sword, as if you were hunting for escaped prisoners. Not all of these men could have seen our faces."

The camp came alive. Three men rushed toward Innowen and Razkili, but Razkili bent around the corner of a tent, pretending to search. "Not here!" he called, waving the soldiers on with his sword. "Try that way!"

Innowen watched the three disappear around another tent, then let go a breath and touched his friend's shoulder. "Between us, I'd rather run for it," he confessed. "My knees can't knock when I run."

Keeping up their pretense, they made it past the last row of tents. They had steered a course away from most of the searchers, until the open plain stretched before them. But far to the left, voices were drawing closer. "Now we run," Razkili said, and he gave Innowen a push.

Innowen ran as fast as he could, and the wind rushing by his ears became a cry of desperation. He threw back his head and sucked air in great regular gulps. The pounding of his heart and the roar of his blood made a thunder in his ears so loud he feared his enemies could hear it. The land rose and fell to meet his tread. It rolled beneath him, lifting him gently, dropping unexpectedly. Each step was a precarious balancing exercise in the darkness.

By his side, Razkili ran easily. The sweat-sheen ignited strangely on his bare chest, his arms, on his back and his pumping legs. The moon had come up, a thin slash in the black heavens, and he glowed with its faint light. His hair made a black wake as he ran, and muscles flowed like a thick, hot liquid beneath his skin.

Innowen's breath came even more quickly as he watched Razkili. An odd burning filled his eyes. It spread down his cheeks to the corners of his lips, over his tongue and the roof of his mouth, down his throat. The burning went all through him, setting fire to all his muscles. Then a moment of vertigo seized him, and he tumbled through nothingness head over heels until the earth reached up and caught him.

Innowen felt Rascal's ragged breath hot in his ear as his friend knelt down beside him. "Get up, Innowen!" He grabbed Innowen's arm and tried to drag him to his feet. "Get up, come on!"

Innowen heard it in those words, the barely concealed note of fear that masqueraded as bravado, the tight control barely maintained in Rascal's voice. Rascal would deny it. Probably, he didn't even know it was there. But Innowen heard it, and because he heard it, he clasped his fingers around his friend's bicep and let himself be pulled up. For an instant, they stood close enough to feel each other's heat; then they ran.

Behind them, though, he heard the pounding of horses' hooves and knew they had been spotted. Innowen poured all his will into his limbs, but the jagged edge of fatigue ripped at his chest, and breath came in desperate gasps. A red film seeped around the borders of his vision. Still, he didn't slow down, though he felt as if all his body were drawing into a smaller and smaller core, diminishing with every agonizing step. *Run!* The word beat through his brain like a cadence. *Run!*

A pair of horses raced by them, turned suddenly, and stopped, cutting them off. Their riders leveled lances with polished, leaf-shaped points of bronze. Quickly, another pair of riders flanked them. Innowen spun about, frantically seeking a clear direction, but more of Chohlit's men surrounded them. He stumbled, fell, and the sword spun from his grasp.

He got up again and ran, actually managing to dodge the lances of the two blocking his way as he darted unexpectedly between their horses. But he heard their taunts and shouts as they rode down on him. Something stung him sharply across the back. The flat of a blade, he realized through a haze of pain. He nearly fell again. Somehow, though, he propelled himself onward.

Rascal, where was Rascal?! He cast a glance around. A rider dashed by him, turned suddenly, and stopped. Innowen bounced off the animal's shoulder and struck the ground. Before he could move, a lance flashed down and embedded in the earth barely a hand's width from his groin.

Innowen scissored his legs and knocked the shaft into his hands as he rolled sideways and got his feet under him. Rising, he swung upward with the blunt end.

The blow caught a soldier under the chin. The man tumbled from his horse with a surprised grunt. Innowen didn't know if it was the man who'd thrown the lance. He didn't care. There were far too many to pick and choose. He whirled and struck again, but instead of finding a man, the bronze point bit deep into a horse's throat. The beast screamed and reared, but its rider clung on.

There was no time to finish that one off. Others were on him. From the corner of his eye he saw Chohlit astride a great steed, directing his men with angry shouts and curses. Innowen could spare him no more attention though.

The lance became a blur in his hands as he spun it end over end, deflecting a sword that whistled down at his head, and striking the kneecap of its wielder. Any scream was cut short as Innowen followed through and crushed the man's unhelmeted skull with a blow that flung him from his horse.

Then something exploded in the top of Innowen's head. White hot stars burned holes in his vision, and pain raced the entire length of his spine. His knees gave way, and the lance fell from hands suddenly unable to grip. A smaller explosion sent numbness crawling through the right side of his face and down his neck. A third between his shoulder blades blasted the air from his lungs. The ground raced up at him with startling speed, and dirt and grass filled his open, gasping mouth.

Someone rolled him over, and he saw Chohlit once again. From his horse, the man barked a series of orders, words Innowen couldn't quite understand for the ringing in his ears. Two soldiers approached from the right, dragging Razkili awkwardly between them. Innowen found breath, and managed to raise up on one elbow. Before he could do more, rough hands seized him and hauled him to his feet.

Chohlit slid down from his horse. With a satisfied smirk, he grabbed Razkili by the hair and jerked his head up so that they were eye to eye. Razkili's face twisted in pain, and his cry was a knife that stabbed Innowen's heart. Twice, then, Chohlit lashed out with the back of his hand, and a thick stream of blood poured from the Osiri's mouth. With an animal growl, Razkili tried to kick Chohlit, but the enraged soldier easily sidestepped the blow and threw a savage punch at Razkili's gut. "Hold him tighter!" he directed his two men.

Chohlit bent over Rascal. "You should have killed me," he hissed. His hands locked around Razkili's throat. "Now I'm going to finish what you started, just the way you started it."

Chohlit's finger tightened slowly. Razkili struggled, his eyes widening with fear. The guards held him with his arms outstretched, his back arched to the breaking point, as Chohlit forced him backward.

"Stop!" Innowen cried. With the strength of desperation, he pulled free of the hands that held him. "You cowards!" He had no sword, no lance, no weapon at all, and Chohlit's guards were reaching for him already.

But they were killing Razkili! "Damn you!" he screamed. "Damn you all!"

Before they could seize him, he flung his arms high and whirled, the toes of his right foot digging deep into the soft ground as he turned. "Bastards!" he muttered furiously. He swept his left leg high in a smooth arch, lunged his weight onto it, and sprang erect again, balanced on one leg, his left foot on his right knee.

Tears began to trickle from his eyes, fear for what was about to happen, fear for Rascal and for himself. But they were angry tears, too.

The wind seemed suddenly to rise about him, its voice a terrible melody in his ears. He whirled, snapped his head to the right, and rolled a shoulder up, back, down. He paused, looked about, and knew he had them now. Chohlit's soldiers seemed frozen as they watched him. Innowen touched his palms together over his head and slid one hand seductively down the other arm, leaning far to the side as he did. The wind sang a new note, and a timpani joined it, the heartbeats, he realized with a horrible certainty, of the men around him. Even Chohlit's eyes were on him now. Innowen met his rapt gaze and poured hatred for the man into his dance.

Somewhere behind him, he heard a scream. A body fell across the corner of his vision. He gave it barely a glance but saw the blood that poured from an ugly gash where once a throat had been. With an incoherent shout, another man jumped on the body and hacked it until the bronze blade of his sword bent at an angle and threatened to break. Someone dragged him off the mutilated corpse, but nearby two more men leaped at each other.

Innowen didn't care what the quarrels were. It didn't matter. Chohlit still had Rascal in his grip, that was all he knew. So he danced, danced, whirling, taunting with his body, drawing dark designs in the air with his arms, weaving intricate patterns with his hands and fingers, unleashing the power that, even yet, he didn't comprehend, power that frightened and terrified him. Yet for Razkili's sake he didn't shirk away.

Slowly, a change rippled over Chohlit's features. His hands unclenched, and Rascal sagged unconscious into a heap at his tormentor's feet. With a snarl, Chohlit kicked him in the ribs and looked for an instant as if he intended to follow it with a second blow. Instead, he balled his fists tightly, lifted them up before his eyes, and stared at them with a look of utter loathing. Without warning, he threw back his head and howled a pitiful sound of such soul-wrenching intensity that it caused Innowen to freeze in midmovement. Stunned, he watched Chohlit fall to his knees, clutch his face in his hands, and weep like a spirit in despair.

It was the final crack in the dam of sanity, and chaos surged free. The rest of Chohlit's men turned on each other, and the air vibrated with screams and curses. Then came the clash of weapons. Some, though, would not fight; they fled, wailing, across the open field, pursued by their personal demons. One man ripped away his clothing, took his sword and drew it across his wrists without a whisper or moan, and sat down to watch his life essence flow away. A hideously sublime smile spread across his mouth.

Innowen ran to Razkili's side and cradled his friend's head in his lap. A sob broke from him as he gazed around again and realized what he'd done. But he'd had to, to save Rascal. He hadn't wanted to do it. They'd made him. They'd brought it on themselves!

"What did you do?" The words were like the sound of a serpent slithering through dry leaves. "What did you do?"

Innowen looked up and saw Chohlit. "What did you do to us?" he demanded again, through clenched teeth. He struggled shakily to his feet and drew his sword. Tears brimmed from his eyes, and his face was a mask of grief and pain. He moved toward them, though, lifting each leg and setting it down ponderously as if his feet were huge stones.

Innowen looked around frantically and found a blade in the grass close by. He hugged Razkili closer, shielding his friend with his body, and lifted the weapon high to ward off the expected blow.

A horn sounded from the direction of the camp. Then another and another. Chohlit hesitated. Beneath Innowen, the ground shook suddenly with the thunder of horse's hooves. A lot of horses, he realized. New screams and shouting drowned the horns. Innowen risked a glance over his shoulder as fire rose from the tents.

"Damn you!" Chohlit cursed. "I knew you were spies!"

"Forget us!" Innowen shouted back. "Save your damned camp if you can. Or your miserable hide, whichever you value more!"

Chohlit gave a roar and rushed at Innowen, slamming his sword down. Innowen caught the blow on his own blade. Again, Chohlit struck, without skill or style, and again, Innowen blocked it, but the sheer force of the impact shivered down his arm and shoulder. When Chohlit raised to strike a third time, Innowen moved faster and raked his edge over Chohlit's unprotected shin. The man leaped back with a sharp scream, cut to the bone, blood pouring down his leg.

"Get out of here!" Innowen shouted furiously. "Save yourself, man! Where's your precious rebellion if you let yourself get caught?!"

Chohlit shot a glance at his burning encampment. Then he looked back to Innowen. Gone were the tears; purest hatred burned in his gaze, and Innowen thought he would attack again. Instead, he turned and ran, but not toward the camp. Across the plain he sped, abandoning his troops to the mercies of whoever had attacked them.

Innowen dropped his sword and bit his lip. Not one of Chohlit's men remained to threaten him. Some were dead, or dying. A few were little more than weeping wretches, hugging and rocking themselves on the ground, moaning words that made no sense. Most had simply run away.

"Wake up, Rascal," he urged, bending close to his friend's ear and shaking him gently. "Wake up. We've got to get away, too." But though his chest rose and fell with regular, if shallow breaths, Razkili didn't stir.

The flames in the distance made a beautiful glow as they reduced Chohlit's camp to ashes. Silhouetted against the orange light, Innowen saw a band of riders coming his way. He looked around forlornly. Even if there had been some place of concealment, it was too late to hide. Perhaps it was the horses wandering near that had attracted attention. Or maybe, the weird carnage. In any case, there was no point in trying to run.

Innowen shut his eyes for a moment and gritted his teeth. He almost regretted what he had done. But Rascal was alive, and that was what mattered. Gently, he lowered his friend's head to the earth, rose, and picked up a lance from the grass. Standing over Rascal, he prepared to meet these new riders.

Wordlessly, they made a ring around him, nine in all. Innowen twirled the lance in the showiest pattern he knew, warning enough, he hoped. Then he set the butt on the ground between his feet and leaned on it. He raised an eyebrow questioningly, regarding each of them in turn.

One of the riders was dressed differently from the

others. He wore the same black kilt and green cloak, but over his bare chest he wore thick plates of gold that hung from chains around his neck and waist. The helm that covered his face also appeared to be entirely gold, and a long horsehair crest flowed from its peak.

Innowen addressed him politely, but without timidity. "Neither I, nor my friend," he gestured toward Razkili without looking away, "is part of Chohlit's army. We're travelers newly returned to Ispor. They mistook us for spies." He forced a smile. "We thank you for your intervention."

"I know well enough you're no spy." The man in gold lifted off his helm with both hands. "Welcome home, Innocent."

Innowen stared in disbelief. "Taelyn!"

On the ground, Razkili raised up on one elbow, rubbed his neck as he gave Innowen a queer look, and muttered with a doubtful hint of amusement, "Innocent?"

CHAPTER 6

INNOWEN LAY AWAKE on his cot as daylight seeped through the thin fabric of the tent. Like water evaporating slowly in the sun, he felt the life leave his legs. He squeezed his eyes shut, hoping the darkness behind his lids might keep the dawn away a few moments longer. He hated the sun, hated the bright blue sky and the light of day.

Razkili sat on the ground beside him, watching him, unable to keep the sorrow from his face. He reached out and took Innowen's hand and held it, then lay his head down on the side of the cot. His touch was strangely warm-hot, Innowen thought, like a spark on the verge of becoming fire, and he tried to concentrate on that instead of his legs. Already he couldn't move his toes or bend his knees. He could feel the weight of the woolen coverlet, but little by little even that sensation faded, faded away.

"Rascal." He brushed his fingers through his friend's short, dark curls. Razkili looked up, and their gazes met. "It's done."

Wordlessly, Razkili slipped his hand from Innowen's, got up, and went to his own cot on the other side of the tent. He turned on his side, his face to the wall. Innowen watched him for a long time, watched the swell and sink of his body as he breathed, the shift of

an arm to an easier position, the unconscious bending
and straightening of a leg. He couldn't tell, though, if
Rascal actually slept or if he just strained for a rest that
wouldn't come.

Innowen listened for sounds from the outside.
Taelyn's camp was unusually quiet. The shuffle of feet
as someone passed by, a pair of muffled voices
approaching and receding, a cough from the next tent,
that was all he heard. Well, it was only dawn. The
soldiers would just be rousing.

He folded his arms under his head, and his thoughts
turned back to Chohlit and the experience of the
previous night. He bit his lip, recalling the man who
had slit his wrists and smiled about it. Innowen closed
his eyes, as if he might shut the vision out so easily,
but it remained and wouldn't leave him. Odd, how that
soldier had drawn his sword from its sheath so casually,
levered it across his veins, and sank so gracefully down.
Almost as if he, too, had been performing a dance.

And he, Innowen, had been the piper. The dead
man might have had a family. Maybe he'd had parents
to support. Maybe he'd had just cause for joining an
army that opposed Kyrin. How could Innowen know?
His only thoughts had been to save Rascal.

He stared at his friend's back. He had done the right
thing, the only thing. Yet it felt so bad. He had never
ever purposely danced to hurt anyone before, and he
knew the images from last night would haunt him for a
long time to come. Had he been able at that moment,
he might have drawn up into a ball and never come
out. Instead, he threw an arm over his eyes. Only in
sleep could he hope to hide from the world.

He woke to the sound of arguing voices. Razkili stood at the tent flap blocking the entrance. Innowen couldn't see the man beyond, but he recognized Taelyn's barely patient tones. "It's all right, Rascal," Innowen said, rolling to his side. "He knows."

Razkili glanced at Innowen over his shoulder, hesitating. Then he shrugged and went to sit on his cot. His surreptitious gaze never left Taelyn, though he leaned back on one elbow and drew a foot up onto the edge, adopting a pose of relaxed indifference. But Innowen was not fooled. He knew Rascal too well and could sense his tension.

Taelyn stood for an instant at the threshold and regarded them both. He had never been an easy man to read, Innowen realized, and he suspected that too many years as a slave had taught Taelyn to lock his emotions behind a lot of high walls. Still, he had a fondness for this man who had taken care of him at Whisperstone, and they had become good friends.

"How are you feeling?" Taelyn asked Innowen.

He slapped his dead right leg and cracked a grin. "I'll be better after sundown."

Taelyn rubbed a hand along the dark stubble on his chin. "You both have some pretty ugly bruises. If I'd known Chohlit had you, I'd have ordered the attack sooner."

"You might have gotten us killed," Razkili said sullenly.

Taelyn cocked an eyebrow and folded his arms. His open stare was not hostile, but it was plain he was drawing some conclusion about the Osiri.

"They thought we were spies," Innowen

explained evenly, attempting to draw Taelyn's attention back to himself. "We couldn't seem to convince them otherwise."

Taelyn pursed his lips, then drew a deep breath and visibly relaxed. For an instant, as he sat down on the edge of Innowen's cot, a heavy weariness showed at the corners of his eyes, there but for a moment, then gone. "I don't doubt that," he said, allowing a careful smirk. "Chohlit's a crazy bastard. Burned an entire village three days ago. Caught every man, woman and child first, tied them up, and tossed them back in their homes before he set the fires. Our Third Army caught up with them yesterday. You said you crossed a battlefield? I was supposed to join up with them before they engaged, but we were delayed by a minor skirmish with yet another bunch of rebels."

Innowen nodded. "Chohlit said there were small rebellions all over Ispor. Is Kyrin really so bad a king?"

Taelyn passed a hand over his eyes, then leaned back and stared at the tent's rooftop. "He's no king at all. While drought and crop failure plague Ispor, he sits in Parendur fattening himself on everything he can rake in from the locals. King? Bandit chieftain is more like it. But he manages to maintain an uneasy truce with a handful of nobles, though he and Minarik are constantly at each other's throats over one thing or another. Only the blood they share binds them together."

"How is Minarik?" Innowen asked, reclining. In that same moment, he noticed the leather slave's collar was gone from Taelyn's neck. "And how did you come to command an army? I think things must have changed very much since I left."

Taelyn pursed his lips again and looked thoughtful. "Minarik is not himself," he said at last. "The years have weighed heavily on him, Innocent. He seems constantly distracted. I don't know by what." He leaned forward, braced his elbows on his knees, and stared at the floor. With seeming reluctance, he gazed toward Innowen once more.

"It started just after you left," he continued. "Something occupies his mind, some secret that he shares with no one. When he's not in the capitol fighting with Kyrin, he spends most of his time alone at Whisperstone pacing his chambers or wandering around the courtyard. When Kyrin ordered the nobles to raise armies and quiet the various rebellions, Minarik obeyed, but he freed me and put me in command as an affront to the king." He allowed a tiny smile to turn up the corners of his lips. "Fortunately, I've proven quite good at it."

"We were on our way to Whisperstone," Innowen said, glancing at Razkili. The Osiri still maintained his posture on the far cot as he picked at a hang nail on one finger. Their gazes brushed for a brief moment, long enough for Innowen to know that despite his seeming indifference, Rascal was listening intently to every word and evaluating.

Taelyn's weight shifted on the cot. Innowen had to look to realize the former slave had laid a hand on his knee. He tried to feel something, the smallest sensation, the slightest pressure. But there was nothing, only the evidence of his eyes to tell him he had been touched. "What of the Witch?" Taelyn asked quietly. "Did you find her?"

Innowen shook his head as he closed his eyes. Her face floated in his memory, shining with a strange light as it did that night she came to him. Her voice whispered on the wind that rustled the thin fabric of the tent. He could hear it now on his small cot, teasing him, tormenting. *Dance, my Innocent, dance away the world!* Those words reverberated in the dimmest corners of his soul. They worried him, gnawed at the edges of his dreams when he slept. How many times had he tried to shut them out? Yet an echo always remained to haunt him. And from time to time, in the puff of a breeze or the unexpected rustle of a leaf, he would hear her voice afresh. *Dance,* she said.

"I followed every possible clue," Innowen whispered almost to himself. "To the borders of Ispor and beyond. I sailed the Tasmian Sea and wandered as far as the bright new city called Jeriko with all its wonders. I found no trace of her." He opened his eyes, but it was not the tent he saw, nor Taelyn, nor even Razkili. Rather, he saw gleaming walkways and high bastions of white stone that sparkled in the sun, slender columns of infinite grace and beauty, majestic pyramids, all the marvelous things he had seen in his travels. There were blue mountains hung with mist, and oceans, and proud ships with crackling white sails, and deserts that burned and shimmered. Smells rushed upon him as he remembered, and sounds of blustering crowds, of cattle herdsmen, of caravans and camel bells. Of ships' riggings creaking in the lonely night winds. *Dance!* they all urged him. *Dance!*

He threw an arm over his face, wishing the

memories away. "In time," he continued, "I gave up looking for her. I tried, instead, to find her god and to learn more about Him. I visited temples and questioned priests wherever I went. 'What,' I asked them, 'could they tell me of wooden idols and copper nails?'" He uncovered his eyes, looked at Taelyn, and forced a smile. "All I got for my troubles was a collection of dolls."

Taelyn lifted an eyebrow.

"Now, even those are gone. They were bundled on our pack horse when Chohlit captured us. Gods know where they are now." Innowen gave a little shrug as he lay on his back. "Well, it was a peculiar hobby for a man, anyway."

A soldier came to the tent entrance with a tray, and a rich odor wafted through the air. Behind him came another man with a small field table under one arm. With a nod to Taelyn, he positioned it in the center of the floor and backed out. The first man set his tray down and prepared to serve. "I'll see to it," Taelyn said, dismissing him. The soldier offered a short bow and left without a word.

Taelyn rose and leaned over the table. On the tray were three bowls. Beside each bowl was a steaming, hot cloth. He lifted one cloth, kneeled beside the cot, and carefully wiped Innowen's hands one at a time. The hot moisture felt very soothing. Taelyn used the cloth to massage Innowen's fingers and knuckles, the bones along the backs of his hands, the palms, and the padded areas below the thumbs, even his nails. Taelyn worked patiently, never lifting his gaze from his task. When he finished, he folded the cloth neatly, placed it on the tray, and stood.

"Thank you," Innowen said simply.

Taelyn took a second cloth from the tray and turned to Razkili, who sat up and started to reach for the cloth. But Innowen spoke up. "Let him do it," he instructed. "It's our custom. The host washes the hands of his honored guests before eating."

Razkili looked dubious but raised one hand. Taelyn wrapped it in the warm cloth and worked with the same careful ministrations he had shown Innowen. It was almost funny, Innowen thought, to watch the petulance melt from Rascal's features. "A very pleasant custom," the Osiri confessed as he held up the other hand for cleansing.

Taelyn finished, folding the cloth with the same ritual care and returning it to the tray. He barely passed the third cloth over his own hands, though, before he laid it aside. "There now," he said. "Let's eat." Handing a bowl to each of them, he took his own to the foot of Innowen's cot and began to eat with a wooden spoon. Innowen inhaled the vapors that rose from his bowl, then began to eat also. It was a posset of cooked grains with chunks of pork added, and very tasty.

"Well," Taelyn said when they had scraped their bowls clean, "time to break camp." He tapped Innowen's knee again with affection and prepared to get up. "I delayed this long to give you time to rest and to give us this chance to talk."

Innowen interrupted, not yet ready to let Taelyn go. "You've changed, old friend," he said gently. "You used to chat the days away. Now your speech is crisp and abrupt. And I remember you used to hate horses, but the first time in five years I see you, you're sitting astride one like you'd always been part of it."

Taelyn shrugged. "The slave has become the commander of his master's army." A distant look stole into his eyes, and the lines in his face briefly relaxed. "I go where Minarik sends me," he said, "do what he tells me. Changed? Maybe. But don't fool yourself, Innocent. I don't. I'm still his slave." He collected Innowen's empty bowl, reached for Razkili's and set them beside his on the table.

"You sound bitter," Innowen observed.

"Blame it on the times," Taelyn answered wearily. "You'll find lots of changes around here, boy. You won't like them all." Their gazes locked for a moment, and Innowen looked for some trace of the old Taelyn in those eyes. If there was any, then it was deeply buried. "Well." His host rubbed his hands over his plain black kilt. "Time to get moving. I'll escort you to Minarik. With the loss of the Third Army, I have to report for reassignment, anyway."

Razkili spoke up suddenly. "Do you think you can locate our horses? Particularly the pack beast with Innowen's things?"

"I'll have some men look," Taelyn offered. "We captured most of Chohlit's stock. He'd most likely have put your animals with his." He crossed to the doorway. "We'll march within an hour." He left them then.

Innowen looked over at Razkili. His friend had resumed his semi-reclining leg-up position and pretended to examine a bruise on his forearm. He poked and prodded its purpled edge and ran his fingertips over it as if to test its tenderness.

Despite the growing warmth of day, Innowen drew his coverlet up to his chest. "Rascal," he said, "what's bothering you?"

"Damn thing hurts like all the hells," Razkili answered without looking up, "and I've got a lot more like it just as sore."

Innowen let several moments go by. Still, Razkili didn't look at him or say anything. "What's wrong?" Innowen pressed again.

Razkili sat up suddenly and reached for his sandals. Quickly, he wound the straps around his calves and tied them. "Nothing," he said at last. He stood up. "I'll go find our horses. Your friend won't know which ones are ours. Maybe I can find the packs, too." He paused at the entrance, bit his lip, then turned around. "Innocent," he muttered. "That's a good nickname for you." Then he too was gone.

Innowen frowned as he stared at the waving tent flap. Rascal's footprints were plain to see in the dust at the entrance. Someone else might have thought they belonged to Taelyn or his two men. And some of the prints did. But he knew Razkili's. He knew the shape, the outline.

Wearily, he sagged back down on his cot. He hadn't slept enough. Usually, he and Rascal slept the day away and traveled by night. He drew his arm over his eyes again. Gods, how he hated the daylight.

A fly buzzed in his ear, lighted on his arm, flew off, and settled on his chin. He swatted it away. The heat grew inside the tent. The bedclothes, damp with his perspiration, clung to him. He turned onto his side, but that was uncomfortable. He returned to his back, but the fly was waiting for him.

Innowen gripped the sides of the cot and pulled himself to a sitting position. He followed the fly's progress as it circled in the air and finally landed safely away on the other cot. He cursed it and threw a pillow at it. The fly sprang into brief flight, then settled again on the same pillow, as if to taunt him.

He envied the tiny creature's mobility. So small and insignificant, yet it could not only walk, but fly, while he had to lean forward with his hands and lift each of his uncooperative legs and drop them over the side of his cot as he twisted the rest of his body around. It was almost enough to make him laugh. How clumsy he was, so clumsy he even managed to ensnare one unfeeling foot in the coverlet and nearly fall off the cot.

His loin cloth lay close by on the floor where he'd discarded it when he and Razkili had washed each others' cuts and bruises after their rescue from Chohlit. He bent forward, being careful not to overbalance, snatched it up, and wound it around his hips and through his thighs. His kilt, too, lay close. He wrapped the short strip of soft blue cloth about his waist and pinned it with a delicate Osiri brooch Razkili had given him. Taelyn had said they'd leave within the hour. The least he could do was get dressed and be ready.

His sandals proved a bigger problem. He couldn't spot them. He leaned far enough to see over the head of the cot, then beyond the foot. They weren't there. Nor were they on Razkili's side of the tent. Irritably, he levered his hips off the edge and lowered himself to the dirt floor. He might have waited until Razkili returned, but there was a certain pride involved. He let himself fall sideways, twisting as he did, and catching himself on his palms. As he'd suspected, they were under the cot. He drew them out, pushed himself back into a sitting posture, and took a long breath. Then with one elbow hooked over the cot's edge, he began to crawl back up onto his bed.

When Razkili appeared in the entrance, Innowen was sitting with hands folded in his lap, sandals laced, ready to depart. Only the dirt on one side of his kilt gave any indication of his travails. Razkili's gaze flickered to it, then back to meet Innowen's. "I found our horses," he said quietly. "Even the packs with your collection. And our money, too, where we hid it in the bottom of our sleeping rolls. I guess Chohlit hadn't had time to search our things thoroughly." His gaze strayed again to the stain on Innowen's garment, and his shoulders sagged. "I would have dressed you."

"I didn't need your help." Innowen looked down at his hands.

Razkili took a waterskin from a small peg set in one of the tent's cornerpoles. With his back to Innowen, he unstoppered it, but he didn't drink. For what seemed like a long time he stood with his head hung between his shoulders, the untouched container halfway to his lips. At last, he sat slowly down on the edge of his own cot.

"It's the first time you've ever hurt anyone deliberately." Razkili's voice was a bare whisper. "You danced and made them watch."

"I did it to save you," Innowen answered, matching his friend's soft tone. He wanted to reach out and touch Razkili, but the distance between them was too far. "I didn't know what would happen."

Razkili leaned forward, his elbows on his knees, the waterskin dangling from one hand. "You unleashed their darkest desires."

"But I didn't know what those desires were," Innowen insisted. "They might still have killed us. I did what I had to do."

Razkili stared at the waterskin and took a drink. "I know," he said finally. He passed it to Innowen, and their fingers brushed. "But they saw you dance." He hesitated, watching as Innowen lifted the skin and swallowed. Then, hanging his head, he murmured, "I want to see you, too."

Innowen slammed the stopper back in place. "You can't," he snapped. "I've told you before."

"I know," Razkili said again.

"Why do you keep asking me?" Innowen leaned forward, gripping the edge of his cot. His eyes burned; his heart hammered wildly in his chest. It frightened him the way Rascal kept reviving this argument. "Why?" he demanded. "You know the danger. You know what happens to people. I won't risk it, Rascal!"

Razkili looked at his hands. "I'm sorry," he said thickly.

Two soldiers appeared at the entrance. "Taelyn sent us to break your camp," one of them said as Innowen beckoned both of them inside. Razkili rose, and they quickly collapsed his cot.

"We'd better get out of their way," Razkili said. "Taelyn promised to bring the horses around." He bent, gathered Innowen in his arms, and carried him outside.

Innowen clapped a hand over his eyes to shut out

the blinding sun. Even the red glare that squeezed between his fingers was painful. He clenched his lids tightly and pressed his face into Razkili's shoulder. Little by little, he dared to peek out until his vision adjusted and he could bear the light of day. "I hate the sun," he said to his friend. He glanced around. The camp bustled with activity. Most of the tents were already struck. A line of pack animals and supply wagons had begun to form. "I don't see Taelyn," he said. "Let's go find him."

"Over there," Razkili managed to point with the same hand that supported Innowen's legs. "He's coming our way."

Innowen shielded his eyes from the sun and spied Taelyn leading three horses. "I'm sorry," he quickly muttered in Rascal's ear.

The Osiri pursed his lips and gave a small nod. He started walking, bearing Innowen's weight easily. Innowen drew a breath, let it out slowly, and sucked in his lower lip. It was not a dignified way to get around, being carried like a child, but he called up as much dignity as he could, as he always did. It was better than crawling in the dirt. He locked his arms about Razkili's neck and studied him in profile. The sun glinted off his short black curls. Light bent around his brow and nose and chin, lending him a beatific radiance. He was handsome, was Rascal, and tall and strong. Innowen thanked the gods for the day he found him.

"I believe these are yours," Taelyn declared. He passed the reins of the three animals into Innowen's hand, and gave a curt nod to Razkili. Innowen recognized their mounts and the pack horse. All his bundles seemed accounted for, the sleeping rolls with their money bags, the bags with his dolls, all the little treasures he and Razkili had elected to bring with them to Whisperstone. "We were lucky, Rascal," Innowen said appraisingly.

"Let me have a litter brought and hitched behind your horse," Taelyn offered as his gaze drifted over Innowen's legs. "You'll be comfortable, and you can sleep as we travel."

"No," Razkili said before Innowen could speak. "That way is for the wounded and the dying. Innocent will ride with me."

Innowen glanced at Razkili with an expression of surprise. Razkili looked back at him and grinned. Innowen let go a long sigh of resignation. Some nicknames just couldn't be lived down, it seemed. His chin dropped to his chest for a moment, and when he looked up, Rascal's grin widened, and the powerful arms that bore him hugged him closer.

"He can't sit on a horse," Taelyn protested. "He's crippled. There's no feeling in his legs!"

"He's not crippled," Razkili answered firmly, his eyes narrowing at that word. "Not while I'm here to be his limbs. Now, come take him for a moment, and hand him up to me after I've mounted. He'll ride in my arms. If he's too much for you to lift, call one of your men."

Taelyn frowned disapprovingly, but he stepped forward and took Innowen in his own arms. "Don't you have anything to say about this?" he said with some exasperation.

Innowen watched as Razkili took his horse's reins and swung one leg high and over. For a moment, his friend lay flat on the animal's bare back, and he remembered that Rascal was still probably a bit stiff and sore from the beating Chohlit had given him, but then he pulled himself erect and reached down with one arm.

Innowen shrugged and gave Taelyn his biggest smile. "I say, hand me up to him when he's mounted," he told his old friend. "If I'm too heavy for you, then call one of your men." He winked suddenly and put on a mock-serious face. "I never argue with him."

"I should drop you, instead," Taelyn muttered as he handed Innowen up into Razkili's embrace.

For an instant, Innowen sat sideways on the horse's withers, his balance precarious. Then Razkili twisted and maneuvered him until one leg slipped over the horse's neck, and he straddled the animal like a proper rider. Finally, one strong arm locked around his waist, and he was settled.

Taelyn helped keep the horse steady by holding its bridle strap until Razkili had a firm grip on the reins. "Can you manage a lead line on your other two beasts?" he asked Innowen, and Innowen nodded. Taelyn disappeared briefly and returned with a rope, which he passed through the bridles of their other two horses. He handed the line to Innowen.

"Now, I've spared enough attention for the pair of you," Taelyn said good-naturedly as he brushed dust from his hands. "I've got an army that needs a little bit of me, too." He turned and pointed to a gathering of mounted soldiers. "You wait with that group forming over there, and I'll join you when we're ready to move out." With that, he left them.

"Ready?" Razkili asked.

Innowen settled back, letting Razkili take his

weight. He rested one arm over the arm around his middle and let the hand holding the lead line dangle over Rascal's thigh. Their flesh quickly stuck together wherever they touched, for the day was hot, and already, he had a fine sweat.

Off to his right, a pair of soldiers stared in their direction and whispered to each other. How, he wondered briefly, had Taelyn explained him to his soldiers? He had walked into camp last night. Now, he had to be carried. He couldn't even ride his own horse. Had Taelyn even bothered to explain?

It wasn't important. Let them think what they would. With his free hand, he squeezed the forearm that crossed his belly, feeling the muscle corded beneath the sun-bronzed skin. As if in response, that arm drew tighter about him.

He lifted his head, and the slightest breeze brushed his face. "Ready," he answered.

CHAPTER

7

ISPOR BY DAY was quite different from the Ispor Innowen and Razkili had traveled through at night. Gone were the moonlit mountain peaks and star-speckled rivers, the vast gray and white plains so beautiful in their starkness. Under the sun's searing glare, the land screamed. The grass shriveled into a course brown hair that only grew in clumps and patches. Dust swirled and eddied in the slightest wind. The trees stood like frail and fatigued old men, stooped and twisted, as if even their wilted leaves were too heavy to bear in such torrid heat.

The deeper into Ispor they journeyed, the worse were the effects of the drought. Ponds and small lakes lay like dried-up scabs on the earth, leeched of water, the black silt bottoms turned to caked and cracked depressions where fish scales and tiny bones gleamed. Even the larger lakes and streams shrank away from their banks, leaving rings or stretches of mud where clouds of insects droned.

Innowen stood outside his tent remembering all he had seen that day. Though night had fallen, the air was still warm enough to cause a few beads of sweat to trickle down the valley of his chest. He caught them on his fingertips and tasted his own salt tang as he gazed into the distance.

The tent fabric gave a slight rustle as Razkili slipped out and joined him. "What are you thinking about?"

he asked, touching Innowen's shoulder.

Innowen let go a long breath and rubbed the ball of his thumb over his lips. "I was remembering that deer carcass we passed," he answered slowly. "It must have died from thirst." He stared toward a faint star that hung just above the horizon. He'd specifically chosen this spot for his tent, on the outer perimeter of the camp, facing away from all the others. It was quieter, more private. It made it easier to steal away when he had to later. "Sometimes I feel like that," he went on softly, "like I'm dying of thirst. Only it's not water that I need. I don't know what it is."

Razkili didn't say anything, but his fingers massaged the muscles of Innowen's neck. Innowen leaned his head to the side and closed his eyes, tried to feel nothing at all but the gentle hand doing its work. The wind brushed his nipples, and the dim notes of an unnatural music hovered just at the edge of the night, where only he could hear them. It was almost time.

"I have to dance," he said after a long silence.

Razkili's hand continued to massage. "I know."

"Walk with me," Innowen offered, "but just a little way."

The dry grass made a brittle sound beneath their sandals as they walked through the darkness. Most of the camp was asleep, but as Innowen glanced back over his shoulder, he saw, here and there, the shadows and silhouettes of men who still clustered around a late fire swapping tales, men like himself, he suspected, who belonged more to the night than to the day. He wondered if Taelyn might be among them.

The wind nudged gently at his back, and he walked on. Already, the soundless music of the night played clearer in his head. He reached for Razkili's hand, as if his touch might somehow anchor him and hold him back. Yet that wasn't what he wanted. He loved the dance. Only while he danced could he find oneness with the world. Only while he danced could he truly touch the gods.

At the foot of a low hill, Innowen stopped and looked back. The low fires of the camp could barely be seen. "Wait for me here," he said to his friend.

"Let me come with you," Razkili responded, his voice little more than a whisper, like the rustle of the breeze—a breeze which bore the music that called him.

Innowen let go of his hand. "No." He embraced Razkili, then backed away. "Just wait, and I'll know that you're near. You'll be in my thoughts, and my dance will be for you."

"But I won't see it," Razkili said, his dark eyes piercing Innowen with a sadness and longing.

"The gods will see," Innowen told him. "They'll know it's for you I dance."

He climbed the hill alone. The wind touched his face now with a lover's care, and the music filled him. Legs that were useless by day carried him higher toward a slender moon that just crested the horizon. Step by step he made his way, feeling the strength and blood and power that surged in his limbs. Excitement grew, and his breath quickened.

At the summit, he did a slow turn. In the moonlight, Ispor had found its beauty again. What could daylight show him, he considered, to compare with such a vista of shadow and darkness and pale luminescence, where every shape and movement took on a meaning and identity all its own, where hills were not hills, but the rounded backs of sleeping gods, where gnarly trees were not mere trees, but the willowy fingers of spirits beckoning men's imaginations? Mystery and subtlety, those were the offerings of the night! He made a sweeping gesture with his hand, as if he could stir the gloom and make it swirl like smoke.

On the ground, his shadow in the moonlight made the same motion with its arm as it stretched along the hillside, but to Innowen it looked like an invitation. The wind rushed with a sudden crescendo of music, and he threw back his head. A little cry, like ecstasy, escaped his lips.

The heartbeat of the world became a drum that drove him. He drank its rhythm and poured it out again in pure motion. The night melted as all things real and perceivable fused into a music that entered him, penetrated the deepest parts of him, made of him an instrument for its own physical expression. He invented new geometries with the lines of his body, angles and curves that only flesh could shape, and time collapsed into a single, pulsing moment.

When it was over, he sprawled exhausted on the ground, panting, and dug his fingers into the earth. Though his body rested, his soul still spun to the last diminishing strains. Finally, the music faded away, and the wind was just the wind.

He rolled over on his back. The moon hung isolated and lonely in the black sky. Only it wasn't the moon to him now. It was a face, the face of the Witch of Shanalane.

Innowen blinked, and the illusion vanished. It was only the moon, after all.

He rose, brushed the dirt from his kilt, and looked around for his sandals. He didn't remember removing them, but he was barefooted. A little searching turned them up. He sat back down long enough to put them on and to wrap the soft laces around his calves. At last, he started down the hill.

Razkili lay on the grass asleep where Innowen had left him. One arm was folded under his head, and his features were composed with such peace that Innowen was reluctant to wake his friend. Razkili looked like a child when he slept, free from cares or worries. Innowen half-smiled to himself, and remembering his own nickname, wondered if in slumber he looked half so innocent.

"Rascal," he whispered.

Razkili's eyes opened. Calmly, he sat up and rubbed a thumb and forefinger over his eyes. A few blades of dead grass were stuck in his short-trimmed black beard and in the curls of his hair. He flicked them away. "I saw you dance," he said quietly.

"What!" Innowen's throat constricted with fear, and his hands clenched into fists that he pressed against his thighs. He'd always dreaded that Rascal might break a promise, follow him, and see him dance. He knew how Rascal wanted that.

He swallowed uncertainly.

"I dreamed," Razkili went on calmly, "and I saw you dance. You said the gods would see you, and they let me see, too, this time, by sending the dream." He closed his eyes as if he could see it all again behind his quivering lids. "You were like a cloud chained to earth, struggling to escape back into the sky." He hesitated. "The chain was your shadow. It wrapped its arms around you and held you down with a will of its own. It kept you from achieving the heavens. You danced, and it danced with you. It was almost like a battle. A beautiful, frightening battle between you," he opened his eyes and looked at Innowen, "and yourself."

Innowen gazed toward the summit of the hill where he had danced. Razkili could not have seen him. The distance was too great, the hill too high. So, it was a dream then. Perhaps, as Rascal claimed, sent by the gods. Was a dream enough, though, to satisfy his friend's desire? Or would he want more than ever to see the dance itself?

He held out a hand and pulled Razkili to his feet.

"You're upset," Razkili observed.

"No," Innowen denied, "just tired. We'll reach Parendur tomorrow afternoon." He pointed south in the direction of Ispor's capitol city. "Taelyn will want to start early again, so we should try to sleep tonight."

"Sleep?" Razkili said with surprise. "You? At night?"

"I know," Innowen answered. "But I am weary, and you didn't get much sleep this morning, either. For now, we're traveling with daytimers, so we have to keep their hours."

They drifted slowly back toward camp, kicking at weeds, pausing sometimes to stare toward the stars or the sound of some nocturnal creature, or to watch a thin dark wisp of cloud roll overhead. The night grew cooler. Innowen felt the dry salt sweat crack on his skin.

"Rascal," he said softly as he swatted his way through a swarm of small winged insects that rose suddenly out of the grass. "Remember what you said about a battle?"

"That part of my dream?" Razkili answered. "Between you and yourself?"

Innowen bit his lip. He had never forgotten Drushen or what had happened at Whisperstone. Many were the nights he had lain awake wondering what had become of the old man. Drushen had been a father to him. He'd been a friend. Now Innowen didn't know if he was alive or dead. But he remembered a face twisted with terror and shame, and he remembered a despairing cry that haunted him still, sometimes, when he dreamed of Drushen running from his room.

He feared what might happen if Rascal ever saw him dance. He had to be careful, had to make sure that never happened. He couldn't bear the thought of hurting Razkili, of watching him run away, too, as Drushen had done.

"Innowen?"

Innowen snatched a tall, half-dead weed and began shredding it with his thumbnail. "Never mind," he told his companion. "I was just thinking."

"Always good to practice a new skill," Razkili quipped.

"You should take it up sometime," Innowen said with a grin.

〕〕〔〔

Just before noon, they passed by a small village called Chalandri. The pathetic fields where a few brave stalks of wheat had fought up through the parched ground had not been tended for days. Dead sheep rotted on the hillside. A milk cow half covered with black flies sprawled across a ditch, its throat cut, its blood a dried brown stain on the earth.

The wooden buildings had been torched. Here and there, blackened timbers stood at strange angles, looking like thin broken silhouettes that cringed and cowered from the sunlight. Smoke still curled from some of the ashes. Bits of pottery and shattered furniture poked up. A few stone houses stood, but fire had gutted the interiors, collapsed the roofs, sometimes cracked a wall.

Taelyn halted his troops long enough to search the

wreckage. It didn't take long. He paced about, stirred ashes with a toe, picked up the splintered handle of a hoe, peered at it, cast it down again. He walked into one of the stone houses. The windows and doorway bled with smoke stains and scorch marks from the heat that had raged inside. Moments later, he emerged carrying a rhyton that was blackened with smoke, yet miraculously intact. He tucked it gingerly under one arm as he continued through the ruins. In the center of the village, he raised a hand to shield his eyes from the sun and gazed up and down the street. Finally, he returned to stand beside his horse. Before he mounted, he gave the rhyton a last examination, crinkled his brow, and dropped it. It broke into three egg-shell thin pieces, which were ground into fragments as he and his army rode over them. It was only pottery, and its materials had come from the earth. To the earth it returned once more.

"I didn't see any bodies," Razkili whispered in Innowen's ear as they left Chalandri behind.

Innowen leaned his head back on his friend's shoulder and squeezed the arm that was wrapped around his belly for support. He tried to lose himself again in the rhythm of the horse's motion. But the sun had turned his pale skin a sharp pink. He itched where his flesh touched Razkili's, and every sudden bump or jostle brought a new irritation. "Maybe they were alerted in time and escaped the raiders. We'll probably find everybody safe at Sucrebor."

They rode side by side with Taelyn. Innowen looked over as he tried again to reconcile his memories of the slave with this new Taelyn, this commander of armies. The man's face was a placid mask, even as it briefly turned his way. It yielded nothing, and Innowen wondered just how much he truly knew of Taelyn and the things that drove him.

He closed his eyes and tried to sleep, but through the red glare behind his lids, visions came in small snatches. He kept seeing the charred timbers of Chalandri's houses. Like shadows, he thought, leaning and twisted and broken, caught in the middle of a macabre kind of dance.

Sucrebor, too, lay in ruin.

All down the line, Taelyn's troops fell silent. The smell of death hung in the still air. There were no dead sheep this time, no milk cows. A ragged line of vultures quietly watched them approach, then grudgingly climbed out of the way.

"A little healthy exercise between courses," Razkili whispered morbidly, watching the birds wheel and screech overhead as he followed Taelyn through the village square. He glanced down at an unrecognizable mound of shredded flesh that might have been a man or a woman. "We're but an intermission, and the grand banquet will resume."

More shadows, Innowen thought, as he stared at the dark, soaring shapes. Ugly birds, they were, yet graceful in flight. They circled without effort, dipped and climbed, changed direction with a careful bend of a wing. A thought came to him, unbidden, that described the way they flew. *Another dance.*

They paused long enough for Taelyn to choose two mounted men to ride ahead as scouts. When the twin gleams of their spearpoints could no longer be seen, he waved to his troops. The march continued, and Sucrebor was left behind. The vultures clacked their reddened beaks by way of applause and returned to their supper.

Blackened timbers. Black vultures. Innowen couldn't put them out of his mind. The images gnawed at him.

They overlapped his view of the landscape as if his eyes perceived two scenes, one through the other. *Black as Vashni's armor, as the shadow of the Witch.*

She had a way of stealing into his thoughts at the oddest times.

He wiped an arm over his wet brow, cursing the irritating tingle his touch raised there. He hated the heat, hated the day. *Hurry, night,* he prayed. The sun beat its way across the sky, burning him and stewing him in his own sweat.

The Akrotir Mountains loomed in the south. Taelyn quickened the pace even though most of his soldiers marched on foot. They hadn't made good time. It would be after sundown before they reached the foothills where Parendur nestled.

Innowen's spirits lifted a little. "I'll ride into the city on my own horse," he told Taelyn.

Razkili ground his bearded chin into Innowen's shoulder. "Ingrate. Tired of my company?"

"Not of your company," Taelyn suggested straight-faced, "but maybe of your stink." He wiped sweat from his eyes, then added, "This heat."

"Allow me my pride," Innowen said with a faint smile. He brushed his palm over Razkili's arm. "It's been five years since I've seen Lord Minarik. I'd like to greet him on my feet."

Before they had traveled much farther, Taelyn's scouts returned. The two raced up, covered with dust and filth, their thighs slick with the creamy lather of their horses. They jerked hard on their reins as they met the front of the line, and their poor steeds wheezed with great labored breaths as their riders made report.

Innowen looked at one of the soldiers with particular interest. Veydon, his commander had called him earlier. He was little more than a boy, younger than Innowen or Razkili, though not by much. Yet underneath the grime and sweat was a powerful warrior's body and eyes that sparkled like shards of black ice. They flickered toward Innowen, lingered for just a moment, then darted away.

"Parendur is under attack," Veydon told Taelyn excitedly. "There's an army camped right outside the city's gates and signs of an unsuccessful attempt to breach the walls. Kyrin's First Army is manning the ramparts, though, and so far the gates remain sealed." He paused long enough to take a swallow from the waterskin his commander offered him.

"Kyrin's First!" Taelyn snorted derisively. "That's no more than the city garrison." He glanced around sharply as some of his men chuckled, then turned back to Veydon. "What foe?" he asked with greater patience. "What are their numbers?"

"They fly no banner or flag that we could see," came the answer. "We crawled on our bellies as close as we dared in daylight, but we couldn't tell who they are." Veydon looked thoughtful, then shrugged. "Their numbers are perhaps two thousand men. Cavalry and footmen. No chariots. They've started building siege equipment. Just ropes and ladders, as far as we could tell. Nothing heavier is in place."

Taelyn frowned as he rubbed a hand over his lips and chin. "Almost four times our number," he muttered. "We camp here, then. Spread the word. No fires. All captains at my tent within the hour." He looked at Innowen. "Afraid we'll have to postpone your reunion, boy. I'll send someone to erect your tent." He pulled on his reins, turned his horse, and rode back along the line.

Taelyn's troops worked with astounding speed. In no

time, the camp sprang up, and all the horses were tethered at its center. No fires were lit, but hard bread and handfuls of grain were distributed to eat.

Four soldiers swiftly erected a tent for Innowen and Razkili and set up a pair of cots.

"I wonder what they think," Innowen said as Razkili carried him inside. "They've seen me walk at night."

"The soldiers?" Razkili set him down on the cot that was most shaded from the sun. "Who knows what they think? Who cares? The whole camp surely knows their commander thinks highly of you because he treats you with respect and you ride at his side, even if you ride in my arms. And by now, word has probably spread that you're Minarik's adopted son."

Innowen nodded. "It bothers me sometimes, though."

Razkili put on a patient grin. "You mean all that garbage about being a whole man? That trash you used to spout?"

Innowen grinned, too, then hung his head in mock-humility. "You put up with a lot, don't you, Rascal?"

Razkili picked up a waterskin one of the soldiers had left. "Wash yourself," he said, pulling the stopper free. He took a quick drink, then squirted a stream that caught Innowen unexpectedly in the face. Innowen sputtered, wiping his eyes. When he could see again, his friend was gone, and the waterskin, stoppered once more, lay at his side.

He took a sip, then put the skin aside and sat quietly for a long moment. Slowly, he removed his kilt and unwound his breech cloth. He spread them as best he could over one end of his cot. They were damp with his sweat, but in the heat they would soon dry. He unstoppered the skin again and took another drink, pondering some more before he grabbed the breech cloth back, wet one end of it, and began to clean away the day's grime.

When Razkili returned, Innowen was stretched out naked on the cot with his clothes drying at one end. He watched without a word as Rascal, too, began to undress, but his friend dropped his garments on the ground instead of laying them out.

Rascal rubbed his nose suddenly. "Smells better in here," he commented. "You took my advice."

"It's quiet outside," Innowen said. "What's happening?"

"Taelyn's posted a minimum guard and ordered everyone else to get some rest, sleep if they can, until an hour after sunset." He sat down on his own cot and unlaced a sandal. Holding it up, he sniffed it, made a wry face, and cast it into a corner. "He intends to attack the enemy army tonight. He invited me to his tent to hear his plan, and it's a good one."

Innowen waited until his other sandal was off. "You're going to fight," he said quietly. It was almost an accusation.

Razkili looked up and met his gaze. "It's what I do, Innowen."

Innowen rose on one elbow. "It's what you used to do! This isn't your battle!"

Razkili's eyes narrowed, and one corner of his mouth pulled upward. He drew a breath and let it out. "Taelyn—your friend—is outnumbered nearly four to one. Even if the city's garrison joins the fight, as he's sure it will, that won't balance the odds. I've already offered him my arm. I can't withdraw now."

Innowen stared at him. Razkili was resolute, and nothing he could say would change the Osiri's mind. He knew that too well. He sucked his lower lip, considering the pointlessness of further argument.

Razkili had been a prince and a soldier, the fifth son of Osirit's king, when they first became friends. The fortune of his birth had earned him an education, a warrior's training, and a captain's rank, but with no position at all to speak of in his father's court, and four older brothers before him in line for Osirit's throne, he had left his homeland to travel with Innowen.

Osirit was a long way from Ispor. But Razkili was still Razkili. If he had offered his service to Taelyn, there was no more to be said. And in truth, he could find no fault in Rascal's decision. Quite probably, they both owed their lives to Taelyn.

Innowen bit his lip. "Watch your back, then." He sighed as he lay back down and covered his eyes with an arm.

Razkili broke the silence that threatened to grow between them. "Look at me," he said cheerfully. "I'm filthy, and I smell, though not quite as bad as you did before you washed. Where's that waterskin?"

Innowen opened his eyes and smiled. He'd been using it as a pillow, waiting for his chance. "Right here," he said, unstoppering it. He squeezed with both hands. Razkili gave a yowl, shielded his eyes, and lunged. Laughing, they fought for possession of the skin until Razkili wrenched it away.

"Now your cot's all wet," he chided, rising over Innowen.

Innowen grinned with satisfaction. "So's yours."

"Well then," Razkili said, dropping the skin and sweeping Innowen's kilt and breech cloth to the ground. "We might as well drown in one bed together." He stretched out on his side by Innowen on the narrow cot, folded one arm under his head, and draped the other over Innowen's waist.

Neither said anything more. Innowen looked into Razkili's eyes until they closed softly. Then he watched the delicate quivering of the pale veined lids. Breathing was the only sound he heard. Razkili's chest rose and fell against his. It was warm in the tent, and his sunburn itched where their bodies touched, but he kept still.

"You stink," he whispered.

"Road cologne," Razkili murmured wearily.

Innowen felt the exact moment his friend fell asleep. The arm on his waist suddenly relaxed, and Razkili's face composed itself into a perfect semblance of peace. *Dream*, Innowen wished him silently, *dream the world away*.

There she was again, the Witch, stealing into his thoughts.

Perhaps he shouldn't have come home to Ispor. The land seemed under a curse, and he'd found nothing but trouble. Chohlit, Chalandri, Sucrebor. Now Parendur. And tonight, Razkili would leave him to fight at Taelyn's side.

He hated the day, hated the heat and the bright sunlight. Even more, he feared for Rascal. He touched his friend's side and left his hand there. He could feel the heartbeat within, the breath, and, he imagined, the soul sleeping under his palm.

Strangely, he found himself praying that darkness would never come.

CHAPTER

8

INNOWEN HELD THE reins of their horses while he waited for Razkili to emerge from the tent. Darkness had fallen. All around, Taelyn's soldiers hurried to complete preparations for battle. They moved with speed and surety and relative quiet. Taelyn had changed his order, allowing a few small fires, which dotted the landscape and made a ruddy chiaroscuro of the faces of men who gathered near them. The flames gleamed on the burnished helms and greaves of the higher ranking soldiers as they passed, giving orders in low voices.

A hushed expectation hung over the army. Every sound seemed muted and distant. Even the four-spoked wheels of the light war chariots made little noise as they formed a line at the edge of the camp.

Veydon and three other men approached, their arms full of packs and bags. "Commander Taelyn thanks you for the gift of your extra horse," he said to Innowen. "May we place your belongings inside your tent?"

Innowen nodded without speaking and watched as the four went inside with his collected treasures. Even a poor packhorse was too valuable to be left behind when a common hoplite soldier might be turned into a more efficient cavalryman. Nor did he begrudge its loss, considering the beautiful gift of armor Taelyn had made to Razkili.

The three pack-bearing soldiers emerged and returned to their own preparations. Moments later,

Razkili and Veydon appeared. Innowen regarded his companion with a mixture of worry and approval. The copper greaves and arm braces he wore gleamed with inlaid silver traceries. The new leather that lined and made them comfortable gave off a pungent odor. On his right arm he bore a small round shield entirely of metal, a rarity, decorated in relief with battle scenes. Innowen worried about its weight, though Razkili said nothing. Under his left arm, he carried a bronze helm. Its nasal bar and cheek-pieces nearly met, so closely did it guard the face, and a bright crest of crimson-dyed horse hair cascaded over the top and down the back. From a strap over one shoulder he wore a short, straight-bladed sword. His only other garment, like most of the mounted soldiers, was a brief black kilt.

"Your friend was very generous," Razkili said of Taelyn. "These are finely made pieces. I had to widen the braces a little to make them fit; my forearms are bigger. I hope he won't mind."

The pieces were from Taelyn's ceremonial armor, which explained their beauty and workmanship. The commander had planned to wear them when he reentered Parendur after a successful engagement with Chohlit. Instead, he had offered them to Razkili for the upcoming battle, preferring to fight in his familiar war-worn pieces.

"I doubt the commander would have given them to you," Veydon said with a smirk, "if he expected to have them returned in perfect condition."

"The shield is too heavy," Innowen commented critically. "You should take a wicker shield or one of the wood and leather ones."

"I can manage," Razkili answered. "This metal will turn a point far better."

"Not if you can't get it up in time."

Razkili transferred the helm under his right arm to his shield arm and patted his friend's shoulder. "You worry too much," he chided.

Their gazes met, but Innowen kept his silence. It would do no good to argue. They had done too much of that already. Yet he resented being left behind. While night cloaked the world, he could ride and fight as well as any man. Both Razkili and Taelyn had denied him that right, though, as if he were still handicapped and some kind of liability.

Veydon broke the tension. "I've got to finish my own preparations," he said. He wore neither weapons, nor armor, only the black kilt and his sandals. "But I make you this offer, Osiri. If you are unhorsed you'll need a spear-mate to fight at your back. Mine was killed in the clash with Chohlit, so my back is also bare. Do we suit each other?"

"You honor me," Razkili answered. "Draw your horse beside mine when we join the line."

Veydon nodded, then clasped Innowen's shoulder before he left them. Innowen watched him disappear between a pair of tents.

"I should be your spear-mate," he said to Razkili when they were alone, "instead of watching everything from the safety of some hilltop."

Razkili took his reins from Innowen's hand. There was a stubborn look on his face. "And if the fighting continued past dawn, what then?"

Innowen turned away. "It won't."

"It could," Razkili snapped in a whisper. Clearly, he was tired of the argument. "We've got a good ride ahead of us, yet, and it will be well past midnight when the first arrows fly. Now mount up. We should join the line."

Innowen bit his lip and fumed. "Give me your damned helmet, then. You can't mount with all that."

Razkili looked at him for a moment, then put on a strained grin and shook his head as Innowen took both his helmet and shield and held them while he bellied onto his horse's back. "Thank you," he offered, taking them again.

Innowen gave a bare acknowledgment as he climbed upon his own horse.

A rider passed through the camp, issuing a last call to form ranks. Innowen gave a quick glance around. Most of the fires had been extinguished, and there was no moonlight yet. Shadowy forms moved quietly and quickly among the tents, heeding the calls of shadow captains, streaming out over the dark land, all gathering in a huge mass beyond the edge of the camp. *Like shades*, Innowen thought morbidly, repressing a chill. *As if most of them were ghosts already.*

Razkili tapped his arm to draw his attention and nodded toward that same mass. Innowen bit his lip. There was nothing more to be said. He nudged his animal into motion and headed for the front line.

They were among the last to leave the camp, but as they came around the final tent, they met Taelyn and two of his officers. Taelyn wore the plain gold breast plates and helm he had used in the attack on Chohlit. He sat proudly upon his horse, and the wind streamed his helmet's crest behind him. A sword hung at his right hip, and on his right arm he carried a large round shield. In his left hand he gripped an immense lance. "Ride beside me," he instructed them, and they steered their mounts to his right side, while his officers took up position on his left.

They rode through the ranks in that formation, and

the soldiers parted for them, all eyes turning to their commander. At the rear of the ranks were the nearly naked hoplites, common footmen, who made up the largest part of Taelyn's force. They wore sandals and small black loin cloths and carried short stabbing swords and shields and longspears. The barest leather caps protected their heads, some sewn with rings of metal and some with rows of boars' tusks.

Next came the ranks of the slingmen. These represented the poorest men who could not yet afford good weapons or armor, but who nevertheless had chosen to join Minarik's army. They wore nothing but sandals and loin cloths and pouches on their hips, which held their throwing stones. Some draped their slings around their necks, and some tied them around their waists. Many wore them tied as headbands across their brows until they were needed. A few of these men would be lucky enough to snatch better weaponry from the fallen once the battle began, and if they survived, they might be allowed to move up into the ranks of the hoplites for the next battle.

The archers held the middle position. Like the slingmen, they wore little armor. Many did, however, don the hoplite's protective leather cap, and a few wore braces on their arms. The bows they carried were of several kinds, both curved and recurved, and their quivers bristled with reed-shafted and wooden arrows. Many also carried secondary weapons in their belts, usually daggers or short swords, sometimes axes or crude, stone-headed clubs.

Eighty mounted men made up the cavalry. These were the officers and wealthier troops who could afford horses and better arms. Metal helms, some of elaborate design, covered their heads and necks. Greaves and braces protected their limbs, and a few, like Taelyn, wore plates of copper, bronze, or gold to guard their chests. Some carried round shields, and some the rectangle. Some wore the short sword at their hips, and others the longer bronze blade that tended to bend easily and nick, but offered the extra reach. All carried the long, slender lance, which was a horseman's primary weapon.

As Taelyn rode among them, they raised their lances in salute, and he acknowledged them with a lifting of his own.

At the head of the army were the chariots, each a light, two-horsed wicker unit built to carry one warrior, who was both driver and fighter. Javelins filled permanently mounted quivers on each side of every vehicle, and every driver wore a sword. In all other respects, the drivers armored themselves like the horsemen, except that their helms were metal caps only, and their throwing arms were left bare.

The two centermost chariots moved forward at Taelyn's approach and withdrew to either end of the line, leaving a space for their commander and his companions. Innowen glanced down and discovered why earlier they had seemed to move so quietly. The wheels had been bound with cloth and strips of leather to muffle any noise made by their passage. Taelyn obviously meant to keep the element of surprise as long as possible.

As Taelyn took his place at the fore of his army, another man rode up and quietly positioned himself behind him. Bound across the shoulders of his mount was a pair of large drums. It would be his job to stay near Taelyn throughout the fighting, no matter where his commander went, no matter how thick the battle, and the thunder of his drums would relay his lord's commands across the field.

Suddenly, another horse raced around the farthest chariot and made straight for them. Abruptly, the rider jerked back hard on his reins, stopping before Taelyn.

"Nearly late for the battle again, eh, boy?" Taelyn said without rancor.

Veydon grinned as he tossed an extra lance to Razkili. "Well, old sir," he said, "even in war, one should make a good entrance."

Innowen eyed the young soldier. His muscled flesh gleamed almost as if oiled, and its deep color made a rich contrast against the highly polished bronze of his unornamented armor and against the dark hide of his mount. Like most soldiers, he disdained a riding pad and rode the animal bare, close up to its shoulders, holding the reins low in one hand. It might have been a throne, the way he sat so proudly.

"Especially in war," Taelyn agreed. Then, more sternly, he instructed, "Now take your proper place, horseman. The cavalry is behind me, not in my path."

Innowen spoke up, looking past Razkili. "If you will, Taelyn, as Razkili has offered his service to you, so has this soldier offered service to him as his spear-mate." He looked at Veydon, and the warrior smiled back at him.

"That's well done," Taelyn answered. "Then he may ride at Razkili's back." He looked again to his young officer and added, "but that's still with the cavalry, and that's still behind me." He waited, then, as Veydon rode sheepishly between Innowen and a chariot and took a position beside the drummer. Innowen overheard Taelyn as he tapped Razkili's knee and whispered with an almost fatherly pride, "You've chosen well, Osiri. He handles a lance better than any of my other men."

Then Taelyn turned to the officer on his left side. "Pass the word as we march," he ordered. "If we make the first ridge before the moonrise, a one hour's rest will be every man's reward. Tell them to march well, and march in silence." To the other officer he instructed, "Choose two horsemen for scouts and send them ahead."

They waited until a pair of riders disappeared in the forward darkness. Innowen took the time to study Razkili at his left side. The Osiri looked so calm and steadfast in his armor. Innowen felt naked beside him, no shield on his arm, no lance in his hand. He felt the eyes of the army on his back, and he imagined he heard their thoughts. They wondered why he carried no weapons. They wondered at his courage. They wondered why it was that he walked by night and needed Razkili to carry him like a doll in the daylight. He could hear them, he was sure he could.

He rolled his gaze to the heavens. The Crown of the Gods stretched across the sky, and the Great Scythe hung low in the north. He shivered suddenly and looked again at Razkili. He wanted to pray, but he'd grown convinced that the gods never listened.

Except for one god whose name he didn't know. *There you are again*, he thought, and the Witch of Shanalane was suddenly in his mind, unchanged by the years, as beautiful as his memory could make her. *You protect him, then*, he thought. *Protect us all*.

But she was just a memory, and memories, by themselves, had no power.

A muffled drumbeat sounded just behind him and swiftly faded. Without looking over, Razkili reached across and squeezed his knee. Like a great beast in the darkness, the army lurched forward, eerily quiet but for the hesitant creaking of the chariots and the soft rhythmic impact of hooves and sandaled feet upon the earth.

It was the stuff of songs, Innowen thought, as he felt the breeze caress his cheek. Silent armies, midnight marches, battles by moonlight. But when a song was done, the singer collected his coin, picked up his drink, tuned his instrument, smiled at his audience, quite safe and quite alive.

He felt the wind on his face again. It urged him to dance. *Not yet*, he told it, *not yet*.

The army moved smoothly over flat plainland until it reached the first foothills of the Akrotir Mountains. There, forces broke up into smaller waves which crested each hill and waited for the next wave to start up before descending. They progressed slowly in the darkness, careful to lose no horse or chariot wheel to unseen ruts or holes. No man spoke now, not even in a whisper. From any summit, the night could carry a voice a considerable distance.

The moon floated slowly above the eastern hills. Its weak radiance lit the hilltops and filled the valleys with shadow. Taelyn led the way down into blackness and up again into light. Finally, when they reached a place deep enough and dark enough to shelter all his troops, he called a rest. Waterskins were passed around and abandoned when empty; they wouldn't be carried into battle.

While others dismounted to rest, Taelyn rode quietly to the summit of the next hill. Innowen tapped Razkili's arm, and together they followed. Veydon, too, joined them.

"Another hour's march," Taelyn said in a low voice

as they pulled up by his side.

"You've brought us a round-about way, Commander," Veydon whispered. "These hills are taking a toll on the men and horses both."

Razkili joined the discussion. "Is there no road or pass to this city of Parendur?"

"If you were the leader of a siege force," Taelyn answered with the patience of a father addressing a favorite son, "where would you most likely station your patrols and watchmen? Yes, there's a road, but I want to keep the element of surprise."

"So we come at them out of the foothills," Veydon said needlessly.

Innowen listened with half an ear, but his eyes turned toward the looming darkness of the Akrotir Mountains in the south. He felt their presence like a ponderous weight upon him, and they oozed an oppressive mystery into the air that he could almost smell. He inhaled deeply. Somehow, his sight seemed sharper, and he could make out the jagged outline that challenged the sky. All his senses took on a finer edge. The wind sang upon those far peaks.

"You're very quiet," Taelyn said to him.

"It's this place," Innowen answered reverently. "It commands quiet."

They grew silent and listened to the stillness, twisting with a strange conservation of motion on their horses' backs to gaze in all directions. Each pair of eyes, though, inevitably turned toward the Akrotirs and lingered there.

Razkili reached across the space between them, and his hand settled on Innowen's knee. "We'll have to separate soon," he said gently.

Innowen listened to the wind as it danced down

from the mountains and flowed over the hills and valleys. He felt it coming like a delicate tide rippling the air before it, and smiled wistfully when it brushed over him. "When we find a high hill that overlooks Parendur," he whispered, "there I'll leave you and watch the battle." He gripped the hand on his knee and held it as he turned to Taelyn. "Give my horse to one of your footmen. I won't need it, and another cavalryman will do more damage than a hoplite."

Taelyn nodded. "My thanks, Innocent." He hesitated, considering his next words. "I know where your heart lies, that you would fight with us. But your friend has given the best advice. None of us questions your courage."

Innowen barked a short laugh, then choked it back. "I think your soldiers have more questions about me than they dare to ask even in private." He waved a hand when Taelyn started to protest. "That's not important now, and if there's anyone on the next hill, I bet they can hear everything we're saying."

Taelyn nodded again and wordlessly started back down toward his troops. Veydon followed, but Innowen clung to Razkili's hand for a long moment and stared toward the mountains. He drank in the awesome silence, inhaled it, filled himself with it until he felt as ponderous and unmovable as the ancient stone itself. Only that way could he keep from voicing his worry for his friend. He should be at Rascal's back, protecting him in the fighting. It was where he knew he belonged. But instead, he would watch from a distance, and Veydon would do his job for him.

He gazed hard and long into the Akrotirs. Then he squeezed Razkili's hand once, let it go, and turned his horse down the slope to rejoin the army.

Veydon intercepted him at the bottom. "I'll watch out for him," he said. There was an odd passion in his words, and his gaze bore piercingly into Innowen. "I swear. I will go down before he does."

Innowen's brow furrowed, and his lips drew into a thin line as he regarded Veydon. "Why?" he said irritably. "Why would you do that?"

Veydon smiled weakly and looked away. "Has it been so long that you've forgotten Shandisti? I know you, Innowen. I remember the harvest festivals of our boyhood." He looked back, and there was a softness in his eyes. "Most of the children were cruel to you because you couldn't walk, and I was one of them." He swallowed and glanced away again. Nearby, Taelyn's officers were rousing the soldiers to their feet. The rest break was over. It was time to resume the march. "Call it atonement that obligates me to look after your friend," Veydon continued in hushed tones. "I know how you must depend on him."

I depend on no one, Innowen started to snap, but he bit it back. It would have been such an obvious lie. He stared at Veydon, trying to remember his face. He couldn't. There had been lots of children in Shandisti, and he had gone to the village only on holidays when Drushen would take him. Some had taunted and tormented him, but he'd never paid much heed. There'd always been too many wonders, too much going on during the festivals, even in such a small community, to hold his attention. He shook his head. Veydon held no place in his memory.

"Just guard his back," he said at last. "You could have nobody better at yours." He looked over his shoulder toward the summit of the hill where Razkili sat alone gazing into the distance. Innowen wondered what thoughts were running through his mind.

"We move," Taelyn said, riding up to him. Innowen and Veydon fell in beside their commander and climbed the hill again. Razkili merged into the line as they overtook him. The army resumed its relentless flow toward Parendur.

The Akrotir Mountains grew ever larger until they dominated the southern sky.

Taelyn held up a hand. His drummer remained silent, but the word quickly passed to halt. Two riders descended the hill before them and made straight for the front line.

Taelyn saluted his scouts. "Report."

"Parendur lies just over that ridge," one of them answered. "We still can't identify the army camped outside its walls, but Veydon's estimate of their number is probably correct. Two thousand men. Most are asleep in their tents now with only a token patrol on the perimeter."

The other scout spoke. "We left our horses on the ridge and bellied down as close as we dared," he said. "They are well armed, but discipline seems lax. We saw gambling and drinking, and a few arguments."

"Mercenaries?" one of Taelyn's officers suggested.

"It's possible," answered the first scout. "We heard a smattering of different languages. Isporan among them, so some, at least, are our own people."

Taelyn spat, then turned to his officers. "Tell the archers to ready their firepots and move them into position. Deploy the other units according to plan." He steered his horse around Razkili and whispered to Innowen. "Choose a place on our left flank where you can see," he said gently. "Razkili can go with you to bring your horse back. With the grace of the gods, we'll clasp hands again when this is over, Innocent."

Innowen took the older man's offered hand. "Razkili would tell you to trust in no gods, just your arm and your weapons. Osiri philosophy. It's good advice."

He pulled away and rode east along an old stream bed that had dried up in the drought. Razkili followed. They picked their way carefully in the darkness until Innowen turned right and started up the side of a high hill. He could still see Taelyn's army huddled in the valley behind him.

At the summit, he dismounted. Even in the darkness, Parendur took his breath away, just as it had the first time he saw it. It filled the next valley and sprawled out onto a narrow plain. Watchfires burned at intervals along the top of the city's defensive wall. The shadows that moved there, he knew, were soldiers at their posts.

The plain was also dotted with fires and the tents of Parendur's attackers. He had a good view into the camp. It was still and quiet. A few men huddled around the fires. A two-man patrol passed far below him, more visible by the shadows they cast than by anything else.

"Archers will set fire to their tents from there," Razkili said, pointing. "The confusion will give the chariots time to pull out of the hills and assemble on the plain."

Innowen held up a hand to interrupt him. "Let me watch it," he said. "That will be the best explanation."

"I just want you to realize it's a good plan," Razkili urged. "It will go well. Taelyn is a skillful strategist."

Innowen shut him up by embracing him. "To hell with strategy," he whispered. "You keep your spear level and your sword close at hand. Now get out of here, and take my horse. The sooner this is done, the sooner we can share a jug of wine in Parendur. The finest wine in the world is made right behind those walls. That's probably why these invaders want in so badly."

"Wine sounds great," Razkili answered. "I'll come back for you when the fighting's done. Gods willing…"

Innowen pressed a hand over Razkili's lips. "Trust no gods, Rascal."

Razkili grinned. "Osiri philosophy from you?"

"Forgive me," he said, stepping away. "My mouth didn't know what it was saying."

"It seldom does, my Innocent." Razkili swung up onto his horse and took the reins of Innowen's mount. "I like that name. It fits you." Before Innowen could respond, he wheeled away and rode down the hill.

Almost at once, a rain of fire streaked the night sky, and the darkness hissed, alive with the sounds of arrows streaming flame. Enemy tents began to burn, brightening the land with a deadly light. Still the arrows flew, and the wind conspired with Taelyn as it carried sparks and ash to the tents that arrows couldn't reach.

Men only half awake began to stumble into the open. Shouting and confusion rose in the camp, but noise alone could not hold back the deadly shafts or the hail of stones that plummeted upon them when Taelyn's slingmen joined the fray. Scores fell dead in their tracks with screams frozen on their lips and faces crushed.

Innowen watched in dreadful fascination as the enemy scurried like crazed ants whose hill had been trampled upon. Some ran wailing, directionless. Some dashed back into burning tents to snatch up weapons. A single officer raced back and forth bellowing orders that went unheeded, while flames reflected in the sweat of his bare back and in his wide eyes.

The storm of arrows and stones ceased. Aided by the light of the burning tents, he gazed expectantly toward the narrow plain.

The chariots hit with tidal force. The horses themselves were as deadly as the drivers' javelins. Men bounced helplessly off the animals' powerful shoulders, hooves pounded them into the earth, wheels crushed limbs and bones.

Behind the chariots came the cavalry. Again and again, long lances ripped streams of scarlet from the backs and bellies of Parendur's invaders. The fires made dazzling patterns on the riders' bronze helmets and on the tips of their weapons. Innowen looked for Razkili and found him easily. The pure burnished metal of his shield caught and magnified the fireglow around him. No other carried such a shield. It had to be Razkili.

Taelyn's hoplites swept out of the hills with crazed battlecries, running with their spears before them. Their fierce charge carried them deep into the heart of the camp. The enemy fell like ripe wheat before them as they lunged and slashed with ruthless efficiency.

The din of battle swelled like a terrible song over the field, and over that, a surging roar as fire raged through the encampment. The mountain winds rushed over the plain, whipping the flames to a frenzy. Streamers of burning fabric swirled into the air. Hot clouds of ash and smoke whirled into the night.

Innowen heard the wind, and suddenly, it scorched him like a hot breath as it flashed up the hill, bringing a maelstrom of glowing ash that gurgled and churned around him. He flung up his arms, expecting pain, yet not a spark touched him. The wind whistled in his ears, changing pitch as the gusts rose and fell. A searing snow whirled about him in elusive choreography.

It was madness. Men were dying down below. Razkili and Taelyn were risking their lives. Yet he reached up and drew a graceful arc with his arm. The wind sang, and the ash danced, and Innowen surrendered to it. He flung back his head. A long sigh issued from his lips. A thousand lives below him did a death-dance that sent a rhythm through the earth, and it flowed into him. He felt the pulse and the thrust of it. He moved, or it moved him.

The screams and shouts became a chorus, a minute part of the music of the world. The clash and clang of spears and swords made a timpani. He spun on his toes, his hands weaving intricate patterns as he turned. Wind-blown, tiny points of firelight, like living creatures, turned with him. They leaped, and he leaped into their midst, extending his arms like wings.

Suddenly, the rhythm changed. He gazed down at the battle, though his feet never stopped, his arms never stilled. The invaders had found their weapons, and they fought back as fear turned to fury. Most of Taelyn's chariots were broken hulks. Half his cavalry fought on foot now. Razkili was nowhere to be seen. A new cry went up at the edge of the plain as archers and slingmen rushed to join the fight, seizing up the spears and swords and shields of the fallen to use as their own. Again, he scoured the carnage, seeking the gleam of Razkili's polished shield.

Another cry went up. Atop Parendur's wall, a growing crowd gathered. Innowen shot a glance at the city's main gate. It remained closed. But Taelyn had counted on reinforcements from Kyrin's First Army. Where were they?

The wind blew, spinning him around. He arched to

the side and kicked high, rolled through his spine, and drew himself spear-straight.

Then he stopped, suddenly deaf to the wind and its impossible music.

A huge knight charged through the combat on a black horse. Firelight rippled along the blade of a great bronze sword and on the metal studs of his leather armor. The dark crest of his helm streamed behind him as he rallied the unknown invaders and urged them back toward the open plain.

Innowen's breath quickened, and he clapped a hand to his mouth. His thoughts churned for an instant, then down the hill he raced, along the side of the next, and out toward the battle. At the border of the fighting, he snatched up a sword. The edge was badly notched, the blade bent. He pressed it over his knee and did his best to straighten it. With his weapon, he rushed into the fray.

The invaders, though, were in full retreat, and the dark warrior was nowhere to be seen.

"Vashni!" Innowen screamed as he ran searching among the burning tents. He had not imagined it, he told himself. It *was* the Witch's servant he had seen. It was Vashni!

He cast away the sword when he found a spear at his feet. It was a better weapon. The shaft was solid in his grip. The point glistened wetly.

He ran, dodging the smoldering remains of tents and bodies that blocked his path. Someone lunged out of the shadows. He blocked a spear thrust and brought the blunt end of his own spear up and around. The attacker crumpled with a groan. Innowen didn't take time to finish him. It was Vashni he wanted.

Suddenly, a horse blocked his way. He brought his

point up, prepared to thrust, but a hand swept out, caught the shaft, and held it with an unyielding strength. One of Taelyn's officers peered down at him, frowning. "Easy, son," he said, removing his helmet. "This fight's all but over."

Innowen lowered his spear, and all the energy seemed to ebb from him. "A warrior in black armor," he muttered. "Huge sword. One of their leaders. You saw him?"

The officer shrugged. "You ask about one man out of two thousand. If he wasn't on the business end of my lance, I didn't see him." He leaned down and extended a hand. "Come up," he said. "I'll take you to the commander."

Innowen let his spear fall to the ground and climbed up behind the soldier. He braced his hands on the horse's rump for balance as they moved off across the field. The destruction spread everywhere around them. Here and there, tent poles still burned, though most of the fabric had been consumed. The smell of smoke and blood made a terrible perfume. The moans of the wounded and dying floated eerily as the clamor of battle faded.

They found Taelyn with a handful of his warriors. At first, Innowen thought he'd been wounded, but he soon realized the blood that covered the older man was not his own. The drummer, though he still rode behind his commander, bled heavily from a cut in his side. His rigid features betrayed his pain.

Taelyn glared with an anger Innowen had never seen in him. "He didn't join us!" he raged. "That bastard never opened the gates."

"Kyrin?" Innowen guessed.

"He let us die out here, so long as he was safe behind

his damned walls!"

"But you won," Innowen reminded him, "without Kyrin."

This time the glare was directed at him. "Tell that to the dead men who followed me into this!"

Taelyn led them through the wreckage toward a cluster of hoplites. Little by little, all that remained of his army began to gather. Men drifted out of the smoke and darkness like bloody ghosts, taking substance as they drew closer. Few spoke. Some looked around for comrades and clapped them silently around the shoulders, too weary or too numb to utter greetings.

It moved Innowen deeply, and shame filled him. He had danced while Isporans lost their lives. How could he have done that? What kind of man was he?

A hand touched his thigh, and he looked down at a weary-looking soldier. "Veydon?" he said, as recognition took hold. He sprang off the horse and caught the young officer as he started to collapse. His arm slipped around Veydon's back, and he felt a slick wetness. "Oh gods," he muttered, and Veydon's breath hissed as Innowen lowered him down.

"Just let me rest," Veydon whispered. Others gathered close to see to him. "It isn't bad, but it hurts like the hells."

"He's taken a thrust under the shoulder blade," someone said, turning him on his side, examining his back.

Veydon gripped Innowen's hand. "What are you doing here?" His words came through clenched teeth. "Razkili's gone into the hills to get you."

"He left you like this?" Innowen said in disbelief.

"He didn't know," Veydon reassured him. "I didn't tell him. It didn't seem so bad at first."

"We've got to get him inside the city," said another officer as he knelt down by them.

Taelyn scowled angrily. "We've got to get a lot of men inside. And by damn we will if I have to pull those gates down myself!"

Several men picked Veydon up out of the dirt, but he refused to release Innowen's hand. "We won," he said with a weak half-grin. "It was the wind. It carried the archers' fire through the camp faster than we could have hoped. It was as if the wind was on our side."

The wind. It still blew down from the Akrotirs. Innowen felt it on his face when he looked up. But it held no music for him now. He gazed away into the darkness, walking beside Veydon as his friends carried him. He didn't know where, but he went just the same, pulled along by the hand that held his.

It was a black hell he walked through, a place of lamentation and death, of smoke and fire and gloom. What a fitting place to find Vashni, a man he had first thought a demon. And if Vashni was here, surely the Witch of Shanalane was close by.

He wiped a hand over his lips, then licked them. The salt taste of blood blossomed in his mouth.

CHAPTER 9

INNOWEN COULD SMELL the tension as Taelyn's force at last rode through the city's main gate and into Parendur. He leaned back against Razkili and flicked away a bead of sweat that threatened to sting his right eye. Rascal's arms tightened around him, and they swayed together in rhythm to the horse's stride.

Throngs of Isporans lined the streets, eager for a glimpse of their liberators. Their cheers swelled through the city. Men hurried forward with buckets of water and ladles, offering drink to the victorious soldiers. Others pushed closer to touch them, to run one hand quickly along a leg or foot, before vanishing with a small gasp back into the crowd.

Innowen felt nothing when they brushed his limbs, but he was still grateful to be on a horse. The height and the size of the animal gave him some safety from the human mass. He pitied the poor footmen when they entered the gate.

Though the crowd roared its gratitude, Taelyn's men kept almost silent. Not even the people's jubilance and the spontaneous celebrations that filled every alley and street corner along their course dulled the collective edge of the army's smoldering anger. Beside Innowen and Razkili, Taelyn sat rigidly on his mount, his face a grim mask. He stared straight ahead, not seeming to blink at all, oblivious to the citizens and all their noise.

Once before, Innowen had seen the palace at

Parendur. His heart quickened as he approached it now. In all his travels, he had seen only a few structures to match its grandeur. It stood two stories high. Banks of columns painted red and white supported its porches and parapets. It was not fortified, but sat atop a central hill whose summit had been leveled by the great labor of slaves and workmen. The rest of the city sprawled below it.

As they reached the road that led upward toward the palace, a squad of soldiers from Kyrin's First Army pushed the crowd back. A mounted captain of the guard blocked their way. Taelyn drew back on his reins and raised one hand to signal for his own men to halt.

The captain saluted politely. "Welcome, Commander. The people hail you as the savior of Parendur." He smiled and indicated the throng that tried to press closer. "Kyrin sends you greetings and awaits you in his personal megaron. The rest of your men may quarter with the garrison. We'll feed them well and see to your wounded. You have the gratitude of the entire city."

"To the hells with your gratitude and with Kyrin's greeting," Taelyn snarled. "Who gave the order to keep the gates sealed last night? Or to keep us outside until dawn? Some of my wounded men died because they couldn't get the attention they needed."

The captain looked stunned, then averted his eyes.

"Don't bother to answer," Taelyn told him. "I don't blame the garrison, soldier. I know where the order came from." He turned to one of his own officers, the man who had found Innowen on the battlefield. "See that my men are cared for. The wounded first; they get first food and the best beds, you understand me?" The man nodded. Taelyn looked back at the garrison captain and gestured toward Innowen. "This is the son of Minarik, and the other is his companion. They come with me. I know Minarik is here. It's him I'll see first. Tell Kyrin he can wait until he shits an emerald. I'll not see him." He beckoned to Innowen and Razkili, and they rode up the hill past the shame-faced captain.

At the top, they passed another escort of honor guards who raised their spears in salute and fell in behind the three. They kept a strained silence, though, and wore a kind of beaten expression. "I think they wanted to fight," Innowen whispered to Razkili. "Kyrin must have held them back."

But Razkili's attention was on the palace. The look on his face was rapt. "It outshines anything in Osirit," he said quietly. "Even the palace at Taruisa is not so fine."

"The first time I saw it, I cried," Innowen confessed. "When I lived in my cottage in the woods, Shandisti seemed like a wondrous place to me. I had no concept of Ispor's greatness. Not even Whisperstone, as awesome a place as it is, prepared me for this."

At the beginning of a long, cobbled walkway, they dismounted. Razkili eased Innowen down and cradled him in his arms.

The captain of the escort stepped up. "Sir, if he's wounded, we can care for him." He beckoned two of his men forward.

"Get away," Razkili said, scowling as they reached for Innowen. "I take care of him. No one else."

"Do as he says," Taelyn ordered before the captain could protest. "Don't touch the boy."

Innowen frowned at that word but said nothing. He rested one arm around Razkili's shoulder as the two soldiers instead took their reins and led the horses away.

Taelyn beckoned for them to follow him, and they started down a path, flanked on either side by rows of tall fluted columns of painted stone, which led into the central courtyard. Smaller pedestals with bowl-shaped depressions in their tops stood between each pair of columns. From these came the smell of fresh oil.

The walls of the palace rose around them. At the far end of the courtyard, on the upper terrace, a pair of ladies stared briefly their way, then averted their faces and vanished quietly inside.

In the northwestern corner, a team of sweat-gleaming slaves worked with hoes and spades and buckets of water at the bases of a pair of lemon trees. Innowen watched them over his shoulder as Razkili carried him, then he glanced around at the rest of the courtyard. The drought had done damage even here. The green eucalyptus bushes were edged with brown and yellow. Most of the flowers were shriveled little weeds. The fruit trees bore small infertile nuggets of pulp that would never reach ripeness.

Only an odd kind of faded beauty remained. The air smelled of sweet herbs and citrus, but Innowen realized that was because pots of incense had been placed among the branches nearest the walkway. Wind chimes played a tinkling funereal music over the dying garden. The white cobbles and the sparkling sandstone terraces, the occasional marble benches, all made a powerful contrast to the parched and struggling greenery.

"I wish you could see this in bloom," Innowen said with soft regret close to his friend's ear. "On my first visit, this became my favorite place."

Razkili shifted Innowen in his arms as he nodded somberly.

The entrance walkway from the garden into the palace was also colonnaded. It took a moment for

Innowen's eyes to adjust as they passed from the hot sunlight into the palace. It was very close and warm, and only a little of the outside brightness filtered through narrow slits in the upper walls.

"I've never seen such floors!" Razkili muttered suddenly in amazement.

Colored pebbles made mosaic patterns upon the walkways, all of oceanic motifs. Elaborate sea-flowers and sea-weeds swirled, entwined in one another. Impressionistic fish nibbled at the leaves and petals, swam and played among clams and coral, blew little streams of bubbles. Even in the dim light, the artistry revealed itself.

"It's meant to remind us of another time in our history," Innowen whispered. "The stones were carried from the shores of the Tasmian Sea and through the Akrotir mountains on foot. Ispor was a great sailing power until Wendur, our first capitol, was sacked and destroyed by raiders. That was over a century ago and on the other side of the mountains. Each of those pebbles was hand-painted. Except for private chambers, there isn't a plain floor in the palace. Even the public spaces have floors just as grand as this."

The room they had entered was immense. Huge sealed pithoi jars, taller than any man, lined the walls. Many of the ground level rooms in the palace were used for storage and contained such vessels, which were far too heavy to convey either upstairs or to basement levels. Razkili had never seen their like.

"Olive oil," Taelyn said absently, answering Razkili's unspoken question as he led the way toward a staircase on the room's farthest side. "The jars are full of it. It's a major export for Parendur, that and wine. The banks of the mountains are loaded with olive trees and vineyards. Or were, before this damned drought."

Before they could mount the staircase, a host of servants appeared at the top. Through their ranks stepped another man dressed in fine robes, his perfect black beard oiled and braided, eyes darkly kohled. He raised a hand, the smallest gesture of a wave, and the soldiers who had escorted them inside turned wordlessly and departed.

"Welcome, Taelyn," the man said as he descended one more step and stopped. "It seems you've won a great victory. Kyrin is waiting to congratulate you in his megaron."

There was no courtesy in Taelyn's response. "Get out of my way, Riloosa. It's Minarik I report to, and I can find his chambers without your guidance, so crawl back into your hole." He started up the stairs.

Riloosa blocked his way. "Kyrin is waiting," he repeated. It was a poorly concealed threat. "He's not in a very good mood."

Taelyn reached up, caught the front of Riloosa's robe, and pulled him down another step. At the same time, he ascended a step. They had exchanged places. Taelyn looked down on Riloosa and sneered. "I don't give a gods damn about his mood. My men waited outside the city gates for hours until the sun came up, and some of them bled their lives needlessly into the dirt while you were safe and comfortable in here." His gaze flickered past Riloosa for a moment and settled on Innowen. "So let Kyrin do the waiting now. I'll see him after the sun goes down, or when Minarik orders me to see him. Not before."

Riloosa glowered. His fingers curled around the hand Taelyn still had clutched in his robe. He made a subtle, but visible, effort to free himself and failed, his strength the lesser of the two men. "If you want to keep that hand, release me!" His voice was a controlled whisper full of menace. "I have friends with sharp knives who value my honor and well-being!"

Innowen caught his breath. Stony-faced, Taelyn forced Riloosa to the very edge of the staircase and bent him backward. It wasn't a high drop if he pushed him, but the suddenness of the move surprised everyone, especially Riloosa. His eyes snapped wide, and he flailed his arms to catch his balance.

Taelyn pulled him back to safety. "Life is very delicate, Counselor," he said, smoothing the wrinkle his grip had made in Riloosa's fine garment. "One moment you have it, then you don't. It's that way for all of us." His hand descended on Riloosa's shoulder, and he dug ever so slightly into the soft place under the collar bone with his thumb until Riloosa winced. "All of us," he emphasized. "Even serpents like you."

Riloosa glared at all three of them before he turned and strode up the stairs. Innowen watched him go, knowing with certainty he had made an enemy without saying a word. Rascal's arms tightened protectively about him. His friend knew it, too.

"Who is he?" he questioned Taelyn softly so the servants at the top of the stair couldn't hear.

"The ass end of a snake," came the answer. "Or Kyrin's advisor, whichever is lower." He shouted up to the servants. "This is Minarik's son. Prepare rooms for him near his father's quarters, and see that he and his companion are treated well."

The servants scurried away. He turned back to Innowen and Razkili as they climbed the stairs. "I'll be staying with my soldiers at the garrison after I've talked with Minarik." They started down a long corridor and entered the western wing of the palace. "But listen to me. Watch your backs around here." He looked directly at Innowen. "You wanted to be Razkili's spear-mate on the field. Well, it'll be twice the job here. Out there you knew the enemy. Here?" He shook his head. "This is not the same Parendur you visited five years ago."

"Why should it be?" Innowen agreed. "It's not the same Ispor."

"The deadliest spider weaves a beautiful web," Razkili muttered.

Innowen pinched his friend's cheek and grinned. "Osiri philosophy," he explained to Taelyn. "He's full of it."

"That wasn't Osiri," Taelyn answered with a serious face. "It's a saying that comes from Syraeus."

"So does Riloosa, unless I miss my guess," said Razkili.

A servant appeared from a doorway just ahead and beckoned to them. The rooms prepared for Innowen and Razkili were spacious and airy. A pair of couches ornately carved from white wood occupied the central chamber. Embroidered cushions lay piled upon them. Close at hand stood a small table. A tray of cold meat strips, a cheese, and half a loaf of bread rested there, along with a wine-filled oinochoe jug, whose urfirnis finish gleamed in the sunlight that filled the room. Beyond was an open terrace with a view of the garden. Two bedrooms also opened onto the terrace.

Razkili placed Innowen on one of the couches and propped pillows around him.

Taelyn helped himself to a strip of meat, chewed it, and washed it down with a drink from the wine vessel. A servant emerged from the south bedroom bearing linens. Taelyn caught him by the arm. "A soldier might tip a bottle, but bring goblets for Minarik's son and his friend." The servant nodded and hurried to obey. "Now,

I've got to find Minarik. Take some advice and don't wander around. Rest. You both need it." Tearing a piece of bread from the loaf and popping it into his mouth, he left them.

No sooner was Taelyn gone than Riloosa appeared in the entrance. He intercepted the servant returning with a tray of golden goblets. "I'll take those," he said, dismissing the servant. He stepped across the threshold, walked between the couches, and set the tray on the table. "Are you comfortable?" he asked Innowen as he seated himself on the opposite couch. He poured wine into two of the goblets and offered one to Innowen. He sipped from the other himself. "We have much to discuss, you and I," he added over the rim of his vessel.

"In Osirit," Razkili said dryly, "it's customary to wait at the door until you are invited to enter."

Riloosa spared a disdainful glance at Razkili, then leaned closer to Innowen. "Could you send your slave elsewhere? We should talk in private...."

Innowen bristled. His hand shot out across the short distance and caught the front of Riloosa's already wrinkled robe, and he pulled the Syraean's face even closer to his own. "This is Prince Razkili," he said acidly, "fifth son of Osirit's royal family, and of better lineage than you." Innowen released him and eased back. "You come here to curry favor, and instead manage to insult us both with your first breath." He shook his head and looked away from Riloosa, turning up his nose. "Now we're a bit weary from last night's adventure. We're going to eat this food, drink this very fine wine, and sleep."

Razkili came to the head of Innowen's couch, folded his arms over his broad chest, and glared at Riloosa with narrowed, menacing eyes. "Allow this poor slave to throw him out on his head, Master."

Riloosa set his goblet aside and rose stiffly to his feet. He looked at them both with a gaze colder than any wind that ever blew on the Akrotir peaks. "I really must change my garment," he said silkily. "This one has become unduly soiled."

"An unexpected release of urine, no doubt," Innowen said, as their uninvited guest strode through the door.

"What do you suppose he wanted?" Razkili wondered when they were alone again.

"I don't care," Innowen answered. "I'm too tired to play games. We've only slept in snatches since we arrived in Ispor, and it's catching up with me." He sipped the wine and licked his lower lip. "Can you drag one of these couches onto the terrace? It's cooler there with the breeze."

"Whatever the master wishes," Razkili quipped. He bent over the empty couch and began to drag it.

"Don't do that," Innowen said earnestly.

Razkili set the couch down and straightened. "Do you want it on the terrace or not?"

"Don't call me master," he said, "or anything like that. I don't like it. It's not funny. Too many people think because you bear me about and care for me that I own you. I don't like to hear it from them, and I especially don't like it from you. Please, Rascal."

Razkili grinned. "You *are* tired," he said, dragging the couch again. When it was in place on the terrace, he carried Innowen out and laid him gently upon it. Then he went back to drag the other couch outside, too.

"Bring the wine," Innowen suggested. "We can get drunk quietly before somebody calls us for dinner."

But he didn't get a chance to drink. The breeze blew warmly over him as he leaned back into the cushions.

He closed his eyes and sank into sleep.

〔〕〔〕〔

He awoke aware of a presence on the couch beside him. Assuming it was Razkili, he stretched, yawned, then slowly opened his eyes.

"Welcome home, Innocent."

He sat up quickly. "Minarik! Father!" He threw his arms around the older man, and they embraced.

Five years had marked Minarik. The gray that once had colored his temples had spread throughout his mane. His beard, too, had taken on a cloudy shade. Deep lines radiated from around his eyes and shot across his brow. He was still a large man and powerful, and his grip on Innowen's arm betrayed no weakness, yet there was something different, a vitality that seemed to be missing.

"Did you find our Witch?" Minarik asked quietly.

Innowen pushed himself back against the cushions into a better sitting position and realized he had done so with his legs. He had not even noticed that the sun had gone down. He drew his feet up close and hugged his knees. On the other couch, Razkili lay asleep with his back to them.

He shook his head. "But I have hope again suddenly, when I thought all hope was gone. Five years of searching, and I found no trace of her. Then, last night in the battle, I saw her man, Vashni. I'm sure it was him."

Minarik's eyes smoldered with the dark fire of disappointment. His gaze burned into Innowen. For long moments he stared, and Innowen couldn't bring himself to avert his eyes. He suffered under the scrutiny of that glare until his adoptive father suddenly patted his knee and stood.

"We'll speak of it later, but now we must bathe," he said. "Wake your friend. Kyrin is hosting a banquet tonight."

"In Taelyn's honor?" Innowen inquired, rising.

"I would hardly put it that way," Minarik said, walking to the edge of the terrace and gazing down into the garden below. "As Taelyn always manages to do these days, he's irritated our good and beloved king. But he'll be there. He's the people's hero, at least for the hour, and that'll provide him with a certain temporary safety. Now wake your friend."

They woke Razkili, and Innowen made formal introductions. Afterward, Minarik led them through another maze of lamp-lit corridors, down a flight of stairs to the first level again, out into the garden, and back through another doorway into the palace. They entered a small, bare room with several stone stools placed at intervals.

"Undress," Innowen told Razkili solemnly. All three men removed their garments and sandals, folded them, and placed them carefully on the stools. Minarik approached another door in the opposite wall and pushed it open. The red-gold glow of braziers shimmered on a pool of water within. A sweet incense diffused on the air.

"Once you enter the lustral chamber," he advised Razkili, "do not speak. It's a holy place, a place to cleanse body and mind before we enter the hall beyond, which is both a throne room and a temple to our gods."

Razkili nodded and followed Minarik through the door. Innowen, the last to enter, pulled it closed. A graceful staircase descended into the pool. Naked, they lowered themselves into the cool water and bathed each other. Soft cloths had been left in a basket on the pool's edge. As Innowen lifted one, crushed herbs fell from between its folds. He pressed it to his face and breathed the sweetness, then wet it and passed it over Rascal's back. The fireglow sheened in the drops of moisture that trickled down the Osiri's spine. Innowen caught one on his fingertip, studied it in the ruddy light, then touched it to his tongue.

He felt Minarik's hand and a soft cloth on the nape of his neck and closed his eyes while his father washed him. Then Razkili appeared before him with a cloth, too. The herb scent filled his nostrils, and the texture of the fabric against his skin seemed almost too much to bear. Gooseflesh rose on his arms, and the fine hairs stood on end. He listened, and the only sounds were their breaths and a gentle splashing of water. Even so, there was a music in it, and it reminded him that he must dance soon.

They wrung out their cloths and placed them in another basket beside the first. A second staircase at the pool's far end led out of the water and to a room beyond. Dripping, they passed over the threshold and closed another door.

The new room was brighter than the lustral chamber. Mirrors of copper metal mounted behind four wall lamps cast light into every corner. Five stone benches were the only furnishings. Upon one of them they found a stack of towels and clean white chitons. To Razkili's surprise, their sandals were also there.

"A slave brought them," Minarik told him. "There's a passage from the outer chamber to this one that bypasses the lustral pool. The same slave is at this moment burning your old clothes. They were filthy with dust and blood. I picked these for you."

Razkili thanked him as he slipped the soft, draping

garment over his head and belted it.

But Minarik was the first dressed. "Take your time, Innocent," he said. "I want to test the temperature at the banquet table. I'll return for you."

"Are you expecting some trouble?" Innowen asked.

Minarik raised an eyebrow. "This is Kyrin's party," he answered. "You'd do well to stay light on your feet." He passed through one more door, and they were alone.

"Innowen?"

He turned back to Razkili. "Hmmm?"

"Considering how you looked forward to this reunion, your father seems somewhat reserved."

Innowen hugged his towel around his shoulders and sat down. "I failed him, Rascal," he said quietly. "My quest to find the Witch was his quest, as well. There's some history they share that even I don't completely understand. He expected me to find her."

"But you tried," Razkili reminded him, laying a hand consolingly on his shoulder.

"*Trying* doesn't ease his disappointment." He threw off the towel and reached for the remaining chiton and pulled it on. Then he laced up his sandals. Beneath one of the oil lamps was a small shelf mounted on the wall. Several grooming utensils rested there. Innowen picked up a pale shell comb, instructed his friend to sit, moved behind him, and began to pass it through Rascal's damp hair.

"I've been curious," Razkili began, changing the subject. "Where do you keep your women? I saw two on the terrace when we arrived, and they ran away like deer in a hunter's sights. I've seen none at all except those."

Innowen concentrated on the comb. "Oh, I'm sure you saw some in the crowd when we rode through the streets. And if you traveled through the farming villages you'd find them right beside their men." He drew a part in Rascal's short locks and worked the hair with his fingers. "But in the cities, women are treated differently, like a commodity, kept hidden. High-born women, once they reach a marriageable age, are seldom seen at all, except at prearranged audiences. There will be none at this banquet tonight."

Razkili nodded. "Yet I recall you speaking of Kyrin's daughter."

"Dyan," Innowen remembered. "Yes, but she was a child when I met her, and the rules are somewhat different for girl children. Five years have passed, though. She won't just be wandering around anymore. I wasn't allowed to see her the last time I was here. I doubt if I'll see her this time."

Razkili reached up and caught the comb. "Do you want to see her?"

Innowen looked thoughtful. "I've never forgotten her music," he confessed. "I bought a gift for her in Milas just before I met you. It's in our bags with the rest of my collection. Taelyn said everything would be brought to our rooms. If it hasn't been damaged, I'd still like the chance to give it to her."

Razkili sat Innowen down. It was his turn to work the comb. He slid it with ease through Innowen's straight long hair.

"Have I thanked you," Innowen said, "for taking care of me the way you do?"

"Don't," Razkili answered, giving his friend's hair a twist to wring the water from it, starting his combing again. "I prefer you as an ungrateful wretch."

Innowen changed his tone. "Don't twist so hard," he whined. "And watch the comb, you're raking my scalp. Can't you do anything right?" A sly grin spread over his face, and he resumed his normal voice. "Is that better."

Razkili bent low, wrapped his arms around Innowen, and hugged him. Straightening again, he rapped Innowen's head playfully with the comb.

Minarik returned, closed the door, leaned against it for a moment, and pursed his lips. "The tension is thicker than the gravy," he said. "Kyrin is already seated. Taelyn's here, too, so I have to hurry back. He's my general, after all, though he's inclined to forget that at times." He hesitated, looked at Razkili, then at Innowen. "Anyway, my son, keep your friend close and mind his manners. This isn't a road tavern where you dine tonight, but the very heart and soul of Ispor."

Innowen's jaw dropped. He stared, stunned by his father's own bad manners, while Minarik opened the door for them. A warmth flooded his face as he felt himself blush with anger. He stepped beside his father, placed his hand against the door, and pushed it firmly shut again. "I know you're disappointed that I didn't find the Witch. Take that disappointment out on me, if you must, but you and everyone here will treat Razkili with courtesy." His expression softened somewhat, but a certain confusion lingered. "I've never heard you utter an unkindness, but that was unkind."

Minarik studied him for a long moment, but his stony face masked his thoughts. "I'm sorry," he answered at last. "I meant no offense, but this is a formal occasion. He is Osiri and not familiar with our customs." He pulled open the door again. "Now come. Already food is being served." He left ahead of them.

"Have you noticed," Razkili said off-handedly, "how softly everyone seems to talk around here? Almost in whispers?"

"Let's both fart loudly after the cheese course," Innowen said through clenched teeth.

The throne room was a huge, dark chamber lit by scores of oil lamps and braziers. Just as in the rest of the palace, the floor was a pebble mosaic, but the walls, too, were painted with elaborate sea frescoes, and the low ceiling was covered with stucco swirls and spirals made to resemble delicate shells. Time and smoke from the lamps had dimmed the once bright paint and blackened the tiniest recesses of the ceiling's artwork. Still, the room possessed an immense sense of grandeur.

The actual throne was a pink marble chair built as part of the east wall. Stone benches lined all the walls. Above those, set in deep niches, stood the shadowed sculptures which represented the various gods of Ispor.

"You said this was a temple as well as a throne room," Razkili whispered to Innowen. "I've never heard you talk much about your gods."

"Kyrin is as much a priest as a king," Innowen answered. "The city-dwellers, especially in Parendur, are ruled much more by the formalities of religion. But I grew up in the woods; a small village was the closest thing to a city. We didn't have a temple. With the day-to-day toils, we didn't have much time to carve statues, and sheep and cattle were far too valuable to waste as sacrifices." He cast his gaze over the cold stone figures in their gloomy niches, feeling no life in them at all. "I don't know the names of half of these," he confessed. "I've never had time for gods."

"Yet you searched hard for the Witch of Shanalane and for some trace of her god."

"That's different," Innowen said softly.

A long table with benches stood near the south wall. Kyrin was already seated. Five years had aged him, too, and it startled Innowen to note how strong a resemblance he bore to Minarik. His foster father and Taelyn and another officer stood in one corner talking among themselves. Riloosa maintained a place behind Kyrin and to his right. His eyes roamed everywhere, studied everything. There were other men, perhaps twenty. City officials, priests and minor priests, garrison officers, Innowen figured. He didn't recognize any of them.

Already there was food on the table, but Innowen guided Razkili toward Minarik and Taelyn. There was not even time to introduce themselves to the third man there before Kyrin called them all to sit. At his order, ten slaves entered bearing silver bowls of water with clean cloths draped over their arms. They proceeded to wash the hands of every guest. Only then did they pour wine into each man's cup, and the dinner began.

Razkili lifted his own slender kylix and poured a dollop from it onto the floor. "For those who've gone before," he uttered.

Innowen clenched his teeth, and felt his shoulders draw up. All eyes stared. Mouths fell open, then shut. No one said a word, but slowly they turned toward Kyrin. The king's face screwed up with anger and disgust.

Realizing he'd done something wrong, Razkili quietly lowered his vessel. He whispered to Innowen out of the corner of his mouth. "I thought you taught me…"

Innowen squeezed his friend's leg under the table to silence him.

"That toast," Kyrin said coldly, "is for the outdoors, foreigner. Do you have any idea what it takes to clean the filth from a mosaic floor such as this?"

"Yes, Rascal," Taelyn interjected, seizing the earliest opportunity to make a verbal slash at Kyrin, "by all means, consider the knees of our poor slaves. You only helped save a city; you didn't conquer one."

That, at least, diverted Kyrin's attention from Razkili, and Innowen forced his shoulders back down, though he still ground his teeth.

"Ah, our guest of honor," Kyrin said, raising his kylix. "Let's drink to the city's newest hero and take a lesson from him, that a man may raise himself to a pinnacle even from so low a background as a common house slave."

Cups rose to lips, but hesitated as Taelyn spoke up. "If I have a lesson to teach, my lord, let it be phrased so: A good sword knows no nobility."

King and commander glared at each other over the rims of their wine vessels. Minarik let escape a small sigh and gazed wearily at his son. The rest of the guests looked as if they were considering a quiet slide under the table. It was going to be a long evening. Innowen exchanged glances with Rascal and did his best to relax.

On his right, the coals of a brazier flared suddenly, shooting a popping little flame into the air. Its sudden light faded quickly, and Innowen cast his gaze around the throne room. Lamps and braziers were everywhere, but they were not enough to hold back all the darkness. In the red flickering, he found his shadow on the wall, and Rascal's shadow, and all their shadows cavorting and twisting at the whims of the flames.

Shadows everywhere he looked, and all of them dancing.

CHAPTER

10

ROBIN WAYNE BAILEY

"I DON'T UNDERSTAND," Razkili said when they were alone in their quarters. "How can Taelyn and Minarik speak the way they do to Kyrin? He's their king."

Innowen paced on the terrace. Clouds raced across the night sky, obscuring the stars. The dark shapes of nocturnal birds rode the winds, wheeling and swooping without apparent purpose. In the garden below, the wind chimes sang.

"This is not Osirit," Innowen answered. "Kyrin has no divine right to the throne of Ispor. To rule, he must command the respect and obedience of his generals and the nobility. If he loses that respect, those generals might replace him with another member of the royal family, or more radically, with another general who would then become the first of a new royal family. There is a continuity of leadership Isporans traditionally follow, but if a king proves incompetent, then there are options."

Razkili came out onto the terrace. He leaned against a painted pillar and watched the birds with Innowen as he spoke. "But how can he command respect if Taelyn, or any of his generals, openly insult him before his other officers?"

"It takes a strong man," Innowen told him. "A king must rule by the strength of his character as much as by the strength of his arms. Otherwise, how shall his people regard him, as a king or as a tyrant?" He held up a hand before Razkili could interrupt. "I know, I know.

Taelyn dares a lot to speak so rudely, and Minarik..." he hesitated, then wet his lips. "Minarik has changed in subtle ways. I don't know what's on his mind."

A moment of silence hung between them. The moon shone briefly through the clouds overhead, then disappeared again. "If Kyrin were deposed, your father would be a likely candidate for the throne."

Innowen thought about that and nodded slowly.

"Or if another general was chosen?"

Innowen straightened and hugged himself. The night wind was warm, yet he felt cool. "Taelyn is very popular right now." He started pacing again. "But that's all too simple. Minarik has always been content with his holdings at Whisperstone. It's not ambition that burdens his thoughts."

Razkili turned away and stared across the garden. "These are hard times for your land," he said gently. "Maybe your father thinks he can do better than Kyrin. That wouldn't be the same as ambition."

Innowen didn't respond. The questions were too complex, and he had been gone too long to form quick answers. He stopped his pacing and listened to the wind chimes. In the darkness, the garden appeared as beautiful as it once had, silvered with fleeting rays of moonlight, branches of fruit trees swaying rhythmically, the odor of eucalyptus wafting on the air. Gloom and shadow cloaked all evidence of blight and decay.

Perhaps that was why he loved the nighttime best, when darkness hid the ugliness of the world.

"You haven't danced," Razkili reminded him.

Innowen's mouth curled in a slight smile. Rascal wouldn't let him forget; the Osiri still took care of him. "I know, and those chimes are practically calling my name."

"They make nice music," Razkili agreed. "But it

wouldn't be safe in the garden."

Innowen's gaze swept around the upper terrace above the garden, scanning the darkened apartments. He and Rascal seemed to be the only ones awake. He couldn't count on that, though, and he wouldn't risk being seen. There was trouble enough already in Parendur.

"I know a place," he said at last. He turned away from the terrace and went back inside, crossed their quarters, and headed for the outer corridor. "I'll wait for you," he heard Razkili say as he moved into the hall.

He made his way back to the lustral chamber without encountering anyone. The entire palace seemed to be asleep. He bathed in the pool and toweled himself, then gathered his garments and entered the throne room. It was vast and silent. Only a few lamps continued to burn.

The eyes of Ispor's gods stared down upon him. Slowly, he crept around the huge chamber, wondering if he had done wrong never to learn all their names, never to pay them proper homage. Oh, some he knew, of course. Tremyrin, who ruled the forests. The harvest god, Celet. Shokastis, the god of the hunt. He stood before each of these in turn and bowed his head. But they were only a handful, and many were the deities in Ispor's pantheon. He looked up into the stony faces of those he didn't know and offered a silent apology for his ignorance.

He found his shadow upon the wall. *It's for them we dance tonight*, he told it wordlessly. He looked back to the statues. *And if we dance well enough, maybe you gods will lift whatever curse it is that plagues this land.*

There was no wind to be his music, yet somehow he could feel it blowing, trying to get in. He could hear its moan as it swept through the Akrotirs, and the chimes in the garden were as loud in his ears as they had been when he stood on his terrace. How they tinkled and rang so sweetly. It was impossible, and yet he heard. He embraced his shadow, cast away all thought, and melted into motion.

The gods stood unmoving in their gloomy niches where the light of the lamps barely touched them. When Innowen finished, he looked up into each of their faces one by one. Nothing showed in their carefully sculpted expressions. If he had pleased them, he couldn't tell.

He left the throne room through the same lustral chamber and washed the sweat from his body and from his hair. Dressed, he wandered through the lower level of the palace. An occasional lamp burned here and there to light his way. The pithoi jars loomed like hulking monsters in the darker corners, and the sea patterns in the floor seemed to shift and waver in the dim flickering glow. He found the state room, where Kyrin conducted the day-to-day business of his office, and the kitchens, which were now dark and empty, though warm from ovens that never went cold.

Eventually, he wandered out into the garden. The wind kissed him and rumpled his damp locks. He looked up and turned slowly around. Razkili was not on the terrace. He considered calling to him, then thought better of it. He might awaken others. There was little enough peace in Parendur; he wouldn't be the one to disturb it.

He drifted along the cobbled path. The slender moon was bright now with only a few clouds to diminish it. It touched the flowers like a healing balm and bathed the fruit trees. At the very center of the garden stood a small well. He lowered the wooden bucket. Deeper and deeper it went, and still deeper, until the rope was almost at an end and Innowen feared that perhaps it had dried up in the long drought. But at last he felt a buoyancy and a sudden weight as it began to fill, and he cranked it back up.

He set the bucket on the side and cupped cool water in his hands. The moon reflected there like a beautiful jewel and gradually vanished as the water sieved between his fingers. He cupped more water and captured the moon once more. Then a third time, and this time he drank the moon. It was an amusing, wonderful marvel he'd discovered, that he could actually hold the moon. He looked down into the bucket, and the moon was there, too, so he picked the bucket up under one arm and with a shake of his hand began to sprinkle its liquid light on the parched flowers.

Abruptly, he stopped. A soft flurry of notes quivered on the wind. Innowen wasn't at all sure he'd actually heard them. He listened. There was only the dripping of water beads as they fell back into the bucket from his motionless hand. Then they came again, a gently muffled crescendo that made the wind chimes' music seem like the clacking of sticks.

Dyan. It was her pipes he heard, he knew it. But where was she, where did the music come from? He turned and turned. No lights burned in any of the apartments except his own. A fragment of a song floated down into the garden, and he turned again. Where could she be?

He waited and waited. When he had nearly given up hope, another song began. This time it didn't stop. It settled upon him like a veil, obscuring his senses. The garden itself seemed to shiver. He set the bucket down and shut his eyes, slowly beginning to turn and turn as the piper wove music around him.

When it stopped, he nearly fell down. He opened his eyes, but the garden continued to spin. He fought to steady himself until the dizziness passed. He drew a deep breath and let it out. A bead of sweat rolled into the corner of his mouth, and he tasted his own salt.

Then he screamed inside and shot a glance toward the terrace outside his apartment. Razkili was not there, thank the gods, and all the other apartments were still dark, too.

Innowen hugged himself, though the air was warm, and began to shiver. Rascal hadn't seen. No one had seen him. *You fool!* he cursed himself, and again, *fool!* He looked up at his apartment once more and bit his lower lip to still its trembling. *If Rascal had seen him dancing...* He squeezed his eyes shut and clenched his fists. *How could you be that careless? Stupid fool!*

He ran from the garden back into the gloom of the palace. When he achieved his rooms, he rushed out onto the terrace and found Razkili curled asleep on one of the couches. He looked into the garden. Its beauty was gone; instead, it was a place of entrapment and danger. He glanced at Rascal again, and down at the garden, and at a bottle of wine on a table between the couches. He picked it up and drank while he paced.

When he was quite drunk, he shook Razkili's shoulder. "Wake up," he said thickly. "Let's go to bed."

"Innocent!" Razkili sputtered, rolling over quickly and sitting up. "I'm sorry, I fell asleep."

"Shut up!" he snapped, heading for his bedchamber. "You don't know what you're talking about. You never make any sense. Why don't you ever make any sense?"

He fell atop the coverlet, and the night lasted well into the next day.

〖IIII〗

It was late afternoon when he finally woke up. He felt stiff and sluggish. When he started to swing out of bed and discovered that his legs were useless, he called Razkili.

Moments later, the Osiri appeared at the threshold.

"About time, you drunken sot," Razkili said, grinning. He crossed the room and sat on the edge of Innowen's bed. "Minarik came by, but when he saw you lying there like a slug, he decided to come back later. He brought our packs and baggage, though. Do you want me to carry you to the terrace? There's bread and cheese if you're hungry. Wine, too, if you really want it."

"No more wine," Innowen answered. He reached up and locked his arms around Rascal's neck and let himself be lifted from the bed and carried to one of the couches on the terrace. He settled back into the cushions and drew a thin sheet across his hips. It was a scorching day. The sun's brightness stung his eyes. Razkili brought a tray with dry bread and goat cheese and set it on the small table close at hand. There was also a pitcher with a beautiful urfirnis glaze full of water, and clean ceramic drinking cups.

He heard the scrapings of hoes and shovels and rakes from the garden below as slaves continued their efforts to save the flowers and fruit trees from the drought. Razkili heard it, too. He peered over the side, watching them, and whispered to Innowen. "Have you noticed," he said, "that none of the slaves talk? They can't. Kyrin's had their tongues cut out."

"How do you know that?" Innowen asked from the couch. His head ached, and he rubbed his temples.

"I tried to question the one who brought me breakfast, and he showed me his mouth." Razkili leaned back against a pillar and sighed. "I asked Minarik about it, and he told me they were all mute, every slave in the palace."

"That's sick," Innowen muttered. "Why'd Kyrin do it?"

"No one knows. Your father thinks he's gone crazy."

They sat on the terrace together. The bread and

cheese went untouched, but Razkili brought the bottle of wine, and they mixed it with a lot of water. It proved refreshing, but not too potent, as they traded impressions of Ispor and Parendur and the people they had met.

Slowly, an iodine fire spread across the sky. To the south, they could barely see the Akrotir Mountains over the palace rooftop. The peaks shimmered like flame in the sunset, flame that cooled and finally went out as twilight advanced.

Innowen felt life return to his legs. First, it was just the sensation of the sheet across his hips. He curled his toes, flexed his knees. He bit his lip and sighed with relief and gratitude. It was always at this moment that his fear was greatest, that the sun might set and his limbs would still not move, that the magic, whatever it was, would be gone. But it was *not* gone. He sat up, eased the sheet back, swung his legs over the side of the couch, and stood up. Razkili stepped closer, and Innowen saw in his eyes the same dark fear and the same relief. They embraced wordlessly, laying their heads on each others' shoulders.

A slave appeared from the outer corridor and waited to be recognized. Innowen saw him first and beckoned for him to enter, noting the small wax tablet box he carried in one hand. The slave passed it to him, bowed, and backed up three paces.

Innowen opened the box and read the message his father had scrawled in the soft wax. "We're invited to dinner," he told Razkili, who remained on the terrace, "in Minarik's quarters." He turned back to the slave. "Tell him we'll..." he hesitated then, feeling a slight heat rise in his cheeks. "I'm sorry. You can't tell him anything, can you?"

"Of course, I can." The slave looked him straight in

the eye, all his apparent humility vanished.

"You can talk!" Innowen said with some surprise. Razkili came in from the terrace, a look of confusion on his face. Innowen's brow furrowed. "But we thought—"

"I'm not a slave," the man interrupted. "I'm one of your father's captains, his bodyguard if you will, at least while he's in Parendur. However, it would cause trouble if Kyrin knew how little Minarik trusts him, so I play the slave and keep my mouth shut so no one suspects."

"And carry messages for him?" Innowen suggested. "And spy for him?"

The captain arched an eyebrow and cocked his head at an angle. It was answer enough.

"A man who does not speak hears much," Razkili said.

"Another immortal gem of wisdom from the scholars of Osirit," Innowen noted. "Tell my father we'll join him shortly. As you can see, I'm not quite dressed for dining."

The captain left, and they took time to share one more cup of wine while the evening was still quiet. Then they prepared themselves for supper and walked the empty corridors to Minarik's quarters. Taelyn was there, also.

"How's Veydon?" Razkili asked.

"Better," Taelyn answered, directing them to the table. "There's a woman with him constantly. She sewed the wound and treated his fever. Wouldn't take gold. For payment she wanted a stag, meat to feed her family. Five men hunted half the day. She made a broth from it, though, for Veydon, and makes him eat it, too."

Minarik appeared from another chamber and joined them at the table. At his seat was a bowl of water and a cloth. He carried the bowl to each of his guests and washed their hands. It was a perfunctory gesture, however, performed quickly and without ceremony. He dropped the cloth back in the water, splashing some on the table, as he set the bowl aside. With custom sufficiently observed, he sat, and they began to eat and talk.

"Another army is gathering in the north," Minarik informed them. "I attended Kyrin's court today when his spies made their reports. They're camped where the River Semene flows down from the Akrotirs." He took a sip from his wine cup.

"That close?" Innowen said in surprise.

"Could they be part of the siege force we broke up?" Razkili asked.

"More likely the siege force was part of this larger army," Taelyn answered. "In fact, the siege itself may have been a diversion to prevent Kyrin from noticing the greater threat that was crossing the mountains."

"You think they came from the coast?" Innowen looked from Taelyn to Minarik and took a bite of bread.

"The spies think they gathered there," Minarik answered. "They may have been building their ranks for a long time. But the recruits seem to be from all over, even from lands beyond Ispor's borders."

Innowen, Razkili, and Taelyn exchanged glances. "Exactly what my spies reported about the siege force before we attacked them. Could someone be gathering all the warring factions into one massive army?"

Minarik shrugged as he looked at them one at a time.

When the meal was over and their talk had dwindled to trivialities, Innowen rose, hugged his foster father, and said his goodnights. Razkili followed him back to their quarters. They exchanged no words in the corridors as they walked, and Innowen went straight to the terrace and looked down into the garden.

"All right," Razkili said at last. "What is it?"

Innowen turned a little and leaned against a column. He wore a frown as he folded his arms over his chest and said softly, "We've had two lavish meals since we arrived here, Kyrin's feast last night, and supper with my father just now." He nodded toward the table between the couches. It still held the dried remains of their lunch. "And the servants have kept us well fed on bread and cheese and wine." He looked back at the garden, and suddenly its beauty seemed false and artificial, preserved only by the back-breaking labor of tongueless slaves, who toiled in the sweltering heat of the day. "But I was thinking of the rest of the people in Parendur and Ispor. What did they have to eat tonight? Did they eat at all?"

Razkili leaned against the wall and interlocked his fingers. "Is that why you stopped halfway through the meal?" His voice was little more than a whisper.

"When they brought the meat course," he answered. "It was pork, but the only thing I could think about was the woman caring for Veydon. All she wanted was a stag to feed her family."

Wind chimes whimpered in the trees below. Leaves rustled dryly. Lights flickered dimly in the windows of a few apartments around the garden. Here and there, shadows stirred, causing small eclipses. In the farthest apartment, the lights went out entirely.

Innowen sighed and started back inside, but Razkili caught him and hugged him close. "Thinking of others, my Innocent?" He rumpled Innowen's hair playfully.

He sighed again, but with great drama. "I know, it's not one of my usual habits." He dug his fingers in Razkili's ribs and jumped away. "Be patient. It's a mood that'll pass. Come on, let's light our own lamps."

"Just one or two," Razkili suggested. "Maybe I've been around you too long, but I'm tired of so much light, and you're going to go off to dance anyway."

〖〗〖〗〖〗

Rascal knew him too well, Innowen thought later as he made his way to the lustral chamber and the throne room. The palace was quiet, and he encountered no one along the way. As he stripped and washed himself, he reflected on his first visit to Parendur. The palace had bustled with staff and dignitaries and visitors. Now it seemed deserted by comparison. There weren't even any guards; they had all been assigned to the city walls or to street duty, except for a handful who patrolled the palace grounds. They never ventured inside, though.

He walked to the center of the chamber. It was darker even than the night before. Only four oil lamps suspended from the ceiling provided any illumination, a weak and diffuse light that puddled in the gloom. The banquet table, he noted, was gone, as were the benches for guests. He stared at the empty throne and at the silent gods in their private niches. Again, standing before Tremyrin, Celet, and Shokastis, he made obeisance. To the others, he offered hasty prayers.

If the gods of Ispor heard him, they gave no sign.

He began to dance. The floor was cool against his feet, and he moved mechanically with an unaccustomed detachment. Strangely, there was no music in his head. He neither heard the wind, nor felt it near. Yet he danced. He studied himself, the flow of an arm, the shape of a hand as he drew it slowly through the air, the extension of one leg. It surprised him to feel so little. It was an exercise, he thought, not a dance.

He turned his thoughts inward, away from his limbs, away from the lines and angles he created. Instead, he listened for the beat of his heart, the throb of blood pounding through his body. A warmth spread inexorably through his muscles, a delicious sensation.

There was his dance, deep inside, waiting for him to find it. It wasn't outside; it wasn't his arms and legs, the steps he made or the patterns he weaved upon the floor and through the air. They were only the outward expressions of what lay within.

The choreography of soul. The thought flashed through his head, and suddenly there were whisperings that echoed in every hidden corner of the chamber, whisperings and mutterings that rose and fell with the flickering of the lamps, words that darted by his ears and faded maddeningly before he clearly heard them.

A single, sharp musical note from out of nowhere cut through the whisperings straight to his heart. He flung back his head, and his muscles stood out like strings drawn too tightly around his bones. He held back, though, completely still, waiting for the riff he somehow knew would follow. When it did, he whirled across the floor from one side of the room to the other. Sweat quickly beaded on his chest, on his arms and brow, and began to trickle down. It streamed along his sides, down his groin. As he spun, he flung off a rain that splashed on the floor and the pillars and the walls. He leaped and, at the apex of it, brought his hands together like a crack of thunder.

Music filled him at last. And the gods! The gods seemed to dance around him as he danced. They made a ring, spinning as crazily and wildly as he, never leaving their niches, but dancing just the same.

Gradually, the music diminished, and the gods became just statues again. The last impossible note quavered and faded, and Innowen ended his dance in a gracefully controlled collapse. Tears burned in the corners of his eyes as he lay there, his chest heaving. Whatever the power was that had moved him, whatever the magic, he had never felt it so strongly.

"That was beautiful!"

Innowen sat bolt-upright. That was no muffled whisper, no ghostly muttering. He peered into the gloom toward the throne. In the poor light, it was hard to see. But some shadow-form crept up on the wall beside the great stone chair. The sweat on his body made him suddenly chill. *"Who's there?"*

She rose languidly from the throne. Her shadow stretched up the wall, arched across the ceiling. In the elongated fingers of her silhouette, he saw the pipe and caught his breath.

"Dyan!" he said as she stepped into the light.

"Hello, Innocent!" She put her instrument to her lips and blew a light riff. Smiling, she came toward him.

Innowen scrambled to his feet and backed away quickly. "No, no!" he moaned. "Not you, it can't be you!" He dug his fingers into his closed eyes, then opened them again. It wasn't a dream. Kyrin's daughter came closer, reaching for him. What had he done? What had he awakened in her? He felt the wall at his back and cringed. "I'm sorry, I'm sorry!"

"For what?" she said reasonably, laying a hand on his shoulder. "Innocent, what's wrong? I thought you'd be happy to see me."

Slowly, he looked at her, afraid of what he might find lurking in her face. But there was only concern there, and confusion. He straightened. Her confusion mirrored his own, and he studied her strangely. "Are you all right?" he whispered. He took her hand from his shoulder, squeezed it. A full head taller, he gazed down into the sparkling dark eyes he remembered so well. "How do you feel? What do you want to do?"

She gave an uncertain little laugh. "So many odd questions! Of course I feel fine. How should I feel? I just wanted to see you!"

"In the middle of the night?" He moved back out of the lampglow into the gloom, hoping to hide the shivering that seized him. No matter what she said, how *normal* she acted, he feared her. In fact, she terrified him. There was nothing twisted in her face, nothing threatening in her demeanor. Yet she had seen him dance, and he waited for her darkest desire to take form.

"My father doesn't want me to see you," she told him, brushing strands of black hair back from her face as she glanced demurely at the floor. "That's why he sent me to Milas on the other side of the mountains the last time you came to Parendur." She looked up at him again, rolling her pipe nervously between her hands. "I don't know why he didn't this time. But I happened to be on the terrace with my nurse when I saw you and Taelyn arrive with your escort. Of course, she ushered me inside before I could attract your attention. I'm practically her prisoner, you know."

Despite his fears, Innowen smiled. She spoke as crisply as she played her pipe, and her features moved with amusing animation, a lift of an eyebrow to accent one word, a tilt of the head to stress another, a frown, a conspiratorial grin. She had grown taller in five years, and her body had blossomed. The loose layers of her sleeveless linen gown revealed a woman's grace beneath. Her long black hair spilled down her back and draped her form like a natural cloak. And yet, inside that woman he still saw and heard the child he had met five years before.

His trembling had passed, and he stepped back into

the light. "I don't understand," he muttered to himself. Then to her, "You shouldn't have followed me down here. You don't know the danger."

"But I wanted to see you," she repeated almost petulantly. "And I had to sneak out as it is. I thought my poor nurse would never fall asleep, and I think she's supposed to keep me in my quarters while you're here. Usually, I can go anywhere in the palace as long as I don't leave the grounds. But I wanted to see you dance again. You're beautiful, you know?"

Innowen's heart skipped a beat. "Again?" He swallowed hard, then caught her arm. "You mean you've seen me dance before? When? Where?"

She looked at his hand where he gripped her. "That hurts, Innocent." She said it sweetly, without any animosity or fear, a statement of fact that made him feel like a bully or a fool, and he let her go. "At Whisperstone that first night we met in the courtyard. I watched you from an upper window in the corridor outside my room."

Innowen felt like he was suffocating slowly; his head swam in confusion. "You didn't feel anything? Nothing strange happened?" It was hard to keep a creeping hysteria out of his voice. What if he'd been wrong all these years? What if his dancing had no effect at all on the people who saw him? Had he borne such a burden for nothing? *Maybe he could dance for Razkili.*

"What was supposed to happen?" Dyan answered. "I knew when I saw you that you cared as much for your art as I did for mine." She set her pipe to her lips, blew a stream of air, and her fingers fluttered like birds on a breeze of music. She smiled at him over the reed piece. "I liked you at once, as much as father disliked you." Her smile broadened. "There's balance in that. Dance and music—there's balance there, too. A good dancer needs a good musician."

"You want to play for me?"

She didn't answer in words. She just lifted the pipe and began to make music while she watched him, dared, begged him with those eyes that were darker than the shadows that watched them both.

He tried not to listen. *The danger*, he told himself, *there is still a danger*. He didn't know, didn't understand. Yet she had seen him dance, not once, but twice, and nothing had happened to hurt her. Maybe she was unaffected by whatever terrible power his dancing unleashed. Maybe it was all right. With her, at least.

Her music sang through the chamber, a wondrous music that suddenly filled and nourished him, a food that turned to power and urged him to move, to spin, to fly. Dyan's eyes gleamed at him over her instrument, and the corners of her lips turned upward in a smile of joy even as she played.

He couldn't help himself, didn't want to help himself. It was too powerful. The stones in the walls sang with her melodies, and the echo made an infinite round of every note. It woke the gods in their cold niches, and Innowen's head swirled once more with their muted whisperings.

Dance, they urged him, or perhaps he only imagined it. *Dance the world away!*

So, for the second time that night, Innowen danced.

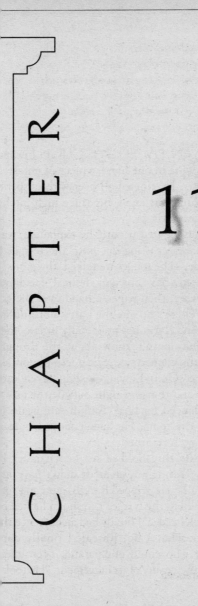

CHAPTER 11

INNOWEN PACED THROUGH his apartment, a kylix of wine in one hand, a piece of untasted cheese in the other. He tingled all over with unspent energy. His breathing was rapid, his voice high-pitched as he talked incessantly.

"I finally figured it out!" he explained, waving his bit of cheese, crossing out onto the terrace, coming back inside. "The longer we talked, the more I realized it. She doesn't have any dark desires!" He drank deeply from his wine, then wiped a hand over the corners of his lips. "There's no one she hates, nothing she seems to want. And Kyrin has practically isolated her in this palace. She doesn't know about the drought or its effect on the countryside. She doesn't know about any rebel armies. Gods, Rascal, she didn't even know about the siege, and that was right outside the city walls!"

"You danced for her?" Razkili said again from the center of the room. He hadn't moved from the spot since Innowen returned.

From the threshold of his bedchamber Innowen answered, "Yes, it was great! It didn't have any effect on her at all!" He gripped Razkili's arm and squeezed it as he crossed to the terrace threshold, looked out, then turned back inside. "I finally had an audience that could appreciate what I do, Rascal. I finally danced for somebody who could understand, even admire, the dance for the beauty of its movement." He took another

drink of wine and swallowed with a gulp. "I *performed!*
And I didn't have to worry about hurting anybody."

"That's why Kyrin cut out the servants' tongues."

Innowen stretched out on one of the couches as he
tossed his piece of cheese into the garden below.
"What's that?" he said, folding his arms under his head.

"That's why Kyrin cut out the tongues of the
servants," he repeated. "He didn't want to take a chance
one of them might tell his precious daughter about all
the misery and hunger in her land, or about all the
murders and burned villages. How do you think she'd
feel if she knew about that woman with her guts spilled
in the road at Chalandri? Or if she'd seen any of those
half-rotted corpses? And what do you think she'd do if
she knew half of Ispor was fighting for the chance to
deball her dear father because he's such an asshole of a
king?"

Innowen sat up and stared. "No, you're wrong."

Razkili glared at him. "The hells I am! The slaves
can't talk. No soldiers are allowed inside the palace—
they might let something slip. She's kept under guard
night and day by a nurse and isolated in some private
part of the palace. Hell, Innowen, she *admitted* she had
to sneak out to see you because her father gave orders
against it!"

Innowen leaped to his feet, spilling what remained
of his wine. Disgusted, he threw the cup down. It
exploded in a shower of ceramic fragments. "You're
blaming Dyan because some slaves had their tongues
ripped out? That's not her fault!" He folded his arms
across his chest and leaned against the jamb. "Why don't
you just admit you're jealous because I danced for her?"

Razkili's eyes narrowed to angry slits. He looked
down at the broken cup and back at Innowen.

"I'm a dancer!" Innowen shouted. "So magic has something to do with it. I still dance! I still create! Well, what good is it to create something if nobody can appreciate it?"

Razkili curled his fists in exasperation. "What is wrong with you?" He stared at his friend, then let out a slow breath. "Can't you see the sickness that pervades this place? The rot eating its way from the inside out? Look at you!" He stormed across the apartment, kicking a pottery shard out of his way as he positioned himself face to face with Innowen. "When did you last give a thought to Vashni? You searched for him for five years, Innowen, five years! Now you come home and find him right outside the gates of your own capitol city. Well, what have you done about it? What are you going to do? If he's here, where's the Witch of Shanalane? Remember her?"

"Remember her?" Innowen answered bitterly. He squeezed past Razkili and retreated to the center of the room. "She made me what I am, gods damn her!"

Razkili followed him relentlessly. "That's just noise out of your mouth, Innowen. *You* made you what you are."

Innowen slammed his fist against a wall. "And what is that, Rascal? Just what am I? *What am I?*"

They stared at each other across the apartment. Neither moved, and the silence stood between them suddenly like a barrier. In that moment, Innowen heard his own plaintive tones, saw all his weakness, all his petty fear and selfishness, and he burned with shame. He wanted to reach out across that silence to Rascal, to touch him and apologize, to be reassured. It should have been easy to make the first move. And yet he couldn't. Instead, he stood and waited and wished that something would happen.

Far away, the dull boom of distant thunder sounded. Razkili blinked, turned away, and walked sadly out to the terrace and gazed up into the sky where the faintest trace of blue overtook the night.

"Innowen!" he shouted suddenly. "Come here, quick!"

Innowen hurried to his side, hoping for forgiveness. His eyes followed where Razkili pointed, and he knew this had nothing to do with their argument. Several lights burned in the windows of the eastern apartments. "Whose rooms are those?" Razkili said urgently.

"Kyrin's," Innowen answered, puzzled. "He has the entire upper level."

"I saw a shadow," Razkili whispered, staring intently, "with a sword."

They watched together. Suddenly a dark form slithered past another window, eclipsing the lamplight. A length of metal gleamed in its hand.

Razkili squeezed Innowen's arm, then took off around the terrace, leaving Innowen behind. Outside a darkened apartment, he leaped a couch someone had left outside and swerved around another obstacle. He disappeared in the gloom for an instant, then reappeared, running hard, making for Kyrin's quarters.

Again, thunder rolled across the night, closer this time. Innowen looked up and frowned. The sky was clear, not a cloud. A few stars twinkled brightly, and in the east... He swallowed hard. Morning was almost upon him.

Yet Razkili was running toward trouble.

He didn't know exactly what, but Innowen felt some sudden danger. That shadow, yes—it moved with deliberate menace. But something more rode the night air, some dark radiance that touched him inexplicably and tingled on his skin. He looked at the sky again where a softening cobalt glow oozed over the rooftop, gave a little cry of desperation, and ran after Rascal.

A high-pitched scream of terror ripped from Kyrin's apartment. Against the lamplight, two silhouettes wrestled suddenly over a blade. Innowen recognized Rascal by the shape of his body and ran faster, his heart pounding as loudly in his ears as the thunder that began to shake the palace stones.

He dashed inside, colliding with another figure that lurched out of the way of the combatants. Starpoints ignited in Innowen's head as he hit the floor. Kyrin's face floated before him as he fought to untangle himself from the heavier, panting man. The smell of urine clung to Kyrin, and he clawed and rolled on top of Innowen, frantic and screaming, and Innowen couldn't tell if his king was trying to kill him or trying to get away. He looked for Rascal, but Kyrin's fingers were in his eyes.

"Get off me, gods damn you!" He smashed his fist against Kyrin's jaw and twisted out from under him. Razkili and the assassin struggled in the far corner of the room. Innowen still couldn't see the man's face. A short bronze sword waved over both their heads, and Razkili had the man's wrist locked in both of his hands. Again and again he brought his knee up sharply into the attacker's side, but with little effect. The bigger man had him pressed to the wall, and growling, he tried to bite Razkili's throat.

Innowen leaped up. With all his might, he threw a punch at the lower curve of the assassin's spine. The man threw back his head and howled in pain, and from behind, Innowen grabbed the soft throat and dragged him backward and down to the floor. Razkili wasted no time and jumped with both feet on the assassin's sword arm. There came a loud crack of breaking bone and a shrill scream.

"Kill him! Kill him!" Kyrin shouted, scrambling to his feet. He ran at the fallen man and dealt him a vicious kick in the ribs before Razkili pushed him back. "He tried to kill me! He dared! My own advisor!"

It *was* Riloosa. He moaned and cradled his arm and struggled to get up, but Innowen took a tighter one-handed grip on the bigger man's throat and dragged his head back even further. Riloosa's weight nearly crushed the breath from him, and sandaled heels drummed against his shins. Innowen dug his fingers deeper into the soft flesh and tangled his other hand in the man's thinning hair. "Stop it!" he hissed savagely. "Stop it, or I'll rip your damned throat out!"

A sound gurgled incoherently in Riloosa's windpipe, and he ceased to struggle. For an instant, Innowen thought he'd inadvertently strangled his captive, but then Riloosa shifted his broken limb and gave another moan.

"Get him to his feet," Razkili said grimly, holding Kyrin at bay with one hand.

"I can't," Innowen answered calmly. Then he smiled. A strange satisfaction surged through him, along with a renewed sense of self-worth. "It's morning."

Razkili bent down and grabbed Riloosa's tunic. "Get off him!" His face twisted with rage and concern for Innowen as he jerked the advisor to his feet. Riloosa screamed again with pain and doubled over, hugging his arm. Kyrin leaped at his would-be killer, but Razkili caught him up short. "Go call your guards!" he dared to order Ispor's king.

Kyrin glared hatefully. "There aren't any guards! Not

in the palace!"

Rascal glared back, raising his voice to match Kyrin's anger. "Then call your slaves, and have them call guards from the palace grounds!"

For a moment, Kyrin looked as if he'd try to hit Razkili, but a blast of thunder unexpectedly rattled the room. Fear danced over the king's features until he realized it was only thunder. He managed to achieve a semblance of composure and went to summon his servants.

Razkili knelt by Innowen. "When?" he asked simply.

"Right after I grabbed him," Innowen answered, grinning. "You thought it was a perfect take-down? Well, it might have been, but dawn and gravity took over."

"And you still held on to him."

The admiration in his friend's voice pushed him to laughter. He sagged back onto the cool floor, grabbed his stomach and shook with mirth. It felt good. *He felt good*. It was the first morning he could remember when the life had gone from his legs and he hadn't given in to a moment of sadness and self-pity. Hells, this time he hadn't even noticed.

Rascal touched his hand. Warmth radiated in that touch, and Innowen drew strength from it, with the reassurance he had hoped for. "Are you all right?" Razkili asked worriedly. Innowen met his gaze, quieted for an instant, then burst into another bout of body-wracking laughter.

Razkili stared, dumbfounded, then grinned and let go a loud guffaw himself. "What a noise, Innocent!" he said in mocking accusation. "You sound worse than the storm!"

As if to make the point, thunder struck again. The vibrations shivered through the floor and the walls. A rhyton trembled on a narrow pedestal in the corner but managed not to fall. Beyond the terrace, a bolt of lightning flashed, and a sudden rain roared on the leaves in the garden.

"What's wrong with him?" Riloosa snarled, backing against a wall for support. His face was pale, drenched in a fine sweat. "Why doesn't he get up?"

"He can't," Razkili explained, and Innowen laughed harder. "He's crippled. And if you try to pick up that sword, you will be, too." He nodded toward Riloosa's blade where it lay a hand's breath from its owner's foot.

Riloosa pretended to ignore the threat. "What kind of a deception do you play at?" he spat. "He ran in here, didn't he? I saw him at the banquet, visited him in his quarters. I watched him dance the other night in the garden."

Innowen felt the laughter in him dry up. He pushed himself onto one elbow, looked from Razkili to Riloosa.

"Get up!" Riloosa urged. "We can still get out of here while Kyrin's gone. I can make you wealthy men!"

A familiar burning gleamed in the adviser's eyes, a fire Innowen had seen before, a light that was no light at all, but the pure darkness of irresistible compulsion. Riloosa's apartments also overlooked the garden. Innowen had made the mistake of assuming since all the windows were black that nobody had been awake to see him. But Riloosa had seen.

He looked at the man with a new kind of respect. Riloosa hadn't tried to fulfill his desire at once, but had resisted it or delayed his action long enough to plan. Innowen had learned the hard way that most men succumbed immediately, no matter the nature of their desire, while a few others, depending on their strength of will, were able to defy the compulsion for a time. Sooner or later, though, all surrendered to their worst wishes.

"Did you want his crown?" he asked softly.

Riloosa harrumphed. "Hells, no," he retorted. The madness seemed to flow out of him. He sighed and sank to the floor. Razkili tensed and started to move, but the advisor put on a faint smile and pushed the sword to the center of the room with his toe. "Only a fool would want to rule this gods-cursed country. I just wanted to kill the pig. His rudeness is intolerable. He insults and abuses everybody. At dinner last night he stabbed a slave because the wine wasn't cool enough." He barked a short, bitter laugh. "Cool enough, in these temperatures!" He gestured with his good arm toward the terrace. "Look, it's finally raining. I think Heaven must have approved of my effort."

The world flashed a violent blue-white. The hairs on Innowen's neck and arms stood suddenly straight on end, and his bones seemed to tingle and burn. A deafening crash split the air, followed by another crash of splintering stone. The smell of burning filled the room.

Razkili leaped to his feet and ran to the terrace. "Lightning!" he called. "It blasted away part of the southern wing!" He shot a glance back at Riloosa. "So much for heaven's approval. That was your apartment."

Without warning, lightning struck again. Razkili cried out, threw an arm across his eyes and flung himself away from the terrace. A belch of flame shot up just beyond the doorway, and a loud crack echoed in the garden as a tree split in half.

"Rascal!" Innowen screamed, and he dragged himself across the floor toward his friend.

"I'm all right," Razkili said, sitting up slowly. He gazed around, blinking, rubbing his eyes.

On his belly, Innowen stared outside. The sky was the color of flint. A gray rain beat down in heavy relentless sheets as blue lightning licked at the world. Thunder surged overhead, pounding and smashing like an impossible surf.

Innowen felt the trembling in the stones beneath him, and the palace huddled into itself with a palpable, animate fear. In the corner, the rhyton fell off its pedestal and shattered. In another corner, a small chair vibrated toward the center of the room.

A distant swelling lamentation rose songlike under the storm, a terrible harmony of tiny screams and wails that beat over the palace gates, into the garden and hallways, frightened, fluttering voices without form or hope. The people of Parendur cried out to their gods and each other, and their shouts became a chorus of despair.

"It's the end of the world," Riloosa whispered, huddling down beside them. He stared outward, his face rapt with awe, cradling his arm and shivering visibly.

A sudden wind shift blew rain over the terrace, drenching them.

"Innocent!"

Taelyn and six of his soldiers rushed into the room. Riloosa shrieked, and his eyes snapped wide with pain as two of them grabbed him and hauled him roughly to his feet.

"I need you!" Taelyn shouted over a thunderclap as two more men pulled Innowen up and settled him piggy-back style on another soldier's back. "The city's under attack, and we've got to get out of here. Minarik and Kyrin and our troops are ready to break out, but you've got to do something first!"

"Dyan!" Innowen shouted back as the storm

attempted to drown his voice. "What about Dyan!"

"She's safe!" Taelyn answered. Then, to his soldiers, "Get him to the gate! Fast! We've got to know! Move!"

But Innowen was not ready to go. "What do you mean, we're being attacked? By whom?"

Taelyn didn't wait to answer, and Innowen barely had time to glance at Razkili.

They ran through the palace corridors, down unfamiliar hallways, down a flight of stairs and into a small courtyard where horses were waiting. "I can't ride!" Innowen called, blinking into the rain that slashed at his eyes. He wiped uselessly at his face. "Put me up with Rascal!"

Lightning made a deadly webwork in the sky as they raced down the hill from the palace and into Parendur's mud-slick streets. Rubble strewed their course, the wreckage of stone and wattle homes that the storm had collapsed. People packed the roads, clutching children and small bundles of belongings. The tallest buildings creaked and swayed treacherously as the sharp wind lashed the city.

The world flashed white and purple as yet another bolt shot earthward. Stone exploded, and the air rumbled with the force.

"The wall!" Innowen shouted in Razkili's ear. "That hit the wall!"

But the wall was clearly their destination. Taelyn's men pushed the crowds out of their path, using the butts of their spears and the size of their horses to make a way. The citizens were more afraid of the storm than of the soldiers and only responded with curses until they looked up and recognized Taelyn, their hero, who had saved the city only days before. He took the lead, riding without speaking a word, and his mere presence parted the obstructing throng.

They arrived at a guard station at the base of the wall and dismounted. Razkili carried Innowen in his arms and hurried up a narrow staircase as Taelyn beckoned them. At the top of the wall, Taelyn pointed outward. "Down there," he said, shouting over the wind, "is that your man?"

Innowen wiped water from his eyes as he bit his lip. A vast army stretched outward over the plain before the main gate. Naked flesh glistened in the rain, bronze spearpoints and swords gleamed with lightning-flash. With every strike of lightning, a great cry went up from the army. They raised their weapons and sent their voices soaring with the thunder as Parendur trembled.

At their head, on a huge black horse, sat Vashni.

"That's him," he answered grimly, "the Witch's man!"

Razkili spoke up. "Watch what they're doing," he said. "Every time the lightning strikes, they point their weapons at the gate and give a shout."

Rascal was right, and Innowen clenched a fist. Suddenly, he remembered his first meeting with the Witch of Shanalane. She'd used a storm to cloak her passage through Minarik's lands, used wind and lightning to smash his house. She'd boasted of her control over it, and of a power so great that, though the storm swept the forest nearly flat, not a drop of rain touched her.

"They're trying to bring down the gate!" Innowen exclaimed. His heart beat faster with the realization that the Witch of Shanalane was near. "This is her doing! She can call the storms!"

"Then where is she?" Taelyn called. The rain had beaten his hair into thick ropes, and the wind whipped them so they writhed like serpents from his head.

"I don't know," Innowen answered shrilly. "I don't see her. She could still be in the mountains, or maybe further out on the plain! But she's here. I *feel* her!"

"If she breaches the gate, there aren't enough troops in the city to resist that army," Razkili pointed out.

"I know," Taelyn snapped angrily. "Blast Kyrin for a fool. Too busy sending our armies after the little rebels. Never considered a big one might come knocking on the gods-damned door!" He headed back down the staircase where his men waited. "Should tie his ass to a post and leave him for the Witch," he said over his shoulder, "but Minarik would never let me have such fun. Let's get to the garrison fast."

Rascal carried him down the stairs. As soon as they were mounted again, they raced through the city. The air crackled and sizzled with electric fire, and the streets shook with explosions. Flames shot up, defying the rain, casting a weird flickering glow against the low clouds.

The garrison was a walled compound within Parendur. Seeing them approach, a pair of guards pushed wide one of the great doors, and they rode inside. Minarik stood in the center of the yard, drenched, yet somehow proud and powerful in his sodden cloak. "How bad?" he said to Taelyn as his commander dismounted.

"Bad," Taelyn answered curtly. "Innocent says it's the Witch. He's sure it's her man, Vashni, at their head. Bulk of the force is at the main gate, but all gates are covered. We want out, then we fight out."

Innowen's jaw dropped, then snapped shut. "You haven't got enough men! You can't engage them!"

Minarik ignored him. "Get everyone who can ride mounted," he instructed Taelyn. "Leave the wounded behind. We won't be able to take care of them. Do it quick, and assemble them here."

"Veydon comes," Razkili said.

Minarik gave him a cold look. "He's wounded. He stays."

"He comes." Razkili handed the reins to Innowen, made sure he was balanced, then slid off the horse's rump to the ground. Innowen quietly tangled his hands in the mane for a more secure grip as the Osiri strode up to Minarik. The two locked gazes for just a moment, a strange test of wills that Razkili seemed to win with ease. He turned to Taelyn. "Where is he?"

Taelyn pointed to a long, low building a short distance across the yard.

"Arrange another horse," he said. "I'll look after Innowen and Veydon both."

Minarik scowled with displeasure. "Just do it fast," he told his former slave. "And have that compound gate sealed and barred now."

"What do we do about him?" Taelyn asked, nodding toward Riloosa, who sat sullenly upon his horse between two soldiers.

"Let Kyrin decide." He spun about, nearly slipping in the mud, but recovered with his dignity intact and marched into a building directly behind him while Taelyn hurried to carry out his orders.

Innowen waited miserably in the rain, perched precariously upon the horse, afraid of falling. If only he'd had time to grab a cloak. His kilt was soaked. The cold rain rilled through his hair, down his chest and back and arms and legs. It filled his ears and stung his eyes. Throughout the compound, soldiers began to scurry, half armored, leading mounts. The great doors slammed closed, causing Innowen to twist around in time to see a huge wooden beam slide into place, guided by four large men.

That caused him to wonder. *How are we supposed to get out?*

A handful of soldiers pulled their mounts up beside Innowen, greeting him with simple nods. He recognized them as Taelyn's men and returned their greeting in kind. Others began to join them, their expressions grim. No one spoke, as if the storm had drenched their spirits as well as their bodies.

A bright flash caused him to shield his eyes. When he took his hand away, Razkili emerged into the yard with Veydon. The young soldier's back and chest were swathed in white cloth, and he walked with one arm around Razkili, but he managed a grin when he saw Innowen. "Nice day," he said, then added, "for a fish."

A soldier arrived with four horses. Razkili helped Veydon to mount one of them, then climbed up carefully behind Innowen again. His arms slid around Innowen's waist as he took back the reins, and he gave a hug. "All right?" he whispered in Innowen's ear, and Innowen nodded. To Veydon, he asked the same question.

"Wet, cold, wounded, and facing a host of thousands." A broad smile cloaked the younger man's discomfort. "It's my kind of party."

"Sure," Razkili said sardonically. "The gods are smiling on us all."

"You mean laughing at us," Innowen corrected.

Taelyn rode up beside them. "I scavenged these," he said, passing swords to Razkili and Veydon.

"What about me?" Innowen said.

Taelyn stared for a moment, then pursed his lips. "I'm sorry, I didn't think you'd be able to…"

"Only my legs are crippled, sir," he snapped in annoyance. "My arms are just fine, and I can use that as well as you." He twisted around to the nearest soldier. The man carried a lance, so Innowen pointed to the blade at his hip. "Give me that," he demanded.

The soldier frowned and looked to his commander.

Lightning snaked through the sky with a hiss and crackle. A blast of thunder followed. Innowen clapped hands to his ears as a dwelling at the farthest end of the compound collapsed unexpectedly. A sharp scream issued from the ruins, and soldiers hurried to drag the occupant free. It was only a corpse they found, though.

"You can't take another man's sword, Innocent," Taelyn chided. "His life might depend on his weapon. I'll *give* you mine."

Innowen clenched his teeth and sighed. "No, damn it," he said sharply. "But next time, don't think so little of me. I'm capable of more than you know."

Minarik emerged into the yard with Kyrin and Dyan. Thick cloaks protected them from the rain, and they hurried to claim their horses. Ispor's king assisted his daughter to mount, and she steered her beast to Innowen's side.

"Hello," she said shyly.

"Get away from him!" Kyrin's face purpled with rage as he grabbed Dyan's reins and pulled her horse away. "He's *abathakati!*" He shot a hateful look at Innowen as he spat out the ancient word.

Innowen recoiled with shock and surprise. "That's not true," he insisted.

But Kyrin hissed again, shaking his fist. "*Abathakati!*"

Minarik steered his horse between his adopted son and his king. "What about Riloosa?" he said. "What shall we do with him?"

Kyrin glared at his Syraean advisor. "He comes with us. I have plans for my sweet, treacherous Riloosa." He looked back at Minarik. "Now open the wall, Uncle, and get us out of this damned rain." He wiped water from his face and climbed upon his horse. "At this rate we'll drown before the invaders break into the city."

"Open the wall?" Razkili whispered in Innowen's ear. Innowen could only shrug. He had no idea what Kyrin meant. His thoughts still dwelled on the king's accusation. *Abathakati.* He repeated the word silently over and over. It couldn't be true, it couldn't.

The remnants of Taelyn's Second Army, complemented by Kyrin's First, which made up the city's garrison force, had crowded into the compound's yard. Overhead, a violent display of electric fire seared through the clouds, and the ground gave a strange, ominous shudder. The horses began to whinney and stamp, and soldiers shot uncertain looks at one another as they gripped their weapons. A frightened muttering rose in the ranks.

Minarik rode between two buildings to a section of the wall where four soldiers waited. They were huge men, Innowen saw, raw with muscle and rippling strength, and their young faces were grim. Minarik spoke to them only briefly, then they lined up shoulder to shoulder and faced the wall. They set their hands upon the rough stone. The muscles in their backs bulged suddenly with strain and effort. Four pairs of sandaled feet slipped, dug, and somehow found purchase in the mud.

There came a sound of grinding stone. A crack appeared in the wall. The four redoubled their efforts, and as one they gave a loud groan and pushed. It was no crack at all, but a doorway. The wall was hollow! Three more soldiers jumped down from their mounts and ran to lend their hands to the task. More tried to follow, but Minarik stopped them. A section of the wall gave inward like a single block, yielding an opening high enough for a mounted man and wide enough to admit a wagon or supply cart.

"Can there be room in there for all of us?" Razkili wondered aloud as Minarik and two of his strongmen disappeared inside.

Veydon sat stiffly on his horse, trying to hide his pain. "I'll bet the entire city wall is hollow. We could hide in there for a long time, then sweep out and catch the invaders unaware while they sleep in our beds."

Within the dark opening, a light flared, then another. Minarik emerged bearing a torch in one hand. He beckoned with the other, and Kyrin rode forward, still gripping the reins of his daughter's horse, leading her close beside him. Taelyn, conferring in private with two of his officers, waved everyone else ahead.

There was plenty of headroom, but Innowen ducked instinctively as they rode inside. A supply of dry torches stood stacked just beyond the entrance, and one of the strongmen passed a torch to Innowen and ignited it from his own burning brand. The old, oil-soaked cloth sputtered and sparked and finally caught fire. Innowen welcomed the bright orange light, but not the foul-smelling smoke the flames gave off.

Farther and farther they rode into the dank space as more men poured in behind them. Innowen decided that Veydon had been right, that the entire wall was indeed hollow. Here and there, they passed pairs of wooden tracks that smelled of aged grease. At each pair, iron rings had been driven into the wall, and coils of thick ropes had been stacked nearby. Portals, he was sure, like the one they had entered. But these led to the outside.

A dry, powdery dust rose from beneath the horses' hooves. A fit of coughing racked Veydon. "I think I preferred the rain," he said, covering his mouth as he coughed again.

"Silence that!" someone shouted with a voice of authority. "No talking, no noise!"

At last they stopped. Then, astride their mounts they waited. And waited. The dust, at least, settled, but the sweat of men and beasts permeated the air. Despite the order for silence, the soldiers began to mumble among themselves. Innowen glanced at Dyan, and she smiled. Even in the faint torchlight, her eyes sparkled. But at her side, Kyrin noticed, caught her wrist and jerked her around. He whispered harshly in her ear, something that Innowen couldn't understand. She looked contrite and hung her head, but from the lowered corner of her eye, she still looked at him.

Razkili squeezed his shoulder. "What did he mean," he said softly, *"abathakati?"*

Innowen thought and chewed his lip. "It's complex," he answered slowly. "A priestly concept. Some believe that anyone who practices magic, or is touched by it, becomes corrupted, incapable of a moral judgment. They are *abathakati*, unable to choose between right and wrong, or even to recognize the difference."

"You're cold," Razkili whispered, and he wrapped his arms more securely about his friend.

A shout from back down the tunnel caught their attention. Taelyn crowded his way past his men to the head of the line. "They've breached the gate," he told Kyrin and Minarik. "Parendur is theirs, and nothing we can do."

"Then we make a run for Whisperstone," Minarik decided. "Nothing can breach that keep." He twisted around and cast a glance back down the crowded tunnel. "Choose two teams of five men. One team rides east to search for any remnants of the Third Army. Send the other team among Ispor's nobility. Tell them to bring anyone they can find. We'll make our stand at Whisperstone."

"But how are we supposed to get out of here unnoticed?" Kyrin snapped. Innowen's torch made patches of ruddy light and shadow on his king's face as Kyrin turned sideways and scowled. "A force this size will attract attention!"

Taelyn stiffened. His eyes narrowed with anger and contempt. "You stupid piece of horse shit." He kept his voice low, perhaps out of consideration for Kyrin's daughter, but he glared unabashedly at his king, and his gaze was full of hatred. "Of course, you'll be noticed. But while you're on your way to Whisperstone, most of these men will stay right here to cover your ass. The invaders are in the streets now. Well, we're going to retake the gate and try to keep them *inside* while you get away. A lot of us are going to die doing that."

"That's enough, Taelyn," Minarik said firmly.

For once, Taelyn spoke back sharply to his lord. "I want him to remember, Minarik. Many of these are the same men he locked outside the gates the last time they saved his ass."

Kyrin straightened his spine and lifted his head high in righteous outrage. "You've insulted me for the last time, Commander," he said loudly. "If you think so highly of the common soldier, then you will personally lead the ones who stay behind, and you will fight in their front ranks." An ugly smile turned up the corners of Kyrin's lips. "And as you go down in the dust with a blade in your gut, do so with the knowledge that you gave your life in my defense."

"Father!" Innowen exclaimed.

Before Minarik could respond, Taelyn held up a hand. "Shut up, Innocent. Any man here will tell this fool I'm always in the front ranks. I never send men where I'm unwilling to go myself. It's a matter of honor this offal knows nothing of."

"Your treasonous tongue!" Kyrin cried, shaking a fist. "You side with the rebels against me!"

"Yes, I'm against you!" Taelyn shouted back, raising his voice for the first time. He pointed to Minarik. "But I'm his man, and he supports you and protects you. Why, I'm damned if I know. He'd make twice the king you are. But as long as he tells me to save your butt, I'll bust mine to do just that. But it's because Minarik asks it of me—not out of any loyalty to you!"

Kyrin shot a look at Minarik. "Uncle, this slave…!"

Minarik turned a cold gaze on his nephew, then on Taelyn. "Enough, both of you." His tone silenced them. "Taelyn, get your teams together. There's not much chance they'll succeed, but they've got to try. Then get men on two of these doors." He pointed to the nearest set of tracks. "Fifty men go out here with us to Whisperstone. The rest, out back there at an exit closer to the gate. We'll wait until you engage and draw their attention. Then we go."

Taelyn let go a sigh. "Gods keep you, Lord," he said softly. He guided his mount back through the ranks, and his voice could be heard giving orders.

Minarik called to the soldiers closest to him. Six men dismounted and approached the wooden tracks.

Two stacks of coiled rope rested beside the tracks where they joined the wall. They quickly uncoiled them, passed them through the iron rings above each track and in teams of three, began to strain.

"Move away a little," Minarik instructed those closest, who only watched.

A huge section of the wall creaked inward. Back down the tunnel, a similar sound echoed in the gloom as men strained with a second portal.

A thin line of blackness appeared around the immense square of stone. "Wait," Minarik ordered, and he slid down from his horse. "Pass those torches farther back," he snapped, waving his hand. "Better yet, extinguish them. Darkness will be our best cloak."

Innowen gave his torch to a soldier who jumped down and rolled it in the dust. A stygian blackness flooded the tunnel, and all whispering and mumbling seemed to stop at once. He held his breath. Razkili's arm tightened around him. He could feel the Osiri's heartbeat.

The ropes snapped tight again, and someone grunted with effort. Again, the stone creaked with movement. Barely visible, Minarik peeked around the edge, then disappeared altogether.

A bright flash lit the borders of the stone, and thunder rumbled as the storm continued to rage. Dimly, another sound reached them. Screaming, Innowen realized, carnage, the sounds of terror reaching faintly over the high wall.

Minarik reappeared in the glare of another lightning blast. He wiped the rain from his face and remounted. "Open it up," he instructed the soldiers who manned the ropes, and the stone slid halfway back inside the tunnel.

Taelyn's voice came out of the darkness. Innowen hadn't seen or heard him as he approached on foot. "We're ready," he said, apparently to Minarik. "Near as we can tell, the gate's wide open and unguarded. They're too busy sacking the city, I guess, to think about their backs."

"Don't worry about their backs," Minarik told him. "Just take the gate and hold it. Keep them inside as long as you can."

Taelyn reached up to clasp his lord's hand, and Innowen imagined him grinning. "I hope they'll appreciate the switch," he said. He tapped Innowen's arm. "I'll say hello to your friend Vashni."

"Stay away from Vashni," Innowen warned, but it was too late. Taelyn was no longer there.

"I'm afraid for him," Innowen confided to Razkili, and his friend said nothing.

Minarik rode to the opening. The lightning silhouetted him as he stared outward, waiting. Back down the tunnel, men and horses began to move, and the dust rose again. The crowding lessened. A slight breeze swept through and faded.

"You've been very quiet, Veydon," Innowen said, unable to see the young soldier, but knowing he waited behind them.

A hesitation. "I should be with my commander," he said sullenly.

"We're going home," Innowen gently reminded, "to Shandisti."

Veydon didn't answer, and Innowen bit his lip. He stared toward the exit. The rear end of Minarik's horse appeared and disappeared in the lightning glow. With a start, he remembered that it was morning. He couldn't walk. Yet the sky outside was eerily dark.

"Let's go!" Minarik rode out into the rain. Kyrin trailed after him, leading Dyan's mount. Innowen, Razkili, and Veydon followed, then the rest of their escort. Now the pain of the city swelled louder over the walls, and the glow of fires gleamed on the low, black storm clouds. Far down the wall, Innowen made out the last of Taelyn's force as it rode in the opposite direction toward the gate. He wiped rain from his eyes.

At Minarik's command, they ran at full gallop toward the foothills of the Akrotir. The wind bit sharply, and the rain stung. The muddy ground splashed treacherously under the horses' hooves. Still, they rushed onward, putting distance between themselves and the city.

Then, off to the right where the plain spread before Parendur's main gate, Innowen spied a small glow. Though Rascal held him tight, he still bounced and jostled, and it was hard to see. He shielded his vision against the rain and stared. "Do you see that?" he cried.

"What?" Razkili shouted back. "See what?"

"Over there!" Innowen pointed. It was just a small glow, moving slowly. Still it sent a tingle through him. He peered, squinting. "Stop, Rascal! We've got to!"

"Forget it!" Razkili's grip tightened around his waist, nearly crushing the breath from him. "There's nothing there!"

Innowen jerked sharply on the horse's mane, but Rascal slapped his arms down and pinned them, then spurred the beast on faster. "It's her!" Innowen screamed. "It's the Witch! Stop!"

"There's nothing there!" Rascal bellowed in his ear

But he could see the glow! She used it to keep the rain off. Yes, and he could see her riding into Parendur alone to claim her prize of conquest. His vision seemed to sharpen as he stared. Darkly blond her hair, and so long, so beautiful, and those same lips like dark roses. He knew it was her!

"Minarik!" he screamed.

But Minarik couldn't hear him over the crash of the storm and the rush of the wind.

CHAPTER

12

THE RAIN CONTINUED to fall. What might have been a blessing on the parched, dry land quickly turned into another kind of nightmare. Water ran in torrents upon the ground, carving deep ruts, washing away what little grass and topsoil remained. Streams swept treacherously over their banks, cutting new courses, spilling out to flood the forests and flatlands.

A thick gray fog lingered everywhere. It clung to the earth like a thick paste, stirred and swirled in the slightest breeze, eddied around the horses' hooves, parted and congealed again at the movement of an arm or leg. In the low places, it was hard to see two men ahead. On the plains the strange shape of a tree would loom suddenly out of the mist, half-concealed, a shadowy monster that made the heart quicken for just an instant.

For three days they rode, taking little rest, eating nothing. There had been no time to supply themselves, and hunting was impossible. The soldiers took it well. Even Riloosa with his broken arm bore his hunger in silence, though his pain carved deep lines in his face, and he cradled his arm as if it were a suffering child. Only Kyrin, of all the company, grumbled and complained.

When the gray day segued toward night, they found copses of trees and spread their soggy bedrolls or wrapped themselves tighter in wet cloaks. Few slept.

There were no fires to gather around; what wood they could find refused to burn. Some of the men curled up together under the scant shelter of dripping branches, sharing body heat for warmth and, perhaps, finding a measure of comfort from the demoralizing fear that gnawed at their hearts. They posted no guards. It was unlikely any pursuers would find them in such weather.

On the third night, Innowen waited, as he had the two nights previously, for Razkili to fall into a troubled sleep. He watched the lines of tension that flowed across his friend's brow, watched the twitching of the eyes, the tightening of the jaw. Rascal's breath came in short, uneven gasps and long, soul-wrenching sighs. Innowen wondered what dreams or nightmares wracked him, and he wondered if it was much of a blessing that Rascal could sleep when so few others could. He clung to Razkili longer than usual that night, their bodies fitting together like spoons, before he slipped his arms free, rose, and stole away toward the edge of the copse.

He had seen rain, and he had seen fog, but never so much of both at the same time. He knew it was the Witch's work. But why did she persist when her army had already taken Parendur? Was it to impede the king's escape? Or was it greater in scope? Perhaps she intended to drown the hopes of all the other rebels and armies that might try to wrest the capitol from her, now that Kyrin was out of the way. Certainly, it would be hard to martial their forces in such weather. They would be paralyzed while she secured her grip on the city.

He tried to wipe his face with his bare arm, then with a corner of a sodden, muddy cloak, which Minarik had given him. It was useless. He was soaked to the bone. There seemed to be no escape from the relentless rain. If only there had been some village along the way to give them shelter.

The ground sucked suddenly at his left sandal. He cursed quietly and tugged his foot free from the ooze.

"Innocent?"

Dyan stepped from behind the last tree. The useless, wet hood of her cloak was cast back, and her dark hair hung plastered to her head. Her eyes were wide, unsure, as she hovered in the shelter of the boll and peered at him. She hugged her pipe close to her chest with both hands, bending over it slightly in a vain attempt to keep the instrument dry. Innowen took a step toward her, and she retreated, placing one hand uncertainly on the damp bark, ready to bolt.

"It's all right," he assured her. "It's me. You managed to get away again?"

Her fear dissolved. "I wasn't sure it was you," she said with relief. "I'm still not used to sneaking around like this. I've never been outside without my father or his chosen chaperon, certainly never at night. Except for the very rare trip at his side, or with my nurse, the palace has been my whole life." She glanced around nervously. "It's kind of scary."

Innowen grinned. "But you're getting used to it. This is the third night. How did you do it this time?"

She giggled as she took his hand, and they started across the plain away from the copse of trees. "Lord Minarik dropped a full wineskin in my father's lap shortly after we stopped. I can't imagine where he got it, and it wasn't my place to ask." She giggled again, a quiet, little girl's laugh. "Well, father's always had a taste for the grape, and when the wineskin was done, so was father."

"You mean he passed out drunk?" Innowen gave her

hand a playful squeeze.

She ignored that. "How did you sneak away from Razkili? He's always around, never leaves your side, and he gives me the strangest looks sometimes."

Innowen frowned. "I don't have to *sneak* away from Rascal." He slipped in the mud. Her grip tightened, steadying him until he caught his balance.

"Don't be so defensive," she teased, moving closer so that their bodies touched as they walked. "I like him, and your affection for him is plain. Even the name you call him by demonstrates that. *Rascal*. That's not a nickname. It's an endearment. Are you lovers?"

Innowen frowned again and moved apart from her. Suddenly, he stopped walking and looked back the way they had come. The copse was an indistinct shadow in the mist and rain. "We shouldn't go any farther," he said. "We don't want to get lost."

Dyan gave an exaggerated sigh. "We're not going to get lost, Innocent. But we'll stop here if you like. And I'm sorry if I pried. I just don't understand you two."

He tilted his face up into the rain. It was cool, but not cold. He felt the rivulets that ran over his chin, down his throat past the collar of his cloak and tunic, felt the water flow upon his chest and belly. It rilled through his hair and down his back. He would have been more comfortable naked; his clothes were thick and heavy and clung awkwardly to his flesh. His cloak was a weight that bent his shoulders.

"You *can't* understand," he told her at last. "The bonds between men are as varied and complex and deep and mystical as any that women ever imagined among themselves. Rascal belongs at my side, and I belong with him. That's all there is to it." They looked at each other for a long moment, then he managed a smile and reached out and tapped the end of her pipe. "Enough of this. Play a tune. Play something to drive away the mist and dry the rain."

"You love him," she whispered gently.

He frowned again, unable to form an answer that would make her understand.

She smiled, and Innowen thought it was the only light in a darkness that threatened to last forever. "Something you can dance to?" she said. She put the pipe to her lips and blew a few soft notes. Innowen glanced over his shoulder toward the copse, but the fog and the rain muffled the music. There was little chance that anyone could hear them. "Yes," he agreed, grinning, "something to dance to."

She closed her eyes and played. A quiet, gentle tune flowed from her, and her fingers worked upon the pipe with an elegant, flawless grace. At first, she stood there in the rain, still as a cool piece of carved ivory, only her fingers moving. Then her head began to move with a barely perceptible rhythm. Next, she began to sway in a subtle, serpentine undulation as she poured out her sound.

Innowen felt the music caress him, enfold, and fill him. He thought he knew the melody, yet Dyan created it anew, enriched and embellished it. It touched him suddenly like a wave, white-capped with a foamy sadness. The high tones were longing and the low tones quiet despair. Each note was a sigh that made a crack in his heart.

The drone of the rain was a moan and a chorus. Innowen lifted one knee, leaned, stretched his arms high overhead, then drew them in and curled into a ball. His flesh became grief and doubt and fear, whatever the music made him, emptiness and uncertainty. The music shaped him. The music gave him form.

A passion filled his dance. He might have slipped in the mud, but his footing was sure. The world whirled around him. He stretched and soared, and the dance became a drug that burned in his veins and sharpened his senses with a razor-edged euphoria.

He danced alone this night, for he had no shadow to dance with him. So thick was the fog that no moon shone through, no stars. He missed his shadow, missed its languid grace and the ease with which it imitated his most difficult moves. It was his friend and his partner, sometimes his confidante, and he could tell it things, tell it things in the language of his dance that only it could understand. But he had no shadow tonight, and the strange taste of loneliness in the music made its absence that much more poignant.

Yet he *did* have a shadow! He almost stopped in surprise when it began to move beside him. No, not *it*. She. Dyan was dancing! Even as he turned, he watched her from the corner of his eye: she moved gracefully, bending and swaying, whirling, never taking the pipe from her lips. Somehow, she had managed to free herself from her cloak without ceasing her music. The rain pasted her pale thin gown transparently to every budding curve of her body. Her eyes gleamed as she regarded him, and the corners of her mouth turned upward in a smile as she blew a new series of notes.

The music took a wilder course, and Innowen drew a sudden deep breath. The sound struck him like a spear thrust, and he flung back his head. He touched the clasp of his own cloak, and it slithered down his body. His tunic came away with a swift upraising of his arms as he pivoted on a sandaled toe. The wind brushed across his bare chest, and his nipples rose in response.

He looked at Dyan, but her gaze told him she was in some world of her own now. Still, her movements mirrored his own. He danced less with his arms, since she could not use hers. He kept his kicks and lifts low because her dress was too restrictive. But he whirled, and she turned with him. He arched his back, and she raised her pipe to the sky.

The rain on his body began to mingle with sweat. The faster she played, the faster he danced, and the faster he danced, the faster she played and danced beside him. He forgot the rain, forgot the mud under his feet, forgot Parendur and the Witch and all the soldiers in the trees nearby. He and his incredible shadow danced, and there was no one else in all the world but the two of them whirling and whirling, faster and faster and faster.

Suddenly Dyan gave a little squawk as she lost her balance and fell. Unhurt though, she hugged her precious pipe between her breasts and rolled from side to side in an uncontrollable fit of giggles, her eyes squeezed tightly shut. "Make it stop!" she wheezed, "everything's spinning!"

Innowen fell on his knees at her side and bent over her, grinning, breathing hard. The rain and sweat ran off the tip of his nose and splashed on her forehead until he wiped at his face. He pressed both her hands with one of his as if he might anchor her until the vertigo passed. Her giggling proved infectious as he stared down at her. Dark mud splattered her hair and skin. Her gown, a slickly smeared ruin, tangled and twisted around her body as she convulsed with laughter.

"You're a mess!" he managed between gasps of laughter, and in response she reached up slyly and filled one of his ears with a fistful of muck.

"Who's a mess?" she countered as he recoiled, and sitting up, she launched another slimy handful that splattered on his neck. He yelped in protest, then hurled himself atop her and pinned her back in the mud. He sat on her chest, his knees pressed against her sides. Laughing, she tried uselessly to push him off, even resorted to poking his ribs with one end of her pipe until he caught that and took it from her.

"I give up!" she squealed. "I give! You're too heavy, and my dress is all tangled. I can't move!" She stopped struggling and lay limply underneath him, her breasts heaving, her giggles gradually subsiding.

Then sharp nails dug into the side of his knee. With her other hand, she gave him a dangerously low short jab and twisted with a surprising sinuous strength. Instantly, Innowen found himself on his back with Dyan on his chest, her knees pinning his arms almost painfully.

"Your pipe!" he exclaimed, for the instrument had slipped from his fingers and lay somewhere in the mud.

She bent over him, her face coming close to his. "My nurse used to pin me like this when I was disobedient," she said in mock sternness. "But when I got a little older, she started winding up exactly as you are now, on your back with your legs beating the air." She rubbed a muddy finger down the length of his nose. "Do you know how funny you look?"

Innowen knew he could unseat her easily, but he

played along, delighted by a side of Dyan he had never seen. Gone was the demure daughter who never looked her father, or any man, in the eyes. Sure, she had sneaked off the two previous nights and played for him while he danced, and they had talked a bit, even laughed a little. But this was another Dyan entirely, and he had not yet recovered from the surprise. "Your pipe!" he tried again. "It'll be ruined!"

"I'll clean it," she said firmly, drumming the tips of her fingers ticklishly on his chest.

It was torture. Innowen stood it less than a moment, then jerked one arm free and trapped her wrist. When he tried to free his other arm, though, she leaned all her weight upon it. They struggled against each other like that, neither gaining the advantage, until suddenly Dyan relaxed.

Her face took on a strangely calm expression as she looked down at him. He saw the gleam in her gaze and a rich moistness there that puzzled him as she leaned lower. Her breath was a flower, and her breasts brushed against his chest through the thin fabric of her gown. He sensed their weight and the warmth they contained. "Innocent," she whispered. Then she kissed him.

He knew a moment of terror and froze, aswirl with confusion as her tongue penetrated him. He couldn't draw a breath; he thought he would suffocate, and still she bent over him, kissing him, stroking his hair, his face, his throat. He reached up to push her away, and his hands found her breasts. She moaned a little, and, afraid that he had hurt her, he pulled back.

Slowly, a warmth began to spread through him. He feared it, but couldn't deny it. His palms returned to her breasts and caressed them through the thin wet material of her dress. As she sighed into his mouth, he accepted her breath with a strange pleasure, swallowing it and opening his mouth wider to take more of her. Somehow, she had found her pipe. She ran it over his body, along his throat, in the hollow place of his chest and over his nipples, down his ribs and hips. The tip of it felt like a hot brand as she passed it over his belly and down the sides of his thighs. He closed his eyes and gasped.

Without thinking, Innowen found the clasp of his kilt and opened it. His breech cloth came away as easily. He pushed Dyan's dress up around her waist and gently rolled her over. Neither of them gave a thought to the mud or the rain. She dragged her pipe along his spine, to the small of his back, and lower as he settled within her, and she exhaled one long, smooth note of pain and pleasure.

After it was over, they stood and let the rain wash the filth from their bodies. Dyan watched him, full of wonderment, never taking her eyes from his form. It made him self-conscious, and though he watched her, too, he stood a little apart, afraid to let her touch him again.

Her gown was a hopeless ruin, but she slid back into it. Her cloak lay close by. When she draped it around her shoulders, it hid most of the damage. Bending over, she wrung water and mud from her hair, then pulled up her hood.

When Innowen was also dressed, she took his hand and laid her head upon his chest. "The palace used to be so full of life and gaiety," she said quietly, "and at night I would watch couples doing that on the terraces where they had dragged their couches to escape the heat of their rooms." Her breath came feather-soft on his sensitive skin. She seemed at once a little girl again, like she had been before their tryst, vulnerable and innocent. It confused him more, and so did his response as he gently wrapped his arms about her. She shivered. "I wondered what it was like." Innowen felt a warm wetness on his chest that he knew was not the rain, and he bit his lip. "I've loved you since that first time I saw you at Whisperstone," she said. "You were a wet, dirty puppy that Minarik had brought home, but I didn't care."

He wanted more than anything to run away, and yet he hugged her closer. "Maybe that's why you can watch me dance," he whispered. "Maybe nothing happens because of your love." Another thought took shape in his mind. Perhaps, Razkili *could* watch him dance. "We should get back to camp," he said distantly, his voice barely audible as he looked through the fog toward the copse of trees.

Hands linked, they started walking. "Have I been too sheltered, Innocent?" she asked with a note of bewilderment. "I wouldn't have thought so, but these past few days prove me wrong. I didn't know how troubled Ispor had become. I didn't know about the drought or the rebellions or anything." She swallowed, and her fingers tightened about his. "I didn't know how disliked my father is by those who serve him. His own men hate him. They'd rather follow Minarik."

Innowen said nothing. What could he say? What could anyone say to a child when it first realized its parents were made of clay, like everyone else, and clay, when wet, was as slimy as the mud under their feet? And didn't every child make that discovery sooner or later, that father and mother were not gods at all, not pillars of strength, or founts of wisdom, but just clay?

He thought of Drushen as he had not done so in some years. It had taken Innowen some time to understand, and a little more time to forgive. He knew now it was his dancing that had made the old man do what he had done. And yet he wouldn't have done it at all if the desire had not always been there, lurking in some small corner of his woodcutter's heart. And that was the way of it. He had raised Innowen, cared for him like his own child, fed and clothed and protected him and loved him—and in his heart secretly harbored a dark desire.

"Remember how the gods made us," he told her quietly, staring into the fog ahead: "...how Enlit, the Good Father, and Bastit, the Dark Father, strove against each other, creating Chaos from their hatred for each other. Yet as they battled, strength against strength, sinew to sinew, each straining to overpower the other, an understanding grew between them, that one could not live without the other, and that, in itself, was a kind of love, and from that understanding came a powerful, passionate coupling. The result of that coupling was Man." He paused long enough to look into her eyes, taking both her hands. "But no one, not all the priests in Ispor, knows which god it was that actually birthed us. Some say it was the Dark Father, because of the evil we do, but some say it was the Good Father, because still we are capable of good things."

"And some say it doesn't matter at all," Dyan interrupted, "because whoever gave us birth, still we're tainted with the seed of the other."

"So it is with Kyrin," Innowen said. "The son of

both his fathers."

"I guess I've only seen him through a daughter's veiled eyes," Dyan answered discordantly. She drew her hands away. "Maybe now, though, I see him too well."

A shrill scream made them stop suddenly. Dyan clutched at Innowen's arm, and he pulled her close as he stared through the fog toward the copse of trees. The scream came again. Then a shouting rose before the scream could fade.

"Come on!" Innowen took Dyan's hand and dragged her along as he ran toward the encampment. They stumbled in the mud and slipped on the slick grass, helping each other. The trees grew closer, and the shouting grew louder. They reached the edge of the copse. Shadowy figures ran among the thick bolls, all in the same direction of the screaming. Innowen followed them.

A confused ring of soldiers had formed on the far side of the camp. With Dyan still in tow, Innowen pushed his way through them to the fore.

Minarik and Kyrin stood nose to nose, shouting at the top of their voices. Riloosa lay on the ground close by, hugging his injured arm, his face a pale twisted mask of agony. He moaned, and his breath hissed through clenched teeth as he rocked himself.

They were not the only source of shouting, however. Just beyond those three, a handful of soldiers kept another group at bay with drawn weapons. Innowen spied Razkili. The point of his friend's sword hovered near someone's throat. More shouting grew among the soldiers in the ring, and Innowen glanced around nervously. How many were Minarik's men, and how many Kyrin's? It hadn't occurred to him before to wonder.

In the center of the ring, Kyrin made a quick side-step and dealt Riloosa a vicious kick. Riloosa shrieked in horror and wrenched his arm out of the blow's range, taking it in the ribs instead. Almost as quickly, Minarik moved, planting both hands on his king's chest, pushing him backward. Kyrin lost his footing in the mud, slipped, and pitched over. He scrambled angrily to his feet again. An ugly sound rumbled through the ranks of soldiers.

Plainly, the argument concerned Riloosa. Innowen tried to focus on what Kyrin was saying.

"He's mine!" the king raged. "I'll do as I please with him, gods damn you, Uncle, and no one's going to set that arm. He used it to raise a sword against me, against his king! And I'm going to see he never uses it again for anything."

Minarik was equally loud and stubborn. "I don't give a frogging damn about his arm! Set it or not, it's nothing to me. Just stop kicking him. It's the middle of the night. At least a few of us are able to sleep, and the rest need a little peace before getting back on a horse again. So stop kicking him, gods damn you, you drunken ass!" He pushed again as Kyrin's foot lashed out.

Dyan squeezed Innowen's hand, but he was barely aware of her at his side.

"I said stop!"

"I'm your king!"

"King of nothing! The Witch has your throne now, and your city and your crown. She'd have your life, too, if Taelyn hadn't pulled your fat out of the fire."

"Ispor is still mine!"

"Nothing is yours! Nothing! Get it through your head, Kyrin. You've lost! She's won. She's finally won. Your sister has the throne now. Your sister!"

"Shut up!" Kyrin glanced wildly at the circle of soldiers. "Shut your lying mouth!" He shook a fist under Minarik's nose, all color gone from his face. "She's not my sister. I never had a sister!" He turned to the crowd, spreading his arms in an appealing gesture. "I have no sister! Minarik speaks an evil lie! Minarik is a traitor!"

"It's no lie!" Minarik shouted at Kyrin. "She was Koryan's firstborn. You know as well as I that Koryan ordered her exposed to the elements before she was three hours old because, fool that he was, he wanted a son first to inherit his crown. But she didn't die. Instead, her nurse fled with her to the island of Mikonos and raised her there. She *is* your sister!"

Kyrin let go a wild cry and threw himself at Minarik, locking his fingers around his uncle's throat. Both men tumbled backward, falling on Riloosa, who let go a shriek of pain. The soldiers stirred uncertainly. Some hands drifted toward sword hilts or tightened around the hafts of spears, but no one moved to assist either combatant as they rolled in the mud.

On his back, pinned between two struggling, screaming men, Minarik scooped a handful of filth from the ground and rubbed it in Kyrin's eyes. His nephew sputtered and flinched enough for Minarik to knock away the hands around his throat, and with a twist, he unseated the once-king and scrambled over Riloosa to his feet.

Kyrin was equally fast. Wiping the muck from his eyes, he launched himself again at Minarik, head down, arms wide and grasping. Minarik caught him by the shoulders and brought a knee up into his chin. Kyrin grunted as he collapsed to the ground, but his arms went around Minarik's legs, and both men were on the ground again, rolling and pummeling each other.

The soldiers had grown tense and quiet, expectant. At once, Innowen realized he was witnessing more than a mere fight. Whichever man emerged from this struggle would rule these soldiers. Kyrin was king, yes, but no king ruled in Ispor without the respect and support of his armies.

Suddenly, a long-bladed copper knife sailed over the heads of the nearest soldiers and splashed in the mud near Kyrin's hand. Innowen caught his breath, then whirled, hoping to spot the man who had thrown it, but to no avail. He turned back to the fight. Kyrin and Minarik also saw the blade. Kyrin reached out for it, his fingertips brushing the hilt. Minarik caught his arm and dragged it away from the weapon. Slowly, he climbed on top of Kyrin and straddled his chest. Kyrin beat Minarik's back with his knees, tried to strike his face with his fists. Instead, Minarik dealt Kyrin two vicious slaps and reached out to claim the knife himself. He raised it high as Kyrin let out a piercing, terrified shriek.

Dyan's nails dug into Innowen's arm as she, too, screamed.

Innowen moved without thinking, shrugging Dyan off, hurling himself forward. His hands closed around Minarik's wrist, preventing the blade from descending. "Father!" he shouted in Minarik's ear. "Don't! No!"

Minarik looked up at him, his eyes glazed with anger and bloodlust. His breath came in ragged gasps, and his lips curled back, exposing teeth. His free hand formed into a fist and prepared to strike, and Innowen readied himself to dodge without relinquishing his grip on his father's knife hand.

Gradually, recognition stole into Minarik's gaze. His anger faded, and his breathing calmed. He turned back to Kyrin, who still held his arms before his face to ward off the expected blow. "You can thank Innowen," he whispered. "You owe him your life." Without taking his eyes off the beaten man, he got to his feet. Only then did he free himself from Innowen's hold and slip the knife into the waistband of his kilt.

Innowen breathed a sigh of relief as his father walked away. He started to follow, glad that the fight had ended. Still, he searched the eyes of the soldiers, wondering what ran through their thoughts. Was it truly over? They seemed listless, uncertain, afraid to look at each other. He remembered a time five years before when Kyrin's troops had dressed in red and Minarik's in green. It had been easy to tell them apart in those quieter times, but the mostly ceremonial uniforms had been cast aside for a warrior's more practical garments. It was no longer so easy to know friend from foe. He couldn't be sure, but those men he thought he recognized as Minarik's appeared to have gravitated to one side of the ring, and those from Parendur, the larger force, to the other.

Dyan stood where he had left her. He remembered pushing her to get to Minarik's side. He owed her an apology. Yet as he approached, her eyes widened, and she gave a shout. "Look out!"

Fire rippled down his back. Without thinking, he whirled and lashed out with the edge of his left hand, even as the other reached around to explore his wound.

Kyrin staggered back a step, rubbing his jaw, glaring. The king's right hand was still curled into a claw, and the nails dripped with blood. "Thank you, *Abathakati?*" he hissed. "Never."

Innowen locked gazes with his king, suddenly loathing the man he saw before him. His eyes flickered toward Razkili on the other side. Rascal stood taut as a drawn bow, ready to move, but Innowen shook his head sternly. He looked back to Kyrin. "A bear did that to me once," he said, wiping at his scratches with the back of a hand. He brought the hand to his lips, and tasted the salty blood with the tip of his tongue. "Your claws are not nearly so sharp." He turned away and passed through the ring.

Minarik was nowhere in sight, so Innowen returned to the small camp he and Razkili had made, curled up on Rascal's spread cloak, and laid his head on a folded arm. A short time later, Rascal stretched out beside him and gathered him close. Innowen welcomed the warmth of the Osiri's body, though he said nothing.

Fingers roamed over his back, exploring, and Innowen flinched. "Does it need attention?" Rascal asked quietly.

"Just scratches," he answered. "They bled a little, that's all."

"I don't have a cloth to wash them," Rascal said, but he pulled Innowen closer until his bare chest pressed against the wounds. There was some comfort in that. "What happened to your cloak?"

Innowen stiffened, remembering where he'd left it, why he'd taken it off, what he'd done. "I was dancing," he explained slowly, uneasily. "When I heard the shouting, I came running and forgot to pick it up."

Razkili raised up on one elbow and peered over at him. "But you'd already danced once tonight when we went walking. I waited for you at the edge of the trees."

Innowen shrugged irritably. "I wanted to dance again. I didn't have to. I just wanted to, all right?" Razkili laid back down and hugged his friend once more. But Innowen sensed a difference in the touch, and his frown deepened. "I couldn't sleep, Rascal," he said. "It's getting to us. It's getting to all of us."

"I know, Innocent," he said. "Shhhh. We'll reach Whisperstone tomorrow. Try to rest."

But he couldn't rest. He stirred restlessly on the damp ground, unable to sleep. Raindrops fell at random from the leaves above, plopping on his face, on an arm or leg, in his ear, driving him to slow distraction. He resented the apparent ease with which Razkili slipped into sleep. Finally, he freed himself once more from Rascal's embrace and got up.

He wandered through the camp, feeling like a ghost as the fog swirled about him. The dark figures of men slumped miserably beneath the trees, heads on their knees, cloaks pulled over their heads or curled fetally on the wet earth. No longer were they paired together as before in warming embraces, but singly isolated, each apart from all the others. A few drifted as he did, faceless shadows moving aimlessly through the thick mist, unable to rest.

He found Minarik, another restless shadow, standing at the edge of the copse, staring into the gray nothingness. His father barely acknowledged him as he glided to his side. For long moments they didn't speak, and Innowen found himself staring outward, too. The swirl and eddy of the mist had a hypnotic quality.

"The Witch is really Kyrin's sister?" he whispered at last. Minarik didn't look at him, though Innowen was sure that he heard. It didn't matter. His silence was answer enough. "Why didn't you tell me?"

The rigidity flowed from Minarik, and he sagged, seeming suddenly older than Innowen had ever seen him. He folded his arms over his chest and closed his eyes briefly. He looked at Innowen at last. When he spoke, emotion weighed heavily in his voice. "How could I tell anyone that the woman I loved and made love with was also my niece?"

Innowen's lips drew into a tight line, and he rubbed his brow with a thumb and forefinger. "She must have known, or did you find it out some other way?"

Minarik looked up at the treetops, and a faint smile flickered over his face. "Oh, she knew," he answered. "But incest was not such a crime in Mikono, where she was raised, and by the time she told me, I was too deeply in love. She teased me about it, but she wouldn't let me go, and I was too weak to leave."

"But you did leave eventually," Innowen said. "Taelyn told me that part."

Minarik went stony again, straightening his spine, turning away from his foster son to seek the ghosts of his memories in the fog. Innowen stayed with him a while longer, trying to discern for himself those vague spirits of the past, but his thoughts were too full of present concerns and fears for the days to come.

He broke the silence with an old question. "You know her name," he said softly. "Tell me her name."

Minarik shook his head. Anger surged up in Innowen's breast, and he clenched one fist. How could Minarik deny him? For five years he'd searched for the

Witch, five years of his life spent on a quest as much Minarik's as his own. "Damn you!" he said, full of bitterness at his father's refusal. "Damn you!" He turned and strode away, leaving his father alone with whatever it was in the fog that so held his attention.

He almost stumbled over Riloosa. The unfortunate former advisor slumped against the boll of a tree, bound fast there with a stout rope passed several times around his waist. He said nothing when Innowen knelt down beside him, but his pain-glazed eyes rolled up sluggishly and fastened on Innowen's face. He covered his injured arm protectively.

"Let me see it," Innowen whispered, touching Riloosa on the shoulder as gently as he could. It occurred to him that he could set the broken bone to spite Kyrin and Minarik both. He had the skill; he'd learned in his travels. He could use sticks for splints and bind them in place with strips of cloth. Kyrin was nowhere in sight. If he worked quietly, and if Riloosa cooperated, he could be done in no time. The difficult moment would come when he manipulated the bone into place. Riloosa might scream and attract attention. "Let me see it," he urged again, trying his best to sound reassuring.

Riloosa pulled up the sleeve of the injured arm. Innowen bent closer, then caught his breath as he recoiled, covering his mouth and nose with one hand. A splinter of bone poked through the puffy flesh just below the elbow. The arm was nearly twice its normal size, and the skin had turned dark. A vein of black ran from the wound all the way up the inside of Riloosa's bicep and disappeared in the folds of his garment. From the puncture around the bone fragment, a thick puss oozed.

"There's nothing you can do for me," Riloosa sighed as he lowered his sleeve. Still cradling his arm, he closed his eyes once more and sagged back against the tree.

Innowen got to his feet and resumed his wandering through the encampment. Riloosa was a dead man, and it was Innowen's fault. Sure, the advisor had hated his employer, even wanted to kill him. But having a desire and acting on it were not the same. Riloosa might never have tried to harm Kyrin, no matter how he loathed him, if he hadn't seen the dance in the garden. But with sight, desire became deed. Innowen had made him attack the king as surely as if he had put the sword in his hand.

He found Rascal awake when he returned to their little camp. Wordlessly, he sat down cross-legged and stared at the fog. Razkili didn't say anything. He just draped an arm around Innowen's shoulders and pulled him closer.

Innowen began to shiver. In the swirling mists, vague shadows started to move, barely seen forms that flitted and slithered through the cool vapors, with faces too far away or too concealed to recognize, yet familiar. They whirled and leaped, floated or flew in the eddies and currents of the fog, dim creatures on the barest edge of his perception. But if he couldn't see their faces, he saw their hands plainly, dark-veined and bloated things that crooked their blackened fingers and beckoned to him.

"Leave me alone," he whispered to them, trembling.

"What's that?" Razkili said uncertainly.

Innowen stared outward, watching the shadow-play. "Nothing," he said, wide-eyed. The fog, the mist, the vapor danced for him, a slow, shifting, sensuous dance that chilled and fascinated him. "Sometimes, I think I see things," he confessed to Razkili. "Maybe it's a side effect of the Witch's healing. But most of the time I think, maybe, I'm just going mad." He sagged back into Rascal's embrace, weary of the interminable rain and the fog and the darkness. For some reason, he thought of Dyan and what he had done with her in the mud and the rain. Then he pushed the thought from his mind.

"Hold me," he begged softly, "hold me."

CHAPTER

13

ROBIN WAYNE BAILEY

THE SMALL VILLAGE OUTSIDE Whisperstone's walls had grown in the five years of Innowen's absence. Many people had moved closer, counting on Minarik's protection to save them from the raider bands and rebels that scoured the countryside, and hoping for his charity and the bounty of his stores to save them from starvation.

There were crude cottages and tents along the road, and farther off lay broad fields, which showed the visible scars of failed attempts at cultivation. Unfortunately, those fields were silvery sheets of water now, and the few scraggly plants that still poked up their heads offered little hope for any real harvest.

The villagers came out to watch as the troops rode past. They were a ragged lot, and hard times showed on their thin, gaunt bodies and threadbare clothing. Women and children turned up their faces, hunting for husbands and fathers that had joined Minarik's army for the few coins it paid and for the grain that service earned their families.

A low moaning went up from some of the women, and from someone, a shriek. From others came cries of relieved greetings as some of the crowd began to run alongside the horses of loved ones who had come home. Atop the gate and along the wall, sentries began to shake their spears and cheer, and more soldiers joined them there, adding their voices as their lord at last returned.

Innowen was too tired to care. He leaned back in Razkili's arms and watched as the massive gates cranked back. Ahead of him, Minarik and Kyrin were first to enter. Straight across the main grounds and to the steps that led to the keep's main doors they rode. Whisperstone's guards pressed around them, taking their reins as they dismounted, reaching up to bear Innowen down and to help Dyan from her horse. Then he was in Rascal's arms again and up those steps and through those great doors. With a muffled boom they closed.

A tomblike quiet filled Whisperstone. A line of slaves and servants stood mutely, ready to take instruction. Innowen recognized none of them as he studied their aged and weather-worn faces. The servants were all old men, recruited, he guessed, from the villagers outside the walls. They had the looks of farmers and herdsmen and lacked the crisp formality of trained slaves or hired domestics.

Still, they moved with swift efficiency as Minarik gave orders. One collected all their cloaks. Another led Kyrin and Dyan away to private chambers, while two others hurried ahead to prepare hot baths. One departed for the kitchens with instructions for the staff there. One led Razkili and Innowen to quarters, while another pair began to clean up the mess the arrivals had made in the entranceway.

Innowen could feel Razkili's fatigue in the way his friend carried him as they ascended a flight of stairs. They both needed rest. He couldn't remember ever feeling so weary or so depressed. He was hungry and dirty, but more than anything else he wanted a soft bed and a chance to close his eyes and forget everything for a while.

They followed a servant, a gnarly old man with neatly cut hair and a white, well-groomed beard, as he led them through the corridors. Innowen half smiled, remembering how magical he had thought Whisperstone was when first he'd come here, how it had seemed more like a labyrinth, its passages dark and unknowable and other-worldly, how the very frescoes that lined the walls had appeared alive to him.

Now, the place seemed dank and oppressive. The dust that covered the floor and hung in the air had a flavor and odor that irritated his senses, and he was acutely aware of the ponderous weight of stone above his head. Shutters that had been closed against the rain had not yet been thrown back, and the smell of stale oil and lamp smoke wafted thick and heavy.

Maybe it had only been his innocence those five years ago that had made it seem such a wondrous place. After all, what had he ever seen of the world, then, but some woods and the four walls of a one-room cottage. He could easily remember the excitement and fear he'd felt that first night here. What a wide-eyed little boy he'd been, what a child.

Or, perhaps, Whisperstone was still a special place. He bit his lip and considered dimly. Maybe his weariness prevented him from seeing it truly, from savoring its mystery. Maybe after some rest, it would once again fire his imagination and fill him with some sense of awe as it once had done. Maybe the tawdriness would melt away, and he would discover that the keep was just as magical as he had found it that first night in all his innocence.

That word kept coming back to him. *Innocence.* Like a small voice inside his head, it mocked him, called his name. *Innocence, Innocent.* He mouthed it, moving his lips soundlessly, matching the cadence of Razkili's footsteps.

He bit his lip again, then laid his head on Rascal's shoulder. He wanted so badly to sleep. He was too tired to think, too tired, so tired....

▯▯▯▯▯

A faint, pitiful scream shattered Innowen's dreamless sleep. He sat straight up in bed, the hairs prickling on his neck. The sound came again, raking through Whisperstone's darkness like the edge of a blade on rock. Innowen flung back the sheets and swung his legs over the edge, barely aware that life had returned to his limbs. He stood and took a step with his hands out before him and kicked a stool with his unprotected toe. Damn, there was no light!

He waited a moment for the scream to come again. His heart thundered in his chest, the blood pounded in his ears. He waited, listening. And waited. At last, he started again to feel his way through his quarters. His hands located the shutters of a window, and he threw them open. A welcome breeze danced over his bare chest, but little illumination spilled inside from the few watchfires that burned along Whisperstone's wall.

"Rascal?" he whispered, turning slowly in the gloom. Where was his friend?

He turned back to the window. Along the wall, the sentries stood in pairs as they kept watch. If there was danger from attack, surely there would be more activity on the wall. What was that scream, then? He leaned a little further out the window and looked as far as he could in all directions. A circle of guards had gathered in conversation near one of the watchfires, and a few others strolled lazily across the main yard, perhaps off duty.

A pervasive quiet returned to Whisperstone, and his fear began to subside. If the sentries were unafraid, then he, too, could remain calm. He would wait for Razkili. Razkili would know what had happened.

He stared beyond the wall. A few lights burned in the windows of some of the more distant cottages in the village. A few gray wisps of smoke curled upward into the night.

Innowen's lips drew into a thin line. Whisperstone had changed forever. Never again would it be an isolated keep. The families that had built their homes in the shadow of its walls would stay, and their children would raise families here, and their children, too. The village would grow into a town, and the edge of the woods would be pushed farther back to make room for larger fields.

He closed his eyes and listened. Yes, he could hear the rustle of the leaves as the wind shivered through the trees. He opened his eyes again. Hard to say if he could actually see the woods. It was so dark. But he could feel it there, old and patient and pervading, part of him, for he had grown up in its heart. He could smell the bark and the dry leaves and the moist earth, though the odors of the forge and the slop barrel mingled in the air, too, like a taint.

Behind him, the door opened, and lamplight suddenly brightened the room. Without leaving the sill, Innowen looked over his shoulder.

"Innocent?" Razkili peered at him, the little flame he carried casting an upward light that limned his face with an eerie chiaroscuro. He moved halfway into the room and set the lamp on a small table. "You're awake," he said needlessly.

"What was that screaming?" Innowen asked as Razkili came toward him. "Where've you been?"

"You passed out as soon as you hit the bed," Razkili told him, "and I was afraid if I slept, too, we might both sleep through the night."

Innowen bit his lip. He knew what that would have meant, and it touched him that Rascal had thought of it.

"So I stayed awake," Razkili continued through Innowen's embrace. "It got kind of quiet, though, and I feared I'd nod off, so I took the lamp to explore for a bit."

"But the screams," Innowen said, crossing to the middle of the room, "didn't you hear them?"

"Of course I heard them." He hesitated, then swallowed. "It was Riloosa. They had to cut off his arm."

Innowen's hands squeezed into fists, and he felt suddenly cold all over.

"He was crazy with fever, and the infection had spread too far. Kyrin's got him in a room downstairs."

Innowen dug his nails into his palms. "Kyrin ordered his arm cut off?"

Razkili nodded as he sat down on the edge of Innowen's bed.

Innowen paced back and forth. The cold he felt dissolved, and the slow fire of anger began to burn within him. He went to a chest where earlier a servant had placed some clothes for them, and he drew out a white chiton, pulled it over his head, not bothering with a loin cloth, and fastened on a belt.

"Why do you care?" Razkili asked suddenly in a strained voice. "As I recall, you didn't much like the Syraean."

Innowen didn't answer. He looked instead for his sandals, then remembered the same servant had taken them away to try to clean off the mud.

He turned back to Razkili. "Show me where he is," he demanded.

Razkili frowned but didn't get up. "What do you think you're doing, Innocent?"

Innowen exploded, grabbing Razkili by the shoulder of his tunic and hauling him to his feet. "I said, show me where he is, gods damn it!" he shouted in his friend's face.

Razkili wiped a bit of spittle from his cheek, and his eyes narrowed with anger. Then his shoulders slumped, and he shook his head slowly. "All right," he said with a calm born of weariness. "All right."

Innowen led the way into the corridor, his jaw set, his fists clenched rigidly at his sides. Razkili snatched up the lamp from the table and followed. From behind one of the many doors in the corridor, voices issued, but Innowen didn't stop to listen or investigate. He stalked on at the very edge of the tiny flame's wavering illumination, his shadow slithering on the floor before him.

The corridor ended in a descending flight of stairs. There, Innowen stopped. Mounted in brackets on the old stone wall was a large round shield whose bronze surface had been beaten into the semblance of a demonic face. On either side of it hung two beautifully wrought copper swords with matching daggers. Innowen slipped one of those daggers from its resting place and ran his finger along the edge. The razor-keen blade equaled half the length of his forearm. He stuck it in his belt and glared wordlessly at Razkili until the Osiri took the lead and continued on.

Rascal guided him through a series of twists and turns. Whisperstone was still a labyrinth, *that* at least had not changed. They descended two more flights of stairs and entered a passage lit by oil lamps that had been suspended by thin chains from broad overhead beams. A faintly odorous smoke drifted in the poorly ventilated corridor.

Just ahead, a sentry stood watch beside one of the many doors. He turned to look when he heard footsteps and watched warily as they approached. A frown flickered over the man's face, and he glanced down uncertainly before finally meeting Innowen's hard gaze.

Innowen wondered if he was one of Minarik's men or one of Kyrin's. Kyrin's, he guessed, since it was Kyrin's prisoner he guarded. Innowen didn't give a damn. He glowered at the soldier, almost nose to nose. "Do you know me?" he asked, but his tone made the question irrelevant. His words were a pure threat.

The soldier blinked with timid consternation as he glanced at Innowen's long dagger. "I know you," he managed.

"Then go back to your barracks," Innowen told him sharply. When the man hesitated, Innowen repeated, his voice an angry hiss, "Go back to your barracks, soldier!"

The soldier shrugged. "This is none of my affair," he muttered. "Me, I got a family I've not seen in months, and fields all gone to hell. The sooner you great lords get to killing each other off, the sooner the rest of us can get back to more important concerns." He made a curt mockery of a bow, then shoved between them and disappeared down the corridor.

"Quite a speech," Razkili said, cocking an eyebrow.

"Quite," Innowen agreed. "See that he gets a bag of

coins tomorrow for his honesty."

Innowen turned toward the door and pushed it open. His anger was gone, lost in the surprising encounter with the guard. Yet he was no less determined as he stepped into the room. The stench of burned flesh and hot pitch hung in the air. Not even the opened window had been able to leech it out. Several lamps provided light, and an unseasonable fire crackled in the small hearth, making an oven of the room.

A bare-chested, leather-collared slave hurried to block their entrance. From the assortment of bandages, steaming pots and bloodied cloths, Innowen guessed he had some responsibility as a healer. It didn't matter. He gently but firmly pushed the older man into the corridor, ignoring his protests, and closed the door again.

Riloosa's ankles had been bound to the end posts of his bed. The sheets upon which he lay were a mess of blood and foul matter and sticky pitch. His clothes had been cut away. He looked frail and withered in his nakedness, not at all the calculating, hard-willed court advisor Innowen had known before. His gray hair seemed thinner, and those darkly glazed eyes seemed barely able to focus as he looked up at Innowen. His lips parted slightly, but no sound came from him. Weakly, his head rolled to the side, and he looked away.

Innowen forced himself to look at the stump where Riloosa's right arm had been. They had taken it just below the shoulder. Black pitch covered the cauterized flesh, but burns were plainly visible on the shoulder and along the right side, caused by whatever they had used for the cauterization, probably a hot torch or a brand from the fireplace.

Innowen pulled the dagger from his belt. He had

brought Riloosa to this with his dancing, and he felt the weight of that guilt like a huge stone around his neck. He had not liked the Syraean, but no man deserved this. He touched Riloosa's forehead; the skin was searing hot with fever. Amputating the arm would not save his life. The infection had eaten far too deeply. Greater agony was all that awaited the advisor, from the poison in his blood and from Kyrin's unforgiving hands.

He had no intention of allowing that. He brushed a finger over Riloosa's cheek, and the old man turned his head to look once more at him. His gaze fastened for an instant on the dagger, then he closed his eyes. His mouth opened slackly, and he let go either a sigh or a little moan.

Innowen fancied it was a sigh of gratitude. He cut the ropes that bound Riloosa's ankles, then sat down on the bed, gathered the old man in one arm, and hugged him close to his chest. Those weary eyes never opened as Innowen pressed his face to the top of the Syraean's balding head. The mouth never tried to speak.

Innowen set the point of the copper dagger to Riloosa's heart and slipped it deep. Another sigh fled the old man's lips, the softest of sounds, like a tiny zephyr that stirred among fallen leaves. For an instant, the Syraean stiffened, then he completely relaxed.

Warm blood spread over Innowen's hand as he pulled the dagger free and dropped it on the floor. Still, he clung to the old man and hugged him closer, as a child might a broken doll, and he set his cheek next to the old man's cheek as tears started to seep from the corners of his eyes. Suddenly, he gave a great sob and buried his face against Riloosa's neck.

Razkili's hands settled on Innowen's shoulders, and

Innowen felt himself pulled away. He refused, though, and clutched at Riloosa's body, twisting away from his friend. "Get out, Rascal!" he cried despairingly. "Get out before someone comes!"

Razkili continued to pull at him, working strength against strength to unwrap his arms from around the counselor's body. "Come on, Innocent!" The urgently whispered words echoed in his ears. "Come on, I'm not leaving you here. He's dead. Let go of him!"

Razkili wrenched Innowen's right arm free and locked his own left arm under Innowen's chin. Innowen sputtered and sobbed as the Osiri dragged him from the bed. With one hand still around Riloosa's chest, he refused to let go. But his grip slipped upward over the shoulder, the bicep, to Riloosa's wrist. Then, the old man slid over the edge of the bed, and his own weight finally broke the hold.

Razkili locked his arms around Innowen's chest and wrestled him toward the door. "We've got to get out of here!" he hissed. Achieving the corridor, he grasped Innowen's arm and ushered him along at a shambling run. Innowen no longer resisted, but let himself be guided. It didn't matter where Razkili was taking him. What was his friend saying in such strident whispers? That didn't matter, either. He stumbled up a flight of stairs. The corridors rushed past, long tunnels of light and dark. His eyes wouldn't focus, but he didn't care. He didn't care.

Only the most primitive kind of awareness told him he was back in his own room again. Like a wraith unable to touch the real world, he floated down upon his bed and sat there, numb.

"Innocent?" Razkili knelt before him and squeezed his hands. "Innocent?"

Rascal's words drifted to him across oceans of mist and fog. Innowen heard, but the effort to answer seemed just too great. He felt Razkili near, but couldn't see him, couldn't see anything but a vast gulf of fear and pain. Blackness rose up, chilling, and froze him. He wanted to return Rascal's squeeze, but he couldn't move, and it didn't matter, anyway. He stared into that gulf, mesmerized by the darkness, oblivious even when Rascal crawled up on the bed behind him and wrapped his arms and legs around him and began to rock him and shed tears, which trailed down Innowen's neck and back.

It was his fault. Riloosa's blood was on his hands, and he couldn't stand that. He saw Riloosa's body floating down in that dark gulf, tumbling, staring back at him. He saw the old man's face clearly, not angry, not accusing, but cold and still, composed in death. Innowen watched, screaming inside, unable to make a sound. He watched it tumble, watched it spin and whirl in that horrible, empty gulf, and soundlessly he screamed again, for he saw, understood, that it was not a random motion. Riloosa—the corpse that had been Riloosa—danced.

It danced for him, and Innowen watched with a dreadful fascination, as if it were his penance.

But his worst desire, whatever it was, stayed buried. Instead, the long darkness began slowly to lift. The gulf faded, and Riloosa faded, and it was only a wall that he was staring at so intently. His hand fell upon Razkili's thigh where it rested on his own, and he stroked it languidly. He didn't try to stop the rocking, but gave in to it, yielded to the soothing rhythm, and accepted consolation.

People envy you for something, never knowing how it eats you up inside. He formed the words in his mind, making them perfect, like a piece of poetry, and carved them in his heart. All his life he had wanted to dance, dance like the trees in the wind, like the birds that wheeled through the sky, like the clouds and the stars as they rolled across the night. Everything that lived danced, and everything that did not live was still caught up in the dance. And Innowen danced, too, and by dancing, became part of everything that was.

But the trees and the wind, the birds, and clouds, and stars, did they pay such a price?

He closed his eyes and ran his palm along Rascal's leg. The fine, soft hair tickled, and the smooth, powerful muscle pulsed with a heat.

"Innowen?" Razkili said softly over his shoulder. But Innowen wasn't ready to talk yet. He said nothing, and after a moment, Razkili laid his head back down against Innowen's shoulder without ever breaking the rhythm their rocking had established.

Innowen sucked his lower lip. He could continue to dance and destroy lives with his dancing, or he could stop…and never walk again. One night, that was all it would take. *Tonight, just don't dance tonight.* Then he would be free. He started at that, almost laughed. He wanted to laugh, but it wouldn't quite come. *Free.* He had thought that walking would make him free.

You are a fool, he told himself bitterly.

He reached back and gently stroked the top of Razkili's head. It was for Razkili most of all he feared, and he knew he should send him away, or drive him away, but he couldn't stand the thought of that, of being alone without him. *Choose*, his inner voice urged, *dance and destroy, or be a cripple.* But what of Razkili? Would he love an invalid?

"I'm sorry," Innowen whispered.

Razkili lifted his head and rested his chin on Innowen's shoulder. "Ummm? What?"

"I've been treating you like a servant," he said apologetically.

Razkili's fingers began to work in Innowen's shoulders, kneading away the tension. His thumbs pressed deep on either side of the spine where it joined the neck and crept up to the soft spot just at the base of the skull. Then they started back down again, slowly, languorously. Innowen's head rolled forward, and he let go a small moan.

"I left the damned lamp downstairs," Razkili said quietly. "Afraid we don't have any light at all."

"We'll have company soon." Innowen drew a deep breath and bit his lower lip. "If the guard didn't talk, the attendant surely did. Somebody must know by now that Riloosa is dead and that I killed him."

Razkili continued his massage. "You did what you had to do." His fingers worked into the soft spots behind Innowen's ears and down the sides of his neck. With a soft sigh, he slipped his arms around his friend and drew him into a gentle embrace. "Speaking of things you have to do, you have to dance. Dawn can't be long off."

I don't want to, Innowen thought, stiffening. *Let the sun come up like this, in this quiet room with Rascal's arms around me. I'm afraid to go on with this curse!*

But he was also afraid to go back, back to being crippled, to being alone and helpless. Vividly, he recalled the night he'd had to drag himself on hands and elbows through a storm and a muddy road to find aid for Drushen. How miserable he'd been, soaked and covered with filth, as he'd crawled along like a drowning worm. Drushen would have died that night if the Witch hadn't come along.

He felt Razkili's warmth curled around him, felt the heart beating deep in the Osiri's chest and the tender strength that pulsed in the arms that held him. He bit his lip again. What if Rascal needed him someday?

"All right," he answered slowly, uncertainly. A huge hand seemed to squeeze the blood from his heart, and he trembled at the decision he'd made. He untangled himself from Razkili's embrace and pushed forward to the edge of the bed. He planted his hands on the side, preparing to rise, then hesitated. A cold lump formed in his throat as he fought to shape words. At the same time, though, his face burned. "Do you love me, Rascal?"

A measureless silence hung over them, darker and deeper than the blackness that filled the room. Neither of them moved, neither of them touched the other. Even the sounds of their breathing stopped. Innowen listened and waited and waited, his fingers tightening in the bedsheet, until he thought he would scream to break the oppressive silence.

Razkili's hand settled lightly on his back. "I love you, Innocent."

Innowen shut his eyes, and his mouth drew into a taut, quivering line. What should have filled him with joy filled him also with a terrible, cloying fear as he pushed himself to stand. He turned, took Razkili's hand, and pulled him to his feet. So close, he felt his friend's feather-soft breath on his face as he inhaled the scent of him.

"Leave me alone in here," he told Razkili. "Stand guard at the door. Let no one enter until I tell you, but shout a warning if it's Minarik." He reached out and pulled Razkili to him. "Now go, and let me get on with it," *before I change my mind*, he added silently, fighting back a strange note of panic. "I won't be long this time."

"I wish I could watch," Razkili whispered.

The note of panic threatened to overwhelm Innowen. He rubbed his hands together as if trying to cleanse them of something. "Don't say that!" he snapped. Then, struggling to control himself, he added "Please, Rascal. Don't say it."

Innowen felt Razkili's hand brush his cheek, then heard his footsteps as he crossed the room, opened the door, and passed into the corridor beyond. Quietly, the door closed.

Alone. Innowen hated it, and he stood in the center of the chamber hugging himself. *Alone.* It was a word of power. It chilled him and made him tremble. The room's sudden emptiness closed in on him like the walls of a box growing menacingly smaller. He dashed to the only window. The shutter was still open, and he stared toward the wall and the flickering watchfires. Yes, a few men still walked their patrols, but they were far away, too far away to matter, just voiceless shadows moving in the night.

Shadows. Without quite knowing why, they reminded him of the Witch, and he clenched his fist. He had seen her close only once, did not even know her name, but she had haunted his life. In his moment of anger, he suddenly resented that. He had spent five years in a futile search for her, walked through many lands on the legs she had given him, and finally returned home, only to find her waiting. He could feel her now, so near, though Parendur was days away.

He shook his head. He knew he had to see her, and he feared. He remembered her voice, the sound of her whisper and her laughter on the wind. He had never forgotten it. Some nights, he still listened for her in the rustle of the leaves or the rush of the clouds across the sky.

He squeezed his eyes tightly shut and covered his ears with his hands. Even when she didn't call him, she *called*.

The breeze blew through the window, kissed his cheek, whispered with a soothing susurrus. Almost against his will, Innowen opened his eyes and listened.

Abruptly, he jumped back and slammed the shutter tight. *No!* he shouted silently at the wind. *I don't want your music tonight!*

Maybe, he thought when the shutters were closed tight, it was the Witch he shouted at.

He backed into the center of the room. There wasn't much space for dancing, and it was dark. He might kick something, or knock something over. Yet there was a kind of grim satisfaction in the thought of a bruised shin or a broken toe. He deserved that and more.

CHAPTER

14

INNOWEN LEANED HIS back against the cool stone of Parendur's high wall and waited for the dawn. By the faint light of the moon he could make out the fine gray ribbon that was the road through the main gate. It stretched across the plain and broke apart, sending smaller roads onward into the valley beyond and into the foothills on either side.

He stared at the gate again and thought of Taelyn. A pang stabbed his heart. Not one of the soldiers in Taelyn's last command had been seen or heard from. No doubt all were dead; theirs had been a suicide assignment.

Cursing silently, he let his head sag forward onto his knees as he drew a few deep, dust-filled breaths. The drought had reasserted itself. The last few days had been scorching, and all evidence of any rain had vanished. Only night brought the slightest relief from the crushing heat. Even so, a fine sheen of sweat dampened his skin.

From high atop the wall came a scuffling and the murmur of low voices. Innowen listened to the changing of the watch guards. Soon enough, the night was quiet again. He stretched one leg out before him, rested one hand on his bent knee, and waited.

The Crown of the Heavens cut a pale swath across the black sky. In the north, the Great Scythe turned slowly, its seven stars blazing. He had known the names of those stars once. Drushen had taught him. In the handle, *Shalaka, Bandal, Paros*. The others eluded him now, though he tried to remember.

Voices came to him again, from above. Snatches of a conversation drifted down from the wall, then faded into silence once more.

He brushed a hand over a small ceramic bowl, where it lay in the dirt beside his outstretched leg, and moved it a little closer. His finger moved idly in the dust. With a start and a pang of guilt, he realized he'd written Razkili's name.

Leaning his head against the wall, he shut his eyes and called up Razkili's features. It was so easy to remember the smell of him, his touch. Razkili had filled his thoughts in the time since he'd left Whisperstone. For five years they'd ridden together. Five days without him had been almost unbearable.

What must Rascal have thought when he read the single word that Innowen had left carved in the wax tablet? *Wait.* That had been the entirety of his message, and then he had contrived to slip away on a pretext, made his way to the stables, left a second message for Minarik with a slave there, and departed his father's keep.

The second message would assure that Razkili was in no way responsible for Riloosa's death. It also promised that he, Innowen, would return to face Kyrin's wrath. He was not running away. There was, however, something he had to do that could no longer be put off. Something he had to do alone.

He turned his gaze up toward the moon again. It was well over half-full. Some nocturnal bird flitted briefly across its face, a dark silhouette, then something more beautiful as it climbed away with the silver light limning its wings.

Please, Rascal, he prayed silently as he watched the bird disappear. *Understand.*

Another sound drew his attention back to the road. The uneven creaking of dry axles and the steady plod of an ox's hooves echoed out of the darkness. It was a few more moments before he made out the dim outline of an approaching cart. It pulled up before the sealed gates and stopped.

Innowen surreptitiously pushed his legs out before him and lifted the small bowl in one hand. "*Selats?*" he said quietly, "a few coppers for an unfortunate cripple?"

An old man peered down at him from his seat on the cart, then slowly lifted his bulk and stepped down with a grunt. "Early for a beggar, you are," he answered finally, offering no coins. "I'm usually the first one here." He reached over the side of his cart and began to unload, pulling down a stool and a potter's wheel, which reeked of strong-smelling clay. He set them by the roadside near Innowen's feet and went back to his cart again. "What's your name, beggar?" he asked as he lifted out a bundle of blankets and spread them on the ground.

"Petroklos," Innowen lied easily, careful to keep his legs still.

The old potter began to place various pots and vessels upon the blankets, knowing even without benefit of a lamp or torch just how he wanted each piece displayed. "Well, Petroklos," he said as he worked. "You're in my spot, now, and if you were another merchant I'd give you a sound drubbing and drive you right off for your impertinence." He turned to Innowen with an oinochoe jug in one hand and shook it at him. "But seeing as how you're a poor miserable cripple, you can beg there and I won't bother you. Mind, though, you don't annoy my customers. What are you doing outside the gates, anyway?"

"Waiting for them to open," Innowen answered truthfully. "Your spot, you say? You're here every morning?"

"Unless it rains, or there's war," the old potter affirmed as he unrolled a small tent and began to erect it near the blankets. "There's been some of both lately, but now the sun's out again as hot as ever, and if the fighting's settled down for a bit, this poor man's back in the business of providing for his family." He flashed a showy grin, pleased with his own speech. "Waiting to get in, lad? Where'd you come from?"

"Kabari," Innowen answered, naming the nearby village where he'd left his horse and the few belongings he'd brought on his journey. He felt inside the rag he wore as a tunic to reassure himself his purse was safe, and the thin dagger he had secreted was still there. "Are things already so normal, with Parendur full of invaders, that you feel secure doing business in the shadow of the city gates?"

The old man used a mallet to drive four metal rods into the ground at the corners of his encampment. That done, he ran a rope through loops at the tops of each rod, and his shop was complete. He paused to survey his work and gave a satisfied sigh. The sound of wheels and voices made him turn—more merchants coming up the road bringing their wares from the countryside. The potter led his wagon around to the back of his tent, unhitched the ox, and tethered the beast to the rearmost rod.

"Normal?" he answered, finally resuming the conversation. He shrugged as he bent to adjust the positioning on his blanket of a tall rhyton, whose urfirnis glaze caught the glint of the moonlight. It was the centerpiece of his display. "All I care about is, is it peaceful? Right now, it's calm enough, so I come here, set up my shop, sell a few pots, and go home. Wife gets fed, children get fed. That's my only worry."

Innowen's brow furrowed as he watched the man rearrange his wares and rearrange them again. "You don't care that King Kyrin is in hiding, and an invader sits on his throne?"

The old potter shrugged again and grunted as he moved the tall rhyton aside to put a huge skyphos bowl in its place. "What's that to me?" he said bluntly. "Kings' business is kings' business, but a poor man's got to look out for himself. You live as long as I have, you'll learn that. It's hard enough, especially in these times, for a man to get by and feed his family. If somebody can keep things peaceable, then let him be king. Don't matter to me what his name is. Kings come and go, but the common people got to make a living." He gave Innowen a long look. "Besides, everybody knows Kyrin got the throne by poisoning old Koryan. Took the crown by murder, he did. Now someone else has taken it from him and made himself king." He wagged a finger at Innowen. "And there'll be someone come along later to take it again."

"It's a woman," Innowen muttered.

The potter looked at him with a show of surprise before he plopped down heavily on his stool behind the wheel. "Hmmmph. Well, the gods will deal with a bitch for not knowing her place. It's still not my worry."

Innowen planted his hands on the ground and pushed up to brace his back more comfortably against the wall. He was careful not to move his legs. That made him grin, however. He hadn't counted on company out here so early. It was hard not to move, and the irony was not lost on him that he had to *pretend* to be crippled—at least until sunrise, which couldn't be far away.

Another merchant had pulled up near the gate and begun to unload his wagon on the opposite side of the road. He marked off the boundaries of his shop with a rope just as the old potter had done. In one corner, he arranged his cobbler's tools and a selection of sandals. In another, he placed a rack of brooms, the handicraft, probably, of a wife trying to help with the family income.

Innowen turned back to the potter. "You say Kyrin poisoned his father?"

"Common knowledge," the potter told him as he wiped down his wheel with a dirty cloth.

"But they say the Witch of Shanalane killed him."

The old potter gave a loud cackle and stopped his work. "Maybe you come from Kabari, now, and maybe you don't. Maybe you don't live around here at all. If you weren't but half a man, I might think you were an agent of this unnatural woman you say is sitting on the throne, and you're trying to test us."

The cobbler from across the street joined in unexpectedly. "That's the tale Kyrin tried to spread across the countryside, boy, blaming that Witch. Maybe some is green enough to believe it, too. But you listen to Rarus, there." He gestured with a wave at the potter. "He's a fool old buzzard, but he's here everyday. So am I, and so are a lot of us. If the Witch of Shanalane had come riding into this city the day Koryan died, don't you think we'd have known it?

We got eyes, haven't we?"

Innowen pursed his lips and tried to think. Was it because he personally disliked Kyrin so much that he found the old man's story easy to believe? Did he simply *want* to believe it? He wondered suddenly if Minarik had heard this story.

"She's here now, though," Rarus said at last. "I got eyes to see that. Didn't know she was the one wearing the crown, I admit, and like I said, the gods will punish her for that arrogance. I thought it was that big one in the black armor, and she was just along for comfort, so to speak." He shrugged and turned away. "Doesn't mean anything to me, so long as things stay peaceable and I sell a few pots."

"That's truth," the cobbler said from the other side of the road.

The first hints of dawn began to color the eastern sky. In the distance, a line of carts trundled up the road, more merchants, craftsmen and farmers, come to sell their products outside the walls of Parendur.

Innowen felt the life seep from his legs. He drew a breath and bit his lip, no longer pretending to be crippled. He could almost feel Vashni and the Witch stirring in their beds on the other side of the wall, rising to meet the day, as if he were somehow attuned to their movements, their spirits. He felt them as surely as he felt his legs dying in the sunlight, and he knew they were near, and that the end of his long quest was finally at hand.

A small village of encampments grew rapidly on either side of the road as merchants and farmers set up stalls and booths and spread their goods for sale. Wagon wheels creaked in the morning. A hammer rang on an anvil. Someone groaned under a heavy burden. Down the road came a line of oxen with a farmer and two little boys waving willow branches to drive them along. The smell of leather rose as the cobbler fell to work. Rarus' potter's wheel began to hum, and the old man began to shape a mound of rich, wet clay.

No one approached Innowen. His beggar's bowl kept them at bay as effectively as a lance or sword.

A shout came from the top of the wall. Wood suddenly grated on wood, and Innowen imagined huge beams being withdrawn by teams of ten soldiers. He waited expectantly, adjusting the rags he'd tied around his elbows and knees, grasping his bowl. He chewed his lip.

The gates of Parendur swung inward. A captain of the guard appeared in the entrance, the horsehair crest of his helmet stirring in a slight breeze. He cast a brief, dispassionate gaze over the motley assortment of traders and vendors, then turned his back and disappeared. Six soldiers with lances took his place, marching to the entrance in single file, then dividing smartly into teams of three. With crisp, sharp strides, they took up posts on either side of the roadway, the massive gates at their backs.

Innowen flopped over onto his belly and crawled, pushing his bowl before him. He kept his head high, both to avoid eating the dust and to study the guards as he approached them. They had the look of several lands. Shaktar, Nimrut, Dardanus, as well as Ispor.

"Out of the way! Out of the way, there, you low-bellied maggot!"

The loud trundle of wagon wheels swelled suddenly in his ears, and the ground seemed to shake beneath him. Innowen rolled hastily out of the middle of the road as a huge cart drawn by four horses and laden with massive pithoi jars bore down on him. The driver leaned from the side of his cart and cracked his whip over Innowen's back. "Idiot!" the wasp-faced man cried angrily.

Innowen flung a handful of dust uselessly after the departing cart, but bit back any invective. He lay there for a moment, breathing heavily, watching the great terra cotta vessels shake and shiver on the wagon bed. They were empty, then, held in place only by stout ropes. If he could secret himself inside such a jar, gaining entrance to the palace might be easy. But no, he had no reason to believe these particular ones were bound for the palace. They might as easily be on their way to a warehouse or some merchant's private stores.

He crawled forward again, this time keeping to the side of the roadway. As he approached the three nearest guards, he paused and held up his bowl. "Selats?" he said, playing his role.

The three looked at him, and at each other, and at their comrades by the opposite gate, and they laughed. "Coppers, you want, beggar?" one of them answered. "Here's copper!" He spun the butt of his lance upward and thrust the burnished point down through the space between Innowen's neck and his outstretched arm.

Innowen glared, but did not flinch. "You shouldn't use a poor beggar so, sir," he commented dryly, running his gaze up the shaft of the lance until he met the eyes of its owner. "I see by the look of you that you're from Dardanus."

The guard fingered the long slender braid that trailed from under his helmet and draped over one shoulder. It was barely as thick as a child's little finger, but according to Dardan faith, it guaranteed his passage to heaven. "What of it?" he scowled suspiciously.

"I visited there once," Innowen answered. He glanced at the guard beside the Dardan and raised one eyebrow confidentially. "Their sheep are better looking than their women, and used accordingly."

Several of the guards laughed in response, but the Dardan gave Innowen a hateful glare and raised the butt-end of his lance. "Filth!" he uttered between clenched teeth as he gripped the shaft of his weapon in both hands and prepared to swing it downward.

Instinctively, Innowen cringed, bringing one arm up to protect his head, realizing too late that he had dared too much. He didn't have his legs now. He was a worm to them, unable to defend himself. He set his teeth against the expected blow.

"Stop!"

The force of command behind the shout was so great that even Innowen obeyed, dropping his arm without thinking about it so that he could look up at the speaker. The breath he'd held leaked slowly out of him, and he felt his heart wither within his chest. He lowered his face and, at the same time, strained to look through the upper corner of his eyes.

Vashni gazed down sternly from the back of a huge black warhorse. He looked just as much the demon as Innowen remembered him on that time of their first meeting. The morning sun cast fiery rays onto the edges of his black lacquered breastplate and one side of his finely crafted helmet, and his huge dark eyes glittered angrily on either side of a narrow nasal bar. His size and strength had actually increased over the years, Innowen was sure.

But more, there was a presence, a power, about Vashni that compelled Innowen to forget any fear that the Witch's man might recognize him. Slowly, he lifted his head again to drink in the sight.

"You have been told." Vashni's voice was the sound of ice cracking at the bottom of the deepest chasm in the world. Yet he spoke slowly, deliberately, as if the air were too insubstantial to support the weight of his words. "Treat these citizens well. You are liberators, not conquerors." He raised one huge hand from where it rested by the reins on his horse's withers and pointed his finger.

The Dardan turned pale, trembling visibly in the shadow of that outstretched limb. He set the end of his lance against the ground again and came to attention as best he could.

Vashni lowered his hand. "Don't give me cause to remember you, Dardan. This is your warning." He looked at each of the guards on either side of the road one by one, locking each of their gazes in turn. He repeated, "You have all been warned."

The thumb and forefinger of his left hand disappeared for just an instant inside the broad metal-studded belt that encircled his waist. He stared down suddenly at Innowen. The hardness seemed to dim in his eyes, and his hand flicked outward.

A gold *cymoren* clinked neatly into Innowen's begging bowl, slid around the rim, and finally settled in the bottom. Innowen stared open-mouthed at the giant figure in the black armor, thinking how strange it was that Vashni had, yet again, after so many years and so many miles, become his benefactor.

But Innowen had a role to play. Carefully, he lifted the triangle-shaped coin with its gently rounded corners between his dirty fingers and bit it with his front teeth. "Thanks, warrior," he mumbled, nodding his satisfaction as he closed his fist around the *cymoren*. That was all he said, holding back a sharp remark about the price of a conqueror's conscience. It wouldn't do to speak too much with Vashni. How good was the man's memory of that night five years ago? Innowen's voice might give him away or spark a remembrance that would spell ruin for his purpose.

Vashni stared at him a moment longer, making Innowen increasingly nervous. Could the Witch's man somehow read his thoughts? Or had he, as he had at first feared, been recognized? Vashni tugged on the reins, turning his mount's head, and rode a few steps closer until his sandaled foot dangled freely just above Innowen's head, and Innowen could see the thin pattern of inlaid gold on his black lacquered greaves.

Innowen fought with himself to keep his gaze in the dirt, yet still he felt that powerful compulsion to look up and meet this man face to face. The sun burned just behind Vashni's head, creating at the same time a bright, eye-numbing corona and a mask of darkness that hid all his features from Innowen.

Innowen wished fervently that it were night and that he had legs to stand.

For an eternity of heartbeats, he waited in Vashni's shadow, but not a word more did either speak. Finally, rider and horse turned and cantered away, leaving Innowen to watch Vashni's broad, proud back and the long streamer of horsehair that trailed from the crest of his helmet down between his powerful shoulders.

"Get on with you," one of the gate guards said at last. "You're blocking the road."

Innowen only half heard. He looked up at the guard, still dazed from the encounter, then over his shoulder to where a group of merchants, including old Rarus, had gathered in the roadway to watch. Already, though, they were dispersing, returning to business.

"Are you deaf as well as crippled?" the guard said again, louder this time, openly threatening. Vashni was out of sight now. It was time for the guards to reassert their authority.

Innowen didn't argue. He dragged himself on his elbows, clutching the *cymoren* in one hand, pushing his bowl before him in the other. Out into the wakening streets of Parendur he went, making his way slowly, keeping as close to the ditches and the walls of buildings as he could, out of the more dangerous paths where carts and oxen and horses ran. For a time he forgot about Vashni and the Witch, forgot about everything, as he concentrated on his safety, avoiding the feet that threatened to mash his fingers, or the wandering hogs and dogs that tried to nip at him.

In this earliest part of the morning, women were allowed outside unaccompanied. They hurried about their duties, eyes cast always downward, their backs bent under bundles and burdens. Their thick skirts swirled the dust as they went by, erasing the prints of their bare feet. The fine clouds of brown powder they raised choked Innowen if they ventured to pass close to him. That did not happen often. Most of them spied him early and cut a circle away, refusing to meet his gaze. For all that he was a cripple and a beggar, he was still a man and a stranger.

A sharp stone penetrated the cloth padding around his right elbow. He gave a quiet yelp. Dragging himself into a narrow alleyway and propping himself up near the entrance, he paused to examine the wound. A small trickle of blood discolored the filthy strippings.

Carefully, he unwound the wrappings and piled them in his lap. He spit on the tip of one finger, placed it against the cut, and leaned his head back against a stone wall. When the bleeding was stopped, he would move on. It was a small wound, but he was mindful of Riloosa and the foul infection he had seen in the dead man's flesh.

He rolled his head to the side and gave a small sigh as he watched the traffic in the street just beyond the alley entrance. It was already hot in the alley, and the air was still. Trickles of sweat began to form on his face. They oozed down his neck and into his tunic. Still, he waited and observed the mingled press of citizens and soldiery that passed in the street.

Suddenly, his sweat seemed to freeze on his skin. He caught his breath and held it, not daring to move, his gaze glued to the entrance. When he did move, it was to turn his head from side to side, wondering if he should crawl farther back into the still-dark depths of the alley or toward the opening to check what he thought he'd seen or to make a run for it.

Rather, a crawl for it, he reminded himself in disgust, opting finally to settle back again and let calm return. He had to remind himself he was a cripple until the sun went down, and on his own. He couldn't afford to act rashly or let panic overtake him. Taunting that Dardan guard had been stupid. Foolish, in fact.

He was no fool.

Hugging himself, he stared back at the alley entrance, this time intently watching the faces of those who passed, watching for one remembered face in particular, fearing it might return while he was still helpless.

He had cause enough, he reflected, to fear Chohlit, and cause enough now to wonder what he had stirred in the man's soul that night on the plain of Kenay when his dancing had destroyed the rebel leader's army. Was he here in Parendur? Why?

Could he have been on the same road, just moments behind me?

Innowen felt for the dagger secreted inside his tunic and drew a measure of comfort from it. It wasn't much of a weapon. Even so, it was more than a beggar would usually have. He fingered his purse beside the dagger and looked back up the alley again. Biting his lower lip, he pulled it out, loosened its strings and dropped the gold *cymoren* into it with his other coins, mostly copper *selats* and a few egg-shaped silver *phalens*. Returning the purse to its hiding place, he leaned back and thought.

Parendur was a big city. Why shouldn't Chohlit be here? Innowen tried to put aside his fears and suspicions, yet they nagged at him. He shouldn't stay in this alley much longer. If Chohlit was actually following him—an unlikely possibility—the man might double back.

He bit his lip again as he glanced up and down the alley. His hand settled on his begging bowl. He lifted it, studied it for a moment by holding it close to his eyes in the faint light, then slammed it forcefully against the wall. It broke into several pieces.

Seizing the largest shard, he ran his thumb along the clean, sharp edge. The rolled rim of the broken bowl made a safe grip. It wasn't as good as a sword or a quality dagger, but if he swung it quickly and surely, he had no doubt that it would cut, and he felt better having two weapons. He thrust the shard down into his knee wrappings. He could get at it quickly there.

Hastily, he wrapped his elbow again. The bleeding had stopped. It hadn't been much anyway, he chided himself. But if he hadn't stopped to tend it, he might have fallen into the arms of his enemy.

He frowned. Vashni and maybe Chohlit in the same morning, both close enough to spit on if he'd dared. Perhaps he had made a mistake in coming to Parendur alone. Well, no matter now. Here he was, and he intended to stay alive.

He flopped over on his belly again and crawled back into the crowded street. He paused long enough to examine the sky, at least the piece of it he could see between the roofs of the buildings that lined the road. It was still early morning. Lots of sunshine left. Lots of time before he was whole.

He crept along with all the strength and speed he could muster, taking the first turn that bore him away from his previous path, assuming, of course, Chohlit would have continued straight ahead. That wasn't necessarily a sure bet, Innowen admitted, so he turned down yet another street, taking a random way, and finding among several burned out buildings the first evidence of the fires caused by the storm of nights before. He continued slowly past, staring at the blackened timbers and scorched stones, and turned down yet another street.

He found himself on the edge of one of Parendur's many small squares. Heat shimmer rose from the paving stones that suddenly lined the way. He was glad it was morning. Later in the day, the stones would be too hot for him to crawl on. They'd sting his flesh too severely. Only sandaled people would walk there after noon.

For now, though, he could tolerate the heat. He set his gaze on the low well that stood at the center of the square. A potent thirst, born of wiggling his way through the dirt and dust, seized him. He waited until he saw no carts, no beasts of any kind that might trample him, then began to navigate a veritable forest of legs and feet toward his goal.

A low circle of stones ringed the well. Eagerly, he dragged himself up, taking all his weight on his forearms, and peered over the side. His lips felt ready to crack, and his tongue stuck to the roof of his mouth.

The well was dry, another victim of the drought.

Innowen wished that he knew all the names of all the gods of Ispor, that he might curse them in the most personal terms.

He twisted his body around and leaned against the well. His useless legs were tangled, and he bent forward to position them better. When he looked up again, another man had sat down beside him on the well's wall. The man was thin as a branch, and he had about him a desperate look. His cheeks were sunken, and his narrow lips were parchment dry. A ragged beard sprouted unevenly from his chin, and his eyes shone with a feral greed. His clothes were little more than tattered rags.

Innowen knew he was about to be robbed. Beggars, especially crippled beggars, were easy marks. It didn't matter how secret his purse was. This man would be happy enough with a tunic that had fewer holes than his own.

His heart thundered inside his chest as the man moved his hand slowly, surreptitiously along the wall toward Innowen's shoulder. It would happen any moment now.

Innowen turned his head and smiled at the man. A puzzled expression turned up the corner of the would-be thief's mouth as he moved his hand casually back to his lap. Innowen waited an instant, then crooked a finger, beckoning the man closer. A furrow appeared between the thief's eyebrows. He looked both ways around the square, which was not too crowded at the moment, then smiled with sudden amiableness and bent down over Innowen.

Quick as he could, Innowen caught the man's collar and jerked with all his strength. Off-balance, he flipped heels over head into the road beside Innowen, grunting in pain as his back struck the hard paving stones. Innowen's right hand tangled in the dirty mop of black hair, lifted the thief's head, and cracked it smartly on the ground to get his attention again. With his other hand he waved the sharp pottery shard in front of the man's eyes before he set it at his throat.

"Next time you plan to rob a cripple," he said as lightly as he could, despite the trembling that coursed through his body, "remember, they may not be as helpless as you think. Now get out of here!"

Innowen let him go, and the man jumped up, shaken and angry. He looked as if he might try to kick Innowen. His fists clenched at his side, and his lips curled back over his teeth. But then his eyes flickered to the shard and to Innowen's own gaze. It was in that moment when their eyes locked that Innowen knew he'd won.

With as much dignity as he could gather, the thief hurried away.

Innowen let go a long breath as he returned the shard to its place in his knee wrapping. The street life of Parendur went on around him, oblivious to what had happened. What was it to any of them if a thief robbed a worthless beggar?

He looked around the square, sure that if there was a well, close by he would find an inn. He was not disappointed. On the farthest eastern side of the square, still in a narrow band of shadow, he spied a sign and started his slow journey toward it.

Before he reached that door, he was twice stepped on by women, whose averted gazes prevented them from seeing him until it was too late. He hesitated there, nursing the fingers of his left hand in his mouth. Finally, he rose up as high as he could and knocked on the rough wooden surface.

A large fat man in a dirty apron answered. His head was bald, and a bright scar ran down from the crown of his brow past his left eye all the way to the lobe of his ear. He looked out, then down at Innowen on the ground and scowled. "Get away from here! No hand-outs!" He started to slam the door.

"I can pay!" Innowen called back as loudly as he dared in the crowded street. "I want a room, not a hand-out!"

The door opened a little wider, and the proprietor poked his head out. "How would a beggar like you come by money to pay?" he sneered. He pushed the door completely open as he leaned against the jamb, filling the entrance with his imposing bulk. He pulled a rag from the waistband of his apron and began to wipe his hands.

"I'm a veteran," Innowen lied, eyeing the man's scar. "It's my discharge pay. I've kept part of it." He glanced back over his shoulder as he dragged his body against the wall and propped himself up.

The proprietor sneered again, still wiping his hands. "Veteran of what?" His eyes narrowed suddenly. "You part of this bunch of animals that's moved in on us?" His bulk took on menacing proportions as he drew himself erect. "I'll kick the guts out of you! Get away from my wall!"

Innowen cringed back, bringing his hands up to protect himself as best he could. "No! I fought to keep them out!" he lied again.

The fat man relented. "You're one of Taelyn's men?"

Innowen nodded. That long night outside Parendur's gate had made Taelyn a hero, and by extension, the men who fought with him. Maybe he could play on that. He didn't like lying, but a crippled beggar had few enough cards to play.

"Get in here then."

To Innowen's surprise, the man bent down and lifted him in massive arms and carried him inside.

The interior was dimly lit by a few oil lamps that dangled on chains from the low beamed ceiling. The smoke from their burning lingered like a wispy fog in the air. A confusing assortment of stale odors assailed the senses. Some tables and chairs lay scattered about. A couple of stools were overturned in a corner. One of the tables had a broken leg and stood at a crazy angle.

"We had a little excitement last night," the

proprietor said gruffly, placing Innowen in one of the safe chairs. "Excuse the mess."

He went behind the bar that stood at one end of the room and returned with two mugs of foaming barley beer. Innowen lifted one and peered at the dirty rim, grateful, after all, for the poor lighting. When his host wasn't looking, he used the ball of his thumb to rub at the place where he intended to put his lips.

"Taelyn," his host said by way of a toast.

Innowen hoisted his mug and drank deeply. Even if the mug was filthy, the beer was cool and washed the street dust from his throat. When he set it back again, half the contents were gone.

"You're a veteran, all right," the proprietor commented. "You one of the wounded that got left behind?"

Again, Innowen nodded. Another lie.

"Can't blame him for leaving," his host went on. "Too few soldiers and too many invaders, and that chicken-shit Kyrin to look after. Actually did us a favor going, the way I see it now. If the fighting had come into the city, it would have been a lot harder on all of us. As it is, that big black bastard that commands them is trying to win us over by being nice to us." He tossed off the rest of his beer, grabbed Innowen's mug, and refilled them both. "Not that it stopped one of his Nimrut mercenaries from raping and killing my youngest daughter a couple nights ago." He came back and sat down heavily in his chair and stared at Innowen.

"What's that I see in your eyes?" Innowen said suddenly. He looked at the broken furniture again and turned back. "What did you do?"

A nasty grin crossed his host's lips. "The bastard that did it had the nerve to come back last night. He had a room here, 'cause we were forced to put some of them up. Still, I didn't think he'd have the nerve to show his face here again. I gave him all the free beer he wanted, and everything else, too. Got him good and drunk." He hesitated, lifting his mug, watching Innowen over the rim. When he set it down again, he wiped his mouth with the back of his hand. "They might find his body in a day or two at the bottom of that empty well out there. Or maybe they won't."

Innowen raised his own mug again in a toast to the proprietor.

"What's your name?" the other man said, changing the subject. "You say you got money?"

"Petroklos," he answered. He pulled his purse from inside his tunic and let it fall on the table. It made a heavy thunk on the coarse wood.

The proprietor eyed the leather pouch. "I'm Baktus. How long do you plan to stay, Petroklos?"

Innowen studied his host and the red scar that trailed down one side of his face, wondering just how much to trust him. Slowly, he opened the purse and took out the gold *cymoren*. He slid the triangular coin across the table and left it beside Baktus' mug.

"Just overnight," he said.

Baktus touched the coin with the tip of one finger, but he didn't pick it up. "That's too much money," he said slowly. "More than a veteran's discharge pay."

Innowen ignored that. "I'd like you, or someone you trust, to pick up a few things for me." He opened the purse again and pulled out the bird-shaped ring which was the sign and seal of Lord Minarik. He placed it on his finger and laid his hand flat on the table. The light from the oil lamps seemed to seek out the ring and dance on its stylized wings.

Baktus' eyes widened with surprise, then narrowed cautiously. He took another drink of his beer, never looking away from Innowen. "You're no cripple," he said at last.

Innowen thought about that. "Maybe you're right," he answered. He leaned forward on the table and peered intently into Baktus' eyes. "Maybe you *are* right."

He grinned, and settled back in the chair with his beer. Baktus grinned suddenly, also, and the two men drained their mugs.

CHAPTER 15

ROBIN WAYNE BAILEY

IN HIS SMALL room behind the bar, Innowen stripped off his rags and washed himself from a basin of precious water, which Baktus had graciously offered. He had slept most of the afternoon away. Now, a tension gripped him—a taut sense of expectation. A single oil lamp filled the room with a soft, warm glow. His shadow made exaggerated movements on the wall before him, as if to tease and mock him.

He stood with his back to the door, laving himself with a soft wet cloth, wiping away the thick dust and grime from his skin. When he wrung the cloth and rinsed it, the water turned brown.

"That was some act," Baktus said from the doorway. Innowen glanced at him over his shoulder. The fat man stood leaning against the jamb with his arms folded over his massive chest. He shook his head as he stared at Innowen's naked legs. "Not many men would've crawled around the street like you did to keep up a disguise."

Innowen dropped the dirty cloth back in the water, causing a few drops to spill over onto the table's rough surface. As Baktus watched him from the entrance, he wrapped his loins with a length of linen fabric.

"Sorry I couldn't offer you a bath," Baktus continued. He leaned against the jamb with his arms folded casually over his thick, hairy chest. "There's just not enough water for that, though. This drought's killing us. I had to take that from our drinking supply."

Innowen finished his winding. "I'm grateful," he acknowledged. "As I am, also, for these garments you obtained for me." He picked up another length of black cloth and wound it into a short kilt about his middle and pinned it with a small copper clasp. Over this, he fastened an unadorned belt of plain leather, which he laced over his navel. "Tell me," he said as he dressed, "do you have any other guests in your inn?"

Baktus frowned. "There's only one other room besides this one. When the invaders first came, they forced their way in on all of us. Inns, private homes, barns—it didn't matter. Had two of them here, too, and no mention of rent, let me tell you."

"What happened to them?" Innowen asked as he sat down on the side of his bed and laced on a pair of sandals. The soles were not leather, but made from pounded water reed fibers. Not Isporan. He wondered silently how Baktus had come by them.

"One soldier found better quarters the next day." He hesitated, looked down, and rubbed his chin with one hand. "The other I mentioned before, the one at the bottom of the well outside."

Innowen finished lacing the sandals and stood up. "Tell me," he said slowly. "Did that one by any chance look like he came from Samyrabis?"

Sheepishly, Baktus shook his head. "I told you," he said, looking askance. "He came from Nimrut."

Innowen suddenly knew where the sandals had come from, and, he assumed, the rest of his new garments. Nimrut and Samyrabis were neighboring kingdoms.

"They're not dead man's shoes," Baktus said defensively, realizing the reason behind Innowen's question. "I mean, he wasn't actually wearing them when I did him. I wouldn't do that to the son of

Minarik." He moved away from the door jamb and pulled himself erect, looking as if he'd done something wrong for which he feared punishment. "That would be terrible luck. I just took them from his room. I mean, why not use them, get some good out of them?" Slowly, he hung his head as he muttered, "The other things came from his room, too." He looked up again, shame-faced and apologetic. "I'll give you back your coin."

"Keep it," Innowen told him, moving close enough to set his hand briefly on the innkeeper's shoulder. "I gave it to you to obtain clothes, and that's what you did." He patted the lacings over his belt and brushed one hand over his bare chest. "Are there any weapons in his room?"

"Everything he brought with him remains," Baktus answered. "If his body is ever found, my story is simply that he never returned here. See, I kept his room and his possessions as he left them. Brigands, rebels maybe, must have dumped him in the well as he came home one night. Or maybe he got drunk and fell in and broke his fool neck."

Baktus disappeared from the doorway only to return a moment later. He carried a short blade in a scabbard of bull's hide. He exposed half of the copper blade before he passed it to Innowen.

Innowen examined the blade more closely. It was an unornamented weapon. Both its edges were keen, though it showed signs where nicks and notches had recently been whetted away. He sheathed it with an approving nod. The scabbard had a stout strap, which he passed under his belt and fastened to a buckle on the bull's hide.

"I owe you much, friend," Innowen said. Going to his bed again, he picked up the black cloak that lay draped across it, another of the dead soldier's possessions. Next, he reached under his pillow and drew out his leather purse. The drawstrings slid open with a gentle tug, and he dipped two fingers within, extracting two gold *cymorens*, which he pushed deep inside his belt so that they rested cool against his flesh. Turning again to Baktus, he set the purse and the rest of its contents down on the table beside the wash basin and stepped away.

"If I return tonight, I may need some of this again. If not, it's yours."

Baktus' eyebrows arched with surprise. Then his brow furrowed. "Petroklos has already paid his rent and more," the innkeeper reminded him. "Times are hard, yes, but I do not take charity."

Innowen shrugged. "You have done me favors, Baktus, important favors. You've earned this. And as I said, I may be back."

Baktus folded his arms across his chest stubbornly. "Take it with you. I don't need charity."

Innowen frowned and shrugged again, but he picked up the purse, hefted it on his palm, then tucked its drawstrings down into the side of his belt. "As you wish," he said with a conciliatory gesture. "Now, if you would leave me, I require a few moments of privacy."

Baktus bowed and retreated to the threshold. "I'll have a taste of beer waiting for you," he said as he prepared to draw the door closed. "It's dark outside, but it's still warm."

Innowen called after him. "Do you have any customers who might see me depart?"

Baktus made a face that was a mixture of amusement and irritation. "Most of the locals are still afraid of your Witch's soldiers. They stay behind their doors and shuttered windows after the sun goes down. And the soldiers, well, you'll find plenty of them about, but mostly at taverns closer to the garrison or the palace. That's all right by me. I don't much want their business."

Innowen waited until he was alone, then set the purse of coins back on the table. Sometimes peasants could be too stubborn for their own good. No customers meant hard times. He understood pride, but Baktus had daughters to think of, too. There were coins enough in the purse to send them to someplace safe until Parendur settled down.

He drew a deep breath as one hand slid along the sword he wore at his side. His palm glided over the coarse bull's hide. It had an almost sensual feel against his fingers and where it brushed his bare thigh.

Beyond the wall of his small room, he heard the wind. He rolled back his head and closed his eyes and listened to see if it bore a whisper from the Witch. It had been so long since he had heard her voice in the wind.

No matter. One way or another, she would speak to him tonight.

He cast his cloak back down on the bed, then checked the door and threw the bolt on his side. Pressing the tips of his fingers anxiously together just below his chin, he glanced once more around his quarters. The room was cramped. He could not move too wildly.

He listened again for the wind. It was there. It was always there, even when others could not feel it or hear it, still it was there.

Dance, it said to him, dance away the world.

〗〇〇〇〇〖

The streets were black as pitch. Here and there, the barest light from a lamp or candle drew a narrow line under a closed door or down the crack between a pair of shutters. Overhead, a peppering of stars shone palely between the rooftops in the utter dark of the heavens. None of it penetrated the stygian gloom of the outer city.

Innowen paused and leaned against a rough stone wall. Unconsciously, he rubbed the fingers of one hand over his chest near his throat in a useless attempt to ease the odd tightening he felt there. He loved the night, yet there was a queer quality to this darkness that gnawed at him. The air felt too thick, too close, and the buildings seemed to press in on him. The streets were so narrow, and the alleys sometimes no more than passages that forced him to inch along sideways with mud bricks at both his shoulders and his nose, never knowing quite when or where he would emerge in the darkness.

It was, he thought, like making his way through a maze blindfolded.

He almost wished he'd taken the lamp that Baktus had offered him. But that would have made him too conspicuous. Soldiers might see him, or thieves, long before he saw them. He didn't want to risk any kind of confrontation. Indeed, despite the heat of the night, he kept his hood up and his cloak pulled about his shoulders. No one would see him unless he wished it.

He moved down the street again, his steps soundless in the soft dust of the road. He made his way carefully, navigating by the narrow strip of stars above him and by occasionally dragging one hand along the walls on either side, choosing any path that took him southward toward the palace.

Once, he nearly fell over an empty rain barrel, but he recovered his balance and caught the barrel before it could make a clatter. Another time, a stool left outside a door by some craftsman caught him in the shin. He bit back a curse at both the pain and the racket, and quickly melted into the darkness before anyone came to investigate, though he doubted that anyone would.

He turned a corner and found himself before a stone stepway that served several upper room apartments. He hesitated, then mounted them quietly.

At the first door, he paused. A thin light oozed under the thick, planked door. Muffled voices whispered on the other side, and soft footsteps pattered back and forth, as if whoever lived within were pacing.

Innowen moved on, climbing to the next and highest apartment. Again, he paused. The light beneath the door was even thinner, and it wavered, perhaps shed by only a single candle. Unmistakable, though, were the soft squeals and throaty moaning he heard as he set his ear to the wooden door. A small grin creased his lips, and he resisted the mischievous urge to pound raucously on the door like an enraged father or brother. For all he knew, it was a married couple within.

He climbed the staircase to the roof and let go a long sigh. The stars spread across the sky now, a glorious panorama, and the tightness in his chest eased. The breeze swirled around him, fluttering his hood and the ends of his cloak. He pushed the hood back briefly and let the playful wind cool his face and dry the thin beads of sweat that dotted his cheeks and brow.

In the south, he could see the outline of Parendur's palace. Its windows burned with the light of mirrored lamps, and pitch-soaked torches burned on its parapets and in its courtyards.

The moon had not yet come up. It would be risky to make his way over the city's rooftops, but this way he would make faster progress. He pulled his hood up again and crept to the edge.

It was little more than a wide step across an alley to the next rooftop. He was careful to land as lightly as he could because the apartments in this part of the city were old and poorly constructed. A careless step and he might plunge through someone's ceiling. Even if the roof was safe and solid, he didn't want his footfalls to disturb the tenants below.

Nevertheless, he moved with greater speed and surety, gaining confidence in his own stealth, until it became like a dance to him, each step with its own timing, each movement with its own peculiar rhythm. His senses seemed to sharpen, as they did when he danced. He could see any obstacles long before they tripped him up.

He flew from rooftop to rooftop across alleys and narrow roads like a dark bird.

Voices from the street below brought him to an abrupt halt. He crouched against a low parapet, rose slowly with his hood clutched close to his face, and peered over the side into the street.

Three men leaned casually against the wall immediately below him, bathed in the light of an oil lamp that hung suspended on leather straps from a tavern sign. The door on their right opened, and another man stepped out, gave the three only a cursory nod as he set a crested helmet on his head, and walked away with a barely perceptible weave. The three watched him go, then resumed their conversation.

Soldiers, Innowen realized. He backed a few paces, then ran, set his foot atop the parapet and leaped into space. For just an instant, he thought he'd misjudged as he hung in the blackness, but then his feet touched the next rooftop. He rolled to soften his landing and rose immediately. Though half tangled in his cloak, he hadn't made a sound.

He crept back to the edge and peered downward again. From his new vantage, he could see the soldiers' faces. Though shadows cast by the overhead lamp obscured the details of their features, he thought they were Isporan. However, the fact that they wore weapons confirmed that they were soldiers, rebels, probably, who for reasons of their own had joined the Witch's ranks.

He turned to face Parendur's palace again, and wondered. Did she feel him coming?

Gradually, as he neared the palace, it became more difficult to travel the rooftops. The streets widened, making the jumps more dangerous, and the parapets that surrounded certain roofs rose higher as he moved into wealthier neighborhoods, where rich men sought to prevent just such intrusions into their dwellings. Finally, Innowen took once more to the streets.

There, he advanced with even greater caution. Many houses hung lamps on wooden pegs outside their doors, and the windows to some shops and inns were unshuttered to encourage late-night customers, most of whom were soldiers. The lamps cast plenty of shadows, though, and he wrapped himself in them.

Murmurs and whispers, sometimes laughter, echoed out to him now as he moved ghostlike through the streets. A pair of guards passed by him, so close he could smell the leeks they had recently eaten. He could have reached out and smashed their skulls together and left them in the road. Instead, he sampled the fabric of a coarse-woven tunic with his fingertips, and savored the experience with a grin as the unknowing wearer continued on.

You are too bold, the wind said to him suddenly as it rustled the hair under his hood. *I could blow your scent to them. Or I could flutter the folds of your cloak so their ears would hear.*

But it was not really the wind, nor the Witch's voice, which sounded so like the wind. It was his own conscience, chiding him for his arrogance and warning him. He slunk back into darkness, determined to avoid anyone else who wandered abroad in the night.

The sound of horses alerted him. Well-hidden at the mouth of an alley, where the stench of slop promised to keep all others at bay, he watched a patrol ride by. Six men, two abreast, they all bore torches to light their way through the black streets. The brilliance of the fire pained Innowen's gloom-widened eyes. He bit his lip and peered through slitted lids, half-expecting, for reasons he couldn't guess, to see Vashni astride one of those beasts.

That was foolishness on his part. The clip-clop of the hooves faded. Innowen slipped from his hiding place and watched the torches and the soldiers disappear around a distant corner. Only then did he wrinkle his nose at the alley's horrid smell. He gave his cloak a sniff to make sure none of the stink clung to it. Satisfied, he hurried away.

A weak cry and a strange, unidentifiable thudding next alerted him. There was no light on the street, though, so no need to hide. He pressed himself against a wall and listened.

The sound came from around the corner. Again the moan of pain, very weak, over and over again. Sometimes sharp, sometimes a bare utterance. And *thud*. Pause. *Thud, thud, thud*. Pause. *Thud*. Then, an ugly laughter. *Thud*.

Someone was being beaten. Innowen closed his eyes, leaned his head back against the hard stone, and let his breath out slowly. He didn't need to look. His head rolled forward until his chin touched his chest, and he drew a deep breath. Cautiously, he strained toward the corner, poked his head around the edge of a wall, and gazed at a scene that sickened him.

Plenty of light spilled through an open doorway. It shone plainly on three soldiers and a naked, broken old man half-conscious at their feet. The soldiers kicked the man repeatedly in the stomach, the back, in the face. A pool of blood gleamed wetly under the poor man's head. His eyes and mouth were horribly swollen and torn. But their victim barely responded now to their brutal blows, except with grunts and groans and a twitching that made Innowen want to vomit.

The soldiers showed no signs of stopping. They laughed, enjoying the torture they inflicted. They would kick the man to death.

Thud. Thud, thud.

Innowen slipped across the roadway and hurried on. There was nothing he could do. He was but one man, and they were three. The old man was probably already dead. If he wasn't, he would be shortly from those injuries.

He made it two more blocks before he turned back.

Thud.

Innowen stepped into the lighted street. This time, one of the soldiers chanced to look up and see him. Immediately, he reached out and caught his comrades by their sleeves. A look of fear crossed over his face, plain to see in the light from the open door.

"Lord Vashni!" the frightened soldier cried, tugging at his friends, pulling them away from the old man.

The name made Innowen freeze. He jerked around to see if Vashni was truly behind him. Then he understood the soldier's mistake. A trick of the night, the black hood, the black cloak…

The tallest soldier possessed better eyesight.

"That's not Vashni, you fool!" he muttered angrily, jerking free of his frightened comrade. To Innowen, he hissed, "Get your arse out of here, stranger, unless you want it carved." He brushed one hand over the hilt of the sword he wore at his waist. "You're spoiling our fun." He gave the old man another kick.

No sound came from the old man. He was unconscious or dead. He couldn't have seen through those swollen eyes anyway. Innowen touched the clasp at his throat, and his cloak slithered over his shoulders to the ground.

The tall one unsheathed his blade. Scowling, he stepped over the old man and advanced down the street.

Innowen's eyes sought the soldier's, and their gazes locked. Languidly, Innowen raised his hands. He shifted his ribcage right, then left, then in a slow, sensuous circle, never moving his hips until the movement with his chest was complete. Next, his hips described the same pattern.

The soldier's step faltered. He licked his lips with a darting tongue, never taking his gaze from Innowen. The point of his sword dipped. Yet still he came on.

Without breaking the gaze that bound them, Innowen rolled his head from side to side and around his shoulders. His arms snaked up and down in the air, weaving patterns. He made a graceful undulation and took a step sideways. He swayed and shifted to the left.

Dimly, Innowen heard the sound of running feet as

one of the other soldiers fled. A loud moaning came from farther down the street, and another sound. *Thud, thud, thud, thud.*

Innowen gazed up into the taller soldier's eyes, and the sword between them lowered completely. They stood close enough now that Innowen could feel the heat of the other man's body, smell his sweat, hear his quick and shallow breathing. Standing directly before the soldier, he made another undulation, flinging his head and his arms back.

The soldier reached out slowly with his free hand. The tips of his fingers touched the flesh just over Innowen's heart.

Innowen steeled himself and gazed deep into the soldier's eyes. Horrors burned in those black pupils, like dancing visions that Innowen could see, and hungers. Hungers that had Innowen's face and Innowen's form.

Shocked, Innowen almost stopped his dance. Instead, he began to turn, slowly at first, then faster as he drew his arms in. One hand closed on the hilt of his sword, and as he came round the next time, he jerked it free and drew the edge across the soldier's throat.

A spray of blood fountained over him as he jumped back. The soldier continued to stare at him as one hand rose to close on the wound. Blood pumped richly between his fingers. Still, he gazed at Innowen, and a terrible sadness settled over his face. Suddenly, he gave a cry of despair. His knees buckled, and he sagged to the street, sprawling forward. Still watching Innowen, he convulsed and died. His blank eyes continued to stare.

Thud, thud, thud, thud.

Innowen shuddered and glanced up. The last remaining soldier, the one who had mistaken him for Vashni, bent over the old man in the street. His right foot worked like a relentless hammer, smashing the corpse again and again, for it was surely a corpse by now. He seemed oblivious to Innowen. All that mattered to him was to kick the old man, and kick, and kick.

Innowen gave a wild cry, raised his sword, and ran down the street, slamming the hilt of his weapon down on the soldier's unprotected neck, sending him toppling with the force of the blow. A cry of pain and surprise issued from the soldier as Innowen straddled him. Twice he stabbed downward, plunging his sword deep into the man's back before his own rage was spent.

He stopped, breathing rapidly, his heart pounding like a furious, caged beast. He wiped a hand across his lips, then licked them. Suddenly, he spit with a gagging sound, his mouth full of bitterness. He stared at the hand he had used to wipe his mouth. It was black with blood.

He shot a glance up and down the street, then at the doors and windows of the upper-level apartments above him, fearful that someone might have seen. There was no light in any of the windows, though, and no sound. The street was eerily silent.

Maybe the sounds of the beating and the soldiers' cold-hearted laughter had driven everyone behind locked doors and shutters. But he couldn't count on that.

The old man was dead, as Innowen had known he would be. There was truly nothing he could have done, and nothing he could do now. All he had really managed was to exact a measure of vengeance for the old man's suffering. Kneeling by the corpse, he felt a flush of sadness. Under the swelling and the cuts and the bruises, there was a kind face. A man who had managed to live so long, he considered, should not have come to such a disrespectful end.

He rose slowly and stared down the street. One soldier had escaped, though perhaps *escape* was not quite the right word. He wondered what he had awakened in the man that had terrified him so. Grimly, he hoped it was something to rival the horrors of hell itself.

He picked the old man up and carried him through the lighted doorway. It was a small apartment with a half bed in one corner. Innowen laid him there and drew a rough blanket up to his waist before he turned away. There was nothing to give a clue why the soldiers had come here, or why they had attacked the old man. The furniture was crude by any standard. There was no food or liquor to steal, no jewelry, not even a candlestick. Innowen shook his head at the senselessness of it and started to leave.

On a small, rickety table, he spied a folded piece of soft linen, the only thing of any possible value. He lifted it up and shook it loose. Plain linen, that was all. A large square. He shook his head again. It made a good enough towel to wipe the copious blood that had sprayed on his body. He wiped his sword, too, before he sheathed it.

He recovered his cloak from the street as he left and fastened it about his shoulders again. He drew it close, not just for its concealing effect. Though the night was warm, he felt quite chilled.

CHAPTER

16

ROBIN WAYNE BAILEY

A SINGLE GUARD stood at the mouth of the road that led up to Parendur's palace. Large and powerfully built, he stood at casual attention with a shield on his arm and a lance in his free hand. A small lantern and a waterskin rested nearby. Its scant light gleamed on his greaves and breastplate and on the helm with its short crest. He wore a sword, too, and a dagger. There was nothing of the ragtag rebel about him. This man was a disciplined mercenary, a professional soldier. Another Dardan, from the look of him.

The swelling moon had just begun its slow flight through the heavens. It shone like a drop of molten gold low on the eastern horizon, barely above the black rooftops. At its zenith it would spill a dangerous light on the city's shadows, and he would have to move cautiously, lest he be noticed. It reminded Innowen, somehow, of the visions he had seen in the tall man's eyes, cold and menacing, and he looked away from it.

Parendur squatted like a citadel on the summit of its low hillock. Gone was the glitter that the daytime sun brought out in the white stone. Hidden was the grace of the fluted colonnades and polished balconies. Now it was a harsh block, all sharp, black lines and cruel angles. The lamplight in the windows was inadequate to illumine the palace's beauty. The torches in the courtyards only mocked its daytime splendor by birthing the shadows and strange flickerings that cavorted on its walls.

Now it was a spider, and the city was its web.

Crouched in the darkened doorway of the building nearest the guard, Innowen whispered, his voice no louder than the soft stirring of the wind,

"Weary soldier, hear my song;
A soft and downy bed is sweet
With dreamy sweethearts to hold and greet
And love to dream of all night long."

The guard reacted at once. His shield snapped up. The point of his lance tipped forward. His head moved ever so slightly as he scanned up and down the street that ran before him. "Who's there?" he challenged with the barest hint of fear in his voice.

Innowen took advantage of the darkness and quickly slipped into another place of concealment. After a few moments, the soldier took a pace forward and stared with greater deliberation into the surrounding blackness. At length, he relaxed, lowered his shield, and returned to his post. Setting his lance aside, he picked up the waterskin, unstoppered it, and took a drink. Then he moved the lantern just a bit closer and resumed his watch.

When the guard was at ease, Innowen whispered again from his place of hiding,

"Heed the beat of slumber's wings;
Strange pleasures lurk in soft repose
To soothe us, like the wind that blows;
Dreams are haunting little things."

Once more, the guard snapped to alertness. "Who's there?" he demanded. This time there was a tremorous note in his speech, and under the rim of his helm, his eyes shifted back and forth, nervously searching the darkness. "Stand forth and show yourself! Are you a man?"

Innowen glided silently into yet another hiding

place and pulled a piece of his hood over his mouth to muffle his quietly spoken words. "A shadow," was all the answer he gave.

It was odd to watch such a physically large man shrink in upon himself, yet that was sometimes the effect of fear. "A spirit, you mean!" the man hissed. "Did the Witch send you? Go away! Why speak of sleep? I'm wide awake!"

> "Round and round, and down we fall;
> Asleep, awake—what does it mean?
> The world you see remains unseen,
> But dreams are true and visceral."

"Do you say I dream?" The guard snapped warily. Once more, he set aside his lance, then bent, picked up his lantern by its thin bail, and lifted it above his head, bathing himself in its pale, pitiful light.

Yet again, Innowen shifted position. The small lantern was no threat to him. "You challenge the shadows," he whispered mockingly, "and they speak back to you. How can that be if you're awake?"

"Hah! Out of poems!" the guard noted, as if the observation were some sort of triumph. "I know the Witch sent you, Spirit, to see if I am alert at my post. She's a sly one for a woman. But you tell her I'm doing my duty."

Innowen didn't reply.

The guard waited. "Did you hear me, Spirit? I said I'm doing my duty. You tell her!" He waited again, expecting an answer. "Spirit?" He lifted the lantern higher still and crept into the street, straining to see through the darkness beyond the light. "Spirit?"

On soundless feet, Innowen slipped around the perimeter of light, past the lone guard, and up the road to the palace. Wrapped in his cloak, he grinned to himself. He'd spent enough time in Dardanus to know its people were a superstitious lot. It surprised him that so many Dardans were working for the Witch. On the other hand, theirs was a hard land, and a hungry man took employment where he could find it.

Innowen stayed well to the side of the road as it ascended and tread in the soft dust, avoiding the cobbled paving, where his footsteps might have made more noise. As he went, he remembered how he had last ridden this way with Taelyn, Rascal and Veydon. They had come in triumph, then, with the cheers of the city ringing in their ears. Now, Taelyn was dead, and he returned alone, like a silent thief.

Quickly, he found himself on the walkway that led into the central courtyard. Slender, fluted columns rose on either side, just as Innowen recalled them. Between each pair of columns stood the low stone pedestals he had observed before with their bowl-shaped depressions filled with oil. A lighted wick floated in each of those depressions, shedding a faint yellow glow onto the walkway.

Wherever the light from the flames touched a column, there was a shadow. Innowen made his way swiftly from one place of concealment to the next, until he was almost to the courtyard itself. There, he paused.

A pair of sentries stood facing into the courtyard with their backs to Innowen. Expecting no danger, they leaned against the walls, lances held in the crooks of their elbows, as they passed the time in whispered conversation. Innowen listened for a few moments, hoping for a scrap of useful information, but the guards spoke only of a dice game and some woman, who was the stake.

Innowen considered his course of action, then

slipped back down the walkway to the road. Crouching, he ran his hands in the dust and along the edge of the road until he found two stones. Clutching them in his fists, he crept back to his hiding place at the base of one of the columns where he could see the two sentries.

Aiming carefully, he flung one of the stones at a nearby pedestal. A loud crack sounded as it skipped on the top, hit the inside rim, and fell into the oil-filled depression with a splash. The small flame sputtered and went out. The shadows around the pedestal undulated into new configurations.

"What was that?" One of the sentries whirled, snapping his lance down into a defensive posture. He stared down the walkway. Turning, the other sentry shifted his grip on his lance, but the frown he wore conveyed only a sense of boredom and annoyance. He spied the lightless pedestal, though, and started toward it. After a moment's hesitation, his companion followed.

Innowen flattened on the ground as they passed his hiding place.

The pair stopped beside the pedestal, stared at the extinguished wick, and regarded each other. "I tell you, Artur," the nervous sentry grumbled to his more relaxed comrade, "if I'd known that Vashni was taking orders from that woman, I'd never have signed up. It's unnatural. She's unnatural. And we can't expect anything but unnatural things to start happening around here. Until we entered the city, I thought he was in charge. He always gave the orders."

The one called Artur rubbed his chin. "Not my place to question it," he answered quietly. He peered around, his frown deepening as he shook his head. "Ispor's not my land. If a woman wants to rule it, what's it to me?

So long as her coin's good and the food's hot, I'll do what I'm told."

"Ispor no longer," the nameless guard muttered. "She calls it Akkadi."

With their attention diverted, Innowen might have skulked into the garden then. They seemed satisfied to begin a new conversation without exploring why the light had gone out. Still, he preferred to lure them farther away. Once inside the courtyard, it might take some time to break into the palace proper. He wouldn't want them returning before he managed it.

From his concealment, he drew back and let the second stone fly. It clattered sharply on the cobbled paving in the darkness beyond the walkway.

The guards glanced at each other once again and stared toward the sound. Wearing an expression of weary resignation, Artur sighed. The two proceeded down the walk to investigate.

Innowen wasted no time, but leaped to his feet and ran from shadow to shadow until he achieved the courtyard. Reaching the spot where the sentries had earlier stood their duty, he looked back the way he had come. There was no sign of the pair. They had gone out toward the road itself, leaving the walkway empty.

As he started forward again, his toe stubbed against something soft. Looking down, he found the guards' waterskin. He licked his lips, hesitated, then picked it up, unstoppered it, and took a hasty sip. The moment the liquid rolled into his mouth, his eyes snapped wide. He almost sputtered, but stopped himself before he made any noise.

Wine, he realized, sniffing the skin's nipple as he wiped his mouth with the back of his hand. Of course, with the drought, the city was short of water. Still, he wondered with a smirk if their superior officers knew. He took another sip, this time prepared for the stronger taste. Now that he knew it was wine, he didn't mind at all.

With a grin, he stoppered the skin and put it back on the ground.

One basin of flame stood in each of the courtyard's four corners, not enough light at all to endanger him. Quickly and quietly, he moved deeper into the garden and crouched behind a thicket of dead rose bushes. The leaves and blooms had long since fallen away, but the tangle of branches and the gloom were sufficient to hide him from all but the most determined eyes. Even if the guards returned now, he doubted they would see him.

In the halflight, at the center of the garden, he made out the fountain where, nights before, he had sat and held the moon. He remembered with an odd sweetness how that silver orb had reflected in the water that he had cupped in his palms. It had seemed a quiet wonder to him, then, that a man could hold the moon, a moment in time that had so impressed itself on his mind that he knew he would never forget it.

To his left were the apartments where Riloosa had tried to kill Kyrin. Lamplight shone in several of the unshuttered windows. The king's megaron was part of those apartments. He had no doubt that he would find the Witch there.

Innowen twisted around and located his own apartment. The soft glow from a lamp shone there, too. No doubt some of the Witch's officers had taken residence in the palace. Most of the other windows were either black or shuttered tight.

Emerging from the bushes, he made his way around the perimeter of the garden, pausing wherever a shadow or a dark niche offered itself. Once, voices at the far end of the courtyard made him stop and listen. It was only the two sentries returning to their posts. Innowen glanced from them up toward the stars, which now seemed to be the objects of their conversation. The stars stared back, like small, cold eyes burning in the blackness. Innowen turned away and hurried to the embrace of the next shadow.

In the wall at the northeast corner of the garden, he found a door just where he remembered it. Squeezing its latch, he leaned his shoulder gently against it and pushed. It opened without a sound, easily, and Innowen slipped inside. The merest breath of wind whispered in behind him before he closed it again.

His heart began to hammer.

How long had he thought about this moment? How long had this one goal guided his life? All the dreams that had ever haunted his sleep rushed suddenly upon him again as he stood in that narrow hall staring toward a dim amber glow, listening, listening....

But there was only the beating of his heart to hear.

Innowen crept toward the glow and emerged into a huge storage chamber. He knew it; he had been here before. Yet in the faint illumination from a pair of flickering, smoky torches, the immense pithoi jars with their narrow bottoms and fat round middles seemed ominous and threatening. Their shadows made strange distortions on the walls and floor, and the gloom that clung to them seemed blacker than any night he had ever known. The air, which should have carried the pleasant scent of olive oil or wine, smelled, instead, of mold.

He looked again at the torches. They suggested that someone had passed this way on an errand, possibly an inspection, or perhaps to fetch something. Lamps would have been used if this chamber were kept lit through the night. Since the torches were still here and burning, that someone might also return. It was best to keep moving.

She would be above him, this time of night, in the king's bedchambers. She would have made them her own, he had no doubt of that. Wraithlike, he moved in the shadows of the pithoi jars and darted between the pair of torches into another corridor where their light didn't follow.

It led him to the antechamber of Parendur's great stateroom. A single oil lamp, suspended on a chain, burned above the massive carved door. Two mighty wooden pillars rose in semirelief on either side of the door, painted, Innowen remembered, bright red. In the absence of daylight, though, they loomed black as old blood, except for small spots of fresher color near the tops where the fireglow touched them.

He looked away from the door and the pillars to the far side of the antechamber. Just where he remembered it, a grand staircase rose into the upper levels.

He crossed the marble floor. Halfway up the stairs, he paused. The yellow glow of more lamps filtered down from above. There were no shadows to hide him on the stairs; he dared not linger. Anyone might suddenly appear above or below him, and he would be discovered.

On an impulse, he pressed his ear to the wall and listened. It should breathe, this palace, these walls, with the sound of the Witch's breathing. The stones should echo with her heartbeat. He set his palm against the wall, expecting a pulse, a vibration, a *warmth*.

But there was nothing, and he didn't understand it. Perhaps it even disappointed him. He bit his lip and continued up the stairs.

The palace at Taruisa in Osirit, where Razkili's father ruled, would not have allowed him such easy entrance, he reflected as he reached the upper level and slid through the blackened entrance of an empty room. Pressing against the inner wall, he paused to catch his breath as he remembered his time in that distant capitol.

In Taruisa, guards stood at every palace entrance, and day or night, hallways were always well-lit. King and queen were protected like national treasures and regarded by some as gods. Innowen laughed suddenly to himself as he remembered. In fact, he had stolen something from that palace—Razkili's heart.

Innowen leaned his head back against the wall, secure in the darkness, and thought of Rascal. Would his lover forgive him for leaving Whisperstone so secretively, without a word?

Lover. He had never used that word before. It felt odd to him.

The soft slap of footsteps in the hall drew his attention. He held his breath and waited until they passed before he eased to the entrance and peered out.

A dark-haired slave, clad in a saffron chiton and leather sandals, carrying a shallow, bowl-shaped reed basket before him in both hands, moved halfway down the corridor and turned a darkened corner.

A whiff of some unusual, sweet odor brushed Innowen's nose, somehow familiar, yet unnameable. Curious, he hurried after the slave, hugging the walls as he moved, though few shadows offered themselves now.

The slave entered an anteroom where a small oil lamp shone on the gleaming threads of a fine gauze curtain. Moments later, Innowen followed, hugging his black cloak as if it were a shield to ward off the light.

The slave continued on, leading Innowen through a small maze of rooms, through the King's megaron itself, where a great stone chair loomed against the west wall, between the statues of Ispor's two most benevolent gods, Vashua, the Sea Father and Skrayt, the Sky Father. The uplifted palms of both deities glowed with the fires of small lamps, whose light cast shadows that fell across Innowen's path like dire warnings.

Staring at those gods and their shadows, Innowen was almost discovered. A second slave, an old man, emerged from the room where the first slave had vanished. Barely in time, Innowen leaped out of the light that spilled through the doorway. With no other place to hide, he flung himself upon the throne, placed his arms upon the great rests, and assumed a most regal pose.

The slave never glanced his way. But from deep within his hood, as he held his breath, Innowen studied this servant. The old man's face was a mask of fear, and those gnarly hands trembled as they wrung around each other.

Innowen waited until the old man passed into the hallway. Alone once more, he rose and melted into the thickest shadow the room offered, where he slowly let out his breath.

He could feel her now. He knew she was close.

He ducked into the next room. Two lamps burned on delicate tables at opposite sides of yet another doorway. Quickly, he looked around for some place of concealment, but the only darkness lay beyond the balcony. This room opened to the outside.

The slave with the strange-smelling basket had not gone outside, though, Innowen was sure. With broad strides, he swept toward the doorway, paused beside one of the tables, then crossed to the other, risking a look into the next room as he did so.

"Set it down here, by the bed, and leave me."

Innowen nearly froze in midstep as he heard her voice. He made it to the other side of the second table with its lamp and, heedless of its amber glow, pressed himself against the wall.

Now, he could feel her heartbeat in the stones, her breathing in his ears. He sank down into a ball on the far side of that table and hid himself under the folds of his cloak, trembling, barely aware when the slave passed by without seeing him.

With one quivering hand, he slid the hood back from his head and listened. Strange stirrings came suddenly from the room beyond. His heart lurched, but he feared to move. She might emerge to take a breath of the night air and discover him beneath the table. Some other slave might appear to answer her call, or to bring her something she had ordered, and give warning.

With an effort, he mastered his fear and forced it away.

Abruptly, the stirrings ceased. The room grew silent. After a while, Innowen crawled from under the table and rose.

He thought of the balcony. There was a good chance it passed outside her room. From there, the darkness of the night might shelter him while he dared to peek inside. To see her, that was what he had come for.

That, and more.

Yet a dreadful cowardice filled him again. In his mind, he saw the shadows of the Sea Father and the Sky Father spilling across his path in the megaron, their arms extended as if to warn him away. He squeezed his eyes shut, and in the darkness behind his lids, he imagined he saw another god, a black idol squatting in the mud, laughing at him, laughing, laughing....

Innowen clenched his fists until the knuckles threatened to crack. *Whoever you are*, he swore silently, *whatever hell you reign in, I will not be laughed at.*

He slipped back into the previous room and out into the warm embrace of darkness. The wind kissed his face and throat and slithered down inside his cloak before he drew it close again. He wiped at a free trickle of sweat as it rolled down his left temple to his cheek.

It was hot. Gods, it was so hot. Even at night, the unending drought tortured his poor country. He stared at all the darkened windows of the palace and wondered how anyone could sleep in such heat.

Again, the sound of footsteps drew his attention. These were not the footfalls of a slave, though. These rang with authority on the marble tiles of the room within.

Innowen moved swiftly now, without thinking, following the balcony as it bent suddenly around a corner. Light spilled through an open doorway from the room just ahead. He took a moment while darkness still surrounded him to peer over the balcony's edge into the courtyard below. Then, gathering his courage, he stole up to the doorway.

At first, he thought he'd found the wrong room. It was brightly lit with many candles and lamps, and richly furnished. The largest bed he had ever seen in any of his travels dominated the chamber. It was canopied and draped with expensive sheer fabrics that stirred ever so delicately in the slight draft and shimmered in the firelight.

But there was no sign of the Witch.

He leaned cautiously inside. Seeing no one, he stepped with sudden boldness into the shadow of a huge wardrobe. From there, he had full view of what had once been the King's bedroom.

Still he saw no one. To whom had those footsteps belonged? Just as he decided to move onto the balcony again, a sound warned him back into his shadow. He pressed against the wardrobe and the wall. An instant later, Vashni strode into the room.

The huge warrior looked around in puzzlement. Even so late at night, he still wore his armor. The glow of the candles and lamps danced on the exaggerated musculature of his black lacquered breastplate and on the gold inlaid patterns that decorated his greaves. On the great bulges of his bare arms and along his strong jawline, there was a fine sheen of summer sweat.

After a moment, a frown creased Vashni's lips. He stared toward the bed, then toward the balcony, and began to walk in that direction.

Innowen bit his lip and gripped the hilt of his sword. Vashni might miss him as he went out to the balcony. But if he turned to reenter...

Then, before Vashni moved two steps, her voice sounded from a darkened antechamber beyond the bed. At first, Innowen thought it was a high, sweet song, but it ended too quickly. Not a song at all. Only two strange foreign words spoken with a musical quality.

The Witch of Shanalane emerged out of the darkness of that room.

A powerful trembling seized Innowen. With a sudden horrible insight, he realized that what he once had thought was love for this woman had somehow, at some time, turned into a powerful, overwhelming fear. For five years he had pursued her. Now, she was but the width of a room away, and he could not—dared not—make a move.

Her hair, which in the darkness and lightning of a storm had once looked blond to him, was, in fact, black as the night, black as any shadow. It swept around her face and over her shoulders in a crazy tangle that he still found oddly beautiful. Her lips were just as he remembered, red as roses. And her eyes...! His first impression was that they glittered like stars. Now, he saw them filled with a peculiar glaze.

In her hand was the reason. She carried the reed basket he had seen earlier in the possession of a slave. From it, she lifted white flower petals and stuffed them into her mouth.

Innowen remembered the sweet odor he had experienced when the slave had passed him. He had not recalled it immediately, but he knew it now by its smell and by its effect.

The flower was called *snowfever*. Some claimed it was medicine, and some claimed it was magic. Some claimed it was a gift from the gods, and some a pretty trap set by Bastit, the Lord of Chaos, to snare the unwary. Whatever it was, those who chewed its leaves or ate its petals dreamed such dreams that some chose never to wake again. *Fever dreams*, the users called them, dreams of flight, or of colors with taste, potent visions of the past or the future, of heaven or hell.

Innowen watched as she lifted another handful. A few petals slipped between her fingers and wafted back into the basket. Like a child with candy, she ate them.

Vashni went toward her. "Mother..."

In his amazement, Innowen's trembling ceased. He had never guessed their relationship. Suddenly, he saw it written on their faces.

The Witch glared. "I've told you not to call me that!" She moved past Vashni and set the basket on a table. When she turned toward him again, she held out a single petal and pressed it to his lips. "Eat," she commanded.

Vashni towered over his mother, yet he obeyed meekly, nibbling the petal from her fingers as a horse eating sugar from its master's hand. As he fed, her other hand touched his thigh and worked its way up under his brief kilt. He closed his eyes and moaned as he swallowed the last of the petal.

"You know what I want," she told him. She pulled his face down to hers and kissed him deeply, almost cruelly, while her other hand continued to explore under his kilt. Vashni moaned again and gathered her in his arms. He lifted her from the floor as if she weighed nothing.

The Witch's legs wrapped around her son. Their kiss seemed to last forever as she worked at the straps of his armor. Finally, he put her down and finished disrobing himself while his mother watched impatiently. He reached out then, and with a wrench, ripped away her thin garment.

The firelight gleamed on both of them as they moved together again. Vashni lifted her once more, and again she wrapped her legs about his massive body. This time, a sharp cry issued from her throat, and she flung back her head.

The nails of Innowen's right hand shattered as he dug them into the stone wall at his back. He knew he should run while they were too occupied to see him. Yet he stayed and watched, fascinated, terrified, like a mouse watching the mating of cobras.

"The bed!" the Witch ordered. Her hands gripped Vashni's hair as if it were a stallion's mane, and she jerked his head around to steer him where she wanted him to go. They didn't separate, nor cease their eager movements, but fell upon the sheets in a blind ardor.

Up where the pillows should have been, the covering slipped back a little. From his hiding place, Innowen saw a pair of hands bound together with a rope that stretched to the edge of the mattress and under the bed.

The Witch screamed commands and orders at her son and lover as they worked furiously together.

Vashni's pantings and thrustings grew embarrassingly loud. Innowen felt a rush of shame as he realized how rapid and harsh his own breathing had become. He watched the Witch, though, and Vashni's gleaming, sweating body, and he watched that unmoving pair of hands above them.

Then the Witch had a dagger in her hand. Innowen didn't see where she'd gotten it. Hidden among the bedclothes possibly. She simply had it. Through the haze of his passion, Vashni saw it, too.

"No!" he muttered, thick-voiced. His thrustings ceased.

The Witch dug the nails of her free hand into his bare backside. "Keep working!" she screamed. Using the same hand in which she held the dagger, she whisked away the covering at the top of the bed.

A man lay there, bound hand and foot. His naked, hirsute form stirred not a whit, though, for all the violence and turmoil taking place on the bed. Scattered around him were a few of the white *snowfever* petals.

Innowen didn't know the bearded face. But he knew the man dreamed a dream from which he would never awaken.

"Not another soldier!" Vashni cried with angry desperation. "My men have served you well!"

"He serves me better now!" the Witch answered savagely.

Vashni ground his body down on his mother, as if he could punish her with his motions. "He doesn't deserve this!"

The Witch didn't answer. Instead, she arched her back and twisted so that she could see the sleeping soldier and continue her rutting at the same time. Her legs locked around Vashni's hips, driving him deeper, preventing him from escaping her embrace.

The dagger made a silver flash above the soldier's throat. A spray of blood fountained upward and splashed in Vashni's hair and on his back. More blood pumped outward. It ran down Vashni's neck, over his shoulders, into the Witch's face and over her breasts. Her body arched in ecstasy, her hands spasmed open, and the blade clattered to the floor beside the bed.

"Minowee!" Vashni screamed, but whether in terror or in lust, Innowen couldn't tell. "Mother!"

The Witch smeared blood with her hands wherever she could touch her son. His back shone black with it, and his buttocks, his sides. His hair dripped. It all ran down onto the Witch.

"I need a man's blood, Vashni!" she cried suddenly. "A man's blood and fluid gives me strength, fills me with a man's courage and power!"

They bucked wildly together while the sheets turned scarlet beneath them. "You already have Ispor!" Vashni grunted.

"Akkadi!" she managed between ragged breaths. "It's not enough to have it. I must rule! I need a man's strength—a man's power—for that. A great Akkadian empire will be ours, Vashni, because I take what I need."

Vashni's back arched, and his head rolled toward his straining shoulders. "When will it end?" he shouted through clenched teeth. "When will it end?"

The Witch thrashed under him. "Now, let it end now!" She raked her nails down his spine. "Come to me, my favorite son. Come, and give me just a little of your strength, too!"

17

CHAPTER

ROBIN WAYNE BAILEY

INNOWEN COWERED IN the wardrobe's shadow. He shivered, afraid to move, though his legs ached painfully.

Some time ago, Vashni had risen from the bed and recovered his things. Innowen had imagined he could hear the dried blood crack on the huge man's skin as Vashni had bent and lifted the dead soldier's body and slung it over one shoulder. Vashni had paused, looked at his sleeping mother with an expression of strange hurt, then taken another pale petal of *snowfever* from the basket and eaten it.

The Witch of Shanalane slept. The sheets under her spent body gleamed moistly with red blood that sometimes, according to the whims of the flickering lamplight, seemed utterly black. So much blood! Innowen was sure if he could creep to the edge and press his smallest finger to the mattress, a crimson pool would seep up and form around the tip. Her body lay streaked with the stuff, her hair matted with it.

He shut his eyes and stuffed a pair of fingers in his mouth as he tried to call up the image of her that he had so long clung to, the memory of her as he had first seen her astride a great horse on the road through the woods to Shandisti. But the image would not come. He knew it was lost forever. Once, he had thought her so beautiful, but he had been young then. No, not young, not really. Just naive.

Well, he had finished his quest. He had found the Witch. He had even learned a few of her secrets. Now he would forget her, if he could, turn his back on this whole sorry business. Maybe he could talk Rascal into returning to Osirit for a while. He wanted nothing more than to be away from here, far away. Ispor or Akkadi, this land was no longer his home.

Slowly, he stepped from the shadow. The Witch didn't stir. She lay there, like a bee at the center of a red, red rose. Or a wasp. Innowen walked to the foot of her bed and stared at her. *I loved you,* he whispered, but the words no longer had any meaning for him. What he had loved had never existed, except in his mind.

A sudden flicker of light made him whirl toward the door, afraid he had been discovered. But it was only the draft teasing a lamp flame, nothing more.

It was then, as his eyes moved slowly around the room, that he noticed and remembered the darkened antechamber just beyond the bed. An overwhelming urge to know what waited there possessed him. It was wrong to yield to it, he knew. He should leave now, head for the balcony, out through the courtyard and escape this city and this woman forever. Yet even as he thought those thoughts, he found himself picking up one of the lamps and stealing toward the darkness.

Under the lintel, he paused and lifted his light higher. His sudden intake of breath cracked the silence before he clapped his free hand to his mouth. It was only armor, standing on a rack, in the far corner. Her armor, he realized. It shimmered in the lampglow, blackened, light-weight metal, inlaid with wild traceries of gold and silver, from Mikonos, he was sure, by the workmanship.

He moved closer to examine and admire it. He

touched the breastplate delicately. It was small, made to conform to her body. There were her greaves, also, and arm bracers, and a helm beautiful beyond any he had seen, with hinged cheek-guards shaped like birds' wings to mask her eyes and face, and a crest of scarlet plumage. Around it all was thrown a white cloak, and over that hung a leather baldric, which supported a white-lacquered scabbard and a sword with a gleaming ruby pommel stone.

He touched the pommel stone with the tip of one finger, tentatively, as if it might snap at him. The Witch had worn such a ruby around her throat once, on a chain.

His gaze turned upward then, and he held the light still higher. Around the room, about head height, a narrow shelf ran. A chill shivered through him.

There were his dolls, arranged carefully and neatly, the dolls he had collected in his five years of travels, the dolls he had carried with him in a bag across a dozen lands and brought to Parendur, only to forget and leave them behind when the army fled to Whisperstone.

Long ago it seemed, he had thought there was magic in such dolls, as people in many lands believed. In Ispor, farmers stuffed dolls with grain and planted them in their gardens, leaving only the heads to show, believing this made the crops grow better. In Osirit, dolls stuffed with fruit seeds were sometimes hung from the branches of fruit trees in the belief this made the orchards bloom and the fruit taste sweeter. In distant Shaktar, men carved dolls from oak and offered them to the spirits of their vast forests. In faraway Samyrabis, the dusky-skinned nobility entombed their dead with hundreds of tiny, intricately carved dolls, believing these would come alive in the underworld and serve the noble's spirit.

This fascination with dolls and magic, he had known

from the first, had been inspired by the Witch's idol, that strange god-figure with its pelt of copper spikes. He had sought that idol as fervently as he had sought the Witch herself.

Now he had found it, too.

It stood now on a recently erected wooden pedestal, similar to those in the courtyard, against the antechamber's west wall. He let out a slow breath as he regarded it. Somehow, he had known from the moment he entered this room it would be here, waiting for him.

It bristled with copper nails, some new and gleaming, others green and black with age. The scorches of countless prayer-fires marred and cracked the wooden skin between those nails. A piece of the shoulder seemed burned away entirely. Yet it still possessed a horrible, primitive beauty.

Why, Innowen wondered silently, unable to voice the question he had so long waited to ask. *Why me?*

The tricky lamplight flashed on the copper heads of the nails in its eyes.

Innowen crept closer. No voice answered him, as he had half-expected. The idol was just an idol, no more than a lump of charred wood. He bent over it, peered at it. Then, taking a step back, he looked down at his own legs. Slowly, he slipped a hand up his left thigh.

How? he wondered, regarding the idol again. *Why?*

But the idol gave no sign, no answer, and Innowen felt a rage swell up inside him that he had never suspected. He grabbed the idol by the nails that protruded from the top of its head and jerked backward, intending to hurl it to the floor. It proved heavier than he would have guessed, though. It rocked on its base and settled forward again. Innowen grabbed it a second time. This time he'd use all his strength, and the abomination would tumble.

Instead, he snatched his hand away with a small cry. A sharp pain blossomed in his palm. With a curse, he closed his fist around the wound, but that only intensified the pain. A fine trickle of blood ran out the bottom of his fist. Opening his hand, he brought his light close.

Deep under the skin was a black splinter. But he hadn't even touched the wood, had he? Only the nails! He pressed the wound to his mouth, wincing, and licked at the crimson that showed so clearly in the lines of his palm as he backed away from the idol.

The hurt had brought him to his senses. He retreated to the far end of the antechamber, taking his small light with him until the cursed thing on the pedestal was once more swallowed by the gloom. He felt it there, barely visible, as if it were somehow watching him. He couldn't be sure anymore of what was real and what was just his imagination. He only knew that he had to get out of this damned place.

He cast a final glance at his dolls on the shelf around the antechamber, and a wave of sadness washed over him. He couldn't take all of them, but a few were special to him. Suddenly, he couldn't bear to leave those few in the Witch's possession.

How to carry them, though?

He saw the Witch's armor, and rubbed his chin thoughtfully. Then, snatching off the white cloak, he spread it on the floor. Next, holding his light high, he searched the shelf for the four dolls he meant to take. He reached for the first one, then winced again as he bent his hand around the splinter in his palm. He had to get that out. But it would take a better light than this lamp, and he'd need a sharp knife. If he wasn't careful now, he'd only drive it deeper.

He took down the four dolls and laid them in the center of the cloak. It was a big cloak, he noted, with ample folds, and there was plenty of room left when he gathered up the corners. For a moment, he thought of taking the rest of the dolls.

A better idea occurred to him.

Suddenly, he wanted the Witch to know that he'd been here. He could think of no better way of telling her than by stealing her armor. He set the lamp up on the shelf in the space where one of his dolls had been. Then he collected the various pieces, even her sword, and placed them on the white cloak.

The lamp, he determined, could stay where it was on the shelf. With his good hand, he slung his burden over his shoulder and slunk back into the Witch's bedchamber.

Just as he passed the foot of her grisly bed, with his thoughts on the fresh air and the warm breeze of the balcony, she sat up and peered at him.

"Hello, spirit of dreams," she whispered thickly. The light from her candles and lamps sheened in her glazed eyes.

Innowen glanced from the Witch to the basket of *snowfever* petals. He looked at her again and moved his head slowly from side to side. Her eyes didn't follow. They seemed focused on his chest. He lifted one arm and moved it across the spot where her gaze seemed fixed. She didn't react.

She had called him a spirit—spirit of dreams. Well then, he would take his cue from that and gamble on the strength of the drug in her body. He answered softly, playing the same game with her he had played with the guard.

> *"The land beyond sleep is sweetest of all—*
> *A thing is never what it seems,*
> *And men are merest dreams,*
> *Pale memories wrapped within a pall."*

The corners of her lips lifted in a tiny, delicate smile, a thing that seemed so out of place on her blood-smeared face. To Innowen's surprise, she answered him in verse, whispering, as her head rolled back a little, and her gaze locked with his.

> *"Dreams are but an alphabet for the language of*
> *our lives.*
> *Those who strive and learn to read*
> *Find endless worlds of want and need*
> *That nightly shift and change and thrive."*

Her eyes made a languorous blink, and the pink tip of her tongue slipped out to moisten the corners of her mouth. "I want, and I need," she told him in a husky murmur. "I know you."

A chill shivered up Innowen's spine. He was suddenly very aware of the bundle he carried. He forced himself to keep calm, to play the game. "Do you know me, Lady?" he answered quietly. "I am a shadow."

"No," she told him. "You are a dream, my Innocent, a dream from long ago." Her smile faltered and faded, and a look of sadness took its place.

"And I know you, Minowee." It was the first time he had dared to say her name, even in his mind, since Vashni had revealed it. She had been the Witch to him—the Witch of Shanalane. He repeated her name again, silently in his head, and pursed his lips. She would always be the Witch.

"I made you to walk," she said. Her head rolled down until her chin rested on her chest.

"You made me a vampire," he answered without bitterness. "I walk the night and sleep by day."

She looked up at that, but still the glaze filled her eyes. She was deep in the *feverdream*. "Is it true?" she said with a kind of muffled wonderment. She shrugged. "My god was always a perverse god. Look what he has made of me!" Her head gimbaled back to rest between her shoulders. A tinkling little laugh escaped her stretched throat. "Queen of the land," she continued, "mistress of a country where women may not rule." Her head came up, and her gaze locked with his again.

"I should have ruled from the beginning," she snapped suddenly. "I was Koryan's first-born. In many lands, the throne would have passed to me. But because I was a girl-child, my father ordered me exposed to the elements, left on a road to die from the night's cold or a wolf's teeth."

Innowen swallowed. How similar her story was to his own, he thought. Had it not been for the blood that smeared her face, he might have found a measure of sympathy. Instead, he watched her carefully for any sign that the *snowfever* had lost its grip on her. When he spoke, he kept his voice low and soothing. "You didn't die, Minowee."

"No, I didn't," she answered languidly. "My mother employed an old nurse to take me to Mikonos before Koryan's order could be carried out, and there in that island kingdom I was raised and taught things that would make your heart shrivel in your chest." Her smile returned. "I see your heart, you know." She hesitated, peering at him with strange eyes that glittered briefly like the stars, as he remembered them. "I had almost forgotten you."

Despite himself, he softened somewhat toward her, and he whispered.

> *"A thousand times I heard you singing in the wind.*
> *Every night when the sun went down and the*
> *breezes came,*
> *I listened, and you called my name*
> *While the moon laughed and the owls grinned."*

He licked his lips and swallowed again. More than just his legs, she had given him a dream and a purpose. Now it all lay shattered.

Her smile widened before her chin settled to her chest again. "You make nice verse for a spirit," she said in a soft whisper. "Did you know that Koryan killed my mother a few years later?" She raised a blood-covered hand and moved it through the air as if there were something invisible there, which only she could see and touch. "I never knew her face; I was only a newborn, after all." Her expression changed suddenly, turning hard, cruel. "But I can see it sometimes, the deed, the murder, like the struggle of two shadows in a room full of darkness, and I hear her gasps. I feel her die."

Innowen watched as her hands explored the outline of some memory, and as her fingers closed around something and tensed and began to choke. Her face contorted, taking on the expressions of both victim and murderer, flickering between rage and terror.

It was appalling to witness, yet Innowen could not turn away. "Did you kill Koryan for revenge?" he dared to ask in the barest whisper.

The Witch's face recomposed itself. Her arms froze in midair, then sank down and hung limply in her lap. "No," she answered in a childlike voice. "Little brother did that. Kyrin killed him. He discovered who I was and came to visit me in the dark of the night at Shanalane. That old nurse never let me forget who my parents were, you see. I'm not sure how Kyrin found me out, but I think it was the ruby."

"The ruby?" Innowen whispered, remembering her sword, which was in the bundle on his back.

The Witch nodded slowly. "The Wendur Ruby. My mother sent it with my nurse to give to me when I grew old enough. In my vanity, I wore it when I returned to Ispor. I think someone must have recognized it after so many years, and they took the news to Kyrin." She looked aside, toward the lamps, toward the basket of *snowfever* petals.

"But it's no matter," she continued. "I have driven Kyrin out and taken the throne that is rightfully mine. All things change, is that not so, Spirit of Dreams? No woman has ever ruled Ispor. But a woman rules now in Akkadi. I've built an army. Soon, I will build an empire."

Her eyes flickered and closed, and her head sank forward again. She sat there in her blood-dyed bed like a doll that someone had propped up and abandoned.

Innowen stared at her as he shifted the burden on his shoulders. "Some dreams are nightmares, Minowee."

She didn't look up, nor did she open her eyes. "That is true, my Innocent," she whispered. "You dreamed of dancing, once, and I told you, *'Dance, dance away the world.'* Do you remember?"

Innowen backed slowly out of the lamplight and toward the darkness of the balcony. He could bear to stay no longer. "How could I remember?" he murmured. "Innowen is not here. I am a spirit, a spirit of dreams, flown in through your window, flown out again."

She wrapped both arms about herself and reclined gracefully back on the stained bed. Her lips moved ever so slightly, and her words floated in the air.

> *"Begone, then, spirit—dissolve away!*
> *Upon this ruddy pillow I am pressed,*
> *With bloody work to plan—no time for rest.*
> *And schemes to dream before the light of day."*

Innowen made no response. The time for games was over. He slipped out onto the balcony and filled his lungs with the clean, fresh air of night. He leaned on the rail and, for a brief moment, thought he might be sick. He gazed up at the sky; the stars shone like cold dagger points.

From within the bedchamber came the faint sound of weeping, and he knew it was Minowee. He bit his lip. How easily she seemed to slip from one role into another—benefactress, murderess, conqueror, lost child. She was the Witch of Shanalane to all who knew her. But alone in her bed, when night's heart beat slowly, she was only Minowee.

He turned her name over and over in his mind. Her name, just one of the secrets he had learned tonight. Minowee. It sounded to him like *little minnow*, and in another time and place, he might have given her that nickname.

But it wasn't another time or place. It was Ispor, and he should have taken her dagger from the floor by the bed where she'd dropped it and cut her throat while she dreamed. That would have been best for everyone. Yet even as he conceived of such a deed, he knew he could never have done it.

For all that she was, all the cruelty she had done,

she still had lifted him out of the mud. Because of her, he walked. Where would he be now if she had not stopped on that road in the forest? What would he be?

He began to move along the balcony, letting distance muffle the sound of her tears, paying little attention to the windows and doorways he passed. None were lighted at this late hour. He went as quickly as he could, finally breaking into a run, wanting desperately to be away from that place.

There was no stairway down from the upper balcony to the courtyard. When he had made his way around to a point almost opposite the Witch's bedchamber, he stopped. The logical thing to do would be to go back inside and make his way out, either through the courtyard or another egress. He couldn't bring himself to do that. The palace was hers now. It smelled of her; it smelled of incarnedined sheets and *snowfever* petals. The very essence of her wafted in the corridors.

Instead, he threw one leg over the rail, then the other. On the very edge of the balcony, clinging with only his injured hand, he cast a glance toward the pair of guards at the garden entrance. Carefully, he bent down as low as he could and dangled the cloak-wrapped bundle he carried in his other hand. It might make some noise when he dropped it, but he would risk it. He wouldn't go back inside.

He scanned the ground below. The gloom was thick, but he spied a bush that still had a few leaves and dropped his bundle upon it. It made only a slight sound. At the far end of the garden, the guards appeared too occupied with their conversation to notice. Innowen let go of the rail and dropped. The soft thud of his landing was too small to carry.

Now he faced another problem. Recovering his

burden, he crouched behind the bush and observed the two sentries. They were the same ones he had tricked to win entrance. He would need a new deception to get past them again. He might even have to kill them, though he didn't like that idea. In that case, he would have to get close enough to do it quickly before they could raise an alarm.

Abruptly, a plan took form in his thoughts.

Undoing the bundle, he spread the Witch's armor out before him. Then he unfastened his own black cloak and set it aside. He picked up the breastplate. The cool touch of it against his skin sent a shiver through him. It was small. It would never do for him in combat, but by loosening its straps, he could wear it. Next, he fastened her greaves over the straps of his sandals. He had to bend and widen the curve of her gold arm bracers to fit them over his larger forearms. When that was done, he cast the Witch's white cloak around his shoulders.

That left only her helmet. He held his breath as he lifted it to his head, fearing it wouldn't fit, and indeed, it barely did so. He opened and closed the wing-shaped cheek pieces, testing the range of his vision. Fortunately, he had shaved at Baktus' inn and had no beard to give him away.

Lastly, he strapped on her sword, then gathered his four dolls and rolled them securely in the black cloak. With a quiet sigh, he stood, still safe behind the bush. His new bundle, much smaller now, he concealed within the folds of the Witch's cloak, which he wrapped about himself and held closed with his injured hand. In his good hand, also kept within the folds, he carried his own short sword, bared and ready for use.

He felt foolish. Sweat began to run down his face

inside the close-fitting helm. He had no idea how he looked, if his disguise was any good. He might not get close enough to use his sword before the guards raised an alarm. He checked himself again to see what improvements he could make, and adjusted the Witch's sword to expose the hilt with its ruby pommel stone.

He took a moment to still a quivering in his limbs and tried to think, instead, of how the Witch would walk, how she would sound if she gave an order, though, of course, if Innowen had to speak, his deeper voice would give him away immediately. At last, he stepped away from the bush onto one of the white-pebbled walkways and strode boldly toward the garden gate.

The sentries heard his tread on the loose stones, stared in his direction, and snapped to attention at once. Innowen waited as he neared them, his grip tightening on his sword, the echo of his breathing inside the too-small helmet loud in his ears.

He watched their faces from behind the masking cheek pieces. He was almost to the gate. They stared not at him, but past him. He went straight up to the guards. *Do it now,* a weak voice screamed inside his head. *Two quick thrusts before they have time to react.* Then he was past them, past the shadowed columns and the flickering stone bowls of oil-fed flame, and down the narrow road from the palace without ever lifting his sword.

At the bottom of the hill, the lone Dardan guard proved no more of a problem. The man paled a little as he recognized the figure walking toward him, then bowed his body almost level to the ground and said nothing, as if it were the most natural thing in the world for the Witch to be wandering abroad this time of night.

Well, Innowen reasoned, perhaps they thought it

was. She was *abathakati* in the eyes of these men, a night-creature, touched by magic.

He walked a maze of streets, putting distance between himself and the Witch, working his way toward the main gate. He had to get out of Parendur, even if it meant crawling across the plain when the sun came up. If he was here when she awoke, he knew in the core of his soul that she would somehow find him.

He glanced up at the sky again, over the rooftops and towers, and wondered at the hour. A disconcerting sense of timelessness filled him. Where was the moon? The night seemed both too long and too short, nor could he correct that sense by observing the stars. They moved tonight in unfamiliar orbits, he was sure, and lied to him with their motions.

How long before the sunrise?

The clip-clop sound of a horse's hooves, muffled by soft road-dust, alerted him too late. A single rider turned the corner and reined up sharply. "My Lady!" the rider, one of the Witch's soldiers, exclaimed fearfully before bowing his head. Keeping his eyes averted, he said, "I apologize, but I didn't see you. The hour is late. May I escort you somewhere?"

Innowen stood in the middle of the road, his thoughts racing. The soldier had addressed him directly. There was nothing to do but play out his role. He kept his voice to a soft whisper, barely loud enough to be heard. "Give me your horse," he ordered sternly. He stepped close enough to strike at once with his sword if the man wasn't fooled.

"My horse?" The soldier answered hesitantly.

"Give me your horse!" Innowen hissed angrily, as he imagined the Witch would do to any who made her repeat a command.

Meekly, the soldier slid to the ground and handed over the reins of his mount. Innowen quickly shifted his sword into the hand that also held the bundle, wincing at the additional strain on his wounded palm. With his good hand, he reached out and accepted the reins. "Now go," he ordered curtly. "Leave me!"

The soldier walked on up the street, scratching his head, but not daring to look back. Innowen waited until the man was out of sight before grabbing a handful of the horse's mane and swinging up astride the beast. He balanced the bundle between his legs near the horse's withers and shoved his blade through his belt so that it rested near the small of his back. Adjusting the white cloak neatly about his shoulders again so that its folds concealed as much of him as possible, he rode forward.

A contingent of guards stood watch at the main gate, but Innowen felt sure of himself now. He didn't hesitate, but rode into the light of their lamps and torches, straight up to the gate itself. The ponderous doors were shut, as he'd known they would be.

The captain of the guard came forward. Surreptitiously, Innowen pushed the ruby-pommeled hilt of the Witch's sword into plainer view. "Lady," the captain said, bowing, then kneeling in the dust.

"Out," was all that Innowen said.

The captain rose quickly and gave orders to his men. Moments later, the great oaken bar slid back, and one of the doors opened just wide enough for a single rider. Innowen nudged his mount forward.

"My men on the wall will see you coming if you return before sunrise," the captain said, walking beside him as far as the gap. As Innowen passed through, the captain called after him. "Be careful, Lady. It is dangerous country for a woman alone."

Innowen's grip tightened around the reins, but he kept the horse to a walk until he was out of eyesight of the guards. Then he drummed his heels against the animal's flanks and ran as fast as he dared, turning off the road that crossed Parendur Plain, and racing toward the looming blackness of the Akrotir Mountains.

Without the city's rooftops to conceal it, the moon hung bright above his shoulder and cast his shadow out over the earth. Its black, distorted shape raced ahead of him over the coarse ground, matching every fluid movement of horse and rider with a subtle grace, as only a shadow could. Innowen bent low over his horse's neck and clutched the bundle between his legs with the injured hand while his other worked the reins.

It was a fool's chase, to run after a shadow, but still he tried desperately to catch himself.

ROBIN WAYNE BAILEY

THE MORNING SUN beat with fierce intensity on Innowen's bare back and shoulders as he rode carefully up a shallow incline. The life had long since gone out of his legs. He kept his balance on the horse purely with his hands, bracing himself on the beast's withers, while the reins dangled loosely between his fingers. It made for precarious riding, so he went slowly, keeping to a northward course, and let the horse pick its way.

Just before dawn, he had paused long enough to make equal bundles of the two cloaks, distributing the weight of the Witch's armor and his four dolls between them. Then he'd bound them together, making a big, clumsy knot, and tossed them over the horse's shoulders, where they jostled now against his unfeeling knees.

On his left, the jagged peaks of the Akrotir Mountains rose in sharp relief against the blue sky. He had never thought of the mountains as ominous before, but now, stripped by the long drought of the greenery that normally covered their slopes, the bare gray stone depressed him. A subtle mist clung to the highest points, not yet dissipated by the swelling heat. Some breeze that played among the peaks stirred and churned those wisps and sent pale streamers drifting outward to diffuse into nothingness.

A pair of birds flew overhead, their calls loud in the crisp air as they spiraled and looped and chased one another. Innowen almost unbalanced himself as he twisted his head around to observe their mating flight.

With a gasp, he caught a double handful of the horse's mane in his right hand and managed to redistribute his weight.

He knew he should find a place to dismount, a safe place where he could sleep the day away. If the horse misstepped, or if he grew careless again and fell off, he wouldn't be able to get back up. For that matter, he thought with a frown, the only way he was going to get down when he did find such a place was to let go and fall.

He looked at the ground and bit his lip. The earth was hard and rocky, as gray as the mountains, with only a few tufts of spiky weeds poking up here and there to remind him mockingly of what grass had once looked like. He decided to push ahead. He would find a better place, if he just didn't fall.

His head still swam with images from the night before. The Witch's murder of the drugged soldier, the bloody love-making with her son, a *snowfever* petal clinging to her lip, a pink tongue gathering and drawing it into her mouth; these visions played over and over again in his mind.

There were other visions, too. Parendur at night, transformed into a kind of black, silent hell. The old man beaten to death in the street outside his home, and Innowen's killing of two of the attackers. He didn't like killing, and yet he had done that so easily.

Over it all lingered one other image, of himself, seen without benefit of a mirror, as only his mind could conjure it, in the Witch's armor, moving like a ghost through a sleeping city, among men who dared not look at him.

Minowee. He whispered the name in his mind, though he dared not speak it aloud, even so far from Parendur, for fear she might somehow hear. *Minowee*, he thought again, remembering how she had come to him out of the storm on a forest road long ago, remembering her as she had addressed him last night, covered in crimson, deep in the *feverdream*. He strove with all his understanding to reconcile the images.

The wind blew down from the peaks and rumpled his hair, brushed over his throat, teased his nipples to tiny erections. The sound it made as it whistled down out of the gray, lonely peaks was the sound of her name, *Minoweeeee.*

"No!" Innowen shouted in sudden defiance, waving a hand before his face as if he might bat the wind away. "You won't possess me! I'm free of you now!"

He gripped the horse's mane tightly in both hands, tangling the reins in his fingers, and nudged the beast to a faster pace. He soon slowed again. With no feeling below his waist, he had no sense of a rider's rhythm, and the bouncing promised to unseat him no matter how he held on with his hands. He licked his lips and felt his breath quicken. An old sense of helplessness threatened him once more.

He rode carefully down one slope and up the next. At its summit, he paused. In the distance, a brown ribbon wound among the hills, all that remained of the Kashoki River, which originated at a point further ahead in the Akrotir foothills and flowed outward across the plains toward the heart of Ispor to join with the River Semene. In normal times, the Kashoki was a great and swift-running river. Now, there was very little water at all between its muddy banks.

A powerful thirst came upon him. He had neither wine nor water with him and had wet his mouth with nothing since that stolen sip from a soldier's bota in the palace courtyard. He steered his horse toward the river, cutting an angling course down the slope and hanging on with all his strength.

Overhead, birds circled in greater numbers, drawn by the river. Unlike the pair he had observed earlier, these were silent in their flight, as if a call or a song was too great an expenditure of energy. He heard them, though, heard the beat of their pinions, heard the rush of the wind through their feathers, and he envied them, who had no fear of falling.

He thought of her again, thought of the soldier's blood pumping onto her heaving, groaning body while Vashni rode her.

Innowen pushed the image violently from his mind, cursed her, and cursed himself. He had to concentrate to keep his balance. His arms were tiring rapidly from supporting all his weight, and his shoulders ached. It would only take a little mistake, and he'd wind up on the ground, flat on his back. What then? The birds above him weren't vultures, but it was easy to imagine they were.

The Kashoki River had dwindled to little more than a thin trickle. Innowen rode down an embankment onto a dry bed of sun-cracked mud. A swarm of gnats and flies buzzed up around his face suddenly. He waved a hand to drive them off. The silvery scaled remains of dead fish lay scattered about, half buried by the insects.

The ground became muddy as he approached the narrow ribbon of water. The tracks of other animals were visible, some still relatively fresh. At dawn and sundown, no doubt, this place teemed with life. He watched particularly for wolf-prints or signs of other predators.

The horse waded out into the river. It was only a stream now, barely deep enough to cover his fetlocks. The beast bent his head to drink, and Innowen nearly lost his seat again as the reins jerked in his hands. The horse didn't care. It was thirsty, and it lapped the water greedily.

Innowen, however, was faced with a problem. He

couldn't get down to drink unless he let himself fall. If he did that, he wouldn't be able to mount again. He could smell the water, so close and yet so far, and his tongue rubbed against the dry roof of his mouth. He thought about his kilt. If he unwound it and dangled an end in the stream, he could soak up some water and suck it from the cloth. He didn't think he could do that without losing his balance on the horse. His breech cloth was useless for the same reason. Besides, he discovered when he felt it with a hand that it was saturated with the horse's lather. Possibly, too, with his own urine.

My belt, though, just might work. Holding the reins in one hand and leaning on his mount's withers, he carefully recovered the two gold *cymorens* he had thrust down between the belt and his skin. These he also shoved into the fist that held the reins. Then, one-handed, he worked at the laces over his belly that held the belt in place. It was ridiculously hard work, as he seemed to be constantly teetering in the air, ready to plunge off. At last, he got it free.

He rested for a moment, putting his weight on both hands, before lowering himself slowly, cautiously forward until he was stretched out along the horse's neck. If the beast bucked up or tossed its head suddenly, it would unseat him for sure. But the smell of the water was too strong. He leaned down as far as he dared and dipped the end of his belt in the river and pulled it up.

He clung to the horse for balance now, one arm wrapped nearly around its long throat, as he raised the end of the belt to his lips. The droplets ran into his mouth, and his tongue strained to catch them all. They brought with them a muddy taste and the slightly bitter tang of leather and tanner's dye, but to Innowen nothing ever tasted so sweet or so good. He dipped the belt a second time and drank again.

It was a clumsy and arduous process, but he managed to refresh himself. At last, he pressed himself upright. He'd let the horse drink too much; he chided himself, as he struggled to wrap his belt around his waist. That only brought new frustration, for he couldn't do it with only one hand, not while the other had to hold the reins and the gold coins and keep his balance. Finally, muttering an oath, he tucked the belt between his thighs and the knot that tied the two bundles together. The coins he shoved down his breech cloth.

He had to find a place to sleep, or at least a place to rest, and he couldn't put it off much longer. Sooner or later, the horse was bound to misstep and throw him, or his own fatigue and carelessness would undo him. Better, instead, to find a safe spot and wait for the sunset to bring life back to his limbs.

He had planned the ride to Parendur with deliberate care, so there had always been a town or village or farm, someplace where he could rent a bed or beg a stable hayloft in which to sleep the day away. But he had fled Parendur in a panic. Only in the few brief moments he had spent atop a hill, watching the sun rise, feeling it warm his face as it chilled his legs, had he chosen a destination. No, not chosen. *Realized.* He'd realized where he'd been heading since leaving the Witch behind.

It was as if fate, a mightier river than the Kashoki had ever been, had swept him up in a current and carried him along. As if the gods of Ispor had set their hands on him and turned him where they wanted him to go.

But Innowen put little stock in fate or gods. If he wanted, he could turn his horse aside. He could choose another course and still find his way to Whisperstone.

He followed the foothills northward because he wanted to. It was his own morbid desire that drove him, nothing to blame on fate or gods.

He turned his left hand over and stared at the thin black streak just under the skin of his palm. The splinter no longer pained him unless he made a fist. It was an evil reminder, though, that a god had, in fact, touched him. What good was all his arrogance and disdain for the gods? He himself was proof of their power.

Still, he lifted his head, and something of a sneer flickered across his lips. None of it mattered. Whether it was his will, or the will of the gods, he knew where he was going.

〗〖〗〖〗

Night descended softly, splendidly, over Ispor. The Crown of the Gods made a milky blaze across the sky, and in the north, the Great Scythe carved a lazy swath. In the south, the Red Beast clawed its way into the heavens; its curling tail, however, anchored it forever to the earth; the harder it strove, the brighter burned the single, bright crimson star, which scholars called Antarios, that made its head. Directly overhead, the Great Swan kept watch over the poor people of the earth and brought them a peaceful summer night's sleep.

Innowen felt some measure of that peace as he followed the Kashoki River northward. Life had returned to his legs again, and he had danced a slow and graceful dance high atop one of the Akrotir foothills as the earliest stars winked into view. It was for them he'd danced, and he'd called them by name, the ones he knew, conjuring them to appear, each in their proper places, to bejewel the night.

He had not slept, though. Perhaps that explained the languid peace that filled him. Or perhaps it was the gentle, rolling motion of the horse that lulled him. Maybe it was the easy trickling of the Kashoki as it purled between its banks. This far north, where the river flowed among the foothills, it carried more water than farther out on the plain where he had first drunk from it.

He had passed the afternoon in nervous watchfulness atop a high hill where he could see in all directions, afraid of wild animals, half afraid that the Witch might somehow find him. By now, she must know of her missing armor. She might have noticed the missing dolls. Perhaps she remembered the dream that had visited her in her sleep. Innowen had no clear idea of the extent of her powers, or if distance was any safeguard against her retaliation. He hadn't thought too much about it in the morning, when balancing on his horse without the benefit of his legs had taken most of his concentration. But in the afternoon, when he had hoped to rest, it had prevented him from ever closing his eyes.

He had decided it was a fear born out of his vulnerability, for as the use of his legs had returned to him, the fear had melted away. Now he thought mostly about his hunger, about his destination, and about the stars that burned so brilliantly, like lamps in the heavens to light his way, and he wished Razkili were at his side to see such stars.

The Great Scythe disappeared as the river took a sudden bend and cut deeper into the foothills. The Kashoki was still little more than a stream. A few good strides would take him to the opposite bank. But it was cleaner, unsullied by the mud of the plains. He stopped, took a drink and let his horse drink, then mounted again and continued onward.

The river led him into a shallow valley, and Innowen paused to study the village nestled there. Lamplights shone in the windows of some homes even at such a late hour, but most dwellings were utterly dark. He rode forward cautiously, nudging his horse with his heels, staying close to the river.

An abandoned pier rose on the opposite bank, and the corpses of broken boats lay scattered about it, half buried in the mud. Once, the Kashoki had been large enough for small boats to navigate, and goods had been shipped up and down the waterway. The drought had put an end to that.

Innowen steered his mount across the river—the water barely came to the horse's knees at its deepest point—and up the other embankment. The horse's hooves clattered loudly as he rode across the land-anchored end of the pier. A few bundles were still piled there, but it was too dark to see what they were, and he had no interest at all in the spilled contents of a pair of shattered barrels.

He followed the river, which flowed into the heart of the village. Empty warehouses rose up on his right side, their great doors open to any who cared to enter, or hanging crookedly on worn hinges. An arched stone bridge was a useless monument to the former greatness of the Kashoki. On his left, more boats lay piled up on the muddy shore, arranged neatly like the bodies of soldiers after a battle.

Some of the homes he passed now were occupied. Windows were opened to catch the breeze. Sometimes, voices spilled out. An argument from this one. A laugh from that one. Once, a small child's face peered out and watched him pass.

He arrived at another bridge and turned right, following the road of which it was part, away from the river. An old man came walking toward him, slouched forward under the weight of a sack he carried slung across one shoulder.

Innowen pulled back on the reins, and his horse stopped. "Is this…?"

The old man passed him by, refusing to answer or even to acknowledge him. Innowen twisted around to watch him disappear across the bridge. With a shrug, he rode onward until he found the village square.

He approached the well that stood in the center of the town. Without dismounting, he looked around. A door slammed off to his left. A pair of voices rose in deep-throated laughter. Innowen observed the two men who stumbled toward the well. They were halfway across the square when they saw him and stopped.

"Well, well, a traveler," said the taller of the two men, a black-haired, bearded fellow dressed in a leather kilt and a ragged tunic. Innowen noted the short dagger on the belt around his waist.

"Who might ye be, comin' here so late in the middle o' the night, now?" The shorter, and obviously younger, man gave off a reek of beer that Innowen could smell as they came closer.

He turned just enough to let them see the sword he wore—the soldier's sword, which Baktus had given him. The Witch's ruby-hilted blade remained wrapped in the bundle with her armor and his dolls. "What village is this?" Innowen asked evenly.

"Shanalane," said the older man, eyeing the sword. "Why, don't ye know where ye're goin', or are ye jus' ridin' around the countryside for the fun of it?"

Innowen ignored the question. "Was that an inn you just came from? I could use a drink and a bite to eat."

"Couldn't we all, now," the younger man laughed drunkenly. "Ye like to buy us a drink, stranger?"

Innowen considered. "Sorry," he said at last. "My poor coins will barely stretch for one meal tonight." He looked the older man in the eyes as he spoke the lie.

The younger one took a half step forward and reached toward Innowen's foot. "That's not very friendly...."

His older comrade caught his arm and yanked him back. "Ferget it, Chaddi," he said, still watching Innowen's eyes. "He's not worth the trouble." Quickly, he ushered a mumbling Chaddi away and down a side street.

Innowen waited until they were gone, then rode toward the door the pair had emerged through. There was no sign or anything to declare if it was an inn or a tavern. Voices sounded loudly from inside, however. He dismounted slowly, keeping the reins of his horse in one hand. In his uncertainty, he thought of knocking on the door, but at last pulled it open.

It was a tavern, all right. A dozen men sat around tables, pouring mugs of liquid down their throats, and holding conversations between gulps. Another half dozen stood in a group at the back of the tavern tossing knives at a painted block of wood. A large sweating man sat on a stool just inside the door. His head was shaved bald, and a small gold hoop gleamed in the drooping lobe of his left ear. He turned and regarded Innowen with a cool, even gaze. "In or out," he grumbled.

Innowen hesitated, mindful of the reins in his hand. "Is there someplace close where I can stable my horse?" he said. "I've come a long way."

The doorman with the earring eyed him again, noting his sword and clothing, peering around the door past Innowen for a look at the horse. "Wait," he answered, pushing Innowen back outside and closing the door in his face.

Innowen frowned, but waited, twisting the reins

around one hand as he idly stroked his horse's neck with the other. He didn't wait long. The door opened, and another man emerged, wearing an apron, which he wiped over both his hands. His hair was black and curly, and his grin reminded Innowen startlingly of Taelyn.

"Hot tonight, isn't it?" the man remarked casually, extending his hand to clasp Innowen's forearm. There was power in his grip, and Innowen liked him at once, finding him a pleasant change from the first four souls he'd met in this village.

"All the nights are hot," Innowen answered. "I'm Petroklos, a traveler."

"And I'm Moryn."

Innowen's head tilted to one side as he studied the man with renewed interest. "That's a Mureibet name," he said.

Moryn's left brow elevated, and he, too, gave Innowen a closer look. "You must be well-traveled, indeed. My father was from Mureibet, but he settled here with my Isporan mother." His grin broadened. "People who know me around here call me Mourn."

The two finally let go of each other's forearms. "Merit said you needed your horse looked after," Mourn remarked, taking the reins from Innowen's hand. "Let me see to him. I'm friends with the owner of the only stable still open on this side of the river, and I'll get you a good price. It's not far. You go on in and have a drink. There'll be food when I get back."

"My thanks," Innowen said, pleased by such hospitality. "Do you have rooms? I haven't slept for some time."

"No rooms, I'm afraid," Mourn answered, biting a corner of his lip. "Shanalane hasn't been able to support an inn for quite a while. Few travelers come this way since the river dried up." He paused, then the corners of his mouth turned up in a renewed smile. "If you like, though, you can sleep with me. I've plenty of room. The bed is soft and big enough, and I won't disturb you."

Innowen hesitated. "That's a generous offer to make to a stranger."

Mourn shrugged. "Anyone who's been to Mureibet must have stories to tell. Me, I've never left this village in my life, except to sail upriver to Kharkus, which doesn't count. Don't worry, Petroklos. You'll earn a night's keep with tale-telling. Now go inside while I get fresh straw and oats for your horse."

Innowen collected his two bundles from around the horse's shoulders, and Mourn led the animal away. Innowen went into the tavern. Choosing a table near the door, he sat down and looked around.

The giant by the door—Mourn had called him Merit—never took his eyes off Innowen. After a few moments, a young girl separated from the group of knife-throwers and approached him. At first, he assumed she was a prostitute. Why else would she be in such a place? But she only asked his preference, "Beer, ale, or wine."

"Wine," he told her, and shortly she brought it to him in the same heavy earthen mug used for beer or ale. Innowen put one of his gold *cymorens* on the table. The girl's eyes widened at sight of it, but before she could make a move, Merit waved her away and shook his head. The girl retreated instantly.

The giant raised his bulk from the stool and ambled over. He covered the shining coin with one meaty hand and pushed it toward Innowen with a frown. "Don't show that around here," he said gruffly. "We don't need no trouble." He turned and took up his perch on the stool, and never looked Innowen's way again.

Innowen sighed and slipped the coin back into his belt. As he raised his mug of wine and sipped, he glanced around the room, wondering why he had come here, what he had hoped to find. Shanalane was something of a disappointment, only an old fishing and shipping town, dried up like the river, which had been its livelihood.

Still, somewhere in the hills close by was the Witch's keep. He didn't understand it, but he wanted to see where Minarik and Minowee had trysted and where Vashni must have been born. Innowen had had time to think on the road here, time to lay their faces one upon the other in his mind, and he had no doubt that Vashni was Minarik's son.

He took a gulp of his wine. The pieces of a great puzzle were, at last, coming together. Yet the picture they would form when all were joined still eluded him.

〖〗

When Innowen woke up, Mourn's bedroom was utterly dark. He had slept the day away, then, and he smiled to himself, for he had not quite figured out what he would say if his newfound friend discovered his unusual problem.

When he tried to slide out of bed, however, his legs refused to cooperate. His pulse quickened for an instant, and he knew a moment of cold fear. If it was night, then he should be whole again. He forced himself to be calm. It must not be night, he told himself. He felt around. Mourn was not in bed, and his place on the sheets next to the wall was cold.

Innowen rolled over clumsily, his legs a heavy, impeding weight. Mourn must have crawled off the end of the bed or stepped lightly over him while he slept. There was no space between the far side of the mattress and the wall. Innowen remembered a window, though, just above the bed. It had been open last night to let the warm breeze play over them while they talked and told tales.

He reached out and sighed with relief as his fingers brushed rough cloth. Mourn had closed the shutters and draped a thick woolen blanket over the window to shut out the sunlight so that it wouldn't wake Innowen. He gave a tug, and the blanket came down. A bright shaft of light slipped through the gap between the wooden shutters. He gave them a push, and they flung outward, flooding the room with daylight.

Innowen dragged himself up on his elbows and peered out. As near as he could tell, it was afternoon at least. He gazed down into the street as a cart trundled by, drawn by a single ox, laden with possessions. A man, a woman, and a dirty child sat on the board huddled close together. It was clear they were leaving town.

Near the well in the center of the square, an old man sat surrounded by a ragged gathering of boys and girls. From the occasional gestures he made, and from the rapt expressions on the children's faces, Innowen guessed he was a storyteller.

Across the square, a door opened and banged closed. A pair of women strolled toward the well with large hydria jars carefully balanced on their shoulders. They talked together as they walked, but when they reached the well they fell silent in the presence of the old man. At first, Innowen assumed it was out of the same deference Isporan women showed any man, but as he watched, he realized the two had only paused from their labors to listen to part of the old one's tale before they filled their jars.

A trio of dogs sniffed their way along the gutters of the street that led to the bridge, searching for scraps. A blackbird sailed through the blue and settled on a rooftop. It watched the dogs and waited for a chance to steal anything they might find. Somewhere, a baby began to cry with a weak voice that quickly surrendered to a mother's soft singing.

Peals of laughter rang out from the children by the well, an unexpected sound that suddenly touched Innowen. For all the suffering in Ispor, life still went on. He gazed at the storyteller with a profound respect. The old man was a bringer of joy in hard times. Innowen could tell, even from his faraway window, that Shanalane's children loved him.

Very close, another door banged shut. Just below the window, Mourn appeared with a bucket, which he carried to the gutter and emptied. The dogs were there in no time, yapping at his heels, poking their snouts into the gutter as he poured. But it was only mop water and old grease. The dogs lost interest and trotted off as Mourn set the bucket down and paused to wipe his face with the end of his apron.

Innowen backed away from the window. If Mourn didn't look up and see him, perhaps the tavern keeper would leave him alone, under the impression that Innowen would sleep all day. That would be easiest. Then, as soon as the sun set, he could simply get up and walk downstairs. He pursed his lips and settled back into the pillows, wondering what he could do to pass the time without drawing attention to himself.

A few moments later, Mourn eased into the room. His face looked weary, but he smiled when he saw Innowen. "I saw the open shutters," he said, "so I guessed you were awake."

Innowen pretended to yawn. "I'm still pretty tired," he lied. "I'll probably stay in bed the rest of the day, if you don't mind."

Mourn wiped his hands on his apron, a habit Innowen realized was compulsive with him. Then he untied it, crumpled it, and dropped it on the floor. He stretched out on the huge bed beside Innowen and let go a weary sigh as he closed his eyes.

Innowen studied his new friend. When they had first met in the street, he had thought that Mourn was older, but as they had talked through the night and now, with sunshine lighting Mourn's face, Innowen realized they were of a similar age. Mourn *looked* older, though. Hard work had lined and toughened his face, and years of travail had peppered his black hair with early gray. On impulse, Innowen reached out and brushed an unruly lock back from Mourn's forehead.

"Why'd you do that?" Mourn said, opening his eyes, twisting his head so that he could look at Innowen.

"You remind me of someone," Innowen answered honestly, thinking of Taelyn. "A friend I lost recently."

Mourn's expression softened. He turned on his side, folding one arm under his head. "Sounds like there's a story there," he said.

Innowen groaned and clutched his stomach with both arms. "No, please! Have mercy!" He made a face and waved his arms crazily to lighten the mood, refusing to give in to the sadness that thoughts of Taelyn brought. "I'm hoarse from tale-telling. Dawn was coloring the rim of the sky when you finally let me quit. You know more about my life than I do!"

The grin faded from Mourn's face, and his eyes took on a distant look. For a moment, he seemed to gaze right past Innowen. "I doubt that," he said quietly.

Innowen crinkled his brow, puzzled by his friend's tone. But Mourn rolled onto his back and stared at the ceiling. Neither of them said anything more. After a while, Mourn moved closer and put his head on Innowen's shoulder. Still, they didn't speak, but lay there in the solitude of the room while random sounds from outside flowed around them and mingled with the sound of breathing.

When Mourn finally got up, he appeared more tired

than before. He bent to collect his apron, and slowly, with his back to Innowen, he tied it around his waist and went to the door. He paused there and turned around. "Would you like me to close the shutters?" he asked. "You'll sleep better."

Innowen shook his head. He could just hear the mumbling of the storyteller by the well, and maybe— just maybe if he listened long enough—the children would laugh again.

"Sleep as long as you want, Petroklos," Mourn told him. "Come down when you like." He started to pull the door closed as he went out.

"Wait," Innowen called, and Mourn opened the door wide enough to poke his head inside. "My name is Innowen, not Petroklos. That's just a name I've been using on this journey." He hesitated and chewed the inside of the corner of his lower lip. "Sometimes my friends call me Innocent."

Mourn regarded him blankly, then his face lit up, and he barked a short laugh. "I guess we all have to bear the burden of some nickname, eh?" He chuckled again as he turned away and eased the door shut.

Innowen listened to Mourn's footsteps on the stairs and, for some time after that, to the sounds of his labors in the tavern below. After a while, he turned on his side and drew the extra pillow up against his body and hugged it tightly, resting his chin on the top of it as he closed his eyes.

He didn't know when he fell asleep for the second time, but when he woke again it was truly dark. The first thing that entered his mind was that he could feel the weight of the blanket on his legs. The second thing was that he hadn't thought of the Witch all day.

He ran a finger over the inside of his left palm, feeling the splinter embedded under the skin. It didn't hurt him as sharply anymore, though there was a tenderness. It seemed to be working its way more deeply into his hand, though, and that disturbed him.

Mourn had apparently slipped back into the room while he'd slept. The short stub of a candle that hadn't been there before burned on a table on the room's far side. Its dim yellow glow provided enough light for Innowen to dress by. He glanced toward his two bundles still by the door where he'd left them, then went quietly down the stairs and into the kitchen.

The rich smells of warm bread and broth almost made him dizzy. There was no sign of Mourn, so he went to the hearthplace and bent over a large black pot to inhale the savory aroma arising from it.

"Careful," Mourn said as he came through the kitchen door. "There's no fire there, but those stones are hot. Brush a toe against them, and you'll lose skin."

Innowen backed up and looked at the five large, flat stones that lined the bottom of the hearthplace and on which the cook pot sat. He'd been too interested in the broth. Now he felt the considerable heat rising from the stones. Innowen had never seen the like before. "How do you do that?" he asked wonderingly.

Mourn set down the tray he was carrying and wiped his hands on his apron. "I like hot food," he said simply. "But it's been too warm, with this drought, to build a fire indoors. So a few years ago I dragged those up from the river. I heat them every afternoon in a fire out back, then drag them in here with those." He pointed to a pair of metal rods that hung on pegs by the rear door. One end of each rod was bent into the shape of a hook; the other ends were wrapped with heavy layers of cloth for grasping.

Innowen grinned with wide-eyed appreciation as he picked up one of the rods and turned it in his hands. "You know, if you drilled small holes in the rocks..."

he suggested thoughtfully.

Mourn came and took the rod from him, and Innowen saw there was a hint of blush in his cheeks. "I tried that," he admitted with shy pride, "but the rocks broke. So I took a chisel and cut notches, instead. It works as well." He thrust the hook end of the rod under the edge of one of the rocks, prodded a bit until he found the notch, and lifted the rock just enough to show how it worked. When the pot started to tilt, he let it down again and steadied the vessel with his sandaled foot.

Innowen marveled as Mourn hung the rod back on its peg. "That's the cleverest thing I've ever seen," he said. "Hot food in summer!" He waved his hand to fan his face. "The kitchen's still hot, but not nearly as hot as it would be if you kept a fire going."

"And the stones cool quicker than coals would," Mourn pointed out. "When the cooking is done, I simply wet them with a little water."

Innowen went to the table where Mourn had set his tray. Several loaves of bread lay there, and he broke off a piece. "I'm starving," he admitted, shoving a crust into his mouth. "How did you come to own a tavern, anyway?" he asked, spraying crumbs.

Mourn frowned and cast his gaze downward. His hands began to work in his apron again. He crossed the kitchen, took a couple of mugs down from a shelf and began to ladle beer from an open keg into them. "Inherited it, I guess you might say," he confessed in a barely audible voice. "Several plagues swept Ispor in the first year of the drought. My mother took sick like a lot of people and died." He hesitated as he hung the ladle back in its place and leaned on the keg without looking at Innowen. "We burned her body a little way upriver where there were still a few flowers growing."

He paused thoughtfully and sipped his beer before continuing. "After her funeral, my father was never the same. One day, he threw a few things in a sack and went back to Mareibet."

"Just like that?" Innowen said, incredulous.

Mourn nodded. "Just like that." He picked up the mugs suddenly, turned around, and set them on the tray. "I've got to take these out to a couple of customers. You come on out, too, and sit down. I'll get you something to go with that bread."

Innowen followed him out into the tavern. While Mourn carried the mugs to a pair of men in a far corner—the only customers, it seemed— Innowen went to the table near the door where he had sat the previous night. Merit's stool was empty, he noted. The big man with the earring was nowhere to be seen.

Innowen leaned his elbows on the table and rested his head on folded hands. He closed his eyes. When he opened them again, the inn seemed full of shadows. His own shadow sat beside him on a shadow chair at a shadow table. Mourn's shadow jumped acrobatically from floor to wall to wall as he moved about the other end of the tavern, serving shadow drinks to shadow men.

The smoky oil lamps that hung from the rafters on leather thongs were responsible. Innowen gave them an evil look. He wished he could blow them all out. Then there would only be darkness. The darkness was beautiful. Senses quickened in the darkness. The stars burned in the darkness. Lovers touched in the darkness.

But shadows—sometimes he hated the shadows. They warped and exaggerated and misrepresented. Shadows were liars.

He leaned his head on his hands again and shaped a vision of Mourn's father turning his back on his son, walking away, walking down a river bank toward some half-remembered, love-forsaken land. But suddenly, it became a vision of himself, and it was his own unknown parent just walking away while the world darkened and a forest closed in and the branches filled with hungry, growling glares.

Innowen looked up with stinging eyes as Mourn set a mug of wine down before him, then a wooden bowl of steaming broth with a plate of bread and a few pieces of crumbly cheese. His new friend disappeared briefly, returning a few moments later with similar fare for himself. He took the seat across from Innowen, and they both began to eat in silence.

The broth was excellent and lifted Innowen's spirits. He sopped the last drop from the bowl with a bit of bread and swallowed it, leaned back, and patted his stomach while he waited for Mourn to finish his.

The door to the street opened, and Innowen heard an odd *tap-scrape* that he couldn't quite identify. Merit came in, leading the blind storyteller by the arm. The old man's gnarly cane had made that tapping sound. Merit took the cane from him as he guided the storyteller to an isolated table and sat him down. Leaning the cane against the wall close by the old man's hand, he then went into the kitchen.

The storyteller waited silently, hunched over the table, his hands in his lap. Long strands of wavy gray hair and a grizzled beard hid most of his face, and thick lids drooped over the sightless eyes. He displayed none of the animation now that he had shown earlier as he told tales by the well for the children. Now he seemed frail and tired and small inside the simple, ankle-length garment he wore. Innowen regarded him with curious interest. How still the old man sat!

Mourn reached across the table and tapped the rim of Innowen's empty bowl. "More?" he asked.

"Certainly," Innowen said absently, "but wait a while for this serving to settle."

Merit came back from the kitchen with broth and bread and a mug, which he set before the storyteller. With gruff tenderness, he guided the old man's hands to the food, showing him where bowl and plate and mug were placed, and sat down patiently beside him to help him eat. The storyteller reached for the bread first. His withered hands trembled ever so slightly, but noticeably, as he broke the bread and brought it to his lips.

Mourn said something that Innowen didn't understand. "What?" he muttered. But even as Mourn repeated himself, Innowen pushed back his chair and rose to his feet.

The old man reached for the mug, and Merit helped him find it. The weight of the vessel only intensified the trembling of the hand that held it.

Innowen moved away from his chair and crossed the floor, ignoring the warning look that Merit gave him. A strange sensation of intangibility floated over him, and the rest of the world disappeared. He leaned on the table and bent to peer at the old man's face.

Now it was he who trembled.

"Oh my gods," he whispered, feeling as if a hole had just opened in his chest. "Drushen?"

CHAPTER

19

ROBIN WAYNE BAILEY

INNOWEN WAVED A hand before Drushen's sightless eyes. Despite the old man's blindness and all the gray hair and the beard, there was no doubt it was his former guardian. But what had happened to his eyes? "Drushen!" he exclaimed, grasping the old man's shoulder. "It's Innowen!"

Drushen turned his face upward toward the voice, his jaw falling slack. A violent tremor suddenly seized the old body and shook it like a child's doll. A low moan escaped his lips, a sound that rose in pitch, becoming a frightened keening. The mug slipped from his hands, spilled its contents into the lap of his garment, and clattered to the floor. Drushen lunged away from Innowen's touch, tumbling sideways off his chair. One hand grasped for his gnarled cane, which leaned against the wall, while he waved the other frantically to ward off any who approached him. Merit caught his arm and tried to help him up, but Drushen batted him away and struggled to his feet.

"No!" Drushen moaned. It was the sound of a man staring into the face of terror. "No!" He swung his cane with both hands, carving a wide *whooshing* arc in the air before him as he staggered in the direction of the door. He collided with a table, nearly falling over it as Merit, Mourn, and Innowen tried to surround him. Quickly, though, he recovered, lifted a chair in one hand and flung it.

"What did you do to him?" Merit cried angrily as he ducked a swing of the cane and danced back out of range.

"Nothing!" Innowen cried. "He's my guardian!"

Merit froze, giving Innowen a look of utter dread. "Oh gods!" he muttered, before giving his attention once more to Drushen. "Oh gods!"

Innowen had never seen his oldest friend so terrified. It scared him, and he stood back in hurt confusion watching as Mourn and Merit, now joined by the tavern's two customers, managed to trap the old man and disarm him of the cane. Still, he struggled and fought in their grips. "No!" he keened. "No! No!" And almost as if there was still some vestige of sight in those ruined, fear-widened eyes, they sought out Innowen and locked on him.

All it had taken had been the sound of Innowen's voice. Drushen was like a canary caged with a hawk, fluttering wildly about in a desperate panic to get away. He kicked and scratched with only feeble effect until the others finally bore him back against the wall and pinned him there. Still, he moaned and cried, and tears streamed thickly down his face, until Merit gathered him in his huge arms, hugging him against his body and crooning to him like a mother with an injured child.

"Drushen," Innowen said softly, coming closer. "It's all right. It was my fault, not yours."

Merit scowled over his shoulder, warning Innowen away, and Mourn caught Innowen's arm. "Leave him alone," Mourn told him. "Merit will take care of him. He's taken care of him for years. You can explain to me what this is about."

Innowen let Mourn pull him back to their table while Merit led the sobbing Drushen out into the night. The two customers mumbled their goodnights, and

Mourn thanked them for their aid, offering free beers if they returned tomorrow. They readily agreed. Mourn closed the door after them.

He and Innowen were alone. Innowen caught his head in his hands and leaned on the table, remembering that awful last night he and Drushen had spent at Whisperstone, his first dance there, and the dark thing it had compelled Drushen to do. The memory of it burned in his mind, and he squeezed his eyes shut to stop the tears that tried to seep out.

"Maybe you're not ready to talk yet," Mourn said with some sympathy. He reached across the table and collected Innowen's mug. "I'll refill your wine."

When Mourn came back, he set the mug in front of Innowen, leaned back in his chair and propped his feet up on a corner of the table. Instead of waiting for Innowen, he started the conversation. "Drushen's very dear to most of us," he said, talking into his own mug. "Since he came here five years ago, most of the town—those who remain—have come to love him. He entertains everyone with his stories. You claim he was your guardian?"

Innowen ignored the question. "He's blind!" he said, as if fully realizing the fact for the first time. "How? How did that happen?"

Mourn merely shrugged. "Merit probably knows," he answered. "I don't. He was blind when he stumbled in here. I thought he was a beggar, but Merit knew him and took him in." Mourn paused to take a drink of his wine. He wiped his lips with the tip of a finger before setting the mug down and wrapping his hands around it.

"Then, a few months later," he continued, tilting his head as he peered at Innowen, "along comes Lord Minarik, himself, riding in with five of his men. None of them ever spoke to Drushen as far as I know, or went anywhere near him. But before they rode out, they left coins with Merit to insure that Drushen was kept decently, and a rider comes from Whisperstone with a fresh purse every month." He leaned back in his chair again. "Ah, I see I've touched something there!"

Innowen tried uselessly to hide his shock. He leaned forward intently, half out of his chair as he gripped the edge of the table. "Minarik? What's Minarik got to do with this?" He kicked his chair back and stood up. Pacing, he wiped a hand through his hair. "Mourn, I don't understand any of this! What's going on?" He stopped pacing suddenly and stared toward the door. "I haven't seen that man in five years!" He hung his head and covered his face with his hands. "Oh gods, Drushen, what have I done to you?"

The door creaked open and closed softly. When Innowen opened his eyes, Merit stood there, watching him. Slowly, he came to the table and glanced at the mugs of wine. Then, like a bladder gently collapsing, he gave a little sigh, his shoulders sagged forward, and his back rounded. He trudged away from them and into the kitchen. When he returned moments later, he carried a wine cask that only he could have managed. He set it down beside the table and smashed the lid with two blows from his great fist. "I'm buying," he muttered. He went back to the kitchen long enough to grab an extra mug, which he dipped into the cask.

Innowen bent impatiently over the table. "Merit, how do you know Drushen so well? And what's Minarik—"

Merit held up a hand, silencing Innowen, while he raised the mug to his mouth and drained it. Red wine trickled down the corners of the giant's lips, over his chin, and dripped into the thick mat of hair on his chest, where the scarlet droplets caught the gleam of the lamps and congealed like shining blood.

R O B I N   W A Y N E   B A I L E Y

"Drushen was born here," Merit answered at last, wiping his mouth with the back of one hand as he refilled the mug with the other. "We grew up together, me a fisherman, him a woodcutter, like our fathers before us. Now pardon me, while I savor this fine-tasting tea again." He drained the second mug from top to bottom, his throat muscles working as he swallowed with great noisy gulps.

"Oh, I know you, all right," he said to Innowen when the second mug was finished. "I know you *now*. I never would have let you in here had I known you before, but it's too late, so I'm just going to get good and drunk, instead."

"Where's Drushen?" Innowen demanded indignantly. "I've got to talk to him. I've got to find out what's going on!"

Merit watched over the edge of the cask as his mug refilled a third time. "He won't talk to you, boy," Merit answered condescendingly. "Don't you see he's terrified of you? I've got him calmed down a bit, but I had to lock him in his room so he can't get out. And I took out anything he could hurt himself with, too, 'cause I think he would, knowing that you're here."

Innowen felt his anger growing and struggled to control it. It was almost as if Merit were taunting him purposely, and he didn't like it. "Well, what happened to his eyes? He's blind!"

Merit turned a cool gaze on Innowen as he lifted the full mug from the cask. But he had overfilled it. The red wine ran over the mug's rim, down the handle, staining Merit's meaty fist. A ruby-colored rivulet ran down the giant's arm to his elbow. "He plucked them out himself," Merit answered with chilling calm. "He told me. His story sometimes varies, but either he saw something so beautiful he couldn't stand it, or something so terrible he couldn't face it again." He lifted the mug, then hesitated as his gaze left Innowen's face. "It drove him away from Whisperstone, whatever it was. He wandered around for a while, blind, before finally coming back here."

Innowen fought to control his emotions. He thought back to that night in Whisperstone's courtyard, how he had danced freely and with abandon for Drushen, striving to surprise and delight his guardian with his new legs. For so many nights after that one, he'd lain awake wondering what had become of Drushen. Now he knew, and the pain and guilt were more than he could bear!

He sank down into his chair and fell forward onto the table, barely aware of Mourn's gentle hand on the back of his head. "It wasn't his fault," he wept. "None of it was his fault!"

"Tell me the story," Mourn said softly to Merit. "I don't know any of this. I've never questioned you as long as you did good work here, but I want to know the truth."

Innowen sat up and pulled himself together. "Tell *me*, Merit," he asked quietly, picking up his own mug of wine. "Please."

Merit frowned and looked glumly down at the tabletop. He shifted uncomfortably, his bulk too large for the chair that held it. He lifted his mug, then set it down again without drinking. "All right," he said at last, "I'll tell it then, and tell it straight, and afterward we'll all get drunk together." He looked directly at Innowen. "It isn't your fault, either, boy. You remember that. Isn't none of it your fault."

Innowen knew that wasn't true, but he kept quiet and settled himself to listen. He drained his mug. Without saying anything, Mourn took it from him, refilled it, and placed it in his hands.

"Some years back when a lot of us were a lot younger, and you two weren't born yet, a very beautiful young woman came from the island kingdom of Mikonos and settled here." Merit's eyes rolled up inside his head as he leaned back and remembered. "Oh, she was fine as any dawn you ever saw, and she colored her hair bright gold, the way Mikonos women know how to do."

"The Witch of Shanalane," Mourn said.

"Yes," Merit agreed, "only she wasn't called that, then. We only knew she was a great lady with great powers. She never harmed anyone. Instead, she treated us when we were sick and looked out for the village like she was a mother to us all, making sure the river was always full of fish and the catch was always good, making sure the town never flooded when the rains fell too heavily up in the mountains and the Kashoki swelled up like a pregnant woman's belly." Merit took a thoughtful sip of his wine and set the mug down. He drummed his fingers lightly on the handle as he shook his head. "We never did know her name, so some of us started calling her the Witch of Shanalane, as if she was our own personal good-luck charm, and it sort of caught on."

"Her name was Minowee," Innowen whispered.

Merit repeated it. "Minowee," he said. "It's pretty. And I guess Lord Minarik thought so, too, when he rode through here one day and caught a glimpse of her. After that, he came a lot—Whisperstone isn't but a day's ride from here—or a night's, as the case may be—and it became plain to folks soon enough that the Witch had taken a lover."

Innowen got up and began to pace again with his mug in his hand. "I know that part of the story," he confessed. "Minarik told me, himself."

Mourn had been sitting quietly for some time. At

that, he looked up with interest. "How is it that you know an Isporan lord well enough to receive that kind of confidence?" he asked.

"Another complication of this same story," Innowen said, not missing the irony of his remark. He began to twist the ring he wore—Minarik's ring—around and around his finger. "Minarik is my adoptive father."

Merit leaned forward on the table, fixed Innowen with a piercing gaze, and waved toward the cask with his mug. "You better refill your cup, boy," he said, and he waited for a puzzled Innowen to comply. Only then did he continue. "Most folks around here who still remember will take bets that Minarik is your real father."

The mug fell from Innowen's hand.

"I can see I'm going to have to mop tomorrow," Mourn commented. "First Drushen's mug, now yours."

"That's not possible," Innowen muttered, his eyes glancing about the room like nervous moths before a flame. "The Witch had a child, a son, by Minarik. But his name is Vashni. I've seen him. He even looks like Minarik."

Merit smirked. "Haven't you looked in a mirror, boy?" He took a drink of wine and rose to his feet, nearly bumping his head on a suspended oil lamp. He touched it with one finger and set it spinning on its thong. All about the room, the shadows began to dance.

"I remember the night," Merit said solemnly. "No other pregnant woman in Shanalane was even close to delivering, the night the Witch's child was born. Her cries were terrible, and half the countryside heard her when the labor was worst. She finally gave birth just before midnight, an ill-omened time." He closed his eyes for a moment as he continued to speak. "There were other omens, too. Two barges broke loose in the river for no reason that night. A warehouse caught fire and burned the owner's two sons." He opened his eyes again and looked at them both. "I remember my father caught two fish on the same hook that day."

Innowen smacked his hand against the table with an impatient *thump*. "But what's all this got to do with Minarik being my father? Are you saying the Witch of Shanalane is my mother?"

An uncomfortable silence filled the tavern, a silence perforated only by the sputtering of the small flame in the oil lamp spinning near Merit's head. Only Mourn remained seated. He, too, backed his chair and slowly stood as they all looked at each other.

"You say you've seen the Witch's son," Merit said. They all spoke softly now, almost in whispers, aware that they uttered secrets that had been hidden for years. "Vashni, you called him. Well, I believe you, because there were lots of strange stories of a boy-child. Things like baby cries at odd hours, or childish laughter in the woods near her estate. Some people thought they heard the Witch singing lullabies sometimes late at night. But no one ever actually reported seeing the boy."

Mourn moved around the edge of the table to stand by Innowen. "I still don't see what that has to do with Innowen."

Merit let go a slow breath and folded his arms across his great wine-soaked chest. "Like I said, no other pregnant woman in the town was even close to her time when the Witch gave birth." He paused and looked directly at Innowen again. "Yet, the same night, Drushen found a newborn baby on the old east road. It couldn't move its legs at all, and somebody had left it there to die, exposed."

Innowen bit his lower lip and took a quick gulp of his wine.

"Drushen always had a bit of a soft heart," Merit continued. "And he didn't have any family here, since his parents had both died some years earlier. He left Shanalane that night with the baby, and none of us ever saw him again until he returned here five years ago."

Innowen paced back and forth, his fists tightly clenched. The palm of his left hand burned as it clamped down on the splinter buried in its flesh, but he used that pain to focus his thoughts, deliberately increasing the hurt. "It can't be!" he shouted at last. "Vashni is the Witch's son!"

"Innocent," Mourn said reasonably, using the nickname Innowen had confided to him. He held up two fingers. "Two barges. Two deaths. Two fish." He paused, and the shadows seemed suddenly to veil his face. "Two babies," he whispered. "Twins."

An icy shiver ran down Innowen's spine. A memory came into his head of three thugs beating an old man to death in a Parendur alley. One of those men had mistaken him for Vashni. He had thought it funny, then.

Mourn picked up his own wine mug and carried it around the table to refill it at the cask. "You said the baby Drushen found was malformed," he said to Merit. "Yet Innowen is whole. How could he be that baby?"

Despite the summer heat that filled the tavern, Innowen shivered again.

"I can't explain that," Merit answered, watching Innowen carefully. "But it's clear to me from all that Drushen has said, this is the child he picked up from the road that night."

"But it's not clear that I'm the Witch's child!" Innowen snapped, turning to face them. "Or Minarik's. There's still some doubt."

Merit dipped his mug to refill it again and raised it

in an unspoken toast to the shadows that hovered so near. "The doubt is no smaller," he said pointedly, "than the allowance your father gives me for Drushen's upkeep. And that's quite generous."

Innowen sat down in his chair, but he pushed the wine mug away. For all the liquor he had drunk, his head was remarkably clear. He didn't want it to be. He wanted the embrace of a thick fog around his thoughts, anything to dull and blot the visions that took form in his brain. But the wine couldn't help him tonight.

"Did Drushen tell you what happened between us?" he asked Merit in a hushed voice. "Did he say why he ran away from Whisperstone that night?"

Merit hesitated, then nodded.

"Don't blame him," Innowen said firmly. "You've got to make him understand that it wasn't his fault." He wished he could see Drushen again, talk to him. He could explain to Drushen about his dancing, about its effect on any who watched. He could make him understand. But the old man's fear was too great, and he had no wish to cause him further pain. "I'll tell you something to help him understand," Innowen said at last, "and when you've told him, tell him also that I love him, just as I always did when I was little and he took care of me. Tell him that for me, and make him believe it."

Merit and Mourn both nodded, and Innowen told them how, between the sunset and the dawn, a crippled baby could walk. When he finished his tale, he twisted the bird-shaped ring around his finger. "Now, it's more important than ever that I get home," he said.

Merit drained his mug one last time, then volunteered to make the trip to the stable to fetch Innowen's horse. As he moved toward the door, his step betrayed no hint of the quantity of wine he had consumed. Innowen followed him as far as the door and watched him disappear into the night. When he turned around, Mourn was nowhere to be seen. His friend reappeared shortly, though, bearing Innowen's sword and the two bundles he had made from the Witch's cloak and his own.

"Let's move out by the well," Mourn suggested, refusing to let Innowen carry the bundles.

The square was dark and silent. The only light came from the tavern's open door. The doors and windows of all the other shops and apartments were black, utterly lightless. No one stirred in the square; no one appeared to stir behind the shutters. It was as if the town was in rehearsal for its eventual death.

The air was too warm. Overhead, though, the pale stars shone in a cool patch of black sky. Innowen and Mourn sat down on the side of the well, and each tilted back his head to look at the stars.

"Moryn," Innowen said, breaking the silence, "you've got to get out of Shanalane. Pack what you have and leave. Leave Ispor. There's a decay eating at this land, a corruption that spreads from person to person, and thing to thing. It hasn't touched you, yet, but it will, if you stay."

Mourn looked down at his hands in his lap. "Where would I go?" he said modestly.

Leaning closer, Innowen touched his friend's shoulder and squeezed it. "Go find some stories of your own," he urged. "And lay in bed some night and tell them to a handsome stranger." He gazed around the square at the uneven line of black rooftops, gaunt against the starlit sky. Slipping one hand inside his belt, he retrieved the two gold *cymorens* he kept there. He pressed them into Mourn's hand. "These can get you a long way, if you spend them wisely."

Mourn stared at the pair of triangular coins. The

shiny metal glinted dully in the square's gloom. He closed his fist around them and craned his head back again. "As far as the stars?" he asked.

Innowen leaned over and kissed Mourn lightly. They embraced, then, speaking no more, until they heard the quiet *clip-clop* of Innowen's horse as Merit led it into the square. Innowen rose, picked up his bundles from the place where Mourn had set them, and adjusted them over his mount's withers. Next, he strapped on his sword and took the reins that Merit handed him.

"Remember," he whispered into Mourn's ear just before he mounted. "Your father walked away. So can you."

He left them in the square, taking the north road through town that Merit said would bring him to the Witch's old keep. When the last outbuildings were behind him, and night had swallowed Shanalane, the road swerved gently toward the river and followed its bank.

A few scattered pine trees rose up on either side of the river. Their feathery branches made a raspy susurrus as the wind blew through them. Off to his right, a low, ruddy moon shone through the branches like a half-closed eye that disinterestedly followed his progress. A few more nights, and it would be a full moon, and he would be in Whisperstone to share it with Rascal.

The Witch's keep rose suddenly on the opposite bank of the river. He might have missed it in the dark if he hadn't been watching for it. Its roofs were low and flat, barely visible over the wall that encircled the grounds. Innowen steered his horse across the narrow ribbon of water and up the muddy bank to the keep's once-great entrance.

The gate was a ruin. One great wooden door lay shattered on the ground as if a massive fist had smashed through it, ripped it off, and cast it down. The other hung at an unlikely angle on twisted hinges. A chill crept up Innowen's spine as he rode past them. It seemed inconceivable to him that someone had dared to vandalize the Witch's home.

Inside the gate, slender white pillars that once had lined a pebbled walkway lay broken and overturned. Black cracks in the sides of the gracefully fluted stone showed like gaping old wounds in the moonlight. In the center of the yard, a fountain was also overturned and shattered. The lawn, no doubt carefully tended at one time, had become wild with weeds and high grass. Sticking out of the thatched tangle, though, were pieces of weather-spoiled furniture too heavy for thieves to carry.

Innowen felt like an intruder as he rode across the grounds, though the place was clearly abandoned. He watched the top of the wall and the roofs; his gaze rapidly scanned every shadow, every dark nook and cranny. He should have brought a torch, he told himself. Yet, somehow, this didn't feel like a place where light would be tolerated. It was a temple to darkness and mystery, and the Witch had been its priestess.

And now, he had come, an adherent.

Something shiny lying in the grass caught his attention, and he dismounted to see what it was. Only a bent and twisted copper mirror, whose handle had been snapped off. Time and corrosion had obliterated it's once-polished surface, but a tiny spot remained stubbornly bright enough to catch the moon when he turned it in his hand.

He let it fall to the grass again. Carrying his reins in one hand, he walked toward the entrance of the main house. The pebbles on the walkway crunched conspicuously underfoot and under hoof. There was no reason to fear, he told himself.

He tied the reins around the leg of a huge, broken marble table that someone had apparently dropped from the balcony of the upper level. Like Parendur, most of the estate was of two levels, the upper supported by rows of painted columns. Here, too, the main doors had been smashed inward.

All within was darkness. He went only a few paces inside and breathed the air. It was dust and oppression. The toe of his foot stirred some unseen bit of debris, a fragment of crockery perhaps. He went no further, but stood there until his courage failed him. He retreated outside.

The moon floated just above the wall, barely enough light by which to explore the grounds. As he moved around the eastern side of the house, a sudden movement and a dark shape startled him. He jumped back, one hand clutching at the hilt of his sword, before he recognized his shadow stretched upon the wall and staring back at him from an equally frightened posture. He drew a deep breath and moved on.

He was not looking for anything. His original intent had been only to see where the Witch had lived. Now, there was a greater reason. Could it be that he had been born here? A child should have some memory of the place where it was born, but he had none. All he saw in his mind was a dark road, and that was no memory, he realized, only an image put there by his anger.

He moved past several outbuildings whose walls had been caved in. The tall weeds scratched at his legs, but he ignored the irritation, examining each ruin as closely as he could without light.

Behind the main house, he found another pathway. It, too, had once been colonnaded, but like the other path, its columns were now shattered chunks of stone. With a suddenness, he realized that no vandals had done this damage. It was too systematic, too thorough.

This was Kyrin's work. No doubt, after chasing the Witch from her home that rainy night five years ago, the new king and his men had come here and shattered her gates, pillaged her estate, seized anything that pleased them, and destroyed the rest. The townspeople would never have done this. To hear Merit talk, they had loved the Witch, thought of her as a mother and a protector. Nor would common thieves have broken down the walls, as well as the doors, of the outbuildings. Mere vandals might have broken the fountain and *some* of the columns, but not every single one.

No. Everywhere he looked now, Innowen saw Kyrin's handprint.

His hands curled into fists. He had never hated a man as he hated Kyrin. Koryan's son, or not, he was no fit ruler for Ispor. The land deserved better. Mourn and Merit, Baktus and Rarus deserved better.

But did they deserve the Witch in Kyrin's stead?

There was no reason for him to waste any more time here. There were too many questions whose answers lay at Whisperstone, and no one would keep those answers from him any longer. He went back around to the front of the estate and stood with his hands on his hips, looking up at it. Moonlight edged its points and angles, making the darkness behind its splintered doors and broken shutters seem even darker.

It was a temple, yes, he thought again, and if there had been anything to make a fire, he would have burned it all to the ground.

As he gathered his horse's reins and started back down the walkway, the wind blew across the grounds, causing the weeds to shift and rustle. He thought he heard the laugh of a child, and turned around suddenly, remembering Merit's stories. But when the wind blew again, he knew where the laughter came from. It laughed at him, the wind, as it brushed across his face like the breath of old ghosts.

Shut up, he told the wind, speaking to it, as he so often did, as if it knew his thoughts. He turned his back resolutely on the ruined estate and mounted his horse. *I know the night is passing. But I will not dance here, not on this cursed ground.*

He rode through the gates. Halfway across the Kashoki river, he stopped and slid off his horse again, and washed himself quickly in the water, before he climbed out on the opposite side. It was more than the dirt of Shanalane he wanted to wash from his body, but that would not be as easy. Nor could water accomplish the task.

Now he danced in the road, not to the wind, but to a music born of his own anger. It sang, rising from within, drowning out the rush of air and the shaking of the trees. Every line and angle and turn of his body described power; every gesture screamed.

It was a dance that shouted defiance at the squat, black structure watching in silence on the far side of the river.

CHAPTER 20

INNOWEN HAD SPENT too much time at the Witch's estate to make it all the way to Whisperstone before the sun came up. The sky was turning indigo in the east when he came upon an abandoned farmhouse and decided to wait out the day there. He tied the horse to a spoke of a broken cart wheel, which lay against the front of the house near the door, took down his bundles and the water bota that Mourn had given him, and went inside.

The house was a single bare room with a dirt floor. Not so much as a stool remained. Innowen set down his things and opened the crude shutters on the only two windows to let in the breeze. Then he leaned on the sill of the one facing east, and watched the colors of dawn spread across the sky. Just before the sun appeared over the distant horizon, he sank down with his back to the wall, put his sword across his lap, closed his eyes, and slept.

When night fell again, he drank and washed his face with the last of his water and thought about the fitful snatches of dreams he still remembered from his sleep. He was hungry, but he hadn't thought to bring food from Mourn's tavern, so he took his bundles, mounted his horse, and left the farmhouse behind.

The air was still hot, as if day were reluctant to release the earth, though darkness had come. The landscape was cragged with broken weeds and dead bushes and clumped patches of grass that sprouted sticklike from the cracked, gray soil. In every direction he looked, the land had the same texture as the skins of mummies he had seen in ancient Samyrabis.

Why not? The land was dead. Ispor was dead.

But what of Akkadi? What of the Witch's dream? Could she bring life to a dead land again?

Such were the thoughts that troubled him all the way to Whisperstone. He barely noticed when the hills became plain, and the plain became forest. Before he quite realized where he was, he rode into the village that had grown outside Whisperstone's walls.

It was early for him, but most of the villagers were already abed. This was just one more thing that set him apart from normal people, he reflected morosely. The ride had done that to him, caused him to look inward too deeply, to those places that were often better left alone.

Sometimes, when he passed a door, he heard voices. He paused in the road to listen, and rode on, feeling cold despite the heat. What might it have been like, he wondered, to never have met the Witch or Minarik, to never have left that cottage where he and Drushen had lived? What happiness might he have found in that simple life, the lives these villagers lived?

He bit his lip and made an ironic smirk. Drushen would be dead of snakebite, he reminded himself, and he would probably have starved to death. That would have been his simple life.

Watchfires burned all along the top of Whisperstone's walls, and pacing sentries moving back and forth before the flames cast giant, distorted shadows on the ground below. Innowen stopped to watch those huge, strange shapes and the tiny little men above, of which they were part. He looked over his shoulder. The moon was not yet up. The moonlight would fight the fire. Which way would the shadows go then?

He rode up to the gate.

"Who's there?" a voice called down from atop the wall.

"You know me," he answered. "I am Minarik's son."

There was a scramble on the wall and some muffled shouting. A moment later, there came a scraping of wood as a great bar was drawn back and one gate opened inward wide enough to admit him. A soldier greeted him and held out a hand to grasp the horse's bridle while four other guards closed the gate again and returned to their posts.

"Welcome home, Innocent."

Innowen blinked, at first not recognizing the soldier who addressed him. Suddenly, he smiled. "Veydon!" he said. "I didn't recognize you under that helm." He threw a leg over the horse's head, slid to the ground, and embraced his friend. "You look well. Your wound...?"

Veydon grinned and rolled his shoulder. "Healed enough to let me take a turn at watch," he said.

"But the night watch?" Innowen raised an eyebrow. "You could have pulled better duty."

Veydon clasped Innowen's arm warmly. "I knew it would be moonlight or the stars that lit your way home, Innowen. Not the sun. Rascal knew it, too. He saw you from the wall before I did. I think he sensed your coming."

Innowen glanced around the grounds. Everywhere there were tents and camps, soldiers huddled around fires, stacks of lances and weapons, barrels and carts of supplies. And shadows. Shadows everywhere.

"He's waiting for you," Veydon said.

Innowen nodded, pushing aside the awful foreboding he felt. He kissed Veydon's cheek, then took his bundles from his horse and surrendered the reins. "Don't tell anyone I'm back until morning," he said. He slipped across the crowded grounds, up the marble steps, and entered the main hall.

There was no one to take note of him as he made his way up to his rooms. He pushed the door inward quietly, closed it, and set his bundles down.

Razkili stood naked before the window, framed in the glow of the watchfires, his back to Innowen, his arms and shoulders gleaming as he anointed himself with sweet-smelling persimmon oil from a tiny jug. His right hand, dripping the rare and precious substance, rubbed languorously from his left ear, along his neck and down his chest as he turned slowly to face Innowen.

"Are you angry?" Innowen asked uncertainly.

Razkili shook his head. "You've ridden a long way," he said quietly. "You must be tired. Let me rub you."

Innowen took off his garments and his sandals and stretched out face down upon the bed. Freshly crushed mint leaves had been pressed between the sheets, and the scent rose through the thin fabric. He folded his arms and put his head down upon them to inhale the fragrance.

Razkili brought over a small table upon which sat a pitcher of wine and a single kylix for drinking. He put there also the pot of persimmon oil when he had poured a measure of it into his palm.

Neither of them spoke while Rascal worked the knots out of Innowen's neck and shoulders. Innowen closed his eyes and let the tension seep out of him, trying to keep at bay the images and memories of his journey and certain suspicions that lingered relentlessly at the edge of his consciousness. But the massage only seemed to bring them into sharper focus. When Razkili went to work on his lower back, a few tears leaked from the corners of Innowen's eyes, and when he moved down to his buttocks and thighs, Innowen began to tell everything that had happened.

"There's one more thing you should know," Rascal said when Innowen reached the end of his story. "Kyrin wants your head."

"Because of Riloosa," Innowen mumbled into the sheets. He raised up on his elbows suddenly and took a drink from the kylix. Then he held it up to Rascal's lips for him to drink, too. When Rascal took the vessel, Innowen swung his feet off the bed, rose, and went to stand by the window.

The fires on the wall had a mesmerizing quality. He folded his arms across his bare chest, leaned against the sill, and stared. "Sometimes, I feel like a ghost," he said at last when Razkili came and stood close behind him and looked out into the night with him. "Insubstantial. I see things. I know things. But I'm part of nothing. I belong to nothing."

Rascal wrapped his arms about Innowen and pressed their bodies together. "You're part of me," he said.

Innowen swallowed and leaned his head back on Rascal's shoulder. "Your eyes are right beside mine," he whispered. "We look out the same window." He swallowed again. "But what do you see when you look on the face of night?"

"You," he answered without pause. "I see you, whole

and beautiful. I see all the places we've been together, and I remember the things we've done."

Innowen gave a low chuckle. "My Rascal with the golden tongue," he said. "It was a mistake to leave you behind."

Razkili squeezed him, lifted him from the floor and shook him. "There are no mistakes in life," he answered. "Just lessons. Make sure you learn from this one."

"Ugh!" Innowen cried, struggling playfully. "Osiri philosophy at this hour!"

"Still feel insubstantial?" Rascal said in his ear as he set him down again.

Innowen grew quiet once more as he looked beyond the window at the watchfires, the tiny soldiers upon the wall, and the shadows they made. Whisperstone was full of shadows.

"Sometimes," he repeated honestly, turning serious again. "As if I can't really touch anyone or anything."

Rascal turned him around and kissed him. "I'll show you how to touch," he promised. "I will."

〖〗〖〗〖

Veydon woke Innowen by gently shaking his shoulder. He'd brought a tray with a platter of cold roast pork and bread and a mug of steaming barley broth. The sky beyond the window was bright blue, and Innowen guessed it was near noon. There was no sign of Rascal.

Veydon helped Innowen sit up, propped a cushion between his back and the headboard, and balanced the platter on his lap. Innowen looked at the food, and his mouth watered. He was famished. It surprised him, though, when Veydon lifted a warm, wet cloth from the tray and began to wash Innowen's hands.

"Are you my host, now?" Innowen teased.

Veydon nodded. "My way of saying, 'welcome home.'"

Innowen smiled and accepted Veydon's ministrations. "Have you seen Rascal?" he asked.

Veydon pushed the mug of broth into Innowen's hands. "He got up early this morning," Veydon said, sitting down on the side of the bed. "There was something he had to do, but he'll be back before evening."

"Be back?" Innowen said. "He's left Whisperstone?"

"Eat!" Veydon ordered sternly. "Don't worry about Razkili. He's all right. On the other hand, Minarik knows you've returned, and he wants to see you." He gestured at the platter. "When you're finished with that, I'll help you dress and carry you down to the Great Hall."

Innowen lifted a slice of pork to his lips, but his eyes took on a hard look. "No," he said abruptly. "Tell Minarik I'll receive him in the courtyard in the gazebo."

Veydon frowned. *"You'll receive him?"*

Innowen nodded and began to eat, ignoring the uneasy expression on Veydon's face. In no time at all, he finished the last scrap of meat and the last crust of bread. He drained the barley broth from the mug and wiped his lips.

"Now," he said, handing the platter to Veydon, who set it on the table. "I want the finest cloth you can find for my kilt wrap. If my father wants to see his son, then I'll come in a manner that befits my status." He leaned forward and grasped Veydon's arm intently, pulling him closer. "Find something for me, Veydon."

Veydon's brows narrowed as he met Innowen's gaze.

Then he pulled back a bit. "This isn't vanity, is it? I see a scheme in those eyes." He stared a moment more, then let go a sigh. "Well, let's do it properly, then." He stripped the covering sheet from Innowen and draped it over one arm while he moved the platter from the table. He spread the sheet over the table and turned back to Innowen. "First, I'll oil and scrape your skin. Then fresh oil for your hair. I don't know what's spinning around behind those eyes of yours, Innocent, but if you want to look like a prince, leave it to me." He rubbed his hands together and grinned mischievously. "Prince, hell. You'll look like the finest whore in Jeriko."

Innowen folded his arms across his chest as Veydon lifted him from the bed and set him on the table. "When did you ever see a Jeriko whore?" he said in a teasing scoff. Innowen gripped the edges of the table to keep his balance.

"Shut up," Veydon ordered, "and don't go away. I'll be right back."

Before Innowen could point out how unlikely it was that he would go anywhere, Veydon was out the door. Innowen gripped the table tighter, leaned slowly forward and looked at his legs dangling in the air over the table's edge. There was nothing to do but wait for Veydon's return. Interestingly, though, that old feeling of helplessness, which he had known so often in this very room, no longer seemed to be with him, and that made him smile.

As he sat there, he began to wonder what could have taken Rascal away from Whisperstone, but before he could give it much thought, Veydon came back with a pair of male attendants dressed in white kilts. They bore scrapers and oil pots and mirrors and perfumes and stacks of soft towels. "All right, let's get to work," Veydon said, pushing Innowen onto his back on the table. He was clearly enjoying himself. He clapped his hands, and the attendants moved to either side of Innowen, spreading their grooming utensils near Innowen's head. "I give you a crow," Veydon said to the pair. "Give me back a peacock."

The attendants bowed their heads reverently toward Veydon, then looked at each other across Innowen, who was stretched between them like a banquet feast. One of them lifted a razor and ran a thumb along its edge. "Shave him," he said, passing the razor to the other attendant without so much as a glance at Innowen. "Shave everything."

Innowen's eyes widened, and he heard Veydon's short laugh as the door closed suddenly.

Alone with Innowen, the attendants chuckled lowly. Then they were on him. They shaved away his thick, stubbly beard, clucking to themselves as they took turns dragging the razor over his face and throat. Innowen breathed a sigh of relief when they stopped there and set the tool aside to take up the oil pots. Four hands massaged olive oil into his skin. It felt wonderful, and he slowly relaxed into a languid state as they worked on him. After a time, each attendant picked up a stone scraper and scraped the oil away with short, rapid strokes, shaking the excess from the blades and rinsing them in basins of water.

When his front side was done, they flipped him over and repeated their cleansings on his other side. Not even the spaces between his toes were sacred to these two. Though they began every new movement or phase of their ministrations with an almost menacing roughness, the attendants were surprisingly gentle and thorough. When the oil was scraped away, they rubbed his flesh briskly with the towels until he tingled all over.

One of them found the remains of Razkili's persimmon oil, and they used that to make his hair shine. Next, they bound his curly locks behind his neck with a thin gold cord.

Innowen was sitting up on the table again while the two applied perfume when Veydon returned. "Look at this," he said with pride. He held up a bolt of the most beautiful blue cloth Innowen had ever seen.

"Where did you get it?" he asked with awe as he ran his fingers over the soft material, noting with admiration the subtle interweaving of silver thread among the blue, which created a startling play of light on the fabric.

"Kyrin's daughter overheard me questioning the slave who cares for Minarik's wardrobe," Veydon explained, "and she offered this." Veydon gave a little cough, and added in a lower voice, "She also sends her greeting and requests to see you at your convenience."

Innowen bit his lip thoughtfully. He had brought back a gift for Dyan, one of the four dolls, which still lay in the bundles by the door. But first, he had business with Minarik.

He wrapped his loins with a fresh loin cloth. Then, while the two attendants held him up, Veydon set about winding and draping the blue fabric over his body. Around Innowen's waist, he fastened a belt of large, linked gold circles so long that, once tight about him, a length of it still hung down across his lap to his knees. It jingled lightly every time it moved, and shimmered in the sunlight that came through the window.

"I think you're ready now," Veydon said approvingly. He turned to the attendants. "Thank you, friends. I'll see you on the wall tonight."

"Soldiers?" Innowen muttered as the two headed for the door. The two stopped, turned back toward him, looked at each other, and laughed again. Chuckling, they left without another word.

"That shaving bit was pretty good, wasn't it?" Veydon said with a smirk. "I'll carry you down to the courtyard now." He picked Innowen up with little effort. "Then I'll go find Minarik."

As they prepared to leave the room, Innowen remembered the bundles and their contents. "Wait," he said suddenly. "There's something I want."

A short time later, Innowen was waiting alone in the gazebo. An oinochoe jug full of warm red wine and two deep skyphos bowls for drinking stood on a nearby table within his reach. The greenery that once had covered the gazebo had long since died. Only dry, brown vines draped its framework now. Innowen waved a hand to drive away a fly.

It didn't take Veydon long to find the Lord of Whisperstone. When Minarik strode across the courtyard and stepped up into the gazebo, there was a look of irritation on his face. Before he said anything, though, his gaze fell on Innowen's lap and on the Witch's ruby-pommeled sword, which rested there. His jaw gaped. Then, slowly, he sank down in the seat opposite Innowen.

Minarik let out a slow breath. "It's scorchingly hot," he said, gazing away briefly before his eyes returned to the sword. "I see you found her."

Innowen regarded Minarik coolly, remembering the first time they had sat here together like this so many years ago. He twisted the bird-shaped ring on his finger, watching Minarik observe him as he did so. "I found Minowee," he answered matter-of-factly.

Minarik pursed his lips as he settled deeper into his chair. "So, you've learned her name, too." He steepled his fingers and peered at Innowen over the tips. "What else?"

Innowen had played this over and over in his mind, always keeping his answers cool, his manner smug and superior. He had achieved what Minarik himself had never managed. He had found the Witch of Shanalane.

Instead, a red rage boiled up unexpectedly inside of Innowen. He leaned forward in his chair. "You stone-hearted bastard!" he shouted with vehemence. "Why didn't you tell me you were my *real* father? Why this charade of adoption?" He pulled the ring suddenly from his finger and threw it with stinging force. A startled Minarik flung up his hands to guard his face. The ring struck him in the chest and clattered to the gazebo's wooden floor. Stunned, Minarik gazed down at the ring, but made no effort to retrieve it. He turned back to Innowen.

"It seems you learned a lot in Parendur," he said quietly.

"And more in Shanalane!" Innowen told him in a low, ugly voice as he fought for his self-control.

Minarik looked away again, then closed his eyes. "Shanalane," he murmured as if to himself. "Gods, that was such a long time ago." He sagged sideways in his seat and cradled his head in the palm of one hand. He just sat there like that for a moment while Innowen seethed. At last, Minarik pulled himself erect again.

"Minowee told me she was pregnant the same night

she told me who she really was," Minarik explained. His moment of regret or sadness or whatever it was he had felt, had passed. Once more, he was Minarik, Lord of Whisperstone, and there was no apology in his voice. "I had been sleeping with the daughter of my brother." He pointed at the sword on Innowen's lap. "She had that ruby to prove her claim. She taunted me with the damned thing. But it was proof beyond doubt that she was Koryan's first-born."

Minarik got up and poured himself a bowl of wine. Almost as an afterthought, he poured one for Innowen and pushed it toward him. "She knew what she had done. She'd known from the very beginning that I was her uncle. She laughed about it." He lifted his bowl and drank. "Sometimes, I swear I still hear her laughing." He took another quick drink. "I ran from her bedroom that night, and I never went back." He glared at Innowen, and his face was suddenly hard as stone, his words furious. "I never let myself go back, though I burned in my soul every night I was separated from her. She was my niece, yet I loved her." His lips curled back from his teeth and gums, and his hands clenched on the arms of his chair. "I loved her, Innowen!"

For a moment, Minarik's eyes unfocused, as though some waking dream had seized him. Then he relaxed and settled back into his seat once more. He let go a deep sigh. "But I meant nothing to her. I was merely the first step in her revenge against the family she thought had so grievously wronged her."

Innowen slammed his fist on his unfeeling thigh. "*Thought* had wronged her?" The dismissive tone of Minarik's final remark filled him with a red rage. "Koryan exposed her when she was born—his own child!— he left her in the open to die because she wasn't a male baby!"

Minarik gave Innowen a look that bordered on scorn. "And she did the same to you, Innocent, because you were less than perfect." Minarik waited for his words to sink in before he bent down and picked up the ring Innowen had discarded.

"When Drushen brought you here," he continued, "I couldn't face him. I was still too hurt, too angry. I had my own schemes to punish Minowee, to avenge myself on her." He waved a hand in a self-deprecating manner. "None of which I ever attempted to realize." His expression turned thoughtful for a moment. Finally, he shrugged. "I wish I could say that it wasn't so, Innowen, that I was a better man. But when I looked down at that little crippled baby in Drushen's arms, and remembered the cruel sound of her laughter, it was easy to convince myself that you weren't really my child at all."

Innowen ran his hands over the sheepskin sheath and the hilt of the Witch's sword. "You just forgot about me? Just forgot I existed at all?"

A small, wistful smile turned up the corners of Minarik's lips. "Not quite," he admitted. "When Drushen decided to stay here and raise you himself, I saw to it that the villagers in Shandisti bought their wood only from him. Didn't you ever wonder why there were no other woodcutters in these parts, why Drushen had no competition?" Minarik took a drink from his skyphos bowl. "I guaranteed his income, you might say. And though I continued to deny you were my son, I still kept an ear out in the village as to how you were doing."

Innowen's jaw ached from gnashing his teeth. "And when *did* you decide to accept me?" His voice dripped with venom. He wanted to understand, but he didn't. He hurt. He hurt so much. And, gods help him, he wanted Minarik to hurt, too. "When you found out that night that I could stand on my legs like a man, that maybe you didn't have a crippled son, after all? Damn you, that next morning must have been as frightening to you as it was to me!"

Minarik held up the ring between his fingers and looked at the sun through it. Calmly, he set it back on the table near Innowen's untouched bowl of wine. "Maybe I'm only accepting it now," he said quietly.

Innowen's right hand clenched around the Witch's sword. "You're so damned regal about it," he hissed.

Minarik gave him a look of genuine surprise. "What would you have me do, Innocent? Fall to my knees and beg forgiveness? Break down and blubber all over you, stain your pretty garment with my penitent tears? You want me to tell you how much I love you?" He shook his head wearily. "I don't know you well enough to love you," he admitted honestly, "but I'll tell you this. I respect you. I respect what you've done." He hesitated, meeting Innowen's gaze intently. "And, son, if my father had ever said that to me, nothing would ever have meant more."

Innowen couldn't form an answer. He felt too confused, too angry. The word *son* burned in his ears. He grabbed his bowl of wine and took a drink, hoping it would somehow quench the fire of anger that yet burned in his heart.

Minarik sighed. "We'll talk more," he said. "We've got a lot of talking to do, I think. But it can wait." He turned away from Innowen and stepped down from the gazebo. At the last instant, though, before he left, he stopped and turned back. His hand rested on the gazebo's framework, causing a fine brown shower of dust to fall from the dead vines.

"Will you tell me," he said softly, and there was finally a note of apology in his voice, an embarrassment that suggested he had a heart after all. His gaze fell fearfully to the Witch's sword. "Is she well?"

The breath hissed between Innowen's teeth as he jerked his head around to glare at his father. He knew exactly what Minarik meant, however subtly he tried to phrase his unsubtle question. Innowen felt the white-lacquered sheath under his hands and thought of the gleaming, sharp blade within. If he had had the use of his legs at that moment, he would have gotten up and used it to kill the monster he saw before him.

"Quite well," he answered, trembling. "Why not? She has her kingdom now. That's all she ever wanted."

A look of pain shot across Minarik's face, and Innowen knew he had drawn blood. Grimly, Minarik started to turn away. But Innowen stopped him. "Now you tell me," he shouted at his father's back. "When did you decide to use me as a weapon against my mother?"

Minarik paused without turning around. Slowly, he raised one hand and pointed toward a high window overlooking the courtyard. "I remember precisely," he answered bluntly. "It came to me your second night at Whisperstone. I was leaning in that window, watching you dance for Drushen."

Innowen paled, unable to say anything more as Minarik walked away, incapable of staunching the unexpected wound or stopping the blood that drained from his heart. He twisted in his chair and stared upward through the brown canopy of vines. So many windows in those soaring walls. How many eyes had seen him that terrible night? How many lives had he unknowingly warped with that one dance?

He seized the oinochoe jug and dashed it to bits on the wooden floor. The red wine splashed up on his legs and feet. It spread over the boards, seeped through the cracks, and ran in a thick rivulet toward the chair where Minarik had sat.

Innowen grabbed his father's ring from the table and locked it in a tight fist. With his other hand, he took up his mother's sword. He hugged them both to his chest, rocking back and forth while great sobs wracked him.

After a while, the tears passed, and he sat still. A feeling of emptiness washed over him. He hadn't told Minarik about his other son, Vashni. He would have to do that. Perhaps that would in some part heal the rift he had just made between them. He slipped the ring back on his finger, and after a while, he wept again, but they were softer tears this time, cleansing tears.

A cacophony of trumpets interrupted him. He sat up suddenly, wiped his eyes, and stared around. Those were the warning trumpets from Whisperstone's walls.

An instant later, Veydon came running into the courtyard. His face was sweating and excited. Without asking permission, he seized Innowen up in his arms.

"What's happening?" Innowen cried. He locked his arms around Veydon's neck and nearly dropped the Witch's sword as his friend bore him away from the gazebo at a fast walk. On the walls, the trumpets sounded again.

"Minarik said to bring you!" Veydon answered through ragged breaths as they entered Whisperstone and made their way toward the front hall and entrance. "Someone's coming. Someone you'll want to see."

They passed outside again and stopped on the top step in the shadow of the great doorway. The grounds were alive with scurrying soldiers who rushed to clear a space among the tents and stacks of supplies. The massive gates creaked as teams of men pushed them wide open. Villagers lined the street beyond, not cheering, but staring dumbly, uncertain of what was happening or if it concerned them, as companies of ragged soldiers rode or walked toward Whisperstone.

On the walls, the trumpets sounded again, and the soldiers there set up a cheer that spread all through the grounds. Innowen, though, saw little to cheer about. The men he saw were a pitiful looking lot. They'd been cut to pieces in some recent battle. They limped and stumbled and helped each other toward the gate, used their lances for walking sticks. The relief on their faces as they filed through the gates was marred by obvious weariness and pain. Numbers of them collapsed as soon as they were within Whisperstone's walls, and Minarik's troops rushed to their aid.

Even the slaves and servants of Whisperstone worked alongside Minarik's soldiers, clearing space, making pallets of blankets, which they had stripped from Whisperstone's beds, for the injured. Innowen spied his father working furiously among them, shouting directions, pushing barrels aside with his own hands, lending his shoulder to move a grain cart.

More and more soldiers poured through the gates, and still Innowen could not see the end of their line as it wound through the village. He wondered how

Whisperstone could possibly hold them all. There were supplies, yes, but for so many? And what of water?

"Look," Veydon said suddenly. "There he is!"

Riding through the gate on a huge black horse, bearing a wounded young soldier in his arms, came Taelyn.

CHAPTER

21

Whisperstone's Great Hall was filled to overflowing. Minarik and Kyrin sat on huge wooden chairs at one end of the room, while Taelyn and his captains crowded close together before them. Dyan sat at her father's feet, pale and subdued, a thin saffron veil covering her entire head. Also present were the captains of Minarik's personal guard and officers from those soldiers loyal to Kyrin, who had escaped with him from Parendur.

Veydon had moved quickly enough to find a chair for Innowen, and the young soldier had taken up a position just behind it. He kept a protective hand on Innowen's shoulder, and his scowl warned away any in the crowd who threatened to block Innowen's view. There were no windows in the hall, and oil lamps had to be lit. The room, already too warm, became hotter still with the presence of so many bodies, and the smell of sweat rapidly fouled the air.

Kyrin glowered, purple-faced with anger. He was not happy to see Taelyn alive. "I ordered you to hold the gate at Parendur!" he railed. "The fact that you stand before us alive is proof of your desertion!"

A general shout went up from Taelyn's officers, but Taelyn himself quieted them with a gesture. He glared with open defiance at his king. "You ordered me to hold the gate *until you got away*," he reminded everyone with a sneer. "Well, you got away, didn't you? And I fought in the front lines—that was your order, too. I survived, though, and got most of my men clear, as well. That's the real reason you're sitting there pissing in your loincloth!"

Minarik interceded, attempting to bring some order to the charged proceedings. He raised his hand, and the hall fell silent. "Finish your report," he said to his commander.

Taelyn raised the back of a hand to wipe away a stream of sweat that ran down his left cheek. "We held the Witch's mercenaries long enough for you to get beyond their sight," he explained gruffly to Minarik. "Then, we lured them in a different direction, fighting as we retreated. After we got away, I did as you instructed me—gathered the remains of the Third Army and all other armies still loyal to that." He tilted his head toward Kyrin, pointedly refusing to acknowledge him with a look. "We've fought three battles in eight days. Some of these soldiers have fought with wounds that would've killed lesser men. When their lances and swords broke, they used rocks and clubs, or they used their hands. Most of us haven't eaten in days."

Kyrin slammed an open palm on the arm of his chair. "Yet you came here to lick your wounds. Fool! You may have led my enemies right to me! Her scouts probably followed you!"

Another rumble ran through the room and quickly turned to shouts. Kyrin's officers pressed closer around Taelyn, but Taelyn's men pushed them back, and the room got very tense. Veydon moved to Innowen's side and put one hand on his sword. Dyan got to her feet and stood behind her father's chair.

Minarik stood up. "Stop it!" he ordered sternly, raising his fist. "Stop this bickering!" The room fell silent immediately, and everyone looked to the Lord of Whisperstone. Minarik turned angrily toward Kyrin.

"You're the fool here, if you think the Witch doesn't know exactly where you're hiding."

Kyrin bristled, but kept his seat. "You dare too much, Uncle," he warned, leaning on the chair arm, peering up at Minarik. "I am still king of Ispor."

"Akkadi," Innowen muttered, too softly for anyone to hear him. He glanced down at the sword on his lap. The ruby on its pommel glittered in the lamplight as it had glittered on Minowee's throat in the lightning that night so many years ago.

He felt another storm gathering now.

"You're king of nothing!" Taelyn exploded suddenly. "Without the consent of the noble families and the armies, no man can rule as Ispor's king!"

Kyrin leaped to his feet, but Taelyn was not yet done.

"Well, there are damned few of the noble families alive, and their armies, what's left of them, are out there!" He gestured beyond the room, toward the main grounds. "They fought with me to reach Whisperstone, because they knew this is where the best hope for Ispor's future lay."

Taelyn turned away from Kyrin to face Minarik. He held out his hand toward his lord. "We'll fight to save this dog's life if you ask us, Minarik. But we beg you! Take the crown yourself! Lead the armies. Ispor needs a great king, not this coward you call nephew!"

A thunder of voices filled the hall as some shouted approval and others screamed for Taelyn's head. Veydon's hand tightened on Innowen's shoulder, but Innowen's eyes were on the crowd. He noted the subtle shifting that took place as men loyal to Minarik and Taelyn surreptitiously surrounded Kyrin's officers. He gripped the hilt of the Witch's sword, ready to draw it if a fight broke out.

Minarik sat down slowly in his chair and rested his chin in his fist. That alone was enough to quiet the hall once more. The air was electric with danger. Everyone strained to hear his decision.

Kyrin spoke up, and though his voice was cold and harsh, it contained a note of desperation. "You wouldn't dare!" he challenged. "I am Koryan's son!"

Minarik looked at Kyrin with utter contempt. "Koryan!" he sneered. "Let me tell you something about my brother—your beloved father. He was little better than a pig, glutting himself on the treasures of Ispor while his people struggled to live. He cast off his first-born child because she was *inconvenient,* and after he finally had his son, he cast aside your mother when she dared to protest his rampant ruttings. Nothing with two legs was safe from Koryan, and no practice was beyond his appetites." Minarik shook his head as he scowled. "Don't invoke Koryan's name to me," he said. "You'll win no points there."

Taelyn took a step closer to Minarik. "Then you'll be our king!" he cried triumphantly, and another shout went up from his supporters.

"No," Minarik answered calmly. He glanced briefly at Innowen. "Unfit as he is to rule, I am more unfit."

Taelyn backed up again, his expression turning to disappointment, then to anger as he prepared to argue with his lord.

Minarik stopped him. "Your report is incomplete, Commander," he said curtly, reminding Taelyn of his place as he reasserted his authority.

"What can be left?" Kyrin raged. "He's led the Witch to us!"

Taelyn glanced dumbly from Kyrin to Minarik. Minarik's refusal had put him off-stride. Even his anger deserted him, and the confusion that took its place was almost saddening.

Minarik righted himself in his chair. It was

immediately obvious to everyone in the hall that it was he, not Kyrin, who was tacitly in charge, and they listened to what he said. "He didn't lead the Witch to us," he revealed coolly. "Why do you think I've been hoarding supplies? Why do you think our forges have been working day and night to turn out weapons?" He paused to let his meaning sink in. "Your sister is not the only one with scouts and spies. I've known for days of a large force gathering to the south of us, just a half-day's march away. I believe they're only waiting for the Witch to join them."

Taelyn hung his head. "We heard rumors," he admitted. "But we personally saw no sign of such a force."

"Not even the valiant Taelyn can fight in every corner of the land at once," Minarik offered generously. "But let's have no more talk of crowns. The simple fact is that Koryan's true first-born has made herself Ispor's ruler, whether we like it or not. At least for the moment. It's no crown, but right now we must fight for our lives." He turned his gaze on Kyrin and on Kyrin's officers, one by one. Then he added, "Let the survivors determine whose brow looks best in gold."

Kyrin clenched his hands at his sides and trembled with rage. Suddenly, he turned away from Minarik and stared out across the room, finding and fixing Innowen with his glare. "This is your fault!" he shouted.

The crowd moved back from Innowen and Veydon as all eyes turned his way. Innowen glanced uncertainly at his father, then lifted his head defiantly as he prepared to face Kyrin. Without a word, he reached up and gently pushed Veydon's hand from his shoulder.

Kyrin pointed a finger. "Look how he sits there with the Witch's sword in his lap!" he said, addressing the crowd. "He went to her in Parendur. That's where he's been. No doubt, he's the one who told her where we are. He's the one who betrayed us. Let him deny it!"

"I didn't have to tell her," Innowen answered calmly before the soldiers' mumblings could swell louder and force him to shout. "She could find you by the smell of your terror." The room grew deathly silent, except for a rude snort from Taelyn. "Yes, I saw her. But it concerned a matter strictly between us."

"You had the chance to kill her!" Kyrin charged. He waved a hand over those gathered in the hall. "You could have spared all our lives with a simple thrust of that blade. But you didn't! You didn't, because you're *abathakati*, like her! Look at you, a twisted little monster who only walks by night. You're not fit to sit in the company of decent men!"

Innowen kept his anger in check. He waited, letting the silence and the tension build, until he was sure everyone was looking at him. Then he spat on the floor near Kyrin's feet.

"Maybe I'm everything you say," he answered scornfully. "But I'm no coward. It's not their lives you're worried about. It's your own. You killed Koryan for his crown, and tried to blame the Witch. Now she's coming for you...." He glanced toward Taelyn, remembering something his old friend had said earlier, and a brief smile flickered over his lips. It faded as he gave his attention back to Kyrin: "...and you're pissing in your loincloth from fear."

Kyrin turned red as his rage boiled up within him. He took a step toward Innowen, raising his fists, but Taelyn made a subtle gesture, and two soldiers suddenly blocked their king's way.

Minarik rose to his feet, too, and stepped closer to Kyrin. "Innowen is my son," he said clearly for all to hear. "Not my adoptive son, but my true-born son, flesh of my flesh and blood of my blood." Minarik allowed himself a small grin at the gape-jawed expression that settled over Kyrin's face. "Yes, that makes him your nephew," Minarik added. "As you can see, he's inherited the family mouth."

Kyrin glared murderously, but it was obvious even to him that the mood of the room had turned against him. "This isn't over!" he hissed. He crooked a finger at his daughter, and she went timidly to his side, daring to cast a glance at Innowen, before her father grabbed her arm and dragged her through the crowd, which parted for them, across the room and out the door. Most of Kyrin's officers quickly followed, but a few remained nervously behind.

Minarik sat down again. "We have a battle to prepare for," he said to his soldiers. "I want the wounded moved inside Whisperstone. When the beds are full, put them on pallets in the formal rooms and the hallways. But move them off the grounds; there's too much to do, and they'll only be in the way out there."

Innowen admitted grudgingly that he was watching a man who could rule Ispor as a king should. Minarik certainly looked the part, sitting in his high-backed chair, giving orders to his assembled warriors. His voice cracked with authority, and his gaze seemed to touch each man as it roamed about the hall. The mood of the soldiers changed noticeably. No one argued or grumbled. They listened with attentiveness, almost eagerly, to the Lord of Whisperstone. They were hungry men, starved for the leadership Kyrin had denied them.

Minarik beckoned to Taelyn, and his captain stepped closer. "The villagers know and respect you," he said to Taelyn. "Tell them the village is not safe. Tell them to come inside the gates, those who will. Those who won't come should flee while they can. The young men who come must be ready to fight, and tell the women they'll have to work. We'll be cramped, but we'll find room behind our walls for as many as we can."

"What about supplies?" Taelyn asked, frowning, considering. "Can we feed everyone through a siege?"

"That will be the hard part of your task, my friend," Minarik answered. "Whether they come or not, you'll have to confiscate anything you think will be useful to us. Food, grain, any stores of water, any weapons. Those who refuse to come inside may keep one skin of water to see them on their way. No more. Take a squad of soldiers you trust to back you up."

Taelyn nodded.

Minarik looked toward Veydon. "Your job is to organize the supplies we already have and the ones Taelyn sends in. Take an inventory. I want a list and your report by morning."

One of Kyrin's officers stepped forward. "We'll need oil and wood for the watchfires," he said.

Minarik scratched his chin. "Oil is in short supply," he answered, eyeing the officer. "What is your name?"

"Sireos," the officer replied. "If I may volunteer, I'll take another squad into the village and dismantle the homes of those who leave. We might also send a couple of wagons on a quick trip into the forest."

Minarik studied Sireos coolly, taking his time to form a judgment about the man. "Wait until morning before you dismantle anything. Those are homes, not warehouses, and some people will be attached to them. Wait until the owners are clearly gone. You needn't wait on the wagons, though. Choose volunteers from among the villagers who join us; they know the forest best." He inclined his head toward Sireos without ever breaking eye contact. "Yours is a valuable suggestion. I thank you."

Sireos gave a grunt and grinned. "Hells, it looks like

my neck's on the line, too."

There was a general laugh from the soldiers at that. Then other suggestions began to fly about the room. Minarik handled them one at a time, giving each one equal consideration. Some men left immediately to begin important tasks. Taelyn was among those, but first he slipped through the crowd and came to Innowen.

He bent down and hugged Innowen about the shoulders. "Good to see you again, Innocent," he said quickly. There was a heavy weariness in his eyes where a deep tracery of lines had formed in the corners. Yet the gleam of excitement also burned there. "And you, too, Veydon. I hope we find time to talk later." He straightened, clapped Veydon's arm, and departed.

Veydon leaned forward and whispered in Innowen's ear. "I'd better take you to your room," he said. "I've got a job, too, and I'd better get started."

"Not my room," Innowen said quietly. It bothered him that there was nothing he could do to help. Not until nightfall, anyway. He put those feelings aside, however. Now was not the time to think of himself. The best he could do was keep out of the way. "Take me to the gazebo. I'll wait for Rascal there."

Veydon agreed and picked Innowen up in his arms. They made it halfway to the door, moving around the edges of the assembly, before Minarik stopped them.

"Where do you think you're going, Innowen?" Minarik called firmly, and Veydon turned so that Innowen could face his father. "My son will carry his share of the load around here, like everyone else. You may not be able to walk, but there's nothing wrong with your eyes. You'll take a shift at watch on the wall." He looked to Veydon. "See that a chair is placed at a proper post for him."

Innowen peered at his father, stunned by the

pronouncement, as he attempted to read that inscrutable face. Minarik, though, had already turned his attention to another man.

"He honors you," Veydon murmured as he carried Innowen out of the room. "It elevates you in the soldiers' eyes if he treats you no differently from anyone else. Minarik knows this."

Innowen hugged his mother's sword to his chest with one hand. "I don't object," he answered. "I'm merely surprised."

They encountered a household slave who hurried past them with a sloshing bowl of bloody water. Veydon attempted to stop him, but Innowen interrupted. "Let him go," he said. "If he's seeing after the wounded, that work is more important." They found another slave a few moments later who agreed to come after them with a suitable chair, and Innowen spent the rest of the afternoon on the wall above the main gate, where he could watch the chaos in the village, or turn and watch the slightly more organized chaos on Whisperstone's grounds.

The sun went down almost too quickly. The watchfires were lit, and when Innowen's shift was done, he walked away from his post. Even after nightfall, the preparations continued. The grounds bustled with activity. Huge, eight-foot-tall torches were planted in the earth to add light to the dozens of campfires that burned. Groups of soldiers cleaned and prepared weapons and armor. Other soldiers, working right alongside villagers, made hasty trips back and forth through the gates, hauling anything that might be useful. Innowen weaved among them, eventually made his way inside the great keep, and went to his room.

There was no indication at all that Rascal had returned. The room was exactly as Innowen had left it.

He set down his mother's sword, which he had carried all day. Then, with a sigh, he went to the window and stared outward at the flicker of the watchfires and torches and tried not to worry. Rascal could take care of himself. So what if there was an army massing out there?

He should have been hungry, but he wasn't. He poured a little of the wine that remained from the night before into a kylix and carried it back to the window without drinking. There he leaned against the sill.

He stood like that for some time, watching the scurryings of the people below, waiting for Rascal to return. Finally, he grew tired of the darkness, and he realized, too, that the kylix he held was the same one Rascal and he had shared last night. No slave had come to take it away, and no one had come around to light the lamps.

He picked up his oil lamp from where it sat on a small desk in the corner of the room and went into the hall. The lamps there blazed brilliantly. Careful not to spill the contents, he held his lamp up to one of the flames and took fire from its burning wick.

Back in his room, he placed the lamp down on the table by the bed, climbed onto the soft mattress, and leaned his back against the wall where he could see the door when it opened. Then, by the door, he noticed the two forgotten bundles where he had left them. He got up and carried them to the bed, sat down cross-legged in the middle of the mattress, and began to undo them. Each contained half of the Witch's armor and two of his dolls. He rolled the armor back up in the Witch's white cloak and pushed that bundle under the bed.

One of the dolls, a small ceramic male figurine, had broken under the weight of the breastplate. When Innowen picked it up, its carefully painted head teetered back, fell to the sheets, and rolled down between his legs. He gave a small moan as he picked it up and tried to fit it back onto the doll's body, but the break was too severe, and anyway there was another crack across the doll's left arm. Frowning, he laid the pieces carefully back on the bed and called up good memories of Shaktar, a city-state far to the east where he had bought the doll.

A wan smile parted his lips as he remembered. It seemed fitting somehow that it was the one to break. The doll was an image of *Hopit*, a minor spirit who was supposed to bring good luck to travelers. Innowen had had precious little good luck lately.

Fortunately, his two favorites remained undamaged. He picked them up, one in each hand, and his smile widened. They were incredibly ugly little creatures to look at, with their naked rag bodies made lumpy with hard bean stuffing. Their arms and legs hung limp and much too long for their small shapes, and their fingers and toes were fashioned from oddly-weighted lead pellets. Careful stitches had been sewn into the faces to cause wrinkles and folds around features which had been fashioned from cracked seeds.

The dolls had been made ugly deliberately, and as if to add insult to insult, thin bronze poles had been shoved up their tiny anuses.

Yet Innowen loved them best of all. No other dolls he had seen or collected in all his travels had fascinated him as these had. He held them up to the light.

"What in hell are those things?"

Innowen jerked around to see Rascal standing by the door, apparently healthy, not a scratch on him. There'd been no need to worry about him at all. Therefore, Innowen decided to be mad. "Well, they're not dead rats," he snapped, "so you needn't frown as if they are.

Where have you been?"

Razkili grinned and grabbed a towel from the stack Veydon's soldier-friends had left behind earlier. He rubbed his chest and armpits briskly, and the towel came away damp and filthy. He tossed it in a corner. "Preparing a present for you," he explained. "By the way, I've asked for some food to be sent up. I ran into Veydon, and he explained what's been going on." He came closer and rumpled Innowen's hair. "Can't I leave you alone for a little while without things turning crazy?"

"It's my curse," Innowen answered sarcastically, brushing the offending hand away. It was so like Rascal, Innowen thought. *He worries the hell out of me by disappearing, then tells me it's because he was making me a present!* Well, Innowen wasn't going to feel guilty about being mad. He wrinkled his nose. "Gods, you smell!"

Rascal flashed a big smile, bounced down on the bed, and took one of the ugly dolls. "The aroma of hard work in a hot sun," he replied. He squinted at the doll for a moment, then attempted a comical imitation of its tragic face.

Despite himself, Innowen almost laughed. He managed, though, to keep a straight face. He'd shown only a few of his dolls to Rascal, and never these. He'd bought them in Spyrid in a little town on the coast of the Tasmian Sea before he'd met Rascal.

"I call them my Shadowdancers," he said quietly. "They were the only dolls I bought that weren't supposed to have some magical property. They didn't make the corn grow, they didn't bring you luck, they didn't improve sexual prowess...."

Razkili put on an expression of mock disdain. "Well what good are they?" he interrupted. "Oh, I see." He held his up by its brass rod. "You stick this in a pot of dirt, set it on the window, and they scare away the flies!"

"They teach a lesson," Innowen said simply, ignoring his lover's teasing. "Look." He held up his own doll. "Wretched-looking, I admit. But look there."

He pointed beyond the foot of the bed where the doll's shadow fell on the wall. Razkili had to twist around to see as Innowen set the brass pole against his right palm and began to roll it slowly between his left fingers.

On the wall, the shadow began to turn. Its weighted arms lifted gracefully from its body. One leg lifted higher, too, as if the doll were somehow alive and in control of its limbs. Then the turn slowed, and the arms sank down, and the leg resumed its natural position. It stopped for a moment as if on the points of its toes, seeming to quiver as the oil lamp flickered subtly behind it.

Innowen rolled the metal rod between his fingers again, faster this time. The doll's shadow-arms flung up in a dramatic posture, the one heavily weighted leg lifted high, and it appeared to spin that way on the point of one toe.

By controlling the speed with which he twisted the pole, by stopping and starting it suddenly, Innowen made the shadow dance. "Now you do it with that one," he said to Razkili, indicating the other doll with a nod of his head. Rascal picked it up and began to play. Soon, there were two shadows dancing side by side.

"Don't stop," Innowen said after Razkili had gotten the hang of it. "But here's the lesson. Remember how ugly the dolls are?" From the corner of his eye, he watched Razkili nod. "Yet look how beautiful and graceful the shadows are. Which, then, is the true essence of the dolls?"

"I see!" Razkili exclaimed. His doll danced excitedly as he spun the rod in his hands. "Only their surface features are ugly, but when you understand what they really are, what they can do, and what they're capable of, they're wonderful! That's a marvelous lesson!"

"One that can be applied to people," Innowen agreed. "One that got me through a lot of years of self-doubt." He stopped his doll, cradled it in both his hands and peered into its seed-eyes. "Funny that we need a doll to teach us that, isn't it?" He looked thoughtfully at Rascal, then began to make the doll dance again. "Rather sad, too. There's one more thing that bothers me when I play with them," he added.

"What's that?" Razkili asked without looking at him, without taking his eyes from the pair of shadows on the wall as they pirouetted together.

Innowen stopped again and put his doll down on the bed. "It makes me wonder—whose hands spin us?"

Razkili made a face and put his down, also. "Did I ever tell you that you *think* too much?" he said. He turned back around on the bed, and his knee brushed against the fourth doll, which had lain ignored all this time. "What's this one do?" he asked, picking it up.

It was a slender doll, as long as Innowen's forearm, a lady, all carved from smooth, bone-white wood with a clinging sculpted dress and streaming sculpted hair. Her arms and hands were pressed against her sides in a regal, yet delicate pose. Her eyes were two tiny spots of blue paint, and her cheeks were daubed with red, as were her lips.

Innowen took the figure from him. "That's a gift for Dyan," he said. "You remember. You were with me when I bought this one in Ashmorn." He put the doll's head in his mouth and blew. A high, clear tone shivered through the air. "It's a flute. The Ashmoors believe the music their priestesses make on it brings blessings from their gods."

"I remember," Razkili said, nodding. "Speaking of

gifts, it's time you saw what I've prepared for you." He glanced toward the door and frowned. "I'm hungry, though, and I'll bet you haven't eaten, either. I asked for our meals to be sent up."

Innowen got up from the bed and placed his shadowdancers on his pillows. The doll-flute he set on the table. "I wouldn't expect things to run too smoothly around here," he warned. "No one lit our lamps, either. The servants have their hands full."

Razkili got up, too. "We'll stop in the kitchen and grab something ourselves. Let's go."

Innowen hesitated. "Are we leaving Whisperstone?" he asked, remembering that Rascal had been gone all day.

"Yes," Razkili affirmed, "but not the way you think."

"Then I'm taking a sword," Innowen said, snatching up, not his mother's blade, but the sword Baktus had given him in Parendur. He strapped it around his waist. As an afterthought, he picked up the doll-flute and thrust that into his belt as well. If they were going to the kitchens, he might find Dyan somewhere along the way.

The lower levels of Whisperstone were a marked contrast to the quiet upper levels. Nighttime had not slowed the frantic preparations for war, and people rushed about. The halls were full of strangers. One corridor was lined with cots and pallets for the wounded. Innowen thought he glimpsed Dyan on her way to the courtyard, and thought she glanced his way, too, but before he could call out to her, she hurried around a corner, and Razkili steered him down a different hallway.

The kitchen was nearly abandoned. All the cooking had been moved outside. Still, they managed to find half a loaf of bread, a few crumbs of cheese and some turnips, which they washed down with ladles of water from a bucket. It wasn't very good fare, but they laughed about it.

When their bellies were sufficiently full, Razkili led the way again. Down into the deepest levels of the keep they went, down to depths few visitors ever discovered. They took the last lamp from its niche on the wall and carried it to light their way.

At one particular door, Innowen stopped. In that room he had killed Riloosa to end the poor man's misery. He had killed again since then. Yet the Syraean's death had left a strange, bitter taste that lingered still.

Down more stairs and through dusty corridors they went. Innowen had not visited this level before, and he wondered silently what lay behind the locked doors they passed. There were mysteries to Whisperstone he had not yet explored. Apparently, Razkili had.

Recent footprints marked the soft gray pounce that covered the floor. Mysteriously, those footprints led straight to, seemingly *through*, a solid wall. Barely visible on the discolored stone was a face someone had painted there. The pigment and the once-horrible visage had faded with the years, perhaps with the centuries. It was possible, though, when Razkili held up the torch, to make out the green, twisting snakes which formed the face's hair, the razor-sharp fangs, the eyes that once had burned bright red.

"Can you imagine when this was new," Razkili commented, "coming around that corner with only a torch, not knowing it was here? It would have scared the hair off your chest."

"You don't have any hair on your chest," Innowen answered dryly. But he had traveled enough to know that was probably exactly why the face had been painted there, to scare away snoopers and prowlers.

"Minarik showed me this when I told him what I

wanted to do for you," Razkili volunteered. "Did you know Whisperstone was originally built as some kind of temple?" He moved into the corner, bent down and simultaneously pressed two bricks in the very lowest row. There came a low rumble and the grating of old chains and gears, the grind of stone on stone.

"That was ages ago," Innowen said, watching the wall slide open to expose a yawning darkness. "No one even remembers the sect, or the god they worshipped. They just disappeared."

They stepped across the track on which the massively thick wall traveled, and Razkili stopped to pull a lever that jutted up from the inner floor. The wall slid shut again.

Razkili turned and raised his lamp against the deep darkness. Its sputtering glow revealed an end to the tiled floor just a few steps beyond, and the beginning of bare packed earth. "Minarik says we may use this route whenever we like," he told Innowen, "but he asks that we disturb nothing we find here. Now stay close in the light."

They began to walk. Soon, the smooth stone walls ended, and it became clear that they were in some sort of cave. The ground sloped downward, taking them ever deeper into the earth. The blackness beyond their small lamplight was utter.

"This better be a pretty damned good gift," Innowen muttered.

The path sloped upward suddenly, but only briefly, then down at a sharper angle. For a short distance, the passage narrowed to little more than a crack, and the walls pressed in on them, forcing them to walk sideways with the earth pressing against their backs and chests. Innowen's heart thundered, and he bit his lip, but he trusted Razkili, who had come this way before, and fought down the primitive fear that gnawed at him.

"Look here," Razkili said quietly when the crack had widened a bit. He pulled Innowen into a side-chamber and played the lamplight around.

Innowen gave a short, choked cry. Rotting wooden shelves lined the chamber. Upon those shelves, skeletons and corpses half mummified from age and the cave's peculiar air lay neatly stacked and arranged with a careful, ritual precision. The skulls and faces had all been turned, a trick which had required the breaking of some necks, so that all those dark-socketed eyes stared eternally at the entrance—at Rascal and Innowen.

Innowen shivered and backed out quickly.

"Minarik says there are forty-eight such chambers," Razkili explained, joining Innowen in the passage again, "each containing the remains of forty-eight men, all laid out exactly like this one."

Innowen leaned back against the wall and rubbed his face with both his hands as he tried to get his breath and calm his racing heart. "Who were they?" he wondered aloud.

Razkili touched his arm, indicating they should continue on. "Minarik believes they were the priests who lived here—the ones who vanished—maybe the original builders of Whisperstone. The keep had no defensive wall then. That was constructed much later. He thinks the temple must have been attacked and the priests retreated into these depths."

Innowen did a quick calculation. "That would mean over two thousand priests. What kind of force could make two thousand men retreat into a hole in the ground and entomb themselves in such a grotesque manner?"

Razkili shrugged. "Only time and the gods know,"

he answered. "There are other chambers, some full of supplies that were never used. Apparently, they came down here and felt they couldn't come out again. Your father thinks they finally committed some kind of ritual suicide. It's a mystery."

The walls eventually widened further to allow easier passage, and they walked side by side. Other tunnels occasionally branched off, but Razkili pointed out the faded circles of red paint that marked the main artery.

Suddenly, the walls fell away dramatically, and the darkness before them came to life with thousands of sparkling lights. Innowen gasped and stopped, half afraid, completely awed.

They stood on the edge of a vast cavern whose ceiling dripped with thousands of jagged stalactites. The light of their small lamp, though frail and flickering, fired the embedded minerals and crystals and transformed the gloom to a mesmerizing beauty. In the center of the cavern lay a pool of shimmering black water, utterly still, smooth as a polished mirror.

Razkili led Innowen to it, and they peered into its depths. A single droplet fell from a stalactite above it, startling them as it shattered the perfect surface. But the ripples swiftly ended, and perfection restored itself.

"This is why Whisperstone's wells have never run dry," Razkili explained. "Minarik says there's an underground river that flows all the way down from the Razor Mountains. There are pools like this in several other tunnels, but none quite as lovely."

Abruptly, Razkili set down the lamp and began to remove his clothes. "I promised you I'd bathe," he reminded Innowen.

They bathed together in the icy cold water, whispering in reverent tones that echoed in the loftiness. Innowen thought it was the most beautiful place he had ever seen. He hugged himself, smiling and quivering, as he turned around and around in the water, watching the shimmering minerals. He didn't mind the gooseflesh that rose on his skin or the nearly aching hardness of his nipples. It was almost delicious that he was freezing.

With a half-open palm he launched a barrage of water at Razkili.

"Don't!" Rascal cried with alarm. "Don't! You'll drown the lamp!"

Innowen stopped himself from repeating his attack as he thought of the darkness that would greet them if the tiny flame went out. He cursed himself for engaging in such a stupid and thoughtless act, one that might have doomed them, for he saw by the look of fear on Rascal's face that their lives relied on that light.

"Sorry," he apologized. "I wasn't thinking."

"That's all right," Rascal answered nervously. "I've been this way numerous times now, but never without a light. I suddenly realized that. I don't think I could find the way out in the dark. We could wander down here forever."

They got out and dried themselves with their kilts before they wrapped them back around their waists. When they left the pool to continue through the cavern, Razkili set a faster pace, as if he were eager to stand under open sky once more. "Someday, I'll thread a rope through the main route. That way, if the light ever goes out, we can grab hold and follow it."

Innowen stopped suddenly and held up his hand for silence. "Did you hear anything?" he whispered intensely.

Razkili's brow furrowed as he listened. "Just the drops falling onto the pool back there," he suggested. "The echo can carry quite a ways."

The cavern grew narrower and narrower, becoming a mere cave again. Still, there was room for them to walk abreast, though in places they had to duck their heads to avoid the ceiling. At last, the end of the tunnel was blocked by a huge stone slab that completely sealed them from the outside.

"What now?" Innowen asked patiently.

Razkili approached the slab and ran his hand around the side of it, touching something Innowen couldn't see. Immediately there came a grinding of mechanisms and the clink of chains. The slab fell slowly forward and settled to the earth.

Innowen stared at what appeared to be an enormous staircase. But each step was as high as his waist, and each was carved with a line of unreadable characters. He recognized it as a very ancient form of the Isporan language but could not begin to read it.

"Minarik believes the priests brought their initiates or acolytes to this point. After a long, terrifying journey through the darkness, they faced these steps. On each one is written a question, he says. If they could answer the question, they rose one step. Only by answering all the questions could they reach the top and escape."

"No," Innowen said with a sudden admiring insight. "That's not quite the right interpretation. It's more subtle than that. Not a restrictive test, but an enlightening one. When all the questions were answered, all the answers understood, then they would emerge out of long darkness into light. The symbolism was important, not mere escape."

Razkili nudged him in the ribs. "Hmmmph. And you make fun of Osiri philosophers!"

They levered themselves up onto the first step and then the next. "This place is a marvel of engineering,"

Innowen commented.

Razkili agreed. "Sometimes I think we've forgotten more than we've learned. There are twenty-four steps, by the way. You might note that's half of forty-eight, the number of funeral chambers and bodies in each. Make of that what you will. But the acolyte's final test was a test of strength."

"What do you mean?" Innowen asked. He was beginning to breathe a little harder. If there were twenty-four steps, they were halfway up.

He soon found out. He could only stand in a half crouch on the final step. He ran a hand over the horizontal slab above his head and chewed his lip thoughtfully.

"There's no mechanism," Razkili called out from the step below. "At least, none anyone has found. And there's only room for one person at a time on these higher steps. Just reach up and lift it."

Looking down from the final step, Innowen frowned at his lover. "I suppose you've done this dozens of times yourself."

Rascal grinned and nodded. "You might have to strain a bit. Give it all you've got."

Innowen took a deep breath and rubbed his hands together. He set them against the slab and heaved upward. The weight proved far lighter than Razkili had led him to believe. It flew open on hidden hinges and fell back with a slam. A refreshing breeze surged in around Innowen, and the starry sky greeted him.

"You must be stronger than I thought," Rascal said, smiling at his prank.

Innowen put his hands on either side of the open hole and pulled himself out. He stood slowly and waited for Rascal to join him.

He found himself on a hilltop in the open air under

a bright night sky. The moon hung over the landscape, almost full except for a small missing splinter. It was not ground beneath his feet, but a smooth floor of square marble tiles, one of which was the slab he had pushed open. Broken columns rose, forming a neat square barrier against the rest of the world. Beyond the columns were chunks of old rubble, recently piled.

"These are the old temple ruins on Sparrow Hill," he muttered half to himself. Minarik had shown him this place while teaching him to ride years ago. "The altar used to stand here, almost where our doorway is." He stared south in the direction of Whisperstone, but he could see nothing of the keep in the far distance, not even the watchfires on its walls. "We came all that way underground!"

Three tall wooden posts stood in triangular formation in the center of the floor, perhaps ten paces from one to the other. Innowen knew they shouldn't be there. They had to have something to do with Rascal's gift then. He walked toward them curiously as Razkili climbed out of the opening to the tunnel. "Never close this," Rascal warned. "There's no ring on this side, no way to open it again. It's a long walk to Whisperstone from here."

Innowen only half listened as he examined the mysterious posts. They had been freshly cut from trees and wedged into holes pounded through the stone tiles. Ten slender wires ran from each of the posts, each attached at different heights. They joined a metal cylinder that hung suspended in the air at the center of the triangle formed by the posts. Innowen rapped it with his knuckles, eliciting a dull thunk. It was thin copper. He tried to reach up and touch the wires, but they were too high. They gave the faintest hum when the wind brushed them, like a ship's rigging in a sea breeze.

He turned slowly, examining the construction with a puzzled frown. "What is it?" he said at last.

Razkili's smile threatened to split his face in half. He moved toward the cylinder, reached up inside it, and began to pull out old cloths and hides. As he did so, the vibrating wires began to sing louder and louder in the wind, and the cylinder captured and amplified their voices until the night filled with a wild, incredible chorus. Thirty wires, each of a different length, each at a different angle to the blowing wind, each shifting tones on a fantastic scale according to the wind's intensity—what a magnificent harp it made!

He whirled toward Rascal, awash in the tumultuous sounds, the unbelievable power of the music. It tingled on his skin!

"You can dance here," Rascal said, beaming with pride. "I cleared the ruins myself while you were gone and made this place for you."

22

CHAPTER

ROBIN WAYNE BAILEY

Innowen stood right under the copper cylinder where the notes of the vibrating wires converged. He could barely hear Razkili. The music rippled on his skin, raising gooseflesh, and he threw back his head and made a slow turn, filled with the wonder of it.

He had no doubt: they could hear this wind harp in Whisperstone! He grinned slyly to himself, imagining the superstitious fear it must be causing in some of the people there. Strange music, wailing from the hills, riding the wind!

Razkili joined him under the cylinder. "It's even louder than I expected!" he shouted, trying to make himself heard. "The harder the wind blows, the louder it gets!"

"I noticed!" Innowen answered. Indeed, the wind was picking up, as if the music were summoning it. His hair snapped around his face. The wires screamed. He thought suddenly of the lantern, which Razkili had set on the ground. It was the only light they had by which to make their return through the tunnel. "Better set that inside the trap door," he suggested. Then, "Never mind, I'll do it."

He picked up the lamp. The rising wind had not yet extinguished it, but the flame danced and fluttered dangerously. Innowen carefully shielded it with his cupped hand as he carried it to the open trap, bent down as low as he could, and set it on the highest stair. He pushed it as far into a corner as he could. The flame settled down to a mere flicker in the draft, but it would be safe enough from the wind. As an afterthought, he took the doll-shaped pipe out of his waistband. If he danced, it would be a hindrance.

That brought up another question. What about Razkili? He didn't dare dance with Rascal so close. An irritated frown tugged the corners of his lips. Then a flash of anger shot through him as he realized that must have always been part of Rascal's plan. He had wanted for so long to see Innowen dance.

He turned, disappointed that Rascal would try such an obvious trick, and saw that he was not wrong. Rascal refused to look at him. He stood, instead, with his back against one of the poles, utterly submissive in his posture, with his hands crossed around the pole. At his feet lay a coil of rope.

"What are you doing?" Innowen raged, striding toward Razkili. He clenched his fists at his sides. "No! Stop that!"

Razkili pulled a piece of black silken cloth from deep in his waistband and pressed it into Innowen's hands. It was warm with the heat of Rascal's body, damp with his sweat, rich with the smell of him. His face twisted with an intensity Innowen had never seen before. "Blindfold me!" he pleaded, thrusting his hands behind the pole again. "Then tie me! Don't send me away, Innocent!" He grabbed the cloth out of Innowen's hands and wrapped it over his own eyes, knotting it tight as he shouted. "Look!" he cried. "I can't see anything. I won't see you dance. But I'll be here. I'll be near you, part of whatever you do, part of the music!"

Razkili waited for an answer, his lower lip trembling, his eyes bound shut. He pressed his head back against the pole, his body tensed, the veins in his neck, on his arms, livid and throbbing, his muscles taut. He looked like a man anticipating the lash or the ultimate pleasure of his life, unsure of which, fearing both.

The wind rushed with sudden violence over the hilltop, and when it did, the harp sent a surge of music soaring, swirling, until the world seemed made of sound, nothing but sound. Innowen felt himself melting irresistibly into the music, diffusing into the night. His body shivered, became taut, vibrated like the wires. Whether he wished it or not, flesh and bone and muscle tuned themselves to the incredible instrument Razkili had created. His heart cried to dance. His body demanded it!

Almost of their own will, his fingers loosened the belt that held his sword. The weapon slipped to the ground, the clatter drowned in the sheer power of the music.

Innowen picked up the rope. "Damn you!" he screamed. Helpless to stop himself, he twisted a loop around Rascal's hands, drawing it tight until the cord dug cruelly into the flesh of the wrists. "Damn us both!" he screamed again. Tears poured abruptly from his eyes, angry tears, frightened tears. But he could not turn back now. With brutal knots, he bound Razkili's hands, then jerked his lover's elbows back savagely. Razkili gasped and bit his lip as the rope bit deeply into his biceps.

His lips moved. "Dance!" he begged Innowen, though the wind harp drowned the words. *Dance, dance....*

Innowen put a finger on those lips to still them. Then the finger trailed slowly, tremulously down Rascal's throat, down his chest, parting rivulets of sweat that shimmered in the fine hairs of his belly. His own lips brushed against Rascal's, and a hot wild heat seared his mouth.

With a soft cry, Innowen spun away. Three swift pirouettes, arms flashing out and in, then he stopped with barely contained, explosive power and lifted his head slowly. He closed his eyes, rolled his head, and opened them again. A gasp tore from his throat, evoked by the horrible glory of the sight that greeted him.

The full moon hung in the eastern blackness, full and red as a perfect drop of blood, like an eye that had opened suddenly in the heavens. It watched him coolly.

Somehow it only fed the anger that fountained up within him. He whirled away from the moon, swinging a leg high in defiance, kicking at its solemn face. Then he pushed it from his thoughts and danced with a barbaric fury, the wind harp singing in his ears. Movement flowed from his body, strange movements he had never danced before. He surrendered himself and let the wind and music move him as it would.

What have you created, Rascal? The thought flashed through his mind as he spun beneath the copper cylinder. He arched his back, bent his knees until his head nearly touched the ground. He stared up into the darkness inside the cylinder, a darkness alive and singing. *It's made me a puppet*, he thought as he straightened and leaped toward the wires, his arms spreading like wings. *But who pulls the strings?*

He moved toward Razkili, finding a frightening beauty in the bound figure before him. Rascal's chest heaved and strained, and his breathing came in ragged, barely audible gasps. He faced Innowen, suddenly, as if, somehow, he could see through the blindfold, could see everything. Innowen felt a powerful fear, but he didn't stop. He touched Rascal, brushed his hands over Rascal's shoulders and down his arms. Rascal stiffened at the contact, the breath clutching in his throat. Innowen stared, mesmerized by the thin lines of perspiration on Rascal's cheeks. He pressed closer, swaying. Their bellies touched, then their chests, and they shared sweat. Razkili began to sway against his bonds, matching his rhythm with Innowen's, and he let go a raw sigh that burned Innowen's flesh.

The wind harp wailed like a beast in passion.

Then Razkili's blindfold slipped. He had worked it loose by rubbing his head against the pole. It slithered wetly down over his face, past his chin, down to his neck. Their eyes met. Inside, Innowen screamed, but neither of them stopped.

Rascal had schemed for this moment, hungered to see the dance. Now he became part of it. His dark eyes smoldered and flashed as Innowen put his hands on Rascal's hips and taught them how to move.

The wind danced wildly in the wires, and the harp sang with unimaginable harmonies. Innowen flung back his head and cried out, balanced on that fine line between ecstasy and pain. Unseen hands tugged at him, urged him back from Rascal, and spun him about. The music's volume sawed at his ears, compelling him to dance, driving his body wildly. Again and again, Razkili called his name, but he couldn't respond.

He whirled once more and stopped, striking a pose with dramatic precision, his arms thrust high above his head. The red moon hung in the black heavens between his hands like a huge ball. The music spun him again, and again he stopped. There was the moon, its face turned toward him, watching intently. Yet again he whirled, pivoting on the ball of one foot, three swift tight turns and a sudden, crisp stop with his arms high.

The moon began to diffuse. Red ribbons bled into the blackness of the sky, wafted eerily about in the night air, shifting slowly to the shining color of gold. The streamers swirled gracefully earthward, writhing and twisting, spiraling down to the music of the wind harp. They touched the wires, moved within and without the copper cylinder, danced on the wild wind like strips of fine silken fabric.

Innowen began to spin again, slowly, with his arms held out, his chin tight against his left shoulder. The colors spun with him, faster and faster, whirling about the cylinder, above it, then under it, until they formed a vortex of shifting, blending shapes. Each time Innowen came around, the colors' pattern grew plainer.

He tried to stop, but his legs were no longer his own. "Rascal!" he cried, and over the wind harp's surging harmonics he heard his own name in return. He tried to turn his eyes away from the thing that blossomed beneath the cylinder. Each time he turned, he looked instead to Razkili, and their frightened gazes briefly touched.

A thousand times over the years he had imagined that he could hear on the wind the voice of the Witch or her strange god. But never, since that very first night, when the Witch had spoken with the voice of the storm, commanding him to dance, never had it been more than barely perceived whisperings and murmurings in the rattle of leaves, the shifting of grasses, a pale rush of the breeze in his ear.

In the light of day and the calmer moments of the night, he had dismissed it all as the toys and tinkerings of his own romantic fancy.

But now the wind had a clearer voice, and that voice was the gigantic harp Razkili had built.

Dance with me, said the wind with words of fantastic music. *Dance away the world!*

Innowen's senses melted. He could no longer see Rascal or the red, full moon. It was not dizziness from the turning that prevented him, for his step was sure and balanced when he lunged suddenly and drew his right arm upward in a graceful, sweeping arc that bowed his back and brought his head almost to his heel. He could not perceive even the hilltop or the temple ruins. There was only the wind and the wind harp and himself and a beautiful golden-skinned partner, who mirrored his movements with delicate perfection.

They moved as one, Innowen and the shimmering being, every step exactly matched, every leap precisely measured, touching, pulling apart, coming together. Muscles and limbs extended, flesh and music made a consummate flow of lines and circles and angles. His partner lifted him on one powerful arm, and Innowen arched his body, aware of nothing but the music and the dance.

From somewhere deep inside himself, though, he found the strength to whisper, "You are Minowee's god!"

The wind surged and the harp crescendoed. *Your god,* his partner answered. They whirled toward each other, brushing chests and shoulders. The gleams of golden sweat droplets clung to Innowen, mingling with his own human sweat. *I am Khoom.*

In Parendur, he had found the Witch. Now, at last, he had found her god, to whom he owed thanks for giving him his legs. For five long years he had searched for them, and it had all come to this. "You don't look like the Witch's idol!" he gasped.

Her heart is not your heart. Khoom swept Innowen into his arms, and they whirled, faces close. A god's breath came sweet against his mouth, then a god's lips, softer than Innowen could have imagined. The light of full moons gleamed in Khoom's eyes. *She sees me in one form*, Khoom said. They spun apart until only their fingertips touched. *You see me thus. This is the essence of your heart, Innowen, of your faith.*

Innowen hardly knew what to say. Khoom was beautiful, a matchless, graceful dancer. He flowed effortlessly from lyrical extensions to movements of breathtaking, explosive power, golden muscles rippling under golden flesh, sparks of light bursting from the droplets of his sweat as a sudden turn or gesture flung them off. Innowen followed him rapturously, pushing himself beyond all his known limitations, dancing as he had never danced.

This is a dream, he thought to himself, *a fever dream.* That made him think of the Witch, and he remembered the question he had forgotten to ask her. "Why me?" he cried over the singing of the wind harp.

Khoom smiled as he danced. *Why not?* came the answer. *It is delicious irony that you are Minowee's son, and she does not know it.* A sound almost like laughter shivered through the wires and echoed away into the dark eternity.

It was true, then, Innowen realized without faltering.

The Witch was his mother. He wrapped his arms about himself and let the rolling motion of his head over his left shoulder lead the rest of his body into a slow spiral that took him down to the ground. He lay there for a brief moment, then arched his back and sat up. Khoom caught his extended hand.

Your mother saw the future in a bowl of water, Khoom said, lifting Innowen to his feet, spinning him, bending him in his arms. *You will dance away the world, my Innocent, as she foresaw.* The laughter from the wind harp came again, more powerful than before. The copper cylinder shuddered, and the wires wailed. Khoom smiled again as he pulled Innowen's face close to his own. *But not the world she thinks.*

"I don't understand!" Innowen shouted. He flung out his arms, leaping higher than should have been possible, and Khoom was there before him, eyes shining, arms wide, inviting.

You will, the god answered, *in time. You are a sweet tool, my Innocent, fashioned by my hand, and I will do fine work with you.*

Innowen felt a strange chill. "Tool?" he said, puzzled. For the first time, he faltered.

Khoom gave him a look, then spun up into the sky, turning, turning, climbing higher where Innowen could not possibly follow. Until now, they had danced as partners together. Abruptly, that ended. Khoom hung in the air, turning slowly, gracefully, on the tip of one toe, saying nothing. The movement alone mocked Innowen by reminding him of his human limitations.

A sudden pricking pain blossomed in the palm of his left hand. Innowen winced, squeezing his eyes shut briefly. When he opened them, the world he knew had returned. He found himself on the hilltop under the wind harp, standing on a marble floor with the temple ruins scattered around. He stared at his palm, at the black splinter embedded under the skin.

Behind him, Razkili screamed his name. Innowen whirled around.

Khoom stood between them. The dance was over. Innowen saw Rascal beyond Khoom's shoulder. He wanted to rush to his lover's side, but he hesitated, his gaze meeting, locking with the god's as the wind harp turned suddenly shrill.

Your mother has been a faithful worshipper, the wind proclaimed. *But a mortal cannot live forever. Even a god cannot change fate. You must take her place, Innocent. Become my priest and spread my name in this new land. My worshippers are few in Mikonos, where other gods hold sway. You will make them many here in Akkadi, and I will grow strong on their faith.*

Khoom took a step toward Innowen, but Innowen backed away, staring. What was that protrusion in the god's chest? Why had he not seen it before? There, there was another in his shoulder.

Khoom stopped, but he beckoned to Innowen. *For this, I will bestow a god's full favor upon you, Innocent. I will make you to walk in sunlight as well as in darkness, and we will dance together as we have this night. You will have power, power to beggar that which I have given the Witch, your mother.*

There was another protrusion in Khoom's right hand, and a cluster of shapes in his belly. The golden light that surrounded him began slowly to dim, making the shapes easier to see. Perhaps they had been there all along, and Innowen had been too blinded.

ROBIN WAYNE BAILEY

I require only a sacrifice to seal our bond, Khoom said. He grasped one of the shapes in his belly, pulled it free, and offered it to Innowen. It was a copper spike. He gestured toward Razkili. *There is your sacrifice*, he said, *all bound and ready to bleed. Give him to me, Innocent.*

The golden light died completely. Innowen gazed with horror at a black man-thing whose body glittered with thousands of copper nails and spikes, the embodied form of the Witch's private idol. To his utter revulsion, it lifted its arms and made a delicate pirouette, still graceful in its ugliness.

"I am no one's tool!" Innowen screamed suddenly. "Not the Witch's, not Minarik's, not yours!" He ran around Khoom to Razkili's side. His fingers trembled like frightened birds as they flew to the knots of the ropes that held Rascal. "I reject you!" he shouted as he worked. "Take back your gift. Leave me crippled. I know you truly now. I'll never serve you!"

His hands freed, Razkili snatched his sword from his sheath, but Innowen pushed his blade down before he could raise it and put himself between Rascal and Khoom.

The god laughed. *Well are you called Innocent, little mortal! You have already served me, and your service continues still, though you know it not. I will have a sacrifice, and before the night is done.*

As he spoke, Khoom's form began to waft away like streamers of black smoke. Still, the wind harp sang with his harsh words. *A god does not break faith with his priestess, so as your mother implored that you would walk, so you will, by night, as I tempered her prayer, and so long as you dance. Reject me, Innocent? You know how to do that. You've known from the first. I will not make you a cripple again. That must be your choice. I will enjoy your suffering as you struggle to make it.*

Nothing remained of Khoom's form. It was to the wind that Innowen shouted as he raised his fist. "All this misery!" he raged. "For what? Why, damn you?"

The wind screeched through the wires until the harp shuddered. *The god has dropped from the sky, my Innocent, and answered all your questions,* Khoom said scornfully. *This pitiful little play is almost ended.*

The wind died instantly. An utter stillness descended on the land, and the harp fell silent. Before Innowen could react or draw a breath, Razkili gave a wild cry and rushed at the copper cylinder. His sword smashed down with a terrible clangor, first denting, then breaching the thin metal. Again, he struck, dealing it another rent. With manic fury, he attacked the cylinder until Innowen pulled him away and wrapped him in his arms.

A random breeze skipped over the wires. Through the crushed cylinder, the wind harp made a plaintive sound, like a child mewling in the darkness.

Now Innowen had a new fear. Razkili had seen him dance. He pushed Rascal back at arm's length and looked at him closely.

Razkili drew a deep breath, folded his hands over his mouth and closed his eyes to calm himself. "It's all right," he said at last. "It's the philosopher in me, the one you're always making fun of."

"What's that?" Innowen asked softly, confused.

Razkili shook himself before he stepped back. "You're so easy to read sometimes, Innowen. I've known my darkest desire since the first moment we met." A wistful half smile parted his lips slightly. "It's you. I left my home for you. I left my family and Osirit for you. For you, I cast aside, not only my royal heritage, but the *duties* that I owed Osirit as my father's son." He swallowed, then clutched Innowen's shoulders, meeting his gaze intently. "And I don't regret any of it. I *chose* this. I *chose* you. I'd steal for you, kill for you, give you the last crumb of bread from my starving mouth. That's why I'm not afraid to watch you dance. I've faced my dark desire." He dragged Innowen closer and hugged him. "Hells, I embrace it every time I embrace you."

Innowen clung to Rascal. "I guess you're normal, all right," he whispered. "You never say a thing in three words if you can say it in thirty. I think we'd better get back to Whisperstone." But he didn't let go of Rascal. Not yet. He held him with all his might and looked up to see if there was a moon in the sky.

A pale, virginal light floated directly overhead without so much as a hint of the blood-red fashion it had worn closer to the horizon. In its glow, Innowen turned up the palm of his hand. He flexed it, made a fist, opened it.

The splinter was gone.

Yet before he could wonder at that, another light on the southern horizon caught his eye. He let go of Rascal and backed up. An odd, flickering glow, yellow-reddish, shimmered in the distance, and it grew as he watched.

"Whisperstone!" he shouted as fear clutched his heart. "It's burning!"

Razkili lifted his sword. The blade was badly bent and nicked from his attack on the cylinder. With a cry of rage, he flung it with all his might toward the glow. "I made this place for you!" he said quietly through tightly clenched teeth. "It was supposed to be a place of peace, a place where we could get away from all that madness!"

Innowen stared toward the flames, his heart racing. "It was beautiful, Rascal," Innowen told him urgently. "The wind harp was a work of art, genius, and we'll remake it someday." He backed toward the trap door in the tile floor, still watching the distant flames over Razkili's glistening bare shoulder. "But I've got to get back there. I've got to get home!"

He turned and ran to the open trap. Dropping down onto the first step, he reached for the lamp and froze. He picked up the light, shined it all around, bent lower and shined it on the next step below.

"What's wrong now?" Rascal said as he peered down through the trap. In his hand he held the sword Innowen had dropped and forgotten.

"Dyan's doll-flute," Innowen shouted back. "It's gone." He jumped down to the next step, crouched, and ran his hand along the stone surface. "Look!" he cried, pointing to a warm smear of melted tallow. "Someone was here with a candle!"

Rascal bent down from the step above him as he pulled the heavy marble tile back into place. "Well, whoever it was, they didn't come up through the trap," he said. "They must have gone back through the passage."

Innowen leaped down the steps with a renewed sense of urgency, and Razkili came swiftly after. At the bottom, he waited and gave the lamp to Rascal, who knew the way far better than he did. They exchanged few words but moved as briskly as they could, Rascal cupping one hand around the small flame to protect it.

None of the cavern's mysteries or wonders delayed them. All Innowen thought about was the fire on the horizon, and the Witch of Shanalane, and Khoom's words, *I will have a sacrifice, and before the night is done.*

At the far end of the tunnel, Razkili gave the lamp to Innowen and bent to operate the mechanism that opened the hidden door. As it eased back, Innowen spied more droplets of melted tallow on the dusty floor, more proof that someone had followed them from Whisperstone to the temple ruins.

"Who else knew about this doorway?" Innowen called behind to Razkili.

Rascal stepped quickly into the hall as the door began to rumble closed again. "Minarik," he answered, "and Veydon, who helped me with some of the wind harp's construction."

Innowen bit his lip as he hurried through the corridors to the stairs that would carry them out of the keep's subterranean levels. When they reached lighted hallways, he began to run. The lamp's wick was quickly extinguished, either by the sloshing of the oil or by the wind of his passage. They encountered no one until they reached Whisperstone's great entrance hall, which was full of wounded soldiers on cots and cloth pallets and the people who attended them.

Here, the smell of smoke hung heavy in the air. There was no sign of fire, however, nor did the busy servants and slaves appear overly concerned. Innowen set down the lamp and pulled open one of the great doors.

A crackling curtain of fire shimmered against the black sky, sending smoke and sparking ash swirling upward into the heavens. It was almost beautiful in its fury. "It's the village," Innowen said with a sense of relief as Rascal pressed into the doorway to see. "The fields, too. The Witch has set fire to them."

Hundreds of soldiers lined the top of Whisperstone's wall, some with buckets of water close at hand. Above the massive gates, a squad of Minarik's men were hard at work maneuvering huge barrels of water, which they poured over the side to wet the doors and keep the flames from them.

A cloud of gray smoke blew across the grounds. Innowen closed the door before it drifted inside. A different sense of purpose filled him. His mouth set in a determined line as he turned to Rascal. "There's nothing we can do out there," he declared. "Let's go find that flute."

Razkili resisted. "Why's that so important now?" he demanded, smacking Innowen's sheathed sword against his palm. "They could use our help out there. Suppose some of those sparks blow over the wall?"

"There are plenty of men out there!" Innowen insisted, trying to keep his voice low. He eyed the wounded nearest him and a pair of servants within earshot. "Minarik and Veydon will be out on that wall. You know that! I want to search their rooms. I have to know which of them has it."

Innowen turned away, but Razkili caught his arm and started to protest. Angrily, Innowen pulled free. "Think, damn it!" he hissed, glaring. "Whoever took that flute probably saw me dance."

Razkili squeezed his eyes shut briefly as the import of Innowen's words sank in. "They might have it on them," he said, finally.

"Maybe," Innowen agreed, "but we can find that out

after we search their rooms. I've got to know which of them has it." *Who knows what I might have awakened*, he thought fearfully. He knew Minarik's obsession. It was the Witch, of course. But what of Veydon? What was his darkest desire?

Innowen and Razkili rushed down a corridor and out into the courtyard. They were halfway across it, running for a door in the northwest corner, when a sound from the gazebo brought them up short. Another riff of music danced sweetly into the air and laughed at them.

The two men crept toward the vine-covered structure. Razkili wrapped one hand around the hilt of the sword as they peered inside.

Dyan sat motionless, unveiled, her eyes focused on something far away. The missing doll-flute at her lips, her fingers suddenly did a quick dance. Another flurry of notes issued forth. She paused again, unaware that she was observed. Suddenly, a rich music rushed out from her, and she began to sway sensuously without rising. Her loose dark hair swung over her shoulders as her eyes fluttered closed. Her piping climbed a wild scale and plummeted. The courtyard's peculiar construction caught the sound and magnified the echoes as they soared upward.

"Khoom!" Innowen cried. "He's here!" He leaped into the gazebo and snatched the pipe from Dyan's hands. Still, her fingers continued to dance, as if on an invisible instrument, while the echoes sang in time to her swaying. He caught her arms, forced them down to her sides as he called her name.

At last, her eyes snapped open. She stared into his face. Then she began to laugh. Frightened, Innowen beckoned to Razkili, who set his sword aside. They knelt down before her, each holding one of her hands as the laughter ebbed and tears started seeping from her eyes. Her dress was filthy, Innowen noted, and spots of tallow showed on the front of her hem.

"She's the one who followed us," Innowen whispered, full of concern. "She saw everything."

Razkili rubbed and patted the hand he held. "She's seen you dance before, though. You said it didn't affect her, that she didn't have any dark desires."

Innowen swallowed hard as he looked at Dyan. Her tears came in steady streams now. They rilled down her cheeks, dripped from her chin and dampened her bodice as she rocked ever so slightly and gave little shudders. She made no sound, however, none at all. Her gaze turned toward Innowen, and he saw her terrible pain.

"Gods forgive me," he murmured, shaking his head. "I should have realized before. I've been such a fool."

All of a sudden, Dyan pulled her hand free from Razkili. She leaned forward with the grace of a wounded bird, slipped her arms around Innowen and clung to him with all her might.

Innowen pressed his head into her neck and felt her tears fall on his head and face. "People change, Rascal," he said in a voice heavy with regret. "Desires change, too. These have been hard days and tumultuous times for us all. Who knows what thoughts have occupied her mind?"

Razkili stood and backed up a step. His sigh was audible. "Her thoughts have been of you," he said quietly. "She loves you, too. I haven't been unaware of it."

Innowen freed himself enough to look at Rascal over Dyan's shoulder. In a deep part of himself, he knew it was true. He had closed his eyes to it for a long time. But she must have seen him growing closer and closer to Rascal. How must she have felt?

"Look at her eye," Razkili directed.

Innowen eased Dyan back so that he could see her face. Without a lamp or candle, he hadn't noticed before. Her right eye was swollen and purple. "That must be why she veiled herself for the council this afternoon," Innowen muttered. "Only Kyrin would have dared this."

"You said something about Khoom," Razkili reminded him.

Dyan's tears had stopped. She sat on the chair limply, like a doll that some child had propped there and abandoned. Her gaze had fixed on a spot on the floor.

"I don't know," Innowen said, rubbing his eyes wearily as he rose to his feet. "I don't know. I just heard the music, and she started swaying, and all I could think about was the wind harp and my dancing." He shook his head and caressed Dyan's soft hair with the palm of his hand. "I just don't know anymore."

They were quiet for a long time. Innowen held Dyan's hand and stroked her hair while Razkili leaned against the side of the gazebo. Only the faint smell of smoke reminded him that there was another world beyond the courtyard, but he ignored it. Let others fight the fire and the Witch tonight. He had Dyan and Razkili to care for. Nothing was more important than that.

After a while, he held out one hand to Rascal. Razkili smiled weakly and interlaced his fingers with Innowen's. "Let's get her inside," Innowen whispered. "A sip of wine might help her, and some sleep. We could all use some sleep."

Together, they helped Dyan to her feet. She looked into both their faces and walked passively between them as they left the gazebo and started across the courtyard.

But suddenly, a door opened. Kyrin emerged with four of his followers. He paused when he saw them. His face contorted with anger. "Get away from her!" he ordered. He made a sharp gesture, and his men quickly surrounded them. Innowen saw Razkili glance toward the gazebo and realized he had left the sword there. They were unarmed.

"I said get away from her, damn you!" Kyrin crossed the short distance between them and drew the back of his hand across Innowen's cheek. Razkili shouted a deep-throated curse and leaped at Kyrin. Before he could strike, however, hands seized and wrestled him to the ground.

At the same time, Dyan screamed and threw herself against her father. He batted her aside with a growl, and she crumpled to the pavement. "You little bitch!" Kyrin raged. "I told you to stay away from him, but you disobeyed me!"

Innowen's face stung, but he could do nothing. He had only the doll-flute in his hand, and a sword hovered dangerously near his throat. He glanced at Razkili. Three men had him down, and their swords were out, ready for use. They only waited for Kyrin's order.

Dyan rose stiffly to her feet and glared at her father. "Leave him alone," she warned. There was nothing demure in her voice. Her eyes narrowed as she clenched her fists.

Kyrin gave a low chuckle. "Leave him alone? I

should have killed this *abathakati* bastard the first time I saw him." He turned to face Innowen. "You've mocked me once too often, boy. My uncle isn't here to protect you now." He drew his own sword and set the point of it against Innowen's chest. He had only to lean on it.

"Well, cousin," Innowen answered, putting on a contemptuous smile, meeting Kyrin's gaze unflinchingly. No matter what, he wouldn't grovel for this man's pleasure. "After Koryan, killing me should barely tweak your conscience."

Kyrin's face contorted again, but then he, too, smiled. "Believe me, boy," he murmured, "that didn't tweak my conscience at all."

Razkili struggled on the ground until the point of a sword came to rest on his throat. "Minarik will have your head!" he shouted at Kyrin.

Kyrin only grinned. "I see no reason when I leave here," he said to Innowen, "that Minarik shouldn't suffer your same fate. I should have taken care of him long ago, and his lapdog, Taelyn, as well."

The man behind Innowen tensed, and Innowen felt the cold touch of steel under his chin. "Let's get it over with before someone comes along," said a voice near his ear.

"No, Father!" Dyan hurled herself at Kyrin's feet and flung her arms around his waist. "I beg you! Let them live! I'll obey you, I swear I will! I'll do anything!"

Kyrin bent over her, lifted her chin and smiled a cold, hateful smile. "Dearest daughter," he said.

"Dearest Father," she answered. There was no sweetness in it. Abruptly, she made a sharp thrusting motion with her right arm. The smile vanished immediately from Kyrin's face. His eyes widened, and his mouth twisted in pain. He gave a choked cry of despair and staggered back. Blood spurted between his fingers as he clutched his chest. An instant later, he fell.

Dyan stood up. Her father's blood stained the front of her dress. In her right hand, she grasped the incarnedined dagger she had snatched from his belt. Her eyes gleamed with a frightening excitement. "Dearest Father," she repeated.

Kyrin's followers stared at his body. Uncertainly, they released Innowen and Razkili and sidled away from them. For a moment they lingered, unsure of their course. Then, without a word, they ran from the courtyard.

Rascal scrambled up and dashed for the sword he'd left in the gazebo. Innowen went to Dyan's side. She stared at him, grinning darkly as he pried the small blade from her stubborn grip. Suddenly, she opened her hand, surrendering the weapon to him. At the same time, she snatched back the doll-flute and hugged it to her breasts.

A cold fear seized Innowen. He thought he had seen something, something that terrified him. He caught her right hand again and pried at her fingers. "Let me see!" he urged, struggling with her. "You can keep the flute. Keep it! Just let me see your hand."

Almost shyly, she opened her hand, and Innowen gave a cry of distress. A tiny black streak showed in the fleshy part of her palm, a splinter embedded just under the skin.

Razkili came to his side at once. "What is it, Innowen? What made you cry out?"

Razkili hadn't seen; he didn't know.

Innowen showed him Dyan's palm. "Khoom has had his sacrifice," he said slowly, nodding toward Kyrin's body. "Just as he said he would."

Dyan's gaze flickered over both their faces as she gathered her dress and began to wipe the blood from her hands and the bloody prints from the flute she held so delicately. "I'm not sorry, either," she said evenly. She rose to her feet and stood, lifting her head with dignity, her face enrapt. "Khoom is a wonderful musician. Can't you hear his piping?"

She put the doll-flute to her lips and blew a gentle riff, answering a music no one else could hear.

CHAPTER 23

ROBIN WAYNE BAILEY

AS THE SUN came up, Minarik's forces waited tensely upon the high wall for an attack that never came. Above the gate, Innowen sat between Razkili and Veydon, who stood. Wisps of smoke curled up from charred timbers, all that remained of the village beyond the gate, and the wind filled the air with powdery ash. In the west, the drought-tortured forest continued to smolder and burn, but the wind had carried the flames away from Whisperstone. It would burn for a long time.

With the village gone and the few struggling crops consumed by the fire, a wide, blackened field was all that separated Whisperstone from the forest.

Taelyn paced around the rampart like a great cat, nervous, ready to fight, but lacking a foe. Minarik made sudden, brief appearances, muttered a few encouragements each time, and disappeared. His nephew's death had strangely distressed him, but the fact that the slayer had been Dyan, his niece, had distressed him more.

Among the soldiery, there was an almost tangible relief that Kyrin was dead. Most of his supporters had gone to Minarik at first light and offered him their loyalties. Taelyn had brought the crown from Kyrin's rooms, but Whisperstone's lord had pushed it aside.

For now, Innowen had thought.

The only excitement of the day came at noon. Vashni rode slowly out of the forest toward Whisperstone's gate.

The sun gleamed on the black, lacquered finish of his breastplate and greaves, on the polished metal of the round shield he carried and on the tip of his lance. The horsehair crest of his helm shifted and stirred in the breeze. His white thighs flashed against the black body of his huge warhorse. Halfway across the ashen field, he stopped. For some time, he waited, staring at the men on Whisperstone's wall. After a while, he began to pace his mount back and forth in an arrogant display.

Above the gate, an archer raised his bow, but Minarik stayed the soldier's hand.

"It's a challenge," Taelyn muttered to Minarik. "Let me answer it."

Minarik shook his head as he folded his arms over his chest. "Not yet, old friend. The Witch seeks to worry our nerves a bit by withholding battle. Let us withhold this from her."

For half the afternoon, Vashni pranced below. He called nothing, shouted no words or insults. His presence was insult enough. Minarik stayed upon the wall as long as Vashni stayed below. He kept his soldiers quiet, refused to let them taunt or mock the solitary rider, denied the archers who might have brought Vashni down with a well-placed shot. He merely watched, his eyes dark and hard.

Finally, Vashni trotted closer. The worst archer on the wall might have slain him, had Minarik allowed it. He lifted his lance and hurled it with all his might. Through the air the shaft sped. It struck the gate and quivered there as Vashni insolently turned his back and rode away into the forest.

A collective sigh rose from the soldiers on the wall. "Post a regular watch," Minarik told Taelyn. "There will be no battle today." He left the wall.

"If that black warrior comes tomorrow," Veydon swore under his breath, "I'll take the challenge."

Razkili lifted Innowen and carried him back to their rooms. Neither had slept. Neither seemed inclined to sleep. A slave came shortly after them, bearing a tray of vegetables, some cheese, and a breadloaf. He set it wordlessly on the table and left again.

While Innowen and Razkili ate, the sound of piping floated faintly in the corridor. Minarik had locked Dyan in his own quarters. Innowen, though, privately doubted any lock could hold her. He knew the power of the god she had given herself to. He shivered and set aside the crust of bread he held, no longer hungry.

"I will not dance tonight," he said quietly without looking at Razkili. Beyond their lone window, the sun made its patient way toward the west, and the clouds of night began to gather.

Rascal and Innowen curled up together on the bed, front to back, the folds and bends of their bodies matching perfectly. Rascal's arm draped across Innowen's belly, and his breath warmed the back of Innowen's neck as it slowed and steadied.

Alone, Innowen watched the coming of night, aware of the exact moment when life returned to his legs. He didn't move them. He felt Rascal's knees behind his own, his thighs against his own thighs. He felt Rascal's warmth, the pressure of his touch.

Through the stillness, the sound of Dyan's flute drifted again, light and haunting, like a piece of ghost-music. He listened to it, recalling the first time he had heard her playing as he wandered the halls of the keep, and the first time he had seen her in the courtyard. A pang touched his heart, a regret for a way not taken, or for something that never could have been.

Intermittently, the music stopped, then started again. Stopped, then started. *As if,* he thought privately, *she were holding a conversation.* He stiffened and clenched one fist in the sheets.

How easy it would have been to give himself to Khoom. If only the god hadn't asked for Razkili. *If only.* How long would it have been before Khoom twisted and bent and blackened his soul as he had his mother's?

Innowen tried to imagine a woman named Minowee separate from a woman called the Witch of Shanalane. Sadly, he failed. The Witch was what she was. No fantasy of his would ever change her. His only part was to accept or resist her.

But he had already made that choice, hadn't he? She was on one side of Whisperstone's wall with her army. He was on the other with another. But *when* had he made the choice? *Why* had he made it?

Khoom had spoken of the Witch's fate. Innowen hated the word with all its implications of helplessness. Yet he feared that some power beyond his control was driving him inexorably to confront his mother.

He slipped free of Rascal's embrace, padded across the darkened room, opened the door and went into the hallway. Dyan's music echoed more clearly there, and he paused to listen until she stopped abruptly. Then he made his way down to Whisperstone's deepest level, snatching a lamp on his way, and opened the secret door to the strange cavern as he had seen Rascal do. At the cold, clear pools, among the crystal stalagmites, he bathed, and setting aside his vow for at least one more night, he danced.

The next few days passed much the same. Each morning, Vashni rode up to the walls and pranced arrogantly within bow-shot on his huge black horse. Minarik's soldiers grumbled and muttered, but

Whisperstone's lord kept them under control and refused to answer the challenge. On the fourth day, some of the Witch's troops walked out of the forest to the edge of the burned field and watched Vashni's display. Their taunts and jeering laughter echoed sharply over the distance, and Minarik's soldiers grumbled louder.

"Let me answer his challenge," Taelyn asked his lord.

Veydon said, "Let me."

But Minarik gave no answer, just fixed his gaze beyond the forest, and everyone knew the black-armored figure below meant nothing to him. It was the Witch he was waiting for. It was as if he could see her when he gazed outward, and a haunted look stole into his eyes. He said nothing, but sometimes his lips moved and soundlessly shaped her name.

Each day, Innowen vowed he would not dance again, and each night he broke that vow. He spent less and less time on the wall and more time in his room listening to Dyan's piping. He never saw her. Minarik kept her locked away. Yet her music floated through the halls, filling the keep. It never ceased now. Day and night she played on the doll-shaped flute, sometimes softly, sometimes with notes so crisp and crackling they threatened to shatter the stones of her prison.

On the seventh day, Innowen sat on the wall above the main gate beside his father. Vashni paced below, the crest of his helm stirring in the wind, sunlight glimmering on the bronze point of his lance. The Witch's troops no longer bothered to conceal themselves at the forest's edge. Closer and closer they came, kicking dust and ash with their sandaled heels, as they minced and danced and mocked Whisperstone's soldiers, who shifted uncomfortably and impatiently at their posts, like horses straining at the bit or dogs eager to begin the hunt.

Taelyn and Veydon stood apart from the others, whispering together in close counsel as they glared at the scene below.

"She has time on her side, Father," Innowen at last said quietly.

Minarik's gaze did not waver. "She will make the first move," he answered.

Innowen felt the frustration rising within him. He pointed toward Vashni. "This is her first move!" he hissed in a tight whisper.

Minarik's mouth set in a stubborn line as he gave a bare shake of his head.

Innowen clenched his fists in his lap and gave up. There was no reasoning with Minarik. But time *was* on the Witch's side. The food supplies in Whisperstone would not last forever. And there were bodies piled in the stable—Kyrin's body, and the corpses of some soldiers who had not survived their wounds—that were beginning to stink for want of burial or burning. There were other factors, too. Minarik could not hide behind Whisperstone's walls and keep the respect of his men.

Innowen watched as Vashni launched his spear through the air. It *thunked* into the wooden gate and quivered among all the others he had placed there, one at the end of each day. *My brother*, Innowen thought to himself as Vashni rode away. *My brother*. Yet how different they were. Vashni had grown strong and powerful, arduously developed his body, and made himself a warrior. Innowen wondered if he might have had such a body had he not been born crippled and left in the road to die. *My brother*, he thought to himself again as Vashni disappeared into the forest, drawing his mother's troops after him.

He wondered if Minowee would ever attack.

Whisperstone's walls were strong, but if she had the patience, she only had to sit back and wait. Minarik's wells might hold plenty of water, but food was a different problem. With so many soldiers and villagers to feed, things would get tight very quickly.

When Vashni was gone, Minarik rose from his seat and left the wall. Razkili appeared at Innowen's side and offered to carry him away, also, but Innowen declined, preferring to watch the spectacular sunset and the great red ball that burned in the western sky. A warm wind blew a great cloud of swirling ash across the sun's waning face, and for an instant, the entire world shimmered. Innowen felt his breath catch in his throat. Then, as the wings of night folded over the earth, he lifted himself from his chair and walked away at Rascal's side.

Later, as they lay together in their rooms, they listened to the haunting music from Dyan's pipe. "I wonder if Minowee knows," Innowen whispered, "that Khoom has chosen a new priestess?"

Razkili answered in a similar whisper, the only voice they seemed to use anymore in the presence of Dyan's piping. "I wonder," Rascal said darkly, "if Khoom will answer when your mother tries to call him."

Innowen curled into the crook of Razkili's arm and twisted to look into his face. In the glow of the single lamp, Rascal's eyes gleamed. "You're thinking of Parendur," Innowen said.

Razkili dug his fingers playfully into Innowen's ribs, evoking a squeal, which made them both stop and lay still. They listened. The music continued from Minarik's chamber. They hadn't disturbed it, then, but they lowered their voices another notch, anyway.

"It's annoying when you know my thoughts," Razkili told Innowen as he drew him closer. "I was thinking of

Parendur. She didn't hesitate to attack or use her magic to smash those walls. What's she waiting for?"

Innowen shrugged. He'd pondered the same question. "Maybe she knows a siege will work."

Razkili made a rude, low-throated sound. "That's not her way."

Innowen didn't answer. He waited until Razkili fell asleep, then he slipped away to dance.

Sunrise found them on the wall again at their usual watch above the gate. Minarik's eyes were ringed with dark circles. Obviously, he hadn't slept. A handful of grain and a few crusts of bread were served to them, along with mugs of watered wine. Along the wall, the soldiers were more restless than usual. Innowen noticed it at once. Something in their bearing alerted him, and when they glanced Minarik's way, it was with a thinly veiled hostility. When Veydon appeared on the wall, he kept his distance.

"Where's Taelyn?" Minarik asked suddenly. Louder, he called the same question. "Where's Taelyn?"

No one answered Minarik. Veydon shrugged, pursed his lips, and approached his lord. "Sleeping," he said, and though he tried to hide it, a harsh note lurked just beneath the surface of his words. "He walked the watch all night."

Innowen knew at once it was a lie. He glanced at his friend, but Veydon withheld his gaze and returned to his former place without further comment. At Innowen's right side, Razkili shifted uneasily and leaned on the lance he carried.

In midmorning, Vashni rode out of the forest on his black steed. A fresh wind whipped the horsehair crest of his helm, and the sun glinted on his armor's polished finish. His lance rested casually upon his thighs as he approached. Again, Innowen tried to feel some bond of kinship as he stared down at Vashni. There was only the faintest of tugs at his heart, and he distrusted that.

Why, he wondered silently, had he not yet told Minarik that Vashni, too, was his son? Why was he withholding that? Was he protecting Minarik somehow? Or was he protecting himself? Since their conversation in the gazebo, there had been so little chance to talk with his father. At least that was an easy excuse.

At the edge of the forest, the Witch's soldiers began to appear. They sauntered out onto the field in Vashni's wake, but unlike the night-armored warrior, they stopped safely beyond bow range. Their jeering shouts, however, crossed the distance quite clearly as they brandished their swords and beat their lances against their shields.

A movement on Veydon's part caught Innowen's eye. His friend from Shandisti had drifted close again, but he bent a little at the waist as if straining to see over the wall's edge without being obvious about it. Innowen turned his attention to all the other troops lining the top of the wall. They were too quiet, their sudden tension plain to see. Minarik sensed it, too. The Lord of Whisperstone rose to his feet.

Innowen leaned forward as Vashni brought his mount to a halt. The black-armored warrior stared upward. It seemed to Innowen that Vashni looked straight at him, that even through the slitted helm, their gazes touched.

A sound shivered through the stone beneath Innowen's feet. The great beam that barred the gate scraped suddenly back. The gate swung open briefly and boomed shut. Its vibration traveled up through the stones, through his chair and into his arms on the armrests.

Minarik leaped to his feet as a tremendous cheer went up from the troops along the wall. Below, a rider raced outward from the gate, resplendent in gold helm and breastplate, on a huge white stallion. Innowen recognized that armor. He had seen it once before on Razkili.

He caught Rascal's sleeve. "Get me up!" he said. "Get me up!" Razkili bent down and encircled his waist with an arm and swept him up as if he were a baby.

Taelyn jerked hard on the reins he held in one hand. The stallion thundered to a stop, its hooves kicking clouds of dust as it tossed its head and shook its shining mane. Then it stood absolutely still.

A hush settled suddenly upon the field. Neither Minarik's troops nor the Witch's army at the forest's edge dared to utter a sound. Taelyn and Vashni faced each other over a distance of twenty paces. No breath of wind stirred, and even the sun seemed to wait upon them as they eyed each other.

Suddenly, Taelyn raised his lance high and gave a terrible shout. Vashni did the same and beat his heels against his horse's flanks to drive it forward. The two warriors charged at each other, and when the space between them was halved, Taelyn flung his lance. It flashed through the air, missing Vashni's head. At the same instant, Vashni let fly his own lance. The point narrowly missed Taelyn's head, but the heavy shaft caught him a glancing blow on the shoulder, knocking him sideways. Taelyn threw out a hand, struggling to catch his balance on the horse's bare back, but he fell anyway, crashing to the ground, and rolled frantically out of the way as Vashni rushed by.

It took a moment for Vashni to turn his mount. Taelyn leaped to his feet and ran for his lance, which jutted from the earth at a shallow angle. Vashni bore down on him, the black horse's hooves pounding furiously. Taelyn hurled himself desperately for the lance, grabbing it in both hands as he rolled forward and onto his feet. In the same motion, he flung the lance again.

Vashni's horse gave a piteous cry as the shaft sank deep into its breast. It stumbled and fell forward, and the sharp snap and splinter of wood sounded like a blast of brittle thunder. The horse screamed again as it rolled over on its own neck.

Vashni arched through the air with a dancer's skill, catching himself on his hands as he struck the ground. Unharmed, he rolled to his feet and grabbed for the sword at his waist. Taelyn's sword cleared its sheath at the same time, and the two men ran at each other.

Their blades clanged twice. Then Taelyn caught Vashni's descending wrist with his empty hand. Before Vashni could react, Taelyn's sandaled foot shot upward into his ribs. The black-armored warrior gave an audible grunt and stumbled back. Taelyn gave him no time to recover. With a shout, he rushed at Vashni, and their bronze blades clashed together in a flurry of blows.

Atop the wall, Minarik and Veydon watched side by side. "You planned this with him, didn't you!" an enraged Minarik shouted.

At first, a reluctant Veydon held his tongue. Then he unleashed the anger he'd kept in check so long. "Yes! Someone had to answer that arrogant fool's challenge. I would have ridden out today, but Taelyn took it upon himself. He claimed the right, he said, to fight for you— to wash your honor clean of this mockery!"

"My honor!" Minarik spat with savage contempt. But he turned away from Veydon and stared toward the combat. "I didn't want this!"

"You could have prevented it." Veydon's voice was cold and hard. "You could have taken up the crown and ordered him. He would have obeyed."

Vashni and Taelyn circled each other, trading ringing blows with their swords. When they crashed together bodily, Vashni's greater strength won out. Taelyn fell backward and threw himself aside as Vashni's blade sank into the dust where he had just been. Scrambling up, he swept his free hand over the loose earth. Simultaneously, Vashni stooped low. As if with the same thought, both men flung ash into the other's eyes. Blinded, both stumbled back, sputtering and wiping at their faces.

The black warrior's vision cleared first. Vashni advanced on Taelyn. The sun flashed on the bronze length of his blade as he drew back. Rubbing his eyes, Taelyn reacted much too late. With a sharp, underhanded thrust, Vashni plunged his sword upward under Taelyn's breastplate. He held it there a moment, and the two combatant's stood frozen in a fateful tableau, gazes locked.

A spasm seized Taelyn. His head sagged backward, and his sword fell from his grasp. Vashni thrust his blade in deeper, leaning on it, until it would go no farther. When he jerked it free, Taelyn sagged to his knees, clutching his bowels. Rich blood poured liberally through his hands as he looked toward the top of the wall.

Minarik let go a long, despairing wail as Vashni ripped off Taelyn's helm and clutched a handful of hair. He raised his sword, and it paused in the air to catch the light before it whistled down. Thrice Vashni chopped before Taelyn's head came free. Holding his prize, he marched slowly back and forth before the walls of Parendur while a mighty cheer went up from the ranks of the Witch's soldiers.

In a rage, Minarik rushed from the wall, calling for his horse. Several of his generals hurried after him, trying to dissuade him from a rash act, but he wouldn't listen. He flung off the robe that covered his armor as a young soldier brought his gray mare from the stables.

He threw himself upon its bare back and clutched the reins. "Give me a lance!" he shouted to the top of the wall, and someone tossed one down to him. Catching it with sure skill, he balanced it under his arm. "Open the gate!" he ordered. "Open it!" Four men hurried to obey. It was barely wide enough before he dashed through it.

"He'll be killed!" Innowen said fearfully to Razkili.

Razkili held him tightly and whispered, "Then you'd better think about what your first order will be as Whisperstone's new lord."

Vashni saw Minarik and the long point of a lance rushing toward him. Instantly, he dropped Taelyn's head and ran for his own lance, which angled up from the ground a short distance away. Dust flew up from his feet, and his arms pumped furiously. Minarik bore down on him with swift speed. Vashni reached his lance, pulled it from the earth. In one smooth motion, he turned, balanced himself and threw.

Minarik gave a cry as Vashni's point slammed through his body. A collective groan of dismay went up from the soldiers on the wall, and Innowen screamed as he watched his father fall and lay still in the dust.

Vashni hesitated, breathing hard as he stared at the fallen form. Slowly, he walked toward it, his sword in his hand. The gray mare, uncertain of what it should do, snorted and trotted out of his way. Vashni picked up his lance. The point gleamed, red with Minarik's blood. He cast it down again and knelt beside the fallen lord of Whisperstone. Vashni paused to remove his own black-lacquered helm, and he set it down by Minarik's body. Then, tangling one hand in Minarik's hair, he raised his sword.

Minarik's eyes snapped suddenly open. Before Vashni could react, he twisted and struck, plunging a concealed dagger deep into Vashni's neck. The black knight leaped up and stumbled back, blood gurgling from the wound and rushing down over his armor. With one hand he tried uselessly to stanch the flow as he watched Minarik rise.

A new, jubilant cry of triumph went up from the soldiers on the wall. But Innowen was not so joyous. At first, he'd thought his father had faked it all, but the crimson stain on his side was real.

Minarik took the sword from Vashni's numb grip and clutched it in both his hands. An almost pathetic fear filled Vashni's eyes, but he stood rooted to the spot, waiting for the blow, unable to run. Minarik made a show of drawing back. The muscles in his arms and shoulders corded as he widened his stance. The blade flashed, and a spray of red fountained. Vashni never made a sound. Minarik struck twice more before the body hit the ground. Then he stood over it, glaring. His rage had not yet abated. Like a madman, he raised the sword and swung it down with all his might, hacking Vashni's corpse to pieces while tumultuous shouts of approval rose from the wall and angry cries issued from the Witch's troops.

I never told him, Innowen thought. A deep sadness replaced the terror that had filled him a moment before. He averted his eyes from the butchery, unable to watch. *It's his own son he's just killed, and he doesn't know it. His son. Now, he must never know.* He wondered, was this why he hadn't told Minarik? Had he sensed this coming tragedy? He gripped Razkili's arm with a trembling hand.

Abruptly, the cries from the far side of the field grew louder and more savage. The Witch's troops rushed suddenly forward. At the same time, the great gates of Whisperstone flung back, and a force led by Veydon charged out to surround Minarik. Archers on the wall let fly their shafts, and the air whistled with the whirling of slings.

There was no order to the chaos. The clash of weapons and battlecries and moans made a terrible music, and the sound of it filled Innowen's ears. More men poured out through the gate to join the battle. A cavalry troop charged out of the forest. Warriors fell, and the earth gorged itself on blood. A cloud of dust and ash floated up and hung over the field as if it were a pall. Even the unarmed villagers under Minarik's protection rushed out to join the fray, seizing up the weapons of the fallen, wielding them with unskilled fury.

Innowen watched as Veydon and a circle of men worked their way backward toward Whisperstone's gate, ruthlessly cutting down all who tried to stop them. Two men had Minarik's arms around their shoulders, and they half dragged him to safety inside.

"I'll carry you down to him," Razkili said with a strange quietness.

Innowen tried to read Rascal's face. Usually, he knew what the other was thinking, but not this time. Razkili's jaw was set, the muscles in his cheek clenched until they showed through the skin. "Are you going out there?" Innowen asked with some trepidation.

Rascal shook his head as he bore Innowen down a narrow flight of stone steps. A soldier running past nearly knocked them down. "I've had enough of fighting," he said grimly. "My only thought now is to protect you. I'm beginning to wonder if I can do that in this country of the damned."

They couldn't get close to Minarik. His generals and physicians quickly surrounded him, lifted him on blankets and carried him into Whisperstone. Veydon lifted his helm and wiped sweat from his brow as he watched his lord borne away. He turned toward Innowen and Razkili. Blood covered both his arms and the sword in his hand.

"How bad?" Innowen asked.

Veydon frowned and shrugged. "The spear pierced his side. If they keep the wound clean, and there's no infection, he might live." He pushed his hair back with one hand, set his helm back on his head, and fastened the chin strap.

"Stop," Innowen said suddenly. "Go back on the wall. Sound the order to disengage."

Veydon stared. "What?"

"Disengage!" Innowen ordered forcefully. "Look out the gate, man! Even the villagers are fighting. It may look good right now, but that's not even a fourth of the Witch's army. If they come at us full strength we can't afford to be caught out there. Now call them back!"

Veydon snarled, but he knew the truth of Innowen's words. He hurried to obey, climbing the steps two at a time to seek out a trumpeter above.

"Not bad for your first order, my lord," Razkili said sullenly as he watched Veydon go.

"Minarik isn't dead yet!" Innowen snapped. "Don't call me *lord*. Someone's got to be sensible, though. Damn his generals! They should be out here giving the orders, not inside holding his hand!"

"The privileges of rank," Rascal muttered, "always include the safest, farthest retreat from the actual fighting."

It was Innowen's turn to snarl. "Then carry me back up so I can see what's going on. This day is far from over."

A blast of trumpets rang out from atop the wall, three long ascending notes repeated over and over. Down below, the villagers looked around in confusion until they saw Minarik's troops break off, one by one, and make their way toward the keep. The Witch's warriors fought after them, but archers and slingmen atop the wall drove them back.

Innowen watched with an odd sense of detachment as his father's people surged inside and his mother's soldiers withdrew to the concealment of the forest. He scanned the field. It was littered with the bodies of men and horses. There was no trace of Vashni's body, though. He would have recognized the black armor. No doubt his comrades had carried it away for a decent funeral.

Razkili set him down in Minarik's high-backed chair. Below, though he could not see them, the courtyard rang with the excited voices of his soldiers and the villagers as they celebrated what they, no doubt, considered a victory. He could see no victor. Yes, they had rescued Minarik. But they had lost Taelyn and lots of other worthy men, and despite Veydon's optimism, Minarik might still die if his wound infected.

No, he could see nothing to celebrate. He rested his chin heavily in his hand as the great doors of the gate below boomed closed and the bar scraped home. A wind swept across the field and blew away the pall of dust. The wind seemed to whisper something as it passed, but he could not understand its words.

"I am half sick of shadows," he murmured to himself as a cloud crossed the face of the sun.

CHAPTER

24

Innowen entered the courtyard and walked toward the gazebo where Razkili waited for him. He wore his mother's golden armor and the white cloak he had stolen from her. The light from four tall torches that lit the courtyard shimmered and danced on the breastplate and greaves and arm braces. He carried her helm tucked under one arm. On a belt around his waist, he wore her sword in its white-lacquered sheath.

Razkili sat on a bench near the gazebo. He leaned forward, his elbows on his knees, as he twirled a cup of wine between his hands. His eyes were closed, his lips slightly parted. Innowen approached him quietly.

"Rascal?"

Razkili sat up with a start. "Innowen," he responded. "I didn't hear you." He looked up toward a particular window high above. "I was listening to her music."

Lost in his own thoughts, Innowen had barely noticed Dyan's piping. It floated on the night wind, sweeter and softer than he had ever heard it before. There was a sadness to it, a melancholy that made him forget briefly where he was, what was happening around him.

"What will Minarik do with her?" Razkili said suddenly as he rose to stand beside Innowen.

Innowen shook his head. "He has many options. She saved our lives, but she killed her father and Ispor's king."

Razkili gazed back up at the window. A single light

burned in the room beyond it, and Dyan's shadow swayed back and forth in rhythm with her music. "I never wanted any harm to come to her," Razkili said.

Innowen looked at him. "What do you mean?"

Razkili looked away, then took a sip of his wine. "I knew how she felt about you," he answered at last. He gave a shrug of his shoulders. "I was jealous."

Despite the seriousness of the admission, a small grin turned up the corners of Innowen's mouth. "You never said anything about it," he said softly.

Rascal shrugged again. "What was there to say?" He stared back at the window and the shadow of the piper. The wan lamplight flickered as if in a draft. "Now, I'm afraid for her."

"I'm afraid for all of us," Innowen confessed. He took the cup from Razkili's hand and sipped the wine. "The Witch will come tonight. I feel it in the air, somehow, as surely as I feel this vessel in my hand. She'll come tonight to avenge Vashni."

For the first time, Razkili seemed to notice the armor Innowen wore. He ran his eye up and down it appraisingly and folded his arms over his chest. "You've told Minarik?"

Innowen nodded. "I didn't want to," he said. "He can barely walk with his wound, but he's already on the wall, watching and waiting." He hesitated, handing the winecup back to Razkili, who set it down on the bench. "When one of the physicians tried to stop him, Minarik nearly killed the poor fool."

"He hates the Witch that much," Rascal said, "that he would risk bleeding to death to see her."

Innowen bit his lip. "Or loves her that much. Who knows? Love and hate. After so long, maybe they've become the same thing to him."

Razkili adjusted his own sword on his hip, and they walked across the courtyard, their sandaled heels ringing on the paving stones. Suddenly, Rascal halted and caught Innowen's shoulder. "The music," he said quietly. "It's stopped."

They both stared back at the lit window above, then at each other. Without another word, they walked through Whisperstone and out across the crowded grounds where soldiers huddled around campfires sharpening weapons or polishing armor or grabbing a hasty meal of barley broth and bread prepared by the women. Upon the wall, twice the usual number of men stood watch. Bundles of arrows were stacked everywhere, and stones were piled high for the slingmen.

The moon, no longer perfectly full, but still quite bright, cast a pale wash over the blackened field. During the afternoon, a squad of soldiers had ventured beyond the gate to gather the bodies of their comrades and to collect weapons and usable pieces of armor from the fallen enemy. The ground, however, was still littered with numerous corpses.

The forest beyond the field was silent. The moon dusted the tops of the trees with silver, and the breeze caused the leaves to ripple like the surface of the sea.

The soldiers turned to acknowledge Innowen as he passed them at their posts. By seizing command earlier in the day, he had somehow risen in their regard. Before, they had avoided or tolerated him for Minarik's sake, sometimes eyeing him suspiciously, aware of his strange curse. More than once he had heard the half-whispered word, *abathakati*, behind his back. That had all changed. Now they nodded to him. A few greeted him by name.

His father sat stiffly in his high-backed chair above the main gate. He wore no armor, just a kilt and a thin cloak. Even in the torchlight, his face was pale and drawn, and droplets of sweat beaded his brow. A swath of bandages enwrapped his middle, and he kept one hand pressed over the wound. Veydon stood behind him with a couple of pillows under one arm. He just shrugged and shook his head when he saw Innowen, indicating Minarik had refused such comforts.

The Lord of Whisperstone turned his head ever so slightly toward Veydon and dismissed him with a gesture. Razkili drew off a few paces as well, following his spear-mate.

When he and Innowen were alone, Minarik stared back toward the dark forest. "Do you feel her?" he said to his son. "She's coming. The night tingles with her presence."

There was a strange quality in Minarik's voice that frightened Innowen. He set his helm aside as he knelt at his father's right side and touched his arm. "Maybe we can stop this, Father," he said earnestly. "Give her Kyrin's body. When she sees that he's dead, perhaps she'll be satisfied."

He didn't believe it even as the words tumbled from his mouth. Vashni was dead. Minarik had hacked him to pieces. The Witch wouldn't stop now until the last stone of the keep was cracked asunder.

Minarik covered Innowen's hand with his own and leaned close to his son. Pain reflected in Minarik's eyes, and he winced as he settled himself. With a frown, Innowen reached up and snatched one of the pillows from Veydon and thrust it down between the arm of the chair and his father's side, prepared to stifle any protest from his father. Instead, Minarik smiled tolerantly.

"Should I give her Kyrin's crown, as well, and let her rule Ispor, my son?" Minarik asked pointedly. "Should I deliver our country into the hands of this woman who has torn it apart with mercenary armies and rebels? How many villages has she destroyed, Innowen? How many farms and homes has she burned?"

Innowen bit his lip as he squeezed his father's arm affectionately. He feared suddenly that nothing could stop the Witch, that Whisperstone would be crushed, and with it, his father. He feared losing what he had only so recently found.

"Was Kyrin a better ruler?" Innowen asked stubbornly. "Ispor suffered under his heavy hand, father. He tilled the ground and sowed the seeds of rebellion himself. He burned his own share of villages. Don't defend him."

Minarik snorted and sagged back into his chair. "Defend him?" he sneered. "He murdered my brother— his father. What a family we are!"

Innowen clenched his father's arm with both hands and leaned forward intently. "Then try to stop this!" he appealed. "What's a crown, but a piece of metal. Minowee is my mother, and you're my father!"

A long sigh slid from Minarik's lips, and he clutched gently at his wound. "And you're caught in the middle," the lord admitted. He stared out again at the forest. The leaves, dusted with moonlight, rippled in the breeze. "My poor Innocent," he said sorrowfully, "a crown is more than mere metal. It is a symbol of responsibility. A king must be responsible for the well-being of the weak and the less fortunate. That's the responsibility our family has carried for many years now." He closed his eyes briefly as a spasm of pain shook him, but he waved off any assistance.

"I can't give that crown to your mother," he said when the pain had passed. He cast a glance to either side, as if to assure himself they were still alone. "I loved her once. You know that. I loved her with all my heart and soul—gods forgive me—even after I discovered who she was. But I had to tear myself away." He swallowed, then tried to sit up straighter in the chair. He turned his head again to meet Innowen's gaze. "She's evil, Innowen. Even the good she does has a dark side, and that darkness always comes to the fore. She's not in control of her power. Her power controls her."

Innowen felt Razkili's hand suddenly on his shoulder. Despite their whispering, he could see by the look in Rascal's eyes that he had overheard, and he knew what his lover was thinking. The Witch had made him to walk, yes, and made him to dance. Once, that had been his most fervent wish, to dance. But he knew, too well, the dark side of that. Razkili knew it, too.

Minarik stared at Razkili for a moment, as if resenting the intrusion. Innowen, however, drew strength from that touch. He caught Rascal's hand and squeezed it, refusing to let him withdraw again.

Minarik shrugged. At last he continued. "I can't surrender Ispor into her hands," he said grimly. "I am not king, but I'm the son and brother of kings, and I'm responsible for my people. Think of them, Innowen." He directed his gaze outward again, while the wind rumpled his hair. He sat up straight, and the pain seemed to vanish abruptly from his features. When next he spoke, there was no weakness in his voice. "Reflect on your own life, and think of them."

Veydon interrupted suddenly to direct their attention toward the forest where a line of torches moved among the trees. Silently, the Witch's soldiers emerged and took up formation on the field. The torchlight glittered on helms and greaves and breastplates, on lance points and swords and the metal rims of shields, and there was a terrible beauty to it. Innowen could not count the men. At a guess, they were five times Minarik's force.

"It begins," Minarik murmured. "The final act."

Veydon raised his right arm and cut a sharp arc through the air. The trumpeter blew a single blast. At that signal, every archer and slingman in the keep took a place along the wall. Inside the grounds below, soldiers, never far from their horses, mounted and armed themselves with lances while footmen with swords formed ranks behind the main gate. The doors to Whisperstone slammed closed, sealing in the women and children from the village.

Innowen clutched his father's shoulder with one hand and bit his lip. With his wound, Minarik could be of little help on the wall, but Innowen knew better than to suggest that he withdraw. Instead, he walked a few paces away, begged a shield from another warrior, and pressed it upon his father. "Use this as best you can," he said.

"What are they waiting for?" Razkili muttered impatiently.

Before Innowen could answer, Minarik spoke up. "Their queen," he said with lofty sarcasm.

Until now, the Witch's troops had formed ranks with deliberate silence. Abruptly, the front line brought up their shields and began to beat their lances on them with a steady cadence. The other soldiers picked it up, beating swords against shields or breastplates, the tips of bows against greaves, arm bracers against arm bracers until the forest and the field and the night rattled with the sound.

Innowen felt his heart suddenly quicken to match the percussion. The rhythm called him with an infectious urging. His right hand thumped in tempo on the back of Minarik's chair while his left clenched and unclenched. He listened, drawn in by the persistent beating, until the sound of it took a familiar form and became a great heart throbbing, pulsing in the darkness.

The realization snapped him out of its spell. He glanced self-consciously at Razkili and Veydon. Apparently, they had not been affected. But he hadn't imagined it. The rhythm was the same as that of a human heart. He felt it again as it tried to seize hold of him.

A bolt of crackling power shot across the heavens, fracturing the black, cloudless sky. Innowen felt the hair rise on his body as he clutched at Rascal and gripped the back of Minarik's chair. All along the wall, soldiers screamed and threw up hands to protect their eyes from the sudden white fury.

Thunderblast followed on the downbeat of the cadence set by the Witch's forces. Unbroken, the rhythm continued. Lance and sword banged on shield, on greaves. Hands clapped. Feet stamped the earth.

Again, lightning split open the darkness, and a searing tongue of white fire licked down at Whisperstone. Minarik's soldiers cried out in fear. Someone stumbled backward, tripped, and fell among the soldiers clustered below. Another threw down his bow and jumped.

Just as before, the thunderblast followed on the downbeat of the strange cadence. Innowen felt a sharp pressure in his ears, and for an instant it seemed as if a giant, invisible hand was trying to crush his chest.

Chaos spread through Minarik's soldiers, both on the wall and on the ground, but the Witch's troops never broke their unholy rhythm.

A moan from his father made Innowen forget his fear. Minarik slumped over the arm of his chair. A growing red stain seeped through the bandage around his waist. He grabbed the pillow Veydon had discarded and propped up his father. Minarik's eyes focused on Innowen's. They were filled with the glaze of pain, but there was fear there, too.

"We are lost," Minarik whispered unevenly, his hand falling on Innowen's shoulder as he tried to right himself in his chair. "We can't fight her magic."

Razkili dropped to his knees beside them. "Break up the rhythm," he suggested.

Innowen stared at his lover. It shouldn't have surprised him that Rascal had noted the connection between the lightning and the shield-beating. Still, it took him a moment to grasp what Razkili had suggested. He leaped up, snatching the shield he had earlier given to Minarik, and drew his mother's sword.

Innowen hesitated only a moment, listening again to the heartbeat rhythm from across the field. Then he slammed the flat of his blade against the shield's face, creating a deliberate counter-rhythm. Razkili drew his own sword, grabbed a shield from the nearest man, and followed Innowen's lead. Veydon, too, understood and began to beat his metal arm bracer against his breastplate as he rushed along the wall urging others to do the same. One by one, on the wall and down inside the grounds Minarik's soldiers took up the new rhythm. Minarik pounded his open palm weakly on the arm of his chair.

Innowen turned again, facing the Witch's troops, as

he raised sword and shield high over his head and crashed them together. He couldn't hear the heartbeat rhythm anymore over the din from his own side, but he could see the steady, unceasing movement of spears and lances in the front ranks.

Suddenly, the entire sky flashed. For one searing instant, night became bright noonday. Innowen felt as if his flesh took fire as he fell to his knees, his scream lost in the tumult of screams around him. He struggled to rise, but his limbs flopped about uselessly until the burning sensation began to ebb.

"Well, that didn't work," he muttered in disgust.

The resultant thunder shook the wall itself, but Minarik sprang to his feet, pointing. "There she is!" he shouted with surprising power and vehemence. He staggered to the edge of the wall, clutching his side, and thrust his finger out a second time. "There she is!"

Razkili and Veydon both helped Innowen to his feet, causing him to wonder if he had somehow borne the brunt of the last bolt, but a quick glance around the wall convinced him that wasn't so. Some were still down, eerily twitching and jerking, creating new and equally ineffective rhythms as limbs and armor scraped upon the stone.

Innowen gazed outward, and all his fear left him, replaced by an icy cold anger.

The Witch of Shanalane sat upon a huge white horse as she rode from the forest to the front ranks of her army. Though her mount kept a walking pace, her black hair streamed wildly in the wind that swirled around her, and the white folds of her gown whipped the air. Her men parted to let her pass, never losing the heartbeat rhythm, until she took her place at their head.

Innowen stared at his mother. Could he see her laughing over such a distance, or did he imagine that? He picked up her sword and curled his fist around its hilt until his knuckles cracked. He remembered bitterly how he had seen her that first time in a different storm, her hair flying, the wind slashing about her, and how he had loved her in that first moment of seeing her. He knew it now for what it had been—a youthful infatuation with beauty, many times intensified by his need to find help for Drushen and by his own perceived inadequacies. She was like no woman he had ever seen.

She was still beautiful and still like no other. But he knew her now with a knowledge uncolored by innocence and fantasies. The images from her bedroom in Parendur still burned in his mind.

A soldier came running breathlessly to Minarik's side. It took Innowen a moment to remember the man's name. *Sireos*, originally loyal to Kyrin. Innowen moved closer to his father.

"That last blast," Sireos said quickly, wiping at his forehead. A thin streak of blood appeared again above his eyebrow. Somehow, he had taken a cut. "It shattered two hinges in the great gates."

"Impossible!" Veydon swore.

"You think so?" Sireos retorted sharply. "Come down and see, then. The wall itself has taken several quite amusing cracks, also around the gate." He backed up, beckoning Veydon to follow.

"Go," Minarik told Veydon. "If what Sireos says is true…" He caught the back of his chair and leaned on it for support. "If what he says is true," he repeated, "report back to me." He waited until both men were gone, then he shook his head and slumped into his chair. "If it's true," he said again, "all hope is gone.

She'll shake the stones down around our heads, and there's nothing we can do about it."

Razkili went to Minarik's side. "Charge," he urged. "Why wait for the stones to come down around you when you have weapons and men willing to fight? Throw open the gates before they crumble. Attack!"

Innowen grabbed Razkili's arm and spun him around. "No," he said, and his voice brooked no argument. "I'm the only one going out."

Razkili's jaw gaped, but before he could protest, Innowen stopped him. "I'm the only one going out there," he repeated firmly. He looked Rascal in the eye. "Remember Chohlit?"

Razkili shook his head furiously. "That was only thirty or forty men!" he reminded with a note of desperation. "There are several thousand out there!"

Innowen went to the edge of the wall and stared outward at his mother. She sat proudly upon her horse, as if she were waiting for him. All around her, her men kept up their cadence. It was eating at Innowen's nerves.

"Exactly!" he snapped at Razkili. "Thousands! At least five times our number. And you want to go out and meet them? That's not a fight! That's barely an honorable suicide!" He slammed his hands down against the stone and turned to face his father and his lover. Minarik's face was utter bewilderment. Rascal's was stark terror.

He addressed his father first. "She has power," he said by way of quick explanation, "and she wants to attack, not with her men, but with her magic. She's showing off." He drew a deep breath, held it, then let it out suddenly as he prepared to confess his most deeply held secret. "But I have a magic of my own, a power she unknowingly gave me. Maybe I can turn it against her. At least I'm going to try."

An ear-splitting crackle filled the air. Another arcane bolt flashed earthward. Innowen gave a cry and felt as if his flesh were ripping away from his bones, as if his eyes were burning in their sockets. He sagged forward in his father's lap, gasping for breath as Minarik's knees twitched against his chest. Screams and shouts rose up from inside the grounds. Flames shot up from one of the outbuildings near the stables where the lightning had struck.

Innowen regained control of himself. Minarik sat slumped over one arm of his chair, clutching his wound, his face contorted in a grimace. Innowen pried his father's hands from the bandages. The red stain had grown, but not significantly. He left his father and bent down beside Razkili. Rascal's eyes were closed, and a bruise mark showed above his left brow where his head had struck the stone, but his breathing was even. *She's just made it easier for me*, Innowen thought to himself as he hugged Rascal and laid him gently back on the stone.

He got to his feet and looked around for his mother's sword and the helm he had dropped earlier. Snatching them up, he ran from the wall, pushing and shoving his way to the stairs as panicked soldiers abandoned their posts and ran in all directions. A terrified archer blocked the narrow steps at the halfway point, refusing to go up or down until Innowen ruthlessly kicked him off.

At the gate, he found Veydon and Sireos, fruitlessly attempting, with the help of a few men who had kept their senses, to reinforce the gate by bracing it with a pair of huge beams.

"The cracks are real!" Veydon shouted to Innowen, "and getting worse!"

"That last one broke a hinge clean!" Sireos informed him.

"Let me out," Innowen ordered. He sheathed his mother's sword and took her helm between both hands.

"What?" the two men exclaimed together.

Innowen shouted at them. "Open the godsdamned gate!" he demanded. "And shut it fast again behind me!"

"I hope you know what you're doing," Veydon warned, pushing his dark hair back from his sweaty face, but he beckoned to several men to push open one of the great doors, and he lent his own shoulder to speed the task.

"Innowen!"

Innowen knew without looking that it was Rascal who called his name. He swallowed hard and took a step toward the gate. Rascal shouted his name again, the edge of fear in his voice sharp enough to cut through Innowen's resolve. He hesitated, biting his lip. Slowly, he gazed up. Hands curled into fists, Rascal stood directly above him on the rampart, ready to jump.

There was little time. Another lightning bolt, another thunderblast or two, and the gates might come crashing down, perhaps even the walls themselves, leaving Whisperstone open to the Witch's army. He looked past the opening Veydon had made for him at the sea of torches and glittering armor. Then he called up to Razkili. "Get everyone off the walls!" he shouted. "You know why! Get them off!" He rushed through the opening before Razkili could say more and heard it thud shut behind him.

Innowen stood in the shadow of the gate where neither the moonlight nor the light from the watchfires above reached. He wondered if his mother had noticed the swift opening and closing of the gate, if she felt him watching her. His eye roamed the ranks of her warriors, and doubt quivered through him. There could be no turning back, though. A cloud of dust and ash swirled up around him in a gust of wind. He sputtered and wiped at his eyes. He had planned to wear his mother's helm. Instead, he pulled up the hood of his white cloak and tucked the helm under his arm. He started slowly across the powdery field.

The shadow of the wall drew a black line across the earth. He stopped suddenly without crossing it. The Witch saw him, he was sure of it. She sat rigidly on her horse, and though the wind whipped her hair and the folds of her garments, she did not move. She stared his way, and he felt their gazes lock over the distance between them. He turned away and scanned the top of Whisperstone's wall. Not a single soldier stood atop it. Only two lonely forms remained to watch him from there. In the glow of the watchfires it was difficult to see their faces, but he was sure they were Minarik and Rascal. He wanted to shout at them, *Get below! Don't look!* But he knew nothing he could say or do would make either of them turn away.

He stepped out of the wall's shadow. A crimson bolt sizzled across the heavens, and the world flashed white for a brief instant. But neither the lightning, nor the thunderclap that followed, had the same power as the earlier blasts. He hesitated, then continued walking across the field.

The Witch raised a hand. The sudden silence was its own thunderclap as her soldiers ceased their rhythmic beating. Innowen bit his lip, uncertain of what to expect. If they charged, he was done for. The

Witch gave no further order, however, and her troops kept ranks.

They all saw him. It was impossible not to see him in his mother's white cloak with the moon shining on him. He pushed the cloak's folds back over his shoulders with his free hand, letting the moon strike the armor he wore, his mother's armor.

Halfway across the field, he stopped. A sea of arms and armor stretched before him. Doubt rose in him again, but he took his mother's helm in both hands and raised it high overhead, letting the moonlight play on it. Then he lowered it again and let it slip from his fingers to lie in the dust.

He wished he could have spoken to her, that he could have walked right up to her. She would have said something like, *You have my armor, thief*, and he would have cleverly answered, *Consider it my inheritance, Mother*, and she would have been surprised to hear him call her that. She might have said, *I thought you were a dream when you came to my bedroom*, and he would have answered, *Real as flesh, flesh of your flesh*.

But he dared not get that close. He knew her power. She might stop him before he could stop her army. They could all see him. He had their attention. Nothing remained for him to do, now, but dance. He touched the clasp of the cloak. The soft cloth slithered from his shoulders and dropped to the ground.

He listened for the wind, and from his memory came an echo of Razkili's harp. He closed his eyes, hearing a note that had no physical sound as he put one toe forward, lifted and spun on it, and settled himself again. He opened his eyes and spun once more with his left leg bent behind him and his back deeply arched.

He stopped. That had been no dance, only a series

of mechanical movements. He stared at his mother, wondering what she must be thinking. His breathing was too quick. He forced it to slow. Did he fear his mother so much? Or did he fear *for* her? *Think of your father,* he told himself sharply, *think of Rascal.* He eyed the line of soldiers with their shields and spears and swords.

Innowen swept his hands forward lyrically as he made a deep lunge. His memory had let go a single echo from the magnificent wind harp. Now he called up its entire symphony from the well of his soul. He moved over the ash, flowing sinuously from one extension to the next. His arms swept upward in a rolling motion that carried him to the tips of his toes and over backward until he caught himself on one hand while the other strained toward the moon. Straightening, he flung out his arms and spun again, dragging one toe in the dust, carving a perfect circle on the pale, gray earth.

The wind rose around him, and with it came a wail of music, like a storm, from out of the night. The wind harp! In his mind, he'd heard it. Now he heard it for real. On Sparrow Hill, on the other side of Whisperstone, it sang to him—with the voices of an angel's chorus or a demon's, he didn't know. But the sound filled him, lifted him. The wind surged. The music it carried crescendoed wildly, and Innowen embraced it as he danced.

The Witch, her army, Whisperstone—it all faded from his awareness. That was always the deepest beauty of it. While he danced, his mind emptied. Worry, fear, troubles, all thought poured out of him like water. The world vanished. Time stood still. Out of this unreality, he carved for himself a new reality, a landscape defined by the power of his muscles and the stretch of his limbs, time created by the rhythm of his movements, the beating of his heart, and the pulse of the blood in his veins.

And sometimes, when it was over, when he stopped, he cried, for the world he returned to could never be as beautiful as the one he made with his dance.

Innowen dropped to the ground, exhausted. His heart hammered in his chest. Sweat made rivulets in the dust and ash on his face, and he licked at a droplet that ran into the corner of his mouth. It had a bitter taste. The music of the wind harp floated in the air, softer now, only a faint and purposeless harmony, hovering, lingering.

Slowly, he lifted his head and waited for his vision to focus. With a sigh, he let it fall again.

The Witch's soldiers stood behind their shields, unaffected, unmoved, as far as he could tell. Bitterly, he smashed a fist against his thigh. Maybe, their darkest desires were all to follow the Witch. Maybe she had protected them, somehow.

A curtain of ash blew up as the wind swept across the field from a new direction. The Witch nudged her horse. Like a pale ghost approaching through layers of mist, she rode forward. Unhurriedly she came, alone, taking her time. Her gaze never left him.

Innowen rose to his feet and waited for her. She stopped a few paces away and looked down at him with a passive curiosity. The wind blew a strand of hair across her eyes, and she brushed it back casually with a slender hand. It seemed a long time that she looked at him before she spoke.

"You look familiar to me," she said at last. "What is your name?"

Her voice came deep and rich as velvet from a

mouth full and perfect as a red rose, just as Innowen remembered it. His lips parted ever so slightly as he regarded her, and all his fear vanished. With his new knowledge, it was easy to see so much of his own face in hers.

"You gave me a name five years ago," he answered slowly. "You called me Innocent."

At first, there was no reaction. Then her eyes widened. She raised a hand and set the tips of her fingers lightly on her lips as she looked at him anew. "I remember now." The wind blew her hair across her face again, and again she brushed it back. A distant look came into her eyes until she shook her head abruptly. "You were the crippled boy that I made walk. I dreamed of you some nights ago. But it was no dream. You stole my armor," she said without animosity.

"More than your armor," Innowen told her. "I stole your secrets, Minowee."

An expression of surprise flickered briefly across her face, but she quickly suppressed it. Or, perhaps it really didn't matter that he knew her name. Suddenly, all the hatred that he thought he felt for her dissolved. He pitied her. It was as Minarik had said. She didn't control her power; it controlled her. Khoom was the one to blame.

The Witch drew her shoulders back proudly and looked down her nose at him. Before she could speak, though, he rushed on. "Your god, Khoom, told me everything. He will desert you, Minowee. Already, he's turned away from you. Your power belongs to another."

"To you?" she said with a soft sneer. "You dance prettily, and a few of my soldiers throw down their weapons and run off." She barked a short, rude laugh.

"Apparently, Khoom doesn't hold you in very high favor, Innocent. I'm going to shake these walls apart. That is power, boy."

So, his dancing had had some small effect after all. Innowen took a firmer stance, as if to block her way. "You'll never take Whisperstone," he said defiantly.

"Take it?" she laughed. "I'll crush it. Kyrin's life, and the crown of Ispor, those I'll take."

"What of Minarik?" Innowen shouted angrily. "Will you crush him, too? Vashni's father?"

It was not surprise, but true rage that twisted the Witch's features as she glared down from her horse. "You little bastard!" she cried. "I should have left you in that wretched storm. You think I don't know it was Minarik who slew Vashni on this very spot? If you had Khoom's power, you could see! The ground we stand on burns red with my son's blood!" She jabbed a finger at Whisperstone. "And no one, *no one*, in there will escape my wrath!"

Innowen opened his arms wide. "Then strike me down," he dared her with a barely controlled fury. "Let the earth burn with the blood of both your sons!"

Her jaw dropped. She leaned forward on her horse and glared. "Who are you!" she hissed.

But Innowen didn't answer. The sound of familiar piping floated down from the top of Whisperstone's wall and settled upon him like a soft embrace.

His gaze locked on the Witch, he drew one arm upward with languid grace and lowered it slowly. The wind changed direction again. The distant wind-harp wailed and Dyan's piping soared. The two musics blended, became one. Innowen rolled his head to the side and swayed. The Witch stared, bewildered.

The music caught him up with an unexpected force. He couldn't resist. The pipe sang, the wind harp screamed, and his body began to dance. He spun and spun until the night became a flow of motion and his senses swam. He tried to find a focus, something to help him balance. As he turned, he glanced toward the wall. There were three figures there, now, silhouetted by the watchfires: Minarik and Rascal and Dyan playing her pipe.

The music didn't stop, but as suddenly as it had seized him, it let him go. The wind harp swelled louder, and the pipe's notes blew faster as the wind carried the sound to the Witch's troops.

Eerily, they began to dance as Innowen had danced, repeating his steps, turning, turning. The weapons fell from their hands; torches tumbled to the ground. Mounted warriors dismounted and began to dance. Thousands of men suddenly heard the music of the pipe and the wind harp and fell under a powerful spell.

Innowen watched in horror. No surge of triumph rushed through him. This was nothing he had done. Only the choreography had been drawn from him. It was the power of Khoom, shaped by Dyan. The soldiers moved like puppets, dreamlike, entranced.

The Witch screamed. Her garments whipped about her like the wings of an angry bird. The wind hurled ash into her face. "What have you done?" she cried. "What have you done?"

Thousands of dancers spread out over the field, faces enrapt, turning, swaying, extending their bodies with unnatural grace and power, unable to stop.

"*Dance away the world,*" Innowen said suddenly, flashing a resentful glare. "You claimed you saw it in my future. *Dance away the world,* you said. Armies would fall before me." He clenched his fists and shook them at this stranger who was his mother. "Don't you see? They're your armies, and it's your world, Minowee. Your world and your rule, your dreams of Akkadi!"

The Witch's hands shot into the air, and she threw back her head. "Khoom!" she screamed. "Khoom, give me power!"

"Khoom has abandoned you!" Innowen shouted. He pointed toward the top of the wall, toward the piper. "There is his new priestess. There! Kyrin's daughter! Your niece!"

The Witch screamed again, a note so shrill it chilled the blood in Innowen's veins. Her horse reared, screaming its own animal cry. Its great hooves crashed down at Innowen, and he jumped back desperately. From somewhere within her garments, the Witch drew a sword. Like a vengeful, taloned bird, she swooped down at him.

Innowen hurled himself aside, rolled in the dust and leaped to his feet. But the Witch bent lower and lower, as if the weight of her sword were dragging her down. He realized she was falling. Her garments fluttered wildly about her, and the blade tumbled from her grip. A great cloud of ash rose as she hit the ground.

Innowen raced to her side. The Witch lay unmoving on her back. An arrow sprouted from her left breast where a dark rose was taking form on her white gown. Kneeling, he bent over her. He touched her cheek, so like his own, and warring emotions began to tear and pull at his insides. He screamed silently, lowering his face to hers, peering into her eyes as her blank gaze filled with the light of the moon.

The gates of Whisperstone sprang open. Innowen gathered his mother in his arms and cradled her in his lap as Minarik's soldiers rushed at the Witch's hapless troops. They gave no cheer, no shouts of battle or triumph that might have drowned Dyan's music. While the wind harp faded, her pipe sang loud through the night.

A grisly harvest began.

CHAPTER

25

A DARK SMOKE rose from the piles of burning bodies. All day it hung thick over Whisperstone. The wall meant nothing to it. It drifted through the grounds, through doors and windows, permeating the great keep with its potent smell. Still, out on the field, Minarik's men worked grimly, feeding the flames with more and more corpses while disappointed carrion birds wheeled and gyred in the sweltering sky overhead.

Sitting in Minarik's chair, Innowen watched it all from the top of the wall, a self-imposed penance, and every body thrown into the flames was like a lash stroke across his back. He'd watched his mother tossed into the fire without ceremony. He'd watched as Kyrin's body was carried from the stables and lofted onto the same pile by a pair of burly soldiers wearing cloths tied over their faces.

Despite the pain of his wound, Minarik came to him twice, and squeezed his shoulder, and stared with him out over the carnage. Neither of them spoke, though, and eventually his father left him alone. None of the other soldiers bothered him. He was *abathakati* again, someone to fear. Razkili brought him water to drink and food, which Innowen refused.

"I will not dance tonight," he said quietly. Razkili said nothing, but ran a hand slowly through Innowen's hair and down the back of his neck.

The sun sank behind Whisperstone. As flames

burned high in the darkness, workers continued to feed the dozens of piles. A terrible red-orange beauty colored the night, and shadows danced liked moths around the fires. Innowen rose from his father's chair, and Razkili placed a thin cloak around his shoulders.

"I will not dance tonight," he whispered as Razkili led him away.

Darkness brought no rest to Whisperstone. Those soldiers and villagers who were not working the fires on the field were busy on the main grounds, working, preparing weapons and supplies by the light of campfires. Already, plans were being made to retake Parendur from the token force the Witch had left in control there. It was an action the soldiers were eager for, and spirits were high as they went about their tasks. In Parendur, the soldiers would again offer the crown to Minarik, and there, Minarik would reluctantly accept and become Ispor's king.

Inside Whisperstone, the slaves and servants, with the help of many of the village women, rushed maddeningly about setting out the feast they had spent much of the day preparing. An air of festivity filled the halls. As with the soldiers, most of them considered the battle against the Witch a great victory, and they went about their work jubilantly.

Innowen moved through them like a ghost until he reached the privacy of his rooms. There, he settled down on his bed and threw an arm over his eyes. Shortly, though, he got up and paced to the window and stared outward. Then he walked to the far side of the room and picked up the burning lamp and examined it. He poured a kylix of wine for himself, took a sip, set it down.

Razkili sat patiently, quietly, in a chair out of the

way, watching.

"I won't dance tonight," Innowen said yet again. He picked up the kylix and drained half the wine within it.

"I know," Razkili answered, folding his hands across his stomach as he met Innowen's gaze. His eyes were wide and luminescent in the glow from the lamp, and there was a serenity in his face that sent a pang through Innowen's heart.

Innowen set the cup down, rushed to Razkili and knelt down before him. "I want you to go back to Osirit," he said heavily. He leaned his head down on Razkili's knee and closed his eyes as he spoke. Slowly, he trailed one hand up and down the side of Rascal's calf. "I don't want you to see me crippled."

Razkili began to work his fingers through Innowen's hair. "I've carried you this far," he said with the barest trace of amusement, pushing the double meaning. "What makes you think I'll leave now?"

"Because I want you to, Rascal," he replied flat-voiced, without feeling. "I've been able to walk at night." He paused, the words catching in his throat. He swallowed hard. "It'll be different when I can't walk at all."

Razkili's grip tightened in Innowen's hair, and he gently shook Innowen's head. "Shut up," he whispered, almost with a chuckle.

Innowen opened his eyes, and for a long time he watched the little lamp flame flickering in the slight breeze that blew in through the window. The sounds of music drifted faintly on the air, soft percussion accompanying bells, as the celebration got under way in earnest. With a start, he realized he'd been listening, not for that, but for Dyan's pipe.

Tonight, though, Khoom's new priestess was silent.

Reluctantly, Innowen freed himself from Razkili's

embrace. "Let's go down to the courtyard," he said, thinking of the gazebo. "I'll wait there for sunrise."

Maybe it was the dead foliage that kept others away. Innowen wasn't sure why so few others came to the courtyard. It was his favorite place, despite the withered flowers and the brown, dusty vines. To him, it was the heart of Whisperstone.

No one had lit the torches. The courtyard was utterly dark, except for the thin light that leaked from some of the upper windows. He climbed into the gazebo and sat down in the same seat he had taken years ago on that day when Minarik had adopted him. That made him smile now. Minarik had always been his father. He wondered suddenly what must have gone through Minarik's mind on that day, and he glanced down at the bird-shaped ring on his finger that his father had given him.

"That's better," Razkili said, settling into Minarik's seat opposite Innowen. "It's the first time you've smiled today."

Self-consciously, Innowen smiled again and tried uselessly to hide it. "You must admit, there's been little to smile about." He leaned his head against the back of the chair and sighed.

"Your country is free," Razkili said reasonably.

Innowen sighed once more. Talking was a good way to pass the time. It would keep his mind off dancing, off the gentle, musical rush of the breeze in his ears, off the dooming approach of the dawn. It seemed to him suddenly that he and Rascal had not talked in a long time.

"Free," he said finally. "What does that mean? One ruler falls, another ruler ascends. Koryan, Kyrin, Minowee, and now my father. Yes, Minarik's soldiers are happy, and these villagers are happy because they've lived so long under Minarik's protection. But do you really think the rest of the people care?" He remembered the potter he had spoken with outside the gate of Parendur and felt a stab of guilt because he couldn't recall the old man's name. "As long as their families are fed and they're left alone to scratch a living for themselves, do you think any of this matters to them?"

Razkili leaned forward. "Do you really think that's all they care about? What about fear, Innowen? They may have all you say they want, a little food, and a few coins, and a house to live in. But what if they can lose it all at any moment on a ruler's whim? What if their safety, on any given day, depends on what side of the bed their ruler rises from? What if they can be dragged from their farms and pressed into service? What if they are taxed into starvation?" He leaned back again and crossed one knee over the other as he clasped his hands. "I think you'll find they care more than you give them credit for."

There was a difference between rulers and tyrants, Innowen admitted silently to himself. He had known Kyrin too well, and he had no illusions about which his mother would have been. He knew her power, had seen the relish with which she wielded it. Ispor would have loved her and despaired.

He rested his chin in his hand and looked away. Even in death, Minowee still had not relinquished her hold on him. She'd haunted him in life, and now her ghost would haunt him. At last, he turned back to Razkili and voiced the question he had feared to ask all day. "Did you shoot the arrow that killed her?" he said.

It was Rascal's turn to look away as he pursed his

lips and considered. "No," he answered.

Innowen drew a breath and chewed his lip. "I didn't want it to be you," he said. After another pause, he spoke again. "Was it Minarik?"

Razkili turned back to him. "Do you really want to know who killed her?" he said with a piercing look. "Do you?"

Innowen looked away again, and his thoughts slipped back to that last meeting with his mother. She would have slain him. He saw in his mind the sword in her hand, raised to cut him down, and the look of fury on her face. Yet she hadn't known. She hadn't really known who he was. "No," he said at last. If it wasn't Rascal or Minarik, then he could be content not knowing. He just hadn't wanted the killer to be his lover—or Minowee's lover.

Strange, he found himself using her name more and more, now that she was dead. Before, she had always been *the Witch* or sometimes, much later and rarely, an impersonal *mother*.

"Innocent?" Razkili leaned forward and tapped Innowen's knee to draw his attention.

Innowen winced. "Please," he said, frowning, "don't call me that. Not for a while."

The music of the celebration drifted into the courtyard, louder and more clearly, yet sweet. The bells' crystal notes perforated the air like tiny knives, and Innowen found himself tapping his foot to the drums' percussion. He stopped as soon as he caught himself and gripped the arms of his chair. It would be so easy to give in. The music called him to dance. It tugged at him. This time, though, he would be strong.

"I love you," he said suddenly to Razkili.

They fell quiet again after that. It was enough that

they waited together, privately watching the stars roll above the courtyard, listening to the wind rustle through the gazebo's dry vines, each thinking his own private thoughts. Little by little, the bells and the drums and the sounds of celebration faded. One by one, as the celebrants went to bed, the lights in the windows winked out, all except one, which was the window of their own room. Finally, even that light flickered out as the lamp exhausted its oil. Still, they waited, speaking little, letting the long silences say more than mere words could convey.

The black sky turned slowly to purple. Innowen watched it, biting his lip. Without quite planning it, he got up and stepped out of the gazebo. His sandals rang on the smooth paving stones as he walked a few paces away. He bent and unlaced the sandal straps and kicked them away. Though the air was warm, the stone was cool under his feet, and he relished the sensation. He flexed his toes, then took a few more steps, marveling at the contact on his skin as his weight shifted from the heel to the ball of each foot.

He looked back at Razkili, who had risen from his chair to watch him—tall, proud Razkili, beautiful Rascal with his perfect body and long, muscled thighs. Then he shot a desperate look at the sky again where purple segued toward violet.

He walked the length of the courtyard and back again, savoring the way his own muscles worked. He paced the circumference. The stone tingled against the soles of his feet. A slow fire warmed his calves and ankles. There was a tightness in his left knee, but that, too, was a delicious pleasure. He wanted to run, but he feared running. It would be too easy to lose himself in the sheer joy of motion, to forget and execute a turn or a leap, and he knew he would not stop.

He looked at the sky again—violet to cobalt blue—and went to Razkili. *Help me*, he pleaded silently with his eyes as he took Rascal's hands and led him like a dance partner away from the gazebo. The heat of Rascal's touch flowed through him as they moved together toward a clear, wide space.

Rascal's arms went around him, pulling him close, and Innowen locked his arms around Razkili's neck. So tight was Rascal's grip that Innowen couldn't move. Their chests rose and fell against each other as they shared breath. The harder Rascal held Innowen, the tighter Innowen clung to Rascal. He pressed his head down on Rascal's shoulder even as his gaze turned skyward.

The night faded away like a dream. Only a few stars remained visible over the courtyard. One by one, they winked out.

"Forgive me," Rascal whispered, laying a damp cheek down on the top of Innowen's head. A terrible trembling ran all through Rascal's body, but he only tightened his grip. It was as if he had decided to try to pull Innowen's body into his own.

Innowen couldn't get away, and he knew now Razkili would never let him go. "Thank you," he muttered gratefully, lifting his face into the soft part of Rascal's neck. "Thank you."

The morning came like a gentle sea foam over the walls of Whisperstone.

For a long time, they stood pressed together, trembling, neither willing to move or speak. Above them, a soft wind flirted through a perfect blue sky. Razkili's right hand shifted up and down Innowen's back. Innowen looked up into Rascal's eyes.

"I'm not supporting you," Rascal said with some confusion.

"I know," Innowen murmured in disbelief. He could still feel the stone under his feet, the touch of Rascal's thighs against his, the tightness in his left knee. Cautiously, he freed himself from Rascal's embrace, half expecting to fall. He stepped back, clutching Rascal's arms. Finally, he let go and took another step backward.

"I can walk!" he shouted suddenly. He jumped up in the air, bursting with excitement. "I don't know why, but I can walk! I'm not crippled, Rascal!" He jumped up again, clapping his hands for joy. He rose on the ball of his right foot and did a triple turn, stopped, flung his head back and let go a laugh.

Rascal laughed too. He executed his own triple turn. "You didn't know I could do that, did you?" he cried joyously. He caught Innowen around the waist and hugged him fiercely. "It's over, Innowen. It's over!"

"It's over for you," a voice said coldly from behind them.

Together, they turned. Sireos strode from a door and crossed the courtyard. In his arms he carried Dyan. It was she who had spoken. Innowen and Razkili moved aside as he bore her into the gazebo and set her down in Minarik's chair. In her right hand she clutched the doll-pipe, which Innowen had given her. Innowen stared at it. Was it his imagination, or had its features undergone a subtle change? It seemed in some respects to resemble the golden figure of Khoom that he had danced with.

Carefully, Dyan arranged her red silken dress over her legs, smoothing each fold to perfection while Sireos stood grimly beside her, his gaze smoldering with suppressed anger as he regarded Innowen and Razkili.

"You are free, Innowen," Dyan said at last, lifting her head with an air of disdain.

Innowen looked at her with an expression of dismay. He knew too well the odd, rigid posture, the way she gripped the chair arms, the way her upper body turned without any reaction from the lower half. "You can't walk," he said with a growing numbness.

"No, I can't," Dyan answered matter-of-factly. "I asked Khoom to let you go." She placed one hand on a thigh and rubbed her palm over it unconsciously, as if her leg was only asleep and she might awaken it. "But He would not. He wanted you, Innowen. He wanted you to be his priest, but you rejected him. And it angered Him that I defended you."

Razkili stepped closer, putting himself ever so subtlety between Dyan and Innowen. "Khoom did this to you because you spoke up for Innowen?"

A strange fire flared in Dyan's eyes as she regarded Razkili, and she paused. When she answered, her voice dripped with disdain and bitterness. "He offered me a bargain," she said. "He didn't believe you when you said you would not dance tonight. You had said that so many times before."

"He heard?" Innowen said, alarmed.

Dyan's mouth curved in a patient sneer. "He is a god, and He has a great interest in you. He hears us now." As if to prove her words, the wind swept down unexpectedly and shook the gazebo, rustled the dry vines, and vanished as suddenly. "He didn't believe you," she continued coolly, "but I did. So we bargained. If you danced tonight, then I would never intercede for you again. You would be His to punish, and I would not interfere."

"But I didn't dance," Innowen told her through clenched teeth.

Dyan raised one eyebrow. "So I won the bargain," she answered stiffly. "You are free of Khoom, and your legs are truly healed. You can walk normally, and never fear the sun again."

"But why can't you walk?" Innowen shouted, confused and enraged. She had used him like a piece in a game with her god. Yet she had done a great thing for him. He was glad he could walk, but not if the price was Dyan's own ruin.

Dyan looked at him as if he were the greatest of fools. He felt the chill that radiated from her, and he felt an unbreachable wall rising between them.

"Khoom is a jealous god," she answered. "Though I am His priestess now, I dared to take your side. My punishment is to bear your curse, walking by night, crippled by day." She raised a hand before Innowen could say anything. "It will not prevent me from doing His work and spreading His worship. With more worshippers, Khoom will grow strong, and I will grow strong as well. That was your mother's mistake. She thought she could keep Khoom for herself, but I will spread His name like a wind-driven fire." Dyan tilted her head, and a tiny, unpleasant smile blossomed upon her rose red mouth. "This land will be His one day. Akkadi will rise on the ashes of Ispor." She raised the pipe to her lips and blew a short riff before lowering it to her lap again.

Innowen felt a shiver up his spine as Dyan motioned for Sireos to pick her up. "Sireos served my father for many years," she said to Innowen from the cradle of the large man's arms. "Now, he'll serve me as Razkili served you."

Sireos stepped arrogantly between Innowen and Razkili, forcing them out of his way. "In serving you,

Mistress, I serve Khoom."

"Wait!" Innowen cried, catching up with them, blocking their way. "Where will you go?"

That little smile again turned up the corners of her lips. "If I remain here, Minarik must pass some judgment upon me," she answered. "I don't hold a grudge against him for it. I murdered my father. He should have me executed, but his heart is soft. Instead, of my own will, I will go to Mikonos. That is where the Witch grew up and where Khoom has some few worshippers. They will teach me things I need to know."

Innowen tried to catch her hand. She had been a dear friend once. He feared for her, and he feared the change that had come over her. "Then you'll come back?" he said with a confusing mixture of hope and dread.

Dyan shook her head. "There are lands besides Ispor," came her response. "I have a great respect for Minarik and will not cause him trouble while he rules. For a time I will wander." She pulled her hand free, and her eyes darkened. "But yes. I will come back. Now get out of my way. Sireos already has our wagon waiting."

Innowen bit his lip as he stepped aside. She stared at him for a long moment, and briefly there was a familiar light in her face, and he remembered the young girl he had first met in this same courtyard.

"I love you, Innowen," she said quietly. Biting her lip, she tapped Sireos' arm, and he carried her toward the door. On the threshold, however, she tapped Sireos again. He paused without turning, and she looked over his shoulder. Once more, her eyes filled with a dark and deadly fire. She waited, letting Innowen feel her full power. In the same quiet voice she said, "I hate you."

When Dyan and Sireos were gone, Razkili came to

Innowen's side. "She loves you," he said simply. "Khoom has taken on more than he knows. She has a will."

"So did my mother..." Innowen answered, staring at the door Dyan had gone through: "...in the beginning." He turned around, walked back to the gazebo, and grabbed a handful of vines. They crumbled in his grip, and he poured the gritty powder on the ground. "For those who've gone before," he muttered. He turned back to Razkili. "How would you feel about readying a pair of horses?"

Razkili pursed his lips thoughtfully and rubbed his chin. "Are we going to Parendur with your father?" he asked.

Innowen shook his head as he folded his arms across his chest. "No," he answered slowly. "I've had enough of soldiers and armies. Minarik will have no trouble in Parendur."

"Home, then?" Razkili suggested.

Innowen considered, and a subtle grin lit up his face. "I'd like that," he agreed. Osirit was a beautiful country of softly rolling hills, green valleys, and gentle rivers, as good a destination as any. "You can teach me some philosophy on the way."

He gazed up at the walls that surrounded the courtyard, high stone walls with square dark windows, and an unspoken dread shuddered through him. Who had watched him from those windows that first night he had danced here? Minarik and Taelyn, he knew. Drushen, too—poor Drushen! Who else?

What had he set in motion that night by that innocent act? What forces had he unleashed? How could he know who was really to blame?

He shut his eyes and shook his head slowly. Such a suspicion was too great a burden to torture himself with.

He had to say good-bye to Whisperstone. This place had held too strong a spell on him for far too long. It was time to break that spell, and there was only one way to do it.

He looked at his shadow on the ground. For the first time in his life, he saw it stretching tall and straight in the sunlight. He reached for Rascal's hand and pulled him closer until their shadows merged and became one. With his mouth near his lover's ear, he spoke words he had said to no one else before.

"Dance with me."

SHADOWDANCE

After completing a Master's Degree in Literature at a small midwestern university, Robin Wayne Bailey spent five years as a planetarium lecturer, martial arts instructor, and performer of folk, pop, and country music in area bars and restaurants.

The author of ten previous novels, including the highly successful BROTHERS OF THE DRAGON trilogy, he was also a regular contributor to the THIEVES' WORLD series and has published short stories in various other anthologies and magazines. He's currently at work on a trio of novels featuring new, original adventures of Fafhrd and the Gray Mouser, characters created by science fiction grandmaster, Fritz Leiber. He resides in Kansas City, MO.

ROBIN WAYNE BAILEY